Joan Pritchard has now retired from her life's work and finds writing an excellent challenge. Busy all her life raising a family and having a career, she now finds she has the time to indulge herself. In writing about historical characters, 'things that go bump in the night' and about weird and wonderful tales in general, she is quite happy with her lot. She has a vivid imagination but also enjoys the research needed to produce 'real people' from history, although she does indulge herself by filling their mouths with words of her own. *Strange and Surreal Stories* in this book will keep you both informed and mesmerised—and there are 20 of them. She hopes you will enjoy!

Enjoy

Joan B. Pritchard

This book is dedicated to my grandson, Oliver, who also has a vivid imagination like myself. So much so, he created a website for me which included these words:

'About the author:

Joan Pritchard is my grandma. By looking at her you might expect that she is just another old granny who likes baking cookies and knitting, but you might not think that she writes stories of historical figures, adventure, and a lot of scary stuff. There are stories about magic treehouses, murder, ghosts, dead people who come back from the grave and a bit of history. Her books may not have any pictures, but they are the craziest tales from a lady with the most powerful imagination.

Oliver Bibbey (age 12 and a ½), grandson of Joan Pritchard.

How could I not dedicate this book to him?

Joan B. Pritchard

STRANGE AND SURREAL STORIES

But Are They True?

AUSTIN MACAULEY PUBLISHERS™

LONDON • CAMBRIDGE • NEW YORK • SHARJAH

A CIP catalogue record for this title is available from the British Library.

ISBN 9781398440845 (Paperback)
ISBN 9781398440852 (ePub e-book)

www.austinmacauley.com

First Published 2022
Austin Macauley Publishers Ltd®
1 Canada Square
Canary Wharf
London
E14 5AA

Table of Contents

The Best Ever Storyteller

When young, he wasn't a particularly clever boy—he was average for his age and only attended Grammar School from age 7 to 13. Prior to that, he'd learned the basics from his mother and so could read and write before his formal education began. He also attended a 'Petty School' where he learned numbers, the Ten Commandments and of course, the Bible. It was a sort of Sunday School, associated with the church. He was eventually joined at the Grammar School by his younger brother, Gilbert. The Grammar was called 'The King Edward VI New School' and was attended by boys from all over the county. There was a standard curriculum for all Grammars set by the monarch, and students studied Latin, Math, Philosophy, Drama, Greek, Law and Classical History.

At the time, girls didn't attend school at all, although some from wealthy and more radical families employed tutors to teach their daughters at home. William's mother was Mary Arden—the daughter of a well-to-do landowner from a lesser branch of an aristocratic family. She came from Wilmcote and married John in 1552. John Shakespeare was an ambitious man and at the age of 26, already a qualified glove maker—he was also elected the town Ale Taster, responsible for observing the regulations regarding weights and measures and food processing. A good position for one so young. In 1568, he was given the post of Borough Constable and from there on progressed to Burgess, Chamberlain and finally Alderman.

At this stage in his life, he would be known as 'Goodman Shakespeare' and in 1568 he held the responsible position of High Bailiff—equal to Mayor, which made him the overseer in charge of all public businesses in Stratford. As such, he would have to be addressed as 'Master Shakespeare'. He went on to acquire properties in Stratford—on both Greenhill Street and Henley Street, the latter being where his son, William, was subsequently born, as were his brothers and sisters.

As a side-line, John began operating as a wool dealer which proved to be a very lucrative business, but it led him to a charge of illegal wool purchases, and he had to appear in Court to answer the charges in 1572. The shame of this stopped him from attending Council meetings and his lack of finances excused him from paying levies towards the Poor of the Parish, something he had always done in the past. Money was so tight at this time and he began to mortgage off his land and this situation endured for almost a decade. This was when his eldest son, William, had to leave school, as the family couldn't afford to pay his fees any longer. His father never held public office in Stratford-upon-Avon again.

In line with the neglected education of women, the only recorded information about Mary Arden was her date of death on 19 September 1608 and the fact that she was 6 years younger than her husband. The Arden family had a distinguished history and could trace itself back to the Norman Conquest, when it had fought in the 13th Civil War, the War of the Roses and been a courtier to Henry V11. Truth to tell, Mary's family probably thought she'd married beneath herself, being a member of the landed classes but marrying the son of a tenant farmer.

She did however produce a family of 8 children, the first 2 of whom unfortunately died in infancy. In these days, women were not considered of much importance, other than running a household which was a lot of work, and of course producing children so parents could have someone to look after them in their old age. Having said that however, Mary Arden had been educated, probably in writing and reading only—but she'd obviously been one of the lucky girls tutored at home. Her literacy was apparent as she'd been named as the Executor of her father's will, and she would often read stories and fables to her own children as they were growing up. She was very good at this and used her imagination to create many characters and making up new stories. William was especially interested in the stories.

This then, was the world into which William Shakespeare was born. He was an actor, a poet and a playwright who became known the world over as the most respected writer ever. Sometimes, in certain of his plays, there is clear evidence of his mother's made-up stories—and so she lived on through his writings.

"Gilbert don't be a baby—you're 11 years old and quite capable of going to school without me. I don't want to leave but I have no option. Just be grateful that father can find enough money to allow you to stay at school—but he can't afford for both of us to go, and I've already had more schooling than you. After all, I'm fourteen now and old enough to start an apprenticeship. At least, I'll be able to earn a few shillings—and it'll all help." William was quite proud that he could help his family, although he knew it would take at least 7 years to complete any training.

"That's all right for you to say—what if the other boys pick on me. I'd be happy to help father too—if I didn't go to school either, it would save him even more money, wouldn't it? Can't you suggest it to him?" Gilbert used his most wheedling tone, but William had already moved on and wouldn't discuss it any further.

"Not interested, Brother!" were his last words.

The town of Stratford-on-Avon was a very pretty place to live. It was the central Market Town of Warwickshire in the heart of England and although the Shakespeare family didn't have as much money as they'd once had, they were still much respected by the other townspeople. And so, the time passed and John Shakespeare slowly began to recoup what he'd lost. By the time he died, his resources were back to where they'd once been.

William was 18 and still had 3 years to serve as in an apprenticeship before he qualified. He continued reading anything he could lay his hands on and became involved with a small, local drama group who liked to put on amateur plays for the local towns. It was something to do and he excelled at it. There, he met a young woman called Anne Hathaway who seemed very taken with the young William. She was 26 years old—the average age for people to marry in the 1700s, so she was quite likely on the lookout for a spouse. William however at 18, was still regarded as a minor by Law and was still to complete 3 years of his apprenticeship. After not much time, they'd formed a relationship and Anne had some unexpected news for William.

"Well, my good man, you have done me a great wrong—and you must put it right," Anne spoke to William with great vigour, although she was afraid of people discovering her secret. She was already almost 4 months pregnant by the time she told him about her condition.

"My God, Anne, what are we going to do? I still haven't completed my apprenticeship—we can't marry as I have no money for us to live on. And your brothers will kill me—actually, my father will kill me first when he finds out. Is there any alternative to marriage that you know?" He couldn't keep the fear from his voice.

"There is no alternative—only marriage and if you don't honour me by that, my brothers, who are prosperous and well respected, will make sure your apprenticeship is the least of your problems." Anne was becoming worried that he was going to desert her in her hour of need? "And the church will accuse you of defying the laws of moral living—you will have to stand up in church and admit your treachery of me." She could see he didn't like that and continued to press her point.

"Are you going to reject me because I am the eldest of my brothers and sisters? Are you going to shame me further, even after you've had your way with me? You must know we must marry as it's socially unacceptable for someone of my standing to have a child outside the sanctity of marriage." Now Anne was in a flood of tears.

There was no time to discuss matters further and William knew he was beaten. Because of his age as a minor, he had to ask Anne's oldest brother for her hand in marriage, something her brother gave willingly—as there were still 7 other children at home to support. Anne was actually relieved that her father had died the year before as he would have been most displeased with her. The family was indeed prosperous and could finance the marriage, which they were happy to do. The Hathaways lived in a big farmhouse called Hewland Farm in the village of Shottery, 1 mile from Stratford and that was where the wedding ceremony was eventually held. (*Hewland Farm is now known as Anne Hathaway's Cottage and is the most visited place in England.*)

To avoid scandal around Anne's pregnancy, William applied for a sped-up proceeding at Bishop's Court in Worcester and requested that the reading of banns was carried out only once, and not the usual 3 times. Corners were cut quite neatly. On her wedding day in 1582 Anne donned her very best set of clothes. Her hair was loose and fell to her shoulders—it was crowned with a garland of herbs and her bridesmaids walked in front of her.

"Anne, you are a picture and no mistake." Two young women from the village accompanied her; she was still too early in her pregnancy for her condition to show, although everyone present actually knew about it. News travels fast in the countryside. The bridesmaids spread rushes before the bride, to protect her marriage shoes from mud. She waited by the farmhouse for William and his male friends to arrive—they were accompanied by musicians playing bagpipes and tabors. As was the usual practice, William had brought a pair of new gloves for all the guests, in exchange for the usual gifts of herbs and flowers. His father John, being a Glover by trade, arranged for the very best gloves to be available.

The wedding party stopped outside the church door and William produced the ring, which was blessed by the Minister before passing it to Anne. The whole party then moved into the church itself and the nuptial mass was said. What Anne didn't see at first were the two figures of a man and woman standing just to the side of the church and watching everything with interest. It was her father and mother, whose joint grave stone stood behind them a few feet away from the church door. Anne came back out of the church, claiming she needed some fresh air but really to have a second look at the pair. She walked towards them and stifled a scream, her hand flying to her mouth.

"Mother—Father, why are you here? I've missed you both so much—and here you are on my wedding day. What's going on? Why are you here?"

Her father spoke first, "I wanted to see you married myself, Anne, and to remind you that your brother has your dowry. He's been looking after it since I died. But also, we're here to wish you the best for the future. It wouldn't have been right if we weren't here for you."

Her mother moved then and leaned forward to kiss her cheek. It was like a will-o-the-wisp kiss which Anne barely felt. "And I wanted to tell you to have a happy life although I'm not sure about this William Shakespeare—he'd still just a lad. You certainly took your time to find him, didn't you—and I see you tricked him. How many months gone are you—3 or 4 I'd say, if not a bit more. I've come to offer my best wishes—I thought I owed you that, after dying when you were so young. Now, you try to make him a good wife—although both your father and I think you've married beneath yourself. Still, that's another matter." Her husband put his arm around her shoulders and led her away.

"Come now, Wife, you've said enough." And they both moved off slowly, disappearing into the trees around their gravestone. Anne knew it had really happened and it left her feeling strange and very sad. She really did miss them, her mother in particular—she could have taught her so much—but that would never be now—and so she returned to the wedding party!

"Well, my dear, the deed has been done." William smiled at his bride and the whole wedding party cheered and threw small flower heads at the couple. The Shakespeares and the Hathaways sat down to share a gargantuan meal and celebrated until long after the bride and groom had retired for the night. Although they spent their first night of married life in Anne's home, they soon departed for William's father's house in Henley Street in Stratford, where Anne was welcomed by all the Shakespeare family. She was happy now—she had her dowry in her reticule, safely hidden from prying eyes. Her father had left it to her in his will—but 'it was not to be given to her until the day she married.' So, her pregnancy wasn't the only reason she wanted to marry the young William—there was the welcome dowry to consider.

"I think I love you more than you love me, William." Anne was always fishing for compliments but that was because she was unsure of her husband's affection. She would always believe he'd married her because he had no option, rather than for love of her. She probably would never know, although she told herself she could live with that, now she had his ring on her finger. She was a married woman with all the dignity it brought. Five months later, Will came home to hear the lusty cries of a baby—it was a healthy girl, and they called her Susanna.

For the next few years, he worked as both a schoolteacher and a lawyer's clerk, both something for which he was eminently suitable. He also worked to support his father's business and even found time to join a travelling band of actors who performed in Stratford from time to time. He also formed a close friendship with a local landowner—one Sir Thomas Lucy—and spent much of his free time in the man's company, where he learned to drink freely and often.

"Well Will, is your second child's birth close now—you must be quite excited?" Sir Thomas wasn't really interested in Will's family, but they had become good drinking companions and spent a lot of time in the Stratford Public Houses.

"Aye, the child is already here—and Anne is as fat and happy as a pig in muck. In fact, she's with child again, so I must wait for that birth now." He looked rather worried at his fast growing family…

A couple of years later—after the birth of his twins—William decided to leave Stratford and travel to London. He needed to earn an income to care for his new family and he believed he would find work, perhaps as an actor, in the world of the theatre. London was famous for its theatres and many talented people went there in hope. Anne was none too happy that he was going so far away, but as he pointed out to her, "You have your children to care for—and I must find a way to make some money. We can't go on living off my father."

William Shakespeare left for London in 1592 and rode there on horseback. He took his younger brother, Edmund, with him—they were going to London to make their fortunes. They found themselves lodgings in Bishopsgate and although he changed lodgings a few times more, wherever he lived was always close to the theatres. The two brothers were able to walk to work in the mornings and found some tavern en route to buy ale and bread. Will met many others who worked at the theatre and learned a lot before he worked there himself.

Initially, he worked as a stagehand and helped the actors dress and rehearse their parts. Both he and Edmund took bit parts in plays and enjoyed the sawdust feel of the stage. At the time, all women's parts in a play were undertaken by young men, and he had to learn the art of make-up and doing women's hair. He did all of this willingly as he believed it to be all part of the learning process.

"Stand still, Peter—your dress is not right—it's tucked down the top of your breeches and your hands are filthy—no young lady would have had such dirty hands." He rouged Peter's cheeks and his lips. "Not bad, young Peter—you'd almost pass for a woman, but don't forget to shave tomorrow or the audience will be able to see your stubble." He was enjoying himself—and for the first time, felt glad about coming to the city. Stratford had seemed so tame compared with the magic of the city.

Whilst on this learning curve, his wife Anne was being tested on how to be a housewife. She'd never been educated, of course—in line with other women at the time—but she did have to find about the cost of things in case she was being short-changed at the markets. She was responsible for running the household and had to learn how to preserve and cook food—the housework was hard work too and was physically exhausting. She had to take care of the kitchen garden— vegetables were necessary and not just because they were good for you but when the farmers had a bad harvest, which happened a lot in the 1590s, food was scarce, and people starved. She found she had to be present in the kitchen, watching over the scullery maid and the cook. She had to do all of this as well as looking after the children and washing the household's dirty linen.

"I really don't know if I can do everything, Aunt." Anne was visiting her old home at Hewland Farm. Her mother of course, had died when she was only 10 years old, so she'd never learned from her the usual housewifely things mothers were expected to teach their daughters. Anne therefore had never learned much but her spinster Aunt had come to look after the house and to take over the care of Anne and her 7 siblings. She'd fitted in well and easily took over the responsibilities of the house. Just now however, she found it difficult to listen to Anne's whining—she was lucky to be married, have a husband and family, and still live in Stratford-upon-Avon. As an unmarried woman, her aunt had had none of these things.

"You must just get on with it, Anne—you're a wife and a mother now and you should be grateful for your lot in life." Aunt Hathaway ran her brother's house with precision and hard work and felt Anne should be doing the same. "When is William due for another visit home?" she asked.

"Who knows, I certainly don't! He obviously loves his life in London and forgets all about us here. Do you know, Aunt, my household expects 3 meals a day and I must oversee the preparation and serving. There are just not enough hours in the day and I can't find the time even to bake bread. When I'm lucky enough to lay my hands on some meat, I must preserve it in salt or smoke it—so many things I have to do. I had no idea you had to do so much to look after a house!" It was doing Anne good, just to have a moan.

"I'll tell you what, my dear—I'll instruct Cook to bake you some loaves for your house—would that help?" Her aunt was tired of her niece's need to unburden herself and she reached some spices from the dresser and gave them to her. "Take these, Anne—you'll soon learn all the little tricks, see if you don't. You use the spices to hide the salty taste of the meat you've boiled in brine— and it's good too for concealing meat that's gone off with age."

"Aunt Hathaway, would it be possible for Bessie to send over some butter and cheese as well as the bread—I have to turn the churn myself and it's so tiring—and Susanna always seems to cry when I need to do the work."

"I'll tell you what, Niece—I'll instruct Bessie to brew some ale for your house too—as she does for here. I'm afraid I can do no more—will that help?" Aunt Hathaway was very long-suffering, and Anne jumped up and kissed her.

"You are kind, Aunt—one day I'll be able to repay you—just wait and see— when William becomes famous in London and gives me more money, I'll share it with you." And she went home much happier than when she'd arrived. She was missing Will however—he stayed in London for too long, in fact she hadn't seen him for at least 2 months. 'I hope he's doing well and sends us some money soon.' Money was very short in Stratford.

London's streets took a bit of getting used to by William and Edmund. Stratford had been so clean and the air so fresh that London was a bit of a shock. The streets were very narrow, so the houses and buildings stared straight into each other, and doors were left open to allow the heat and smells to go outside. Unfortunately, this also allowed the street smells to come inside—and those smells were from rotting food, human and animal excrement which ran in the gutters and animals themselves even wandered freely wherever they wanted to go. Dogs, pigs, horses. sheep and goats invaded not only the streets but also the actual houses. Chickens wandered and flew around squawking loudly, especially when trodden on by a distracted pedestrian.

Every trade imaginable was available, with stalls set up side by side and shopkeepers loudly calling out their wares, trying to steal sales from one another—clanging pots, pans together, sharpening knifes, selling fruit and vegetables. Pimps and prostitutes stood on every street corner. All was in equal abundance. Whatever was needed, could be found there. Different buildings were crammed together with a church next to a stable and a house next to an inn or a workshop—and many of the buildings had to be supported by strong posts in case they collapsed when jostled by the crowds. Some buildings had very shallow foundations. The loud voices of the men and women competed with the noise of carriage wheels on the gravel—and all seemed complete chaos.

"My God, Edmund, this is what you call living—the place is so alive you can almost touch it. I could write so many stories about what I see here—some true and some made-up. It's all so exciting." William was in his element and found the atmosphere magical.

Edmund was less enamoured with the place, "I can't see how we're going to make our fortunes here, Will. If there's money around, then it's well hidden."

They walked on together towards the theatre—happily anticipating the day ahead. The theatre was always exciting, and Will's acting skills were being noticed by a couple of the other actors, although one actor had called him 'an upstart crow', but Will put it down to plain jealousy—and it meant 'he had arrived'. He became friendly with one actor called Richard Burbage—Richard was already an established and popular actor and was the brother of Cuthbert Burbage who owned a small theatre in the city. They got into the habit of meeting each other after the night's performance—taverns were all welcoming places when you had a few pennies in your pocket.

Will always seemed to have just enough for his ale and Edmund liked to come along and copy his big brother, but it was Richard Burbage that Will really liked to talk with. They discussed everything under the sun and Richard talked him into becoming one of the founder members of an acting group called The Lord Chamberlains Men, which was emerging as a strong force in the London theatre world.

"Come on Will—put your money where your mouth is—you say you want to be a famous actor one day and to produce plays of your own—well, this is your chance. You'll be right in the thick of it and meet some tremendous people and"—he playfully punched him on the shoulder—"and you'll be able to learn everything you need to know from me. In fact, I might throw you a crumb now and again—throw you the odd line, I mean!" and that was how William Shakespeare first became really involved with the actors in the London theatres.

He moved his digs too as he found he needed privacy and quiet to write and Edmund was always around to stop him from concentrating on his work. He moved to Liberty of the Clink on Bankside into a property owned by the Bishop of Winchester's Estate. (This would become the area for the Globe Theatre in the future) He didn't stay there long before he moved again to lodgings in the house of Christopher Mountjoy, on the corner of Monkwell and Silver Street. This was in Cripplegate not far from St Paul's. In fact, he moved several times but always found the time to visit his wife and children in Stratford—that was his real home and he only ever used temporary lodgings in London.

He was doing well, and his skills were progressing. He wrote well into the night by the light of a tallow candle and spent a fortune replacing the candles several times in a week. His first plays were dramas and he realised how useful he found the things he'd learned at the Grammar School in Stratford—and the stories and fables he'd heard at his mother's knee.

He made some good drinking friends at this time, but spent most of his free time with Michael Drayton, Ben Johnson and of course with Richard and Cuthbert his brother. The men were writers like himself, but no one could produce works at the speed he could. He liked to visit Anne and the children with no advance warning—he always enjoyed the pleasure on his children's faces when he brought them a small trinket from the city. He was making quite good money and he decided to buy a piece of land in Stratford—as well as a property in London. He was becoming quite an entrepreneur.

"I've just finished a play, Richard, and I think you'd be great as the lead. You're just the right age and I must admit you can act. I've written a small part for myself, but you'd be the main player." Richard eagerly accepted the part, knowing the value of Will's work.

"Why don't you call it a night, Will, and come with me to the tavern—I've heard there's some winsome lasses there now—and the barmaids are something to behold." Richard was on his feet already.

"Now Richard—you know I'm a married man with children—how can I ogle the lasses? You can—you're a free agent." But he went with his friend that night and he did ogle the lasses and the barmaids. In fact, as he stumbled drunkenly on his way home, he was approached by one of the many prostitutes who hung around the streets—and he took her home with him.

He felt ashamed of himself next morning once the girl had gone but common sense told him no one need ever know—but he knew! Unfortunately, that became more normal than before but the drinking and whoring seemed not to undermine his writing ability. His plays were being performed in several theatres at the same time—in the Shoreditch Theatre, the Blackfriars Theatre, the Curtain Theatre and eventually once it was completed, the Globe Theatre itself. He wrote the largest number of his works when he was involved with the Globe.

In fact, he partly owned the theatre—he owned 12.5 % of the theatre, as did 3 of his friends, Richard Burbage being one—and 50 % was owned by Cuthbert. Shakespeare bought another property in London, so rich was he becoming, but as usual he never lived there but rented it back to the friend, he'd actually bought it from. He did this to help the friend—but was wise enough to hold onto the property. As said before, he was becoming a true entrepreneur.

The Globe was making a great deal of money. The people of London loved it—they loved both dramas and comedies and were happy to stand in the open-air section which cost them a penny each—they were called The Groundlings! The wealthier audience could sit in the balconies and paid sixpence for the privilege. The theatre could fit 2,000 to 3,000 as an audience, so the revenue raised for each performance was always significant and there were always extras like fruit or sweetmeats for sale, which increased the takings even more. Theatre life in London was very attractive and it was as though the success of it all, just served to make Will produce even more of his plays and sonnets.

He had written, produced, and acted in plays performed in front of—firstly Elizabeth 1 of England and following that, in front of James 1 when he arrived from Scotland to accede to the English throne. Of course, such people could not be expected to go to the theatre with the common man, so plays were put on in palaces and in large ancestral homes. The name of William Shakespeare was known all over the country—and he still worked as hard as before, the only difference being, he could now afford the expensive tallow candles. He continued to stay in lodgings and never set up a household in London, continuing to visit Stratford as often as he could, after all it was his home.

Anne was now enjoying her life of luxury and had become an excellent home maker. She was still unable to read and write but she made sure her children could do both. Susanna was very good at her letters and sums, and the twins, Judith and Hamnet were quickly catching her up. The family was actually living a life of luxury and even John Shakespeare's fortunes had begun to pick up—it was common knowledge that Will had helped his father with this. He was now earning money at an alarming rate and had bought the largest house in Stratford—he now had quite a portfolio of property and Anne gloried in her new home with all the modern conveniences the old one hadn't had.

One day, she was resting in the garden, Susanna was helping Cook in the kitchen and the twins were playing in the meadow at the side of the house. She sensed her before she actually saw her, but it was definitely her—she hadn't seen her mother since her wedding day. "Good day, Mother, I'm very pleased to see you—I'm afraid Will's not here as he has a new play opening in London. What can I do for you, Mother?" She tried to keep calm although the spirit had really scared her.

"There is little you can do for me, Daughter—it's more what I can do for you. I know your life here is good and that man you married keeps your purse full and your servants well paid. I need you to prepare yourself for something bad that will happen soon." She looked across at the children in the meadow. "Which twin are you most fond of, Daughter? Do you have a favourite?"

"Nay Mother, I love both my children equally—why do you ask me that?" She wasn't sure why, but she felt uneasy and didn't want to hear why her mother had come to see her. It had to be bad!

"You must prepare yourself to lose one of your children—one of your twins. I don't know which one it will be—but I felt you should know what was going to happen."

"I don't want to hear that, Mother—and I don't have to believe you. Look at them," and she pointed at the children running around and playing happily. "I'm not going to listen to you—you were wrong in what you said about William—he has made something of himself—and I don't believe my babies are at risk. I care for them well." She jumped up from her chair and it fell backwards. Her mother disappeared as suddenly as she'd come and Anne ran indoors, feeling the bile rise in her throat. She vomited violently into the wash bowl. *If I didn't know better, I'd think Mother enjoyed that.* Her thoughts were running wild, and she went looking for Susanna and found her in the kitchen—just to give her a hug. She tried to shake off the way her mother had made her feel, but the dark cloud was still there.

In London, Will was visiting as many taverns as he could. He always picked up information from the various atmospheres in such places. He had many drinking cronies with whom he discussed and argued one topic after another. He was leading such a sociable life, it was a wonder he found the time to write so many of his works, all of which were successful with the audiences. Many of his scenes take place in taverns—especially Henry 1V, which is set mainly in a tavern. In fact, everything he learned in London figured in many of the scenes he wrote—and much of the knowledge he'd acquired in his early years played a big part in his works.

"Performing before royalty, Will? Where is it this time? Can King James even understand your plays—I thought he spoke only Scots?" Richard was ready for a fun night at his friend's expense.

"Oh, he understands more than you think—he's a very educated man and he appreciates my work. He has invited our players to perform at Hampton Court in a specially prepared theatre and many of his Court will be allowed to attend. I may even take a part in it myself—I miss my acting." He beckoned the serving wench over and ordered another round of drinks. He couldn't resist patting her gently as she walked away. On his return to his lodgings that night, there was a horse and rider waiting for him. He was given a message in a sealed envelope which had been written by the local vicar in Stratford.

'You must come home immediately, William. Your son Hamnet is seriously ill and has already been given the Last Rights. Make as much haste as you possibly can!'

And he did make haste but was too late. He arrived at New Place in Stratford and jumped from his sweating, exhausted horse, throwing the reins to a waiting stable boy. Anne was standing by the boy's bedside with tears streaming down her face. The boy was stretched out on his bed, his sweet, young, face pale and drawn.

Will fell onto his knees and threw his arms around the boy. "Hamnet—my dear Hamnet—what ails you, Boy?" And he laid his head on the little body and sobbed heartfelt tears. Anne came closer and touched her husband's shoulder—he reached back with one hand and tried to comfort the grieving mother—but he was too upset to reach for her. He stood up and the two of them clung to each other—there were no words left to speak.

"Will, my mother visited me a few weeks ago and warned me this was going to happen. I didn't believe her—but she was telling the truth. The doctor says it's

Bubonic Plague—although only a slight infection, but enough to kill one so young. Susanna and Judith have been kept away from their brother for some time—we can only hope they're safe." She took his hand and led him from the room where they both settled in front of the fire, heads bowed in the very worst kind of sadness.

They buried their 11-year-old son and neither mother nor father ever got over the loss. The girls couldn't understand what had happened to Hamnet and yet not to them. The family were sad and in mourning for a long time. Will had to return to London as there was work waiting for him there—and it was, after all, his income for himself and the rest of his family.

Nearly all his plays were now performed at The Globe Theatre, the first being Julius Caesar. If anything, the terrible incident of his son's death seemed to spur him on to write even more—and he produced many brilliant works. His reputation had spread everywhere, and the people queued for hours to be allowed to see his plays—especially his new ones. He'd always had a playful rivalry with Richard Burbag his friend, but no one could come even close to Shakespeare's brilliance and popularity. He was made for life and was a very rich man.

In 1599, two years after the work had begun, the Globe Theatre was opened for business. The costs of building were met by Richard Burbage and the actual timbers came from the very first permanent theatre ever built in London—in the year 1576 by James Burbage, Richard's father. Before that, actors played out their performances on street corners and in the yards of inns, but the London Council caught onto this and began taxing such events as they were executed within the city limits. So, James built his own theatre outside the city limits and plays performed there weren't subject to taxes. A good way to deal with an unjust tax—unless of course you worked as a taxman.

"Now that was a good idea of yours, Richard—to use the timbers from the old theatre to build the new one. Much cheaper and one in the eye for the Council!" Will was happy at the prospect of his works being performed on a brand-new stage.

"Be fair, Will—it might have been my idea initially, but it was The Lord Chamberlain's Men who arranged the actual deed—and you were involved with it too." Richard felt generous with his praises and knew he needed Will's skills to make the whole enterprise work.

"I think we dealt well with the issue of the land where the old theatre sat. My father had the land on a leasehold only and Mr Allen held the actual lease but refused to extend it when it expired. My cunning father realised that, although he didn't own the land, he did own the building that stood on it. Mr Allen was away from home over Christmas and The Chamberlain's Men took down the old theatre and the builder, Peter Street was contracted to build the Globe—he stored the timbers in his yard until it was time to start building. My family couldn't afford to buy a leasehold on land near the South Bank of the River, which was what they wanted—so shares in the building were sold to you and 3 others—£10 each was a reasonable sum, wasn't it—for a 12.5% share in the Globe?"

"I'll say it was and I felt privileged to be included in the deal. Let's fill our tankards again and drink to future success—London loves us, and we love London!" Will felt like talking and if there'd been a soapbox handy, he would have climbed on it. "My properties are doing well; my family is safe in Stratford—except for little Hamnet—and my writing is still in full flow. What more can I ask for?" And he gulped back the ale, banged the tankard on the table and called for more. "Tell me though—how did he get the timbers across the river—that must have been a gigantic effort."

"Come on, Will, it's not what you know, but who you know. When the weather got a bit better, Street brought the timbers across in a boat with the help of—now I must get this right—The King's men, not Lord Chamberlain anymore. It doesn't hurt to have the patronage of a King; you should know that." Richard was well into his cups but loved how it felt. "And so, the Globe Theatre was built in Southwark, quite near to the Rose Theatre and The Swan Theatre—two of our competitors. It's a good place for the theatre—it's outside the city limits, so no taxes and it's surrounded by animal baiting areas, taverns and brothels." He looked smug and delighted at the prospect of lots of people coming to enjoy themselves and spend their money. His elbow slipped and his chin hit the table hard, but he was too happy to feel pain.

Will couldn't resist saying, "You'll need makeup on that bruise before you tread the boards tomorrow. Street has been an amazing builder, hasn't he? He managed to use the cheapest materials and yet produced a magnificent building." They'd chosen the right builder.

The new theatre was a large, open air structure that covered with a roof around the circumference that covered the seating areas—very similar to, but obviously smaller than, the Colosseum in Rome. It cost six pence for a seat and there were three stories of seats which could take thousand spectators in its 100-foot diameter. In the centre was an open arena called 'The Pit' which held 'the

Groundlings' who paid their penny willingly. In the hot summers, the 'groundlings' were sometimes known as the 'stinkards' for obvious reasons. A large rectangular stage, called an apron, projected into the 'the pit' to allow the players to come amongst the audience. In hot Summer, the players didn't really appreciate this, but the rules were the rules and had to be obeyed.

"The Stinkards are ripe today, Master Shakespeare," one of the lady-boys said, holding a scented handkerchief to his nose. "I swear I feel quite bilious."

"That's tough, young man, but that's why you're paid for each performance—so be grateful." He had no time for such complaints. "You're lucky to have a job in such a lovely theatre and by the look of your dark stubble, you won't be having it for much longer."

He turned away from the petulant boy and shouted at the 'Flagman', "White Flags today, John—take the red ones down." To advertise the type of play to be performed that day, coloured flags were hung outside, white for comedy, red for historical and black for tragedy. "And make sure that crest is secure above the entrance—we don't want it dropping onto anyone's head, do we?" The crest was inscribed with the words *Totus mundus agit histrionem—The Whole world is a Playhouse!*

Will was in a controlling mood that day—he liked to involve himself with every aspect of the theatre and he went looking for the 'Collecting Man'. "And you, Sir, make sure the boxes of money collected from the audience are taken straight to the 'Box Office'—make no delay as that's our bread and butter." Loud trumpets began to sound to tell the people the performance was about to begin, and they should take their seats—for the 'Groundlings' of course, to find a good place to stand.

The plays flew from Will's quill—the first at the Globe was Julius Caesar but there were also *As You Like It, Hamlet, Measure for Measure, Othello, King Lear, MacBeth* and *Anthony and Cleopatra*, to name but a few. Of course, other writers also wrote for the Globe, such as Ben Johnson, Thomas Dekker and John Fletcher—but there was no one to rival Shakespeare—his historical and psychological understanding of life and people was unsurpassable and his knowledge of words incredible—he was responsible for many new words that swelled the English dictionary. Not bad for a boy who left school at 13 when he should have been there until 16. How much more would he have known, had he completed his formal education? A rhetorical question if ever there was one!

The years passed—Will's remaining two girls grew in health, his writing became even more prolific, his wife and home were safe and secure, and his London friends grew even more in number. He was however a heavy and frequent drinker and enjoyed the social life in the city too much. He continued to visit Stratford when he could, and he'd even purchased another property there—to make the best use of his wealth. In 1603, he certainly visited his home and stayed for a while, to try to avoid catching the Black Death or Plague in the stifling air of the city.

London suffered greatly from the pandemic which eventually spread all over Europe, coming initially from China where the flee-ridden rats carried it from country to country—mostly on trading vessels. The Globe Theatre was closed for several weeks. Although the Plague quietened down after time, it still raised its head from time to time, and the theatre again had to close its doors in 1608 because of the same Black Death. Will managed to avoid the disease both times by returning home to the comparative safety of Stratford.

"God, Will, I hope you haven't brought that dreadful plague from London. What if the children catch it?" Anne was quite perturbed.

"Did you want me to stay in London where it's rife—and catch it myself? It's a terrible, cruel disease and hardly one person survives once it touches them. This is my home too Wife and don't you forget it. I pay for everything and everyone in it." He'd been expecting an open and warm welcome and was disappointed at Anne's reaction to his unexpected arrival.

"I'm going to my study—I have some writing that needs my attention." And he was off—it was always thus when he turned up unexpectedly. Their love for each other had diminished with the passing years, probably because of his frequent absences to London, but then she enjoyed the money he earned there and the respectability it had given her. She was now highly regarded by the people of Stratford-on-Avon, and he had found some pleasurable interludes in his sociable life in the city. So, other than as the mother of his children and manager of his household, he had little need of her. However, they were both content in their own ways and soldiered on together, but in their separate ways.

The year 1613 arrived—it was 29 June, and a day William Shakespeare would never forget. In fact, it changed his whole life. The play was about Henry VIII, so the red flags were flying outside the theatre. It's believed to have been the last play that Will ever wrote—but apparently history isn't sure of that. He was not actually in attendance at the theatre that night, but the fire started when some small cannons were fired for effect. No cannon balls were actually used but gunpowder and wadding were—and it caught fire with a piece of scenery, setting alight the thatch on the roof. The actors and audience ran in all directions and the theatre itself burned down in just an hour. The strange thing was that, although it was packed with people, only one man was hurt—and it was more his pride than his body. His trousers caught fire, and someone had to douse them with a bottle of beer—and that was the only casualty on the night the Globe Theatre burned down. All the bricks were left intact and were used subsequently to build a second Globe—a more extravagantly built theatre and less flammable than the first one.

When Shakespeare learned what had happened, it was as though someone had ripped the heart from his chest. He suddenly became lethargic and wasn't even interested in his writing. He said goodbye to all his friends in the city and packed his bags—he was going home to Stratford. He felt lacklustre and the thought of lifting his quill was just too much. He packed his saddlebags and rode his horse back to where he'd been born. The change in the man was incredible although Richard Babbage did try to persuade him to stay.

"We're going to build a new theatre, Will—we have the resources because of the success of your plays. Don't give up now—we need you more than ever—once it's up and running, the people will flock back again with their pennies and sixpences—see if they don't." But it was no use, Will had made up his mind. Lack of energy was the main reason for his decision—and the glorious bubble of his writing had finally burst.

"I have come home for good, Wife—London has soured for me, and I need the fresh air of home."

The stable boy had brought his saddlebags from the yard and laid them before him, "Is there anything else, Master?"

Will told him to give the horse a good rubdown. "He's done well on our journey home, maybe he knew it was for the last time." He spoke sadly to the boy.

"You are welcome, Husband—although you'll have to fit in with our routines here—we're used to doing things in a certain way and running the household needs all my attention." Anne spoke quite dismissively. She'd enjoyed overseeing everything and making all the decisions. She needn't have worried though, because Will seemed unlike the man he used to be and accepted her words with little argument. He was beginning to feel quite unwell and for the first time in his life, he began to experience a lethargy that made him want to stay in bed in the morning. He thought this was something that would never happen, but it did. He still used his study more than any other room in the house—as though one day he planned to start writing again, but it just didn't happen. The great man had written his last masterpiece.

The next few years passed peacefully, and Will settled in well with his family—if he missed London, he didn't mention it—after all, it had been his own decision to leave. He kept in touch with the friends he'd made there—only intermittently of course, as they were still busy in the world of entertainment. He was not short of money however and he, and his family, were able to live well on what he'd made in the city.

His biggest enjoyment since coming home was the existence of his first grandchild—Elizabeth Hall was born in 1608 and was the daughter of Susanna and husband, Dr John Hall. Shakespeare adored the girl and likewise, she adored her grandfather, whose stories kept her on the edge of her seat for hours on end. "Tell me more, Grandad—tell me the one about the Princess who lost her crown, or the one about the wicked Queen who murdered her husband." And of course, he did as he was bid and kept her transfixed for hours. He would sit by the great fireplace and hold her on his knee and when she left to go look for some sweet cake or other, he would turn his attention to Hamnet, who often visited him in his study. The frail little boy would stand by his desk and Shakespeare loved to look at him.

"My Boy, we could have had such exciting times together now that I'm home. I missed a lot of your childhood, but I'm home now—and you visit me so often that I feel quite blessed." He could see Hamnet smile and play with his marbles on the floor. The boy was almost alive—but alas, not quite!

"I'll always come to visit you, Grandad—you tell Elizabeth such wonderful stories—I can hear them too." At least, those were the words he heard his grandson say. The boy still looked as he'd had when he was eleven and Will could feel his heart constrict when he thought of how little life the child had had.

"You'll always be welcome to listen to my stories—come and visit me as often as you can." And the once-great writer would puff away contentedly on his pipe bowl and close his eyes in contemplation. The pace of life was slower, but it was all he could manage these days.

In March 1616, he rose from his bed and called for a servant, "Take this note to Mr Jenkins, the solicitor in the High Street, and wait for his reply. I feel the need to put my affairs in order—it's time I did." And so, he did just that. On 25 March 1616, he signed his Last Will and Testament—it was as though he knew he had only limited time left. In the will, he made several bequests but most of his possessions, including the property in London, he bequeathed to his eldest daughter, Susanna. Many smaller disbursements were left to other people, including his London friends. Richard Burbage, John Hemmings, Henry Condell, who all received 26 shillings and 8 pence. The same sum was left to his close family, including his sister Joan Hart, who lived in one of the properties at New Place alongside his own home. All his silver, he left to his granddaughter, Elizabeth. To Anne his wife, he left her well provided—as his widow and under the Law at the time, she would have been entitled to one third of his Estate—enough to live out the rest of her life in luxury, something she enjoyed doing. He did leave her one thing however, which some people decided was meant as an insult.

His will read 'Item I gyve unto my wife, my second-best bed with the furniture.' He probably meant no slight by this, as the 'second best bed' would have been their marriage bed and the actual best bed was always reserved for guests at the house—so it didn't seem as though he was slighting her—but some people believed otherwise. It was just the custom and traditions of the day. Susanna was the major benefactor of the Estate.

In the first week of April 1616, two of Shakespeare's friends from London came to visit him. Ben Johnson and Michael Drayton arrived unexpectedly at New Place and were invited inside by a flustered Anne. They were great men in their own right and she was worried she wouldn't be able to do them justice. She did look after them though and the three literary men sat up all night, drinking immeasurable amounts of wine and ale. Anne provided meat and cheese and bread to aid their digestion. The conversation never lagged and old stories were dug up and told repeatedly. In the morning, they all slept late and Will had to be excused from breakfast as he was too exhausted after the night's celebrations.

The following week, William Shakespeare died in his bed. He died on the same date and month as when he was born—Born 23 April 1564: Died 23 April 1616. It was a death that he, at least, was expecting and he was only 52 years old. It was believed he died of Syphilis, but there was never any evidence to prove that—just speculation. He lies interred in the Church of the Holy Trinity at Stratford-upon-Avon and in due course, his wife will also lie there. On the grave, there is a curse inscribed on the stone and it is believed it was written by Will himself—on the night of the previous week when he drank his two friends, Ben, and Michael, under the table. The curse reads:

Good friend for Jesus' sake forbeare, to dig the dust
Enclosed here. Blessed be the man that spares these
Stones. And cursed be he that moves my bones.

And although repair work was carried out on the floor of the church in 2008, the workers were careful and swore that no stones or bones were touched in the process. His curse, as a protection for his last resting place, has worked until this day. At least, we assume it has!

Shakespeare's second daughter, Judith gave birth to 3 children after her father's death:

Shakespeare Quiney (born November 1617-died May 1617)

Richard Quiney (born October 1617-died January 1639—with no issue)

Thomas Quiney (born January 1619-died January 1639—with no issue).

Both Richard and Thomas died in the same month and year—both probably Plague victims.

Elizabeth, Will's first grandchild, married twice but had no issue—so there is no direct line from the Bard. He was the greatest writer in the world, whose work lives on today. It is still taught in schools, colleges and universities and performed in theatres in every country. It continues to be read by all and is responsible for the best-known quotes in the English language.

Should there be something you'd like to say, but can't find the words, just read some Shakespeare and you're sure to find them there. What a man he was!

Gloriana—The Greatest Monarch

"Well Sire, my time is getting close, it won't be long now until you see your new son." King Henry and two ladies-in-waiting were helping Anne Boleyn board the Royal Barge on the River Thames.

He smiled and nodded his head, "Now take care, my love, it can be quite slippery here." She settled her heavily pregnant body on the soft cushions, placed there in abundance for her comfort. The year was 1533 and Henry and Anne had been married for just under a year. The King's first wife, Katherine of Aragon, was still alive and in her eyes, still his wife but she'd been banished from court because she wouldn't agree to a divorce from the King.

He had addressed the problem by breaking away from the Pope in Rome and therefore from the Catholic Religion itself. He proclaimed himself Supreme Head of the Church of England and so, he could do as he pleased. His pleasure was to ignore Katherine and marry Anne Boleyn. He had persuaded himself that he'd never been lawfully married to Katherine and now all was well in the Royal Court and Henry was happy to ignore the presence of his one daughter Mary, who'd been born to his first 'wife'. But now the birth of his son was imminent— there could be no doubt that Anne would give him a son and heir. He plumped up the cushions behind his wife's back and said, "Lie back, Madam, and enjoy the fresh air—you already have a fair blush to your cheeks, and I like it well."

The Royal barge arrived at Greenwich Palace and the oarsmen jumped onto the pier to make the landing safe. Anne's ladies helped her disembark and between them, slowly walked her up the path to the main door. It was the month of August—late August—and Anne's baby was due early September. Greenwich Palace had been chosen by Henry for her lying-in—it was his favourite palace. The irony was that he'd chosen it even though Katherine of Aragon had given birth to his daughter Mary in the same palace, maybe even the same room. Henry had never been one to worry about his conscience, in fact many doubted he even had one.

"Sire, I would like to hold my lying-in banquet as soon as possible, as I grow weary very easily. I will be able to say goodbye to all the male courtiers and unfortunately to you also. It might be bad luck if I didn't keep the tradition of celebrating at this point in my pregnancy." They were settled in the Great Hall inside the palace and Henry said, "We'll hold the banquet tomorrow night—that'll give sufficient time for the cooks to prepare wonderful dishes and for the courtiers to travel here. I agree, we must keep up the tradition. Now—would you like to retire to your bed chamber and rest for a while?" It was time for her to adjourn to her bedchamber—in fact, she was rather late in doing so, as this was usually done a whole month before a lady's due date. Henry went on, "I shall speak with the Steward and tell him what I want—don't you worry, just leave it all to me."

He made it sound as though he would prepare everything personally which of course, was a nonsense. He just snapped his fingers and it all happened. The occasion was of great importance as it heralded the birth of the King's son and many fireworks displays, tournaments and celebrations were planned to welcome the new Prince. Anne had her lying-in banquet the next night before she retired to her birthing bed, but before the celebrations began, she took holy communion and asked the King if he would like to join her.

Everyone knew Henry VIII had a temper and they'd seen it on many occasions. His face turned red, his lips trembled, and his hands shook. "What, Madam, you say this to me? Do you forget it was for you that I broke with Rome? No, I will not join you." He realised quickly that he mustn't upset her, and he forced himself to calm down but she knew she'd stepped out of line and told herself to be careful in the future. The banquet took over and the laughing, dancing, eating, and drinking saved the day for Anne—on that occasion. She left the celebrations early as it had been all too much for her—but Henry went on partying into the night. At her bedchamber, she said goodbye to her husband and to all the male courtiers—who were not allowed to enter her bedchamber.

The lying-in chamber had been prepared by the ladies of the court. Around the walls and windows, beautiful tapestries had been hung, in the hope that they would distract the Queen from the labours and pain of giving birth. Whether it worked or not, only she knew—but her ladies waited on her and did their best to make her as comfortable as possible. The Queen mustn't be bored.

The wall tapestries were embroidered in gold and silver—flowers and patterns, but no figures nor animals, in case this upset her. Some of the tapestries told the story of Saint Ursula and her eleven thousand virgins, a subject that was to prove peculiarly fitting for the woman the baby would one day become. The floors were deeply covered with lush carpets, many from France—all was ready for the confinement. The King strutted about the palace like a peacock in full feather and twelve days later, he was informed that Anne had gone into labour. He would soon hold his long-awaited son and heir in his arms.

Anne's labour was of average duration and the baby was eventually delivered with the minimum of fuss. As she gave one last final push, she watched her ladies' eyes—and she knew. It was 3 o'clock in the afternoon when the baby was born and even the day followed the theme of the tapestries—it was the eve of the Feast of the Virgin. The ladies kept their eyelids lowered and wouldn't look her in the face. The baby was taken away to be cleaned and she waited patiently for its return. "Is there something wrong with the baby?" she asked, fearing the answer.

"Oh no Madam, the baby is lusty and quite beautiful with your husband's strong nose and red hair. A veritable beauty, Madam." Yet still they avoided her gaze.

She asked outright, "It's a girl, isn't it? Please tell me I'm wrong Madelaine." And she pointed at the youngest lady there, "What sex is the child—I command that you tell me."

But she already knew before Madelaine said, "It is a beautiful girl, strong and with good lungs. May I fetch her for you?"

Anne looked at the small, red-haired baby and the tears began to fall. "Don't tell him yet—please don't tell him yet—let him live with his happy anticipation a little longer." But in the end, the news had to be taken to the King. The tournaments, the firework display and the celebrations were cancelled immediately—they'd been planned for a boy only. His courtiers became subdued, and no one knew what to say. It had to have been the biggest disappointment of his life and he sank back into a chair, his head in his hands. He was angry and felt let down, so he waited for a while before going to see Anne, to allow him to compose himself. In the end, he visited the new mother and asked the ladies to bring the child to him.

"She is a lovely little child, I can see that, and she has my hair colour, doesn't she?" He held the baby for a few minutes and, glancing quickly at his wife, he left the bed chamber, saying over his shoulder, "Never mind, Anne—we will have a boy next time." It wasn't the words a woman who'd just given birth liked to hear and she just fell back against the pillows, exhausted, sad and knowing full well that she'd let him down.

Letters and placards had been prepared to announce the birth of a Prince, but these were scratched through before being issued—by merely removing the word 'boy' and overwriting it with 'girl.' It was cheaper and easier to do this than to prepare new letters—and the baby had only been a girl after all.

The lusty baby was here to stay however, and she was christened 3 days after her birth on 10th September in the Church of Observant Friars in Greenwich. Her Godparents were important and illustrious notables, such as Thomas Cranmer The Archbishop of Canterbury, Agnes Howard, the Dowager Duchess of Norfolk and the Marchioness of Dorset. The ladies spoke privately within their circle, "I am not happy to be here, nor to be the Godmother of a bastard—sweet baby though she is." It was a belief many people shared.

"Nor am I." one of the others replied, "But what can we do—the King has commanded it." Cranmer kept well out of the conversation as he was always wary of Henry. The baby was named Elizabeth after her two grandmothers—Elizabeth of York and Elizabeth Howard—from either side of her parents' families.

For her very first years, Elizabeth was marginalised at court and kept well away from court activities. She lived at Greenwich Palace for a short time but was moved to both Richmond Palace and then to Nonesuch Palace, both magnificent royal homes. Henry didn't know what to do with her, it seemed. At a very young age, she was finally moved to live at Hatfield Palace, and the house was set up as her personal estate, in fact she was given the palace as her own—it had all the necessary staff, and she had both a governess and tutor. She was the very young mistress of her own home. Money spent on her was sparse however as her being a girl gave her no kudos as far as the King was concerned. The child had very few decent clothes—it was just the same for her half-sister, Mary—and both girls lived very frugally indeed.

Possibly to rub her nose in her precarious position at court, the Lady Mary—not now known as the *Princess* Mary—was ordered to Hatfield Palace to serve her young half-sister. Both girls however received the same excellent education—and little Elizabeth especially soaked up knowledge like a sponge. As she grew, she learned Latin, Greek, Spanish, French, as well as all the other subjects of a classical education, including history, philosophy, and mathematics. A great deal for a child's mind to absorb, but somehow, she managed it.

Elizabeth had a jovial nature and sometimes was accused of being too happy, something which was a miracle, as at the age of two she learned from whispers in corridors that she no longer had a mother. For some reason, the whispers also told her, her father had executed her mother—in fact, he'd had her head cut off. She was too young to understand the whys and wherefores of her Father's mind, but she did have regular nightmares, where her Mother appeared as a headless figure. Something that stayed with her throughout her life.

Although scared by the whispers, she managed to find comfort in, firstly Lady Bryant her companion and then when she was four, by a new governess called Katherine Champernowne, who was a sweet, motherly and very well-educated young lady. The immediate affection between the two grew quickly and Katherine—or Kat, as her young charge called her—came to love the child dearly. She soon became a mother-figure to Elizabeth who loved her in return. Kat stayed with her charge for a long time, but eventually married Elizabeth's cousin, John Ashley—something which made the two closer than ever in the years to come. Kat Ashley remained by her side for a great many years.

One day, she and Kat were working on their sewing. They were still in the study where they'd been studying and chatting in French when Elizabeth suddenly asked, "Kat, have you ever seen my mother?" Kat replied that she had, and Elizabeth went on, "No, I don't mean before my father had her executed—I mean after she lost her head. Have you ever seen her in any of the corridors or perhaps after you've retired to bed?" She spoke very matter-of-factually and looked up from her work expectantly.

"Now, My Lady, you know that's not possible, don't you? The question is a rather foolish one and not one you should be asking." Kat was unsure how to handle this—the child was only four after all.

"All right then, Kat—I won't ask you that—but you must tell me why my father did what he did. I should have had a mother, shouldn't I?"

"Why, My Lady, you have me and I love you dearly." Kat was out of her depth and knew she couldn't talk about adultery, promiscuity, and treason to such a young child. In any case, who knew the real reason the execution was necessary—she certainly didn't. She breathed a sigh of relief when the door opened and Blanche Parry came into the room, carrying a long roll of soft material. She was a Welsh lady who was part of the young Elizabeth's household and, like Kat, stayed with her mistress for the rest of her life.

"Look, My Lady, look what you've been sent—the Lady Anne of Cleves—although no longer your stepmother, now that she and your father have separated but she obviously thinks of you often and considers herself your friend." Anne of Cleves was not Henry's wife for very long and had agreed to have their marriage annulled. In the end, a very wise and pragmatic woman who benefitted from this decision by being showered with many expensive gifts by Henry.

Elizabeth grew up, liking Hatfield, in fact it may have been the best time of her life. Her mother, Anne Boleyn had known the house well—it had once been part of her a family estate, but she'd only visited her young daughter there two or three times before her execution. In effect, both she and Henry forgot all about both Elizabeth and Mary's existence. It may have seemed harsh, but it was a good thing for the girls as they were happy there—well away from the prying eyes of the court.

Both Kat and Blanche liked to look after Elizabeth and were working on a new and special dress for her. It was plum coloured and suited her very well. Elizabeth continued trying to find out more about her mother. She cornered Blanche one day, complaining that Kat wouldn't answer her questions. She was a clever girl and would sometimes play the two favourites against each other to get what she wanted. A normal child really!

"And what question is that My Lady?" Blanche liked the idea of doing where Kat had failed.

And of course, Elizabeth asked, "Why did my father execute my mother? Don't worry, you won't upset me—I never really knew her—I was too young." Blanche decided that now Elizabeth was seven years old, almost eight, and quite a serious girl, perhaps it would be better to tell her the truth.

"My Lady, your father fell out of love with the Lady Anne and decided she was a traitor because she had loving relationships with men other than himself. As you now understand, if this were so, it would be classed as treason against the Crown. And that's what happened, I'm afraid."

She couldn't bring herself to tell the child more than that, especially that one of the men had been Elizabeth's Uncle and Anne's own brother. And that all the men accused of being Anne's paramours had been executed as well. It was a particularly cruel act, but King Henry obviously thought very little of it all, as within a few days of Anne's execution, he married for the third time, to one of Anne's ladies-in-waiting, Jane Seymour. She told Elizabeth none of these small details after all what use would it serve? She knew however, in the years to come, the whole story would reach the ears of the child.

"Thank you for that, Parry, now I feel better informed. By the way, what time are we to expect Prince Edward to arrive? I like when he comes to stay—he spends a lot of time with me, but not with Mary I'm afraid—those two just can't get along together, can they—and yet he is still so young?"

Blanche Parry realised the child had absorbed the information about her mother's execution with no problem at all. Children were so realistic and pragmatic—and Elizabeth even more so. As she left the room, her parting words to Parry were, "It's odd really, my father created a lot of pressure for himself, didn't he?" The girl was wise beyond her years. Of course, Blanche didn't respond.

"Hello, Cousin Elizabeth, and how are you today?" The young Prince Edward had come to stay at Hatfield Palace for a while. They were in the rose garden amongst some of the most beautiful smells and colours imaginable. "I am well Brother but all the better for seeing you." Time had passed with most of Elizabeth's time being spent at Hatfield where she was effectively a prisoner—she couldn't go anywhere without her father's permission—and she only heard news from the royal court in London, when the news was already stale. Although only a child, Edward could be relied upon to tell her about the court. He was only six years on this visit, but he was a chatty child and liked to tell his sister things she didn't know. His tutor was only a few feet away—he never travelled without his tutor.

"Did you know our father is to marry yet again? I quite like her—she's funny and makes me laugh. I don't think you'd know her—she's Catherine Howard and I heard she is related to your mother—and so to you, I suppose."

Elizabeth had produced a bag of sugared almonds from her pocket and gave them to him. "Tell me more, Edward, and you're quite right, I didn't know this." The unbidden thought came into her mind, *Will this marriage last, I wonder*. She doubted it very much.

"But surely she is a very young person—this Catherine Howard." She spoke aloud.

"And that's not all," the precocious child went on telling her what he considered to be court secrets. Elizabeth was astounded—first by how young the maid must be and also because he'd executed her cousin, Elizabeth's mother. Another unbidden thought, *My Father seems to have no conscience at all.*

Elizabeth made it her business to find out more about Catherine Howard. Henry was in his fiftieth year and the young girl was only sixteen or seventeen—and she was a first cousin to her Anne Boleyn and a cousin twice remove of her own. Surely her father would never find reason to harm such a young person—he would be unable to find fault with her. But time would tell.

The two married just a few days after Henry's annulment from Anne of Cleves had been made official. The marriage was conducted on 28 July 1540 at Oatlands Palace in Surry. It was said that he was enamoured of her and gave her anything she asked. She was a very playful girl and seemed able to make him laugh, despite his ulcerous leg which was causing him great pain. He was more heavily built than before and couldn't dance with her the way he'd done with previous wives—but he liked to watch her enjoying herself, especially with the young men of the court. Catherine especially liked her own cousin, Thomas Culpepper, who paid her more attention than was perhaps prudent.

"Why do you dance so often with your cousin?" Henry asked her one evening. Now, a wiser and less naïve person would have recognised the sinister overtone of the question, but Catherine was not much more than a child and continued to favour the same young men over and over again.

Elizabeth was sitting in the rose garden. Blanche Parry and Kat were with her, and she begged them for news from the court. Kat's husband attended court regularly and was always ready to tell his wife of happenings there. "How does my father fare with his new wife, ladies? Is he still as fond of her as I've heard? Come on, Kat, your husband must provide you with details of what he sees when he's at court. If you don't tell me, I may have to punish you." But she laughed as she said it and they both knew she'd never do such a thing.

"I think he tires of her already, My Lady. The word is that she's a maid who's too generous with her favours and you know your father is a jealous man. They've been married over a year now and there's still no sign of a baby—he chose her for her youth and vitality in the hope she'd produce another male to secure his dynasty—but it seems to no avail. He still yearns for that other son as a 'spare' for Edward, you know." Kat said nothing, but Blanche blurted it all out, and enjoyed doing so. She'd never approved of the way Elizabeth had been treated by the King.

Only six months later, Catherine Howard was beheaded on Tower Hill. She could only have been nineteen years old, if that much and yet, Henry still took the decision to execute her. As with her cousin, Anne Boleyn, she was charged with treason based on adulterous behaviour—and as with Anne and her brother, this time Catherine was accused of adultery with her cousin Thomas Culpepper. He was executed before Catherine and his head placed on a spike on Tower Bridge. Brave, little Catherine asked for a wooden block to be brought to her cell the night before her execution, so she could practice laying her head on it. When she gave her last confession, she explained she wanted to die like a queen—with dignity.

A story still told today is that she is often seen running down the long gallery at Hampton Court Palace and screaming for mercy—something she actually did on the day she was arrested… She also shouted that she was not guilty and that she wanted to see the King. This she was denied, and she never saw Henry again. It had been Thomas Cromwell his Minister, who'd left a letter on Henry's seat in the chapel at Hampton, giving details and names of those involved with his wife. Henry turned his back on her and on 13 February 1542, the young Catherine was dead. Her lady-in-waiting, Lady Jane Rochford was also executed for apparently aiding her mistress to seek out different lovers.

When Elizabeth heard the news, she was devastated—she'd been related to the young girl, and it seemed to make her own Mother's execution real again and she felt the loss afresh. Poor little Catherine—she really didn't deserve that. Elizabeth didn't like her father but she loved him out of duty—it may have been at this time in her life that she decided she would never take a husband as she saw them as a dangerous attachment in life. And who could blame her?

And so, on 12 July 1543, Henry married his sixth wife, Catherine Parr—a very reputable lady in her early thirties. She had been married very young and widowed twice before marrying the King. It was fourteen months after he'd executed Catherine Howard and the couple were married at Hampton Court Palace where many of his previous brides had lived. It was the place where the young Catherine had first learned Henry had turned against her and where she'd run screaming along the corridor in the Long Gallery. It obviously didn't bother Henry one little bit.

Despite her earlier marriages, Catherine Parr was childless—so in this marriage, it might have been Henry was looking for comfort only—and not a child. A more mature woman would be less demanding than a young one and it was believed the King was impotent and hadn't consummated his marriages since Jane Seymour, but that can only ever be supposition.

Catherine Parr proved to be a dutiful wife and cared for her husband who was in continual pain. She was a very learned and pious lady and at the time, was the first woman ever to publish more than one book. She was a philosopher and philanthropist—a thoroughly caring wife who had serious debates with a husband who also liked an argument, as long as he was allowed to win. She was shrewd enough however, never to overstep the mark as she was only too aware of how Henry's wrath and fury could suddenly erupt.

After a couple of years, she persuaded him to bring Elizabeth and Mary from Hatfield Palace and settle them back at court. She also persuaded him to renew their hereditary places regarding the Crown—always of course, following Prince Edward. It was a quieter period in Henry's life and his two daughters soon settled at Court, a place where some would argue they should always have been.

"Are you happy here, Sister?" Mary asked Elizabeth one day when they'd both gone riding across the palace grounds.

"I am quite happy, Mary—and what about you?" The two sisters didn't often go out together—they had very different characters—but both liked riding, dancing and music. They still studied together and often practised their languages together—they lived in the same place and had no option but to get on with each other. There would always be an element of distrust between them, with Mary's mother being rejected by Henry in favour of Elizabeth's mother and sent to live in isolation, forbidden even to see her own daughter. Elizabeth too was wary of those around her, having been born to a mother, whose head Henry had removed when she was only two years old. They both had reason to distrust their father and knew they had to be careful whilst under his roof. Elizabeth still preferred Hatfield Palace and escaped there as often as she could, but neither Princess was ever to feel safe,

The years slipped by in comparative calm and all Henry had to deal with was the Catholic and Protestant arguments that continued in the land. Which was better for England—Protestant or Catholic? Princess Mary had been brought up as a Catholic and still was one, but only in private. Elizabeth on the other hand, had been brought up in the Protestant faith to which she still clung. Henry of course was the Supreme Head of the Church of England and his wife, although often sitting on the fence on the question of religion, behaved as a Protestant in line with her husband's wishes.

The King's health was increasingly bad, and he developed more and more problems. Queen Catherine was a good nurse and tended to his ulcerated leg herself. In fact, she was the only one he'd allow to dress the wound. The flesh of his leg was putrefied and emanated such a foul smell that courtiers preferred not to be in the same room with him.

On 28 January 1547, Henry VIII breathed his last. His sickbed was at Whitehall Palace in London, and he was fifty-five years old. As was the custom, his three children were at his bedside, as was Queen Catherine, Thomas Cromwell, and several ministers. None of the children cried as they'd never been given the opportunity to get close to their father, but the Queen was upset as she'd been with him for almost five years. It was reported by some of the people present that the king's last words were, 'Monks! Monks! Monks!'—no one understood what he meant but some have said he must have been thinking about the Dissolution of the Monasteries and all those monks who were driven from their homes and places of worship—driven out into the unknown. But his meaning could only ever be supposition.

King Henry VIII had been planning to use an enormous tomb built in the Renaissance style. A tomb Cardinal Wolsey had built for himself—but when he fell out of the King's favour however, Henry took it for himself. Unfortunately, the tomb was never completed and instead, Henry was laid to rest in a vault in St George's Chapel Windsor beside his beloved Queen, Jane Seymour. The funeral procession had taken two days to travel along the route towards Windsor—the entire way was lined with grieving subjects. On top of the coffin, there lay a remarkably realistic effigy of the King—from the crown on his head to the crimson velvet slippers on his feet.

The cortege stopped for one night at Syon Abbey when half the journey had been completed. A tale was told by one of the first guards to arrive next morning at where the coffin was lying in state—he reported that a dog had somehow got into the Abbey and was licking blood that had seeped from the coffin. He chased the dog away—but the terrible tale persists to this very day.

Now Catherine Parr was widowed for a third time, and she was only thirty-six years old. Before Henry had chosen her for his sixth wife, she had been in love with Sir Thomas Seymour who was Queen Jane Seymour's brother. He knew he'd had to keep a low profile but now he and Catherine free to marry and the strange thing was that she fell pregnant within a few weeks and gave birth to a daughter, Mary. Catherine was destined not to see her baby grow as she herself died on 5 September 1548—of Childbed Fever. Sir Thomas Seymour was later executed on Tower Hill as a traitor in 1549. He had been over-friendly with

Elizabeth and his wife had learned of it. Elizabeth was sent back to Hatfield Palace to live—he had been over-familiar with the young girl and probably planned to marry her. After all, one day she could be Queen.

The reason for his execution was that he was very jealous of his brother Edward's relationship with the young Prince Edward—he wanted to be Lord Protector of England in his brother's place. He attempted to abduct Edward and marry him to lady Jane Grey, but the attempt failed, as did his plan to marry Elizabeth himself and so get even closer to the throne. Nothing went right for the ambitious man however—even at his execution, when his body and head were bundled into a coffin and rushed from Tower Hill, the people standing around dipped their handkerchiefs in his blood. Why they did that, no one knows except that it did happen. His daughter Mary was left orphaned at seven months and by the age of two years, had disappeared from history records. No records show what happened to her and it was thought she'd died whilst still a baby. Strange how history can make people disappear!

Elizabeth left Hatfield and joined her brother, King Edward at court—and so did Mary. They were now both legitimate heirs to the throne should anything happen to Edward. Mary and Edward still did not get on well together—he was a staunch Protestant and she, a confirmed Catholic. They argued every day and Elizabeth had to play the role of peacemaker.

"My dear sister Mary, only a fool and an idiot would believe in Catholicism and all its magic tricks to keep peasants like you entertained." He never minced his words when insulting Mary. In fact, he positively disliked her.

"Come, come now, Your Majesty, don't be so cross with Mary—she has had a difficult life." Elizabeth chastised her brother and pulled his nose gently. However, he wasn't in the mood for fun. Anyone defending Mary was not on his side. He was an ardent Protestant and hated the thought of Catholicism. He took his role as Supreme Head of the Church of England very seriously.

"Sister, don't you realise her sort will cause havoc amongst the people—they won't know which way to turn. Our father made this country independent of Rome and I want it to stay that way." To keep his country safe from Catholicism, he then disinherited both his sisters and removed their names from the line of succession. Instead in his Will he gifted the Crown to his Protestant cousin, Lady Jane Grey. This suited the Lord Protector very well as she was his relative.

"Your Majesty, I am as eager to remain a Protestant as you are, but if we must live together, we must try to do it peacefully. Come now and I'll challenge you to a game of tennis—the afternoon is lovely, and we should be out in the sunshine." Elizabeth could always bring him out of a dark mood—they both got on so well together. "Kat, Kat—where are you? I need to change my clothes." And as usual, Kat was close by her mistress.

Edward however, was destined to have a short reign. He developed a wasting disease which resulted in consumption. His uncle, Arthur Tudor, and Henry Fitzroy, Henry VIII's illegitimate son by Bessie Blount, had both developed the identical sickness in their teenage years and they had died very young. When Edward died, things moved very fast in England and Lady Jane Grey was proclaimed Queen. She was used as a pawn in the game by the Lord Protector, Edward Seymour, and despite her reluctance to become queen, Jane went along with his plan.

Mary, who considered herself to be the rightful successor to Edward, gathered together an army very quickly and Lady Jane Grey was captured and placed in the Tower of London, there to await the executioner's axe. She had been Queen for nine days only and Mary took her place on the throne of England. Elizabeth returned to Hatfield Palace and remained there out of Mary's way. A wise move on her part. The year was 1553 and the new Queen was about to undo her brother and fathers' work and return England to the Catholic religion. This was not popular in the country, and she even changed the Heresy Laws so that a practising Protestant could be accused as a traitor. She had three hundred of her people burnt at the stake, including the Archbishop of Canterbury, who defended the people's right to be Protestant. For these decisions, history awarded her the title of 'Bloody Mary'. She is known as this to this day!

She married Phillip II of Spain who had designs on the English throne, but he soon tired of her and returned to Spain, leaving her alone. She had several phantom pregnancies, one of which lasted over a year, and which made the people view her with suspicion as no baby ever appeared. So concerned was she about her place on the throne, she had Elizabeth taken from Hatfield and placed in the Tower of London. This followed a rebellion—the Wyatt rebellion in the North—with which Mary believed Elizabeth was involved. Elizabeth remained in the Tower for three months, being taken there through 'Traitor's gate' which must have made her very afraid. She was questioned many times, but the intelligent young woman said nothing that incriminated her.

Elizabeth was imprisoned in the Bell Tower and her close servants, Kat Ashley and Blanche Parry, were also questioned—but they said nothing against their mistress. Mary believed her half-sister was involved in the rebellion—but she could prove nothing, and in the end, had to release her. She would have preferred to execute her, but she could find no proof of her involvement in the rebellion—and so, Elizabeth returned unscathed to Hatfield Palace, there to remain in a pleasant and comfortable prison. But it was a prison nonetheless and there were many guards to watch her. But at least she was safe there.

Whilst in the Tower, she was allowed to take a daily walk between the Bell and the Beauchamp Towers and one day, she met a small boy, about four years old. They became friends and Elizabeth liked talking to him but when it was reported to Mary, a message came to the Constable of the Tower that Elizabeth's walks were to be stopped and any contact with members of the public not to be allowed. Harsh and unnecessary but then, Mary was paranoid.

Queen Mary 1st reigned for five years until she was forty-two years old. Her country was still wavering between Catholic and Protestant, she was childless with no heir, she'd allowed her armies to lose Calais which had always belonged to England—and her husband Phillip had deserted her. All in all, her life was challenging to say the least. She had suffered many phantom pregnancies and her constitution was weakened—she caught Influenza—which was killing her people in their droves and on 17 November 1558, she died. The throne could pass to only one person.

On the same day as Queen Mary died, 17 November, Elizabeth was sitting under an oak tree in the grounds of Hatfield Palace—she was reading and eating an apple. A few courtiers from London arrived and bowed low before her, declaring her Queen of England. She immediately fell to her knees and said in Latin, "This is the Lord's doing, and it is marvellous in our eyes." In a few short hours, the new Queen's councillors arrived and gathered around for her first Council of State, and it was held in the great hall at Hatfield Palace.

"Pray sit down, gentlemen, you are all welcome here. I am very pleased to have become the Queen of England and the Supreme Head of the Church." No one knew exactly how long she'd been waiting to say those words, but it was many years. "Please sit here by me, William Cecil—you have always been my trusted friend and advisor." She had changed into a splendid purple gown and for the following week, Hatfield had to play host to the courtiers before joining the procession back to London—they numbered almost 1000 in all.

After that day, Elizabeth rarely visited her home at Hatfield—she'd spent so much of her life within its walls, often very worried about the future, especially when Mary had been on the throne. With her of course, Kat Ashley and Blanche Perry travelled in the procession—they would always be by her side—in particular Blanche Parry as she was unmarried. The procession was not hurried and went at a pace to allow the people to see their new monarch. Elizabeth was popular with the people, and they cheered her whole journey to the capital. She reminded them of Henry, her father and they liked her for that.

There were many pending decisions for her to make and Elizabeth immediately immersed herself in matters of state. Phillip of Spain had recently acquired Portugal and was now King of both countries—now he was turning his greedy eyes on England. Of course, as Mary's husband, he'd already had England, but not as he would have liked—not with Mary on the throne—and he'd never really liked Mary. Now, he asked Elizabeth to marry him, which would have been an easy way to win the prize. Elizabeth refused him point blank.

As the new Queen of her country, she had more serious things to deal with. She was afraid Phillip would stir up the Irish/Catholic problem again and of course, he was such a staunch Catholic. The situation was worth keeping an eye on—and she advised her ministers so to do. In fact, she was concerned about being a prominently Protestant country in a very Catholic Europe. Having said that, she never wavered from that faith.

"Please Lord, guide me in the days ahead. I may be frailer than a man but I am the daughter of Henry and will try my best to emulate him." She knelt in the chapel and spoke to God from the heart. She was then negotiating with the King of Morocco and the Sultan of the Ottoman Empire for a trade deal beneficial to England and the whole business was proving to be challenging. She returned to her chambers and sat down to a breakfast of bread and eggs with a tankard of small beer. She had no appetite however, thinking only of the day ahead—it would be her first court at Whitehall and she had much to achieve. She must impress her ministers; she must control them and she must charm them. She was good at this as she'd been doing it all her life—appeasing but retaining personal control.

Following her breakfast which she barely touched, she called her ladies to dress her. "I must look my very best today ladies—I must show my authority and my strength—but also my virility and purpose." And they set about dressing her. She favoured black and white colours, bedecked with many jewels, something of which she now had in abundance. Many different threads were embroidered over her skirts and the gold and silver ones dazzled the eye.

"I will wear the wooden corset today—it may be uncomfortable, but it keeps me ramrod straight and shows off my full skirts. That's it—fit the sleeves carefully, no join must show—and leave plenty of time to apply my make-up." The ladies used a mixture of white lead and vinegar on her face, her lips were covered with a paint made of egg whites and red dye and her cheeks were highlighted with rouge. "I will wear the darker red wig today as I feel it suits me best—and now bring me my jewels."

She chose a heavy necklace, earrings to match and several broaches. She chose from many rings but always after her formal crowning, she wore her coronation ring on her wedding finger to show she was married to her country and not to any man—something of which she was very proud... Another favoured ring was a ruby and diamond, which she wore often. It contained a miniature painting of both herself and of her mother, Anne Boleyn. When the ladies finally set her ruffs around her neck, she was ready to face the world. "Today I must carry my prayer book and the wristwatch given me by Robert Dudley, Earl of Leicester, whom I have no difficulty in favouring."

She stood to her full height and preened before the mirror. "Well ladies, how does your Queen look today?" And she was reassured by her sycophantic ladies who were rightly proud of their work—and on that day, it had taken all of two hours.

Court was already full of courtiers. On some days, there were as many as a thousand people attending—everyone wanted sight of the Queen. Her favourite and most handsome courtier approached her and bowed deeply. Robert Dudley was also elaborately dressed and had spent almost as much time on his appearance as she had on hers. He had known Elizabeth since they were children and they had played together, so they were not strangers. They talked easily and were interested in the same things.

"Madam, shall we adjourn to the gardens—the air is fresh, and the roses are in bloom," Dudley asked, but William Cecil almost pushed him aside to get nearer the Queen.

"Madam, we have many official matters to discuss today, and I fear the garden would not be an appropriate place for such conversations."

She held out her hand to Dudley and ignored Cecil. "We shall take the air first, I think. It will do us all good." And yet again, she did as Dudley wanted.

And this was the way of court. Such events were held wherever the Queen was but, because of the numbers who attended, it was usually held in her larger palaces. The court would walk through the grounds, admiring many different aspects and whilst discussing matters of court. There were even menageries and people selling things to each other, there were people singing and acting out plays for any who would watch. There were many things to amuse and entertain. Palace gardens were places of interest and entertainment.

"Good afternoon, Sir Francis," she stopped her entourage to greet Sir Francis Drake, who'd recently returned from a voyage of privateering—legal pirating on behalf of the crown of course—and on the Queen's behalf.

"And what have you brought back from your travels to amuse me, Sir? I have been feeling bored lately, so I am curious." She waited impatiently for Drake's reply.

"Madam, I shall come to court tomorrow and bring with me such valuables that will amaze. The journey was well worth the making, and I have left many Spaniards with less than they'd like. There were some rich pickings and my loyal crew made sure they picked well." The Queen had a liking for Drake—almost, but not quite—as much as she had for Dudley. Drake had filled the crown's coffers considerably since she'd officially sanctioned his sea-faring trips. She had given Drake letters, referred to as 'marques'—which confirmed he was acting on behalf of the English crown. He was certainly in a favoured position with the Queen, and she used him significantly in her turn. Before parting from him, she held out her hand for him to kiss—a sure signal of her appreciation and regard.

She turned to Robert Dudley who was scowling with obvious displeasure and smiled at him.

"Robert, why do you not ply me with jewels and valuables as does Sir Francis?" She knew the question would infuriate her favourite and so, she invited Drake to accompany her on her walk. At dinner that evening and amongst great merriment, the Queen flirted outrageously with him to restore his good humour and they left the celebration together—to go no one knew where. It was at this time, that Dudley, growing impatient to become the royal consort of the Queen, was involved in an intriguing incident. He'd married Amy Robsart and she had now become a hindrance in his ever-growing popularity with the Queen.

One day, Amy fell downstairs in her home and broke her neck in the fall. It was a rather suspicious death especially the way she'd broken her neck in the fall—she was young after all. When she was found, her neck was at a strange angle, not as her servants would have expected. Her position had seemed rather suspicious. The incident served to enhance Dudley's obsession with the Queen however and now he was free to pursue her, which he continued to do relentlessly.

Next day, after promising Elizabeth he would bring pearls amongst her Spanish riches, Sir Francis was as good as his word and turned up at court with two sailors who carried an enormous chest. When the chest was opened, the Queen saw huge amounts of sparkling gems, silver and gold plate, jewelled swords, pearls and many rings and broaches. It was an amazing sight and Elizabeth ran her fingers through the treasure, almost as though she would devour them.

"You have done, well Sir, your Queen is pleased with you." And she beckoned the sailors to carry the chest from the room. "Come sit by me, Sir Francis—make room for him, Robert," she told Dudley. She thoroughly enjoyed teasing the man and did it for pleasure, resembling the behaviour of a jealous child. Her demeanour changed immediately when William Ceil approached with several of her ministers. Now was the time for business and she became the autocratic leader in a second, ready to discuss serious matters that could affect her people. And her people always came first in her eyes.

Elizabeth contracted the Smallpox when she was just thirty and suffered for some time. As she was recovering, she developed so many scabs on her face and body that the physician feared for her life. But the good nourishment she'd always had helped her fight off the worst elements of the illness. As she gained strength, Robert Dudley asked repeatedly if he could see her, but she denied him. It was only when she was able to tell her ladies to use even more of the white lead paint on her face to conceal the pox marks, that she agreed to see him. He came slowly into her outer bedchamber and fell to his knees before her.

"Ma'am, I have prayed over and over again for your recovery and God has been good and given you back to me."

"And to my loving people whom I believe may also have prayed for my recovery." Elizabeth was quick to point this out. Although her appearance had undergone such change, he made sure he gave no sign of having noticed and reached for her hand to kiss. Dudley was in a difficult position—he had married in secret for a second time and was again not a free man to pursue her attentions, but that didn't stop him. He'd also had an illegitimate child with another woman, but he continued to act as though a free man and kept his change of status from the Queen. They went on as before and there was little doubt that she was fond of him and would have given him anything he asked for. He was eventually knighted and two years afterwards, he was made the Captain of her Guard—an elevated and superior position.

Although it was Sir Francis Drake who'd first circumnavigated the entire globe—an amazing achievement, it was a new favourite who proved himself to the Queen by leading the attack on the Spanish Armada—when their enormous fleet was defeated just off the French coast. It had been on its way to attack and defeat the English—they were tired of Drake's attacks on their ships and of course fully intended to reform England and return the country to the Catholic faith—under the Holy Father in Rome. England was in imminent danger and the biggest fleet ever put together, was on its way to attack England.

Sir Walter Raleigh was a sailor but also an explorer. He had been to America several times and had attempted to set up a new colony there. The name of his colony was 'Roanoke' and it still exists today, but his attempts to colonise repeatedly failed and in the end, he gave up his plans. On one of his trips to America, he brought back two items which were new to England—the potato and tobacco. In presenting them to Elizabeth, she found them amusing and had no idea how much they would eventually affect life in her country. Of course, the Spaniards always claimed they'd already discovered both these things, but Raleigh has always been given the credit for—after all it was he who'd brought them to England.

Raleigh was also a ship designer and builder, who was known for personally aiding his builders in their work. He designed and built 'The Golden' Hind' for himself and 'The Elizabeth' for the Queen. In fact, he helped design and build many ships for England and in 1588, he was already high enough in Elizabeth's esteem to be made the joint commander of the English fleet to fend off the threat of the Spanish Armada of ships. He was one of her true favourites and she often singled him out for attention at court. Again, this upset the ever-watchful Robert Dudley, who still clung to his hopes to one day marry the Queen and share the English throne.

She dressed in a gown of white velvet and wore a plumed helmet and a silver cuirass (corset). She carried a silver and gold baton and rode a magnificent grey gelding. She'd told her ladies to "Make me look strong and beautiful—make me look as if I welcome the challenges of Spain—and make me look the leader of my people, which I am. This will be my most important speech to date."

At Tilbury Docks in Essex, she walked amongst her people, escorted only by six guards. Lord Ormond walked ahead of her carrying the Sword of State and by her side, rode the Earl of Leicester and the Earl of Essex. Sir John Norreys brought up the rear. She passed through all the squadrons of her army and stopping in their midst, to address them in a speech which she wrote herself:

We have been persuaded by some that are careful of our safety, to take heed how we commit ourselves to armed multitudes, for fear of treachery, but I assure you I do not desire to live to distrust my faithful and loving people. Let tyrants fear. I have always so behaved myself that, under God, I have placed my chiefest strength and safeguard in the loyal hearts and good-will of my subjects; and therefore I am come amongst you, as you see at this time, not for my recreation and disport, but being resolved, in the midst and heat of the battle, to live and die amongst you all; to lie down for my God, and for my kingdom, and my people, my honour and my blood, even in the dust.

I know I have the weak and feeble body of a woman ; but I have the heart and stomach of a king, and a king of England too, and think foul scorn that Parma of Spain, or any Prince of Europe, should dare to invade the borders of my realm; to which rather than any dishonour shall grow by me, I myself will take up arms, I myself will be your general, judge and rewarder of every one of your virtues in the field.

I know already, for your forwardness you have deserved rewards and crowns; and We do assure you on a word of a prince, they shall be duly paid. In the meantime, my lieutenant general shall be in my stead, then whom never prince commanded a more noble or worthy subject; not doubting but by your obedience to my general, by your concord in the camp, and your valour in the field, we shall shortly have a famous victory over these enemies of God, of my kingdom, and of my people.

The troops cheered and shouted, "God Save the Queen. God Save England." And Elizabeth was well pleased with their response to her words.

The Spanish Armada tried to advance on England but strong winds off the coast of Scotland drove them back again and again. There were 130 Spanish ships and they sailed in an arch formation, making it difficult to attack. Elizabeth spoke with her generals, "The Spanish failed badly in the Battle of Gravelines eleven days ago, did they not? Why do they wait—do they either attack us or turn back to Spain in disgrace? The Duke of Parma did not lead his flotilla well, I fear."

At that point the English attacked and fought furiously with the enemy, but the Spanish failure in the earlier battle and the strong winds continually blowing them Northwards, proved too much—and they failed to achieve the defeat of the English fleet. Their intention had been to meet up with their land army and between land and sea, to gain their prize—but it was not to be—the English had triumphed, and England was safe.

The Queen returned to court and ordered there to be the most splendid celebrations. She also ordered a medal to be struck to be distributed to all who'd been at Tilbury Docks and the Archbishop at St Paul's Cathedral gave a sermon, praising the bravery and courage shown by the troops. The words he used included 'God's Winds Blew—and They were Scattered,' referring to the Spanish ships and the North Wind which blew them in the wrong direction. The court was full of happy well-wishers, amongst whom was of course Robert Dudley. Elizabeth had since learned of his treachery and his lies—she knew of his now-living wife, Lettice Devereux. He had however remained at her side at Tilbury Docks and supported her as best he could, so she could no nothing else but allow him to court.

However, their personal relationship was never to be the same again. The lady he'd married had considerable wealth and was a member of the Earl of Essex's family. They were eventually to remain married for ten years until the year of the Armada invasion when Dudley's health hit an all-time low. In the same year he died. Elizabeth was greatly saddened by his death and mourned for a long time, but her own health was not as good as it had once been. Dudley and Elizabeth had been friends all their lives—they'd hunted and rode together for hours on end. She was an excellent horsewoman, but Dudley equalled her. They'd been the best of friends at one time.

They'd attended hunts together, hawking and bear-baiting. Elizabeth especially enjoyed bear-baiting and she liked when any of the party brought down a young doe, as she would be invited to cut its throat 'to bring an end to its suffering.' Animal cruelty was not something understood at the time—and Elizabeth and Dudley took full advantage of its popularity. When he died, just after the Spanish Armada, she was devasted—he lived at Kenilworth Castle, a gift from the Queen and he'd just been about to 'take the waters' when his body gave up on him. It was thought that he died of cancer of the stomach.

But for Elizabeth, life had to go on and she turned to his stepson, Robert Devereux, now the Earl of Essex. He became the last of Elizabeth's favourites and she became very fond of him—but he was ambitious and wanted more and more power. He was the most arrogant and conceited man at court, and he made his main purpose to get the people to love him more than they did their aging Queen, yet she still found his arrogance attractive and he was always welcomed at court.

He was jealous when she made Robert Cecil the Secretary of State, a position he wanted for himself. He was sent however at the head of an army, to deal with the Irish problem, where fighting continued—the Catholics being unable to accept the Protestants who had settled there. They also butchered 1200 English men in 1590 and it was known they were communicating with the Spaniards, who planned to land their own Army in Ireland and fight in league with the Irish—to destroy England once and for all.

Devereux lingered in Ireland for six months and in the end, held a secret meeting with the Irish leader of the revolt, the Earl of Tyrone and they agreed between them that their two armies did not need to engage in battle. This didn't please Elizabeth at all, but she needed him as the Spaniards were also planning another invasion of England and he was put in charge of this. Devereux's force supported by an army from Holland set out for Cadiz to deal with the problem. This was achieved with great success and the Spanish were defeated on their own territory and Cadiz itself was sacked. Yet again, Devereux appeared as a hero in the English people's eyes, and he absorbed their admiration like a sponge.

The Queen was beginning to realise she'd created a monster in Devereux and confided this to Robert Cecil, who had no problem in agreeing. He and Devereux had always been enemies. She was shocked however when one morning before she was even dressed—still in her night clothes, with no make-up or wig—he rushed to London, charged through the guards at Nonesuch Palace and broke into the Queen's inner bedchamber. He'd heard she'd allowed her Secretary of State, Robert Cecil to negotiate with James V1 of Scotland for the English throne when Elizabeth died. He still had hopes that he might inherit the English throne himself. But 'the monster' had possibly gone too far this time.

He was of the new generation and decided then that he had to overthrow the Queen—she'd served long enough and was too old he thought. At a council meeting, he argued with her so much that she reached over and boxed his ears, whereupon he drew his sword, something so heinous a crime, it was unbelievable. It was becoming impossible for them to discuss anything reasonably.

Devereux decided to act. He raised three hundred followers in London including many noble lords—and began a revolt against the Government and therefore against the Queen herself. It lasted a very short time and failed, leaving Devereux to run away from the fight and return to his London home where he was arrested and subsequently put on trial. He was inevitably found guilty of treason and sentenced to death. Elizabeth's last favourite was to be executed and to become the last person ever to be executed on Tower Green.

To the last, he was audacious and arrogant. He came to the place of execution dressed in a black cap and black cloak, which he removed to reveal a scarlet waistcoat with long sleeves. He would not look afraid nor penitent. The executioner took three attempts to sever the head from the body, the news of which reached Elizabeth and she grieved for the man who had once been her favourite. However, he had become a monster and had to be dealt with. He was only 32 years old.

"Ladies, you have not used sufficient make-up—I can still see my pox marks and that ruff is not sufficiently stiff. Really, I expect better of you. I am going for a sitting today and I want to look my very best for the painter. I want my people to still see me as a great and beautiful Queen, so the responsibility is yours to present me as just that." Elizabeth was still as vain as she'd ever been, and she loved the name she had been given by the people—'Gloriana'. It pleased her well.

The years were passing and a new century dawned. In the year 1600, she had been on the throne for forty-two years and was still very popular with the people, although many were angry and annoyed at Devereux's death—he had made it his business to make the people like him and of course she had signed his death warrant. However, things in England were good and that raised the Queen's popularity. Age was beginning to be a problem for her and after the business with Devereux, she locked herself away and grieved for several days, after all his action had been a personal attack on her.

Life seemed so empty for her now and many of those around her had died, including her old friend and servant, Kat Ashley. She was feeling alone and very tired. She took to her room but refused to go to bed but sat upright in a chair. She sat there imagining all those once known to her—but now dead—staring at her from the shadows around the walls. Doctors attending her advised the removal of her Coronation ring from her wedding finger—a ring she'd never taken off since the day of the coronation. They were insistent however as it had become embedded into the flesh of her finger and was bleeding. They feared it would poison her and so the ring had to be cut off.

"I feel I am no longer married to my people now—you have removed the tie between us." she told the doctor who stood there, holding the ring, and looking very guilty. "I am sixty-nine years old Doctor; do you think I have much time left?" she asked the question no one would dare answer. He explained there were ulcers in her throat and that he was concerned she had no appetite, no matter what delicacies were offered to her.

"That's not an answer to my question—but don't worry, I understand. I will not go to bed however; I will rest on the floor." She stood up and stayed on her feet for a stretch of fifteen hours before lying down on the floor, where she stayed for two weeks. She wore the same clothes and never asked for her ladies to change them.

"I know I am fading away." she said to no one in particular. In her sixty-ninth year, Elizabeth had no teeth, her thin hair was falling out and she refused to allow her ladies to bathe her. All her life she had been a vain woman, so this was even more sad for those around her. In the end she agreed to let them put her to bed and at ten o'clock on 24th March, she just fell asleep, having reigned for forty-five years. She died at Richmond Palace in London.

Before her death, Elizabeth refused to give permission to her ministers and doctors to carry out a post-mortem and so the cause of her death was never established, although there was more than one suggestion: One was blood poisoning from the white lead-based make-up known as Venetian Ceruse (the spirits of Saturn) that she'd used nearly all her life. Thirty-one years after her death, it was classified as a poison. (When she died, it was said that she had a whole inch of it still on her face.) The second suggestion was that it was Pneumonia, Streptococcus or Cancer, and the third suggestion was that she died when they removed her Coronation ring which had been deeply embedded in her finger. She died one week after it was removed. It had obviously been a sign to her.

As she lay on the floor, she increasingly suffered from depression especially as some of her closest friends were dead and in her final days, she said she regretted having signed Mary, Queen of Scots' death warrant. "I never did give my consent to my cousin's execution—my ministers tricked me at the time." She told this to anyone who would listen. Her conscience was really pricking. Her embalmed body lay in state in Whitehall Palace for three weeks and she was buried on 28 April 1603.

Thousands of people watched her funeral procession and the effigy on the coffin was so lifelike, people gasped in amazement. Lists were made of the people come to pay their last respects and amongst the nobles, there were the humblest members of the royal household, such as scullery maids, porters and spice makers. Their being there would have pleased the Queen as it showed how much they'd loved her.

She was buried in Westminster Abbey, first in the same vault as her grandfather, Henry VII, but in 1606, James I of England/ VI of Scotland had her body moved to another chapel in the Abbey beside a monument he had erected to her. She was placed in the same vault as Mary—in fact, she was placed on top of Mary's coffin. The inscription is in Latin, but it reads 'Partners in throne and grave, here we sleep, Elizabeth and Mary, sisters in hope of the Resurrection.'

And that was Gloriana's life and death. She was an amazing woman, and virgin or not, she was a great Queen of her country. She was artistic, a great horsewoman and orator, she was educated and capable of speaking several languages. Her people adored her and most of her nobles did too. She made laws, fought wars and protected her realm. At the end of her reign, she had made England a force to be reckoned with and a country respected by the rest of Europe. As her people loved her, so she loved them in return. If any fault could be found in her it was that sometimes she allowed her heart to rule her head—especially in her choice of 'favourites'.

One thought that is worth considering is that when she was born, she gave her father Henry, the biggest disappointment of his life. When he saw her, he was angry, sad, and let down by the wife for whom he'd changed his country's religion and broke away from the Vatican in Rome. It was a great pity he didn't know, the baby whom he ignored for most of her life would become England's greatest monarch and make the country one of Europe's most powerful realms. Perhaps he did know in the end—let's hope so.

He was Known as 'Honest Abe'

They met at a dance in 1839 when he approached her and invited her to dance. He apologised in advance for his lack of dancing skills and she nodded primly. Accepting his invitation, they danced one dance together.

"Thank you, Sir, that was most enjoyable." And she returned to her chair beside her sister, Elizabeth. Her name was Mary Todd and she'd recently left her hometown of Lexington Kentucky, to come and live with her older sister Elizabeth Edwards, in Springfield, Illinois. She was 21 years of age and had reached a very acceptable age for marriage, but she was also a shy and demure young woman, who felt awkward in the presence of men—especially strange men, as this one was. Of course, her coming to Springfield was probably part of an unspoken family plan to allow her to meet young men. In fact, she'd specifically come in the hope that her sister could help her find a beau. It was the way things were done.

Ninian, her brother-in-law, should be able to introduce her to some eligible bachelors, as he was a man about town himself. One of those bachelors had just asked her to dance—he was tall and slim and had unusually large hands and feet—something she couldn't help noticing. He was a 31-year-old gentleman and was called Abraham Lincoln. He was amiable and pleasant and had lovely manners, so she had no hesitation in accepting his invitation to dance.

When the dance was over, he escorted her back to her seat and thanked her. "Perhaps we'll see each other again?" But she didn't reply, and he wandered back to his friend across the room.

"Well?" James asked, "What was she like? I must say she looked rather shy."

Abraham merely looked at him—willing to tell him nothing. "Time will tell." was all he said.

Abraham had been born in the Knob Hill region of Hodgeville, Kentucky from where he and his family moved to Indiana in 1816. They had lived in a log cabin and the family had to work hard to make ends meet. Unfortunately, his mother—Nancy Hanks—had died suddenly in 1818 from drinking contaminated milk from a cow who had been eating a milky plant called White Snakeroot. The poison from the plant was lethal, causing severe diarrhoea, sickness and bloating and she lasted only a few days after falling ill. She had come to America as part of the British colonies settling there and had originally been a native of the town of Malmsbury, in Wiltshire, England. It was commonly believed that Abraham had inherited her strength of character, confidence and speaking skills. He was only seven years old when they moved but it was a move that helped him to forge a future for himself.

His father, Thomas, remarried a widow called Sarah Bush Johnston, who became a second mother to the young boy, who spent only 1 year in formal education as his father couldn't afford more and he had to work hard to care for the family—his father's new wife was a widow with 3 children of her own, so there were plenty of mouths to feed. However, Abraham read everything he could lay his hands on and managed to educate himself primarily through reading. He seemed to absorb information and was always greedy for more.

Mary Todd on the other hand, came from a wealthy family of slave owners whilst Abraham was relatively poor and, following various jobs, he was now a struggling and self-taught lawyer, who had to work hard for his living. At the age of 30, he knew it was time to settle down and adopt a more respectable position in society. Hence, he visited Mary Todd's sister's home in Springfield the next day after the dance, or cotillion.

He said outright, "I've come to see your sister, if I may, Mistress Edwards."

Mary's sister invited him indoors and made him welcome. "Mary is not at home just now—she is calling on a friend in town. I'm sorry you've missed her, but I will tell her you called."

"Oh my God, Sister—has he really been here already?" Mary was blushing when she heard the news. "That is so soon when we have only just met."

"I think you must have made quite an impression on him, Mary—well done." And Elizabeth smiled behind her fan.

It was a full 3 years later when the two finally married—despite a fractured relationship when they stopped seeing each other for a while. This may have had something to do with a previous girlfriend of his—Ann Rutledge—but no one really knew what the quarrel was about. In the Autumn of 1842 however, and after an informal engagement which was just an understanding, they planned to marry in the front parlour of a friend, Reverend Dresser, an Episcopalian

Minister. In fact, Abraham paid him a visit early in the morning of 3 November and told him, "I want to get hitched tonight." Dresser agreed to the request but said he could only make it the following day, to which Abraham replied, "Well, I suppose that'll have to do."

He had asked Mary what kind of wedding she wanted to have and she told him with no hesitation, "Mr Lincoln, I wish for a small and quiet wedding with just family members attending." Luckily, this was exactly what he wanted himself, so 'Mr Lincoln', as his wife continued to call him even after they were married, went to a well-known Jeweller's shop in Springfield and bought a beautiful gold band, which he had inscribed 'A.L. to Mary. Nov 4, 1842. Love is Eternal.'

Although he thought he had sorted out everything with his friend, Dresser, he bumped into Mary's brother-in-law, Nathan Edwards, who, on being told of the impending wedding at Dresser's house, told him in no uncertain terms that, "No, that won't do. I am Mary's guardian and if she is married at all, it must be from my house." On Friday evening therefore, 30 relatives and friends gathered to witness the wedding—their invitations having been dealt with very speedily— and in a pretty, white muslin dress, Mary married her suitor. She wore no veil and carried no flowers, but she did have 3 bridesmaids, one of whom was her sister.

Abraham had a Best Man—James Harvey Matheny who worked at the Circuit Court office in Springfield. He was asked to be Best Man on the very day of the wedding. After waiting almost three years, everything seemed to be done in a great hurry. It should be pointed out however, that there was no need for such haste because of any pregnancy fears, as their first son, Robert wasn't born until 1 August 1843.

As Abraham slipped the wedding band on Mary's finger, he repeated the words, "With this ring I thee endow with all my goods, chattels, lands and tenements."

A booming voice filled with laughter, came from behind him, declared, "God Almighty, Lincoln, the statute fixes all that." The voice belonged to Judge Thomas C. Browne of the Illinois Supreme Court, who was known for his bluntness of manner and idiosyncratic thinking. Abraham was embarrassed and remembered this moment clearly for the rest of his life. As he and his new bride looked out of the parlour window, they saw it was pouring with rain—a not so lucky omen for a bride—but they didn't care, they were happy. After an evening of partying and laughter, Abraham and Mary left the reception and went to live in the Globe Tavern, a very ordinary boarding house where they occupied a small room and took their meals in a shared dining room.

There was an announcement in the Sangamo Journal on 11 November 1842 which read:

'MARRIED—In this city on the 4th instant, at the residence of N.W. Edwards, Esq. by Rev. C. Dresser, ABRAHAM LINCOLN. Esq. to MISS MARY TODD, daughter of Robert Todd. Esq. of Lexington, Kentucky.'

Just two months later, Mary waited for Abraham to come home from his lawyer's office. She couldn't wait to tell him as she knew their surroundings weren't ideal for a third person, but needs must. "Mr Lincoln, we are to have our first child—I know it'll be difficult in this small place but there's nothing I can do about that." Her words were curt and to the point, but she needn't have worried as her husband was delighted.

"That is wonderful, my dear—I hope it's a boy, whom I'll make sure is well educated and not like me—he'll learn from the best and not have to teach himself as I did." Considering how little formal education he had had; Abraham had done well to attain the status of lawyer—something that could be done at the time without formal qualifications. He'd had to take many more menial jobs as well however, just to keep the wolf from the door.

The Lincolns continued to live in the wooden boarding house before moving into a three-roomed cottage and then buying their first home at the corner of Eighth and Jackson in Springfield. Abraham was doing well for himself—he was 33 years of age when his first child was born and Mary just 23—Abraham tended to call his wife Molly or Mother and even 'child-wife.' She continued to call him Mr Lincoln.

He became a Whig Party leader and was elected to the United States House of representatives in 1846, but after a couple of disappointments, he decided not to run for any other office and returned to his legal work. It was 8 years later, in 1854, before he returned to the world of politics—his platform was against the expansion of slavery and on this occasion, he lost out to the Democratic Leader, Stephen A. Douglas in the U.S. Senate race.

A little later however, he stood as a nominated moderate participant in the race for the White House and with almost no support from the Southern slave-owning states, he swept clean the North and was elected the 16th President of America. Contrary to what some people like to believe, Lincoln did not support the abolition of slavery in slave states, but he was against the expansion of slavery into other territories. In fact, his platform promised not to interfere with those states where slavery already existed. When he finally fought his way to the Presidency, it was by a massive number of votes, compared to those who were standing against him. He won almost 40% of the popular vote but obviously did not do well in the South. The election saw the second highest turnout of voters ever in America—the turnout was 82.2 %—an incredible number.

It was at this point and after witnessing Lincoln's landslide, the 7 states in the South officially formed the Confederate States of America. They wanted to secede from the rest of the United States—they were agriculturally based states and used slave labour to support this, so the use of slaves was of paramount importance to them. The North however was more industrial and welcomed new technology—they neither needed nor wanted to own slaves, something they considered to be immoral. Strangely enough, although she came from a slave owning family, Lincoln's wife was a very keen abolitionist and always had been, which was the reason she wasn't on good terms with her family, as they most certainly were.

Despite much talking and arguing, there was no compromise between the North and the South about slavery and secession issues, so Lincoln decided to move his family into the White House in Washington in the year 1860. Mary found the whole prospect of living there daunting and she developed a very nervous disposition. Later, it was thought that it was about this time, she began to develop an early onset dementia—something which got much worse with the passing years. Her health certainly began to suffer more than before.

"Mother—why are you so low? You seem to worry about even the most trivial thing?" Abraham tried to be patient with his wife, but it was a difficult time for him as a new President. "How much more do you want? We live in a beautiful house; we have enough money at last and our children are healthy—what more can you possibly want?"

"I want you to be around more—you're always tied up with meetings and you must travel away from here so many times. I feel lonely and feel people are watching me all the time—just to see if I do anything wrong."

He told her she was paranoid and that no one was watching her, but he was lying, as her frequent bouts of depression made it necessary for some servants to keep a close eye on her—he was worried about what she might do. "Come now Mother—you are a lucky woman and a very special one—you are the First Lady of the United States, and as such, can demand what you need. What more can you want?" His patience was understandably becoming thin.

They now had 3 children—originally 4 children, but Edward (born 1848 was already dead) leaving Robert born in 1843, Willie in 1850 and Tad (Thomas) in 1853. Tad spoke with a severe speech impediment because of a cleft lip and palate, but he was a lively, happy boy whom his father loved and called 'Tad' because he wriggled like a tadpole when he was a baby. He was the only one of Lincoln's sons who never attended school—but was taught privately at home. The boys liked living in the White House and were proud of who their father was. They were even more proud of him when he volunteered himself into the much action—but in his sons' eyes, he was a hero and could wear a uniform.

Mary, often called Molly, was a very well-educated woman who'd attended prestigious schools in Kentucky. Her father mixed socially with political figures and so she had a natural interest in politics. She'd marred Lincoln for love and despite her family's opposition to the marriage, opposition which was based primarily on Lincoln's poverty and for his lack of political status—and she'd agreed to marry him after what they regarded as too short an engagement. Her family, being slave owners, upset her as she was very much against the buying and selling of people. People should be free she believed, and she was an ardent abolitionist.

Abe Lincoln was becoming more and more known for his political beliefs and speeches—he was a great orator and spoke with enthusiasm. His spoken words were always chosen carefully and were solely aimed at the people he was addressing. So enthusiastically did he speak about the rights of slaves that he received death threats from slave-owning Southerners and Mary was called a traitor by her fellow Kentuckians. She felt very alone when she lived in the White House as most of her family fought on the side of the Confederates, so she never saw them.

So, the nervous woman was spied on by the North because of her background and threatened by the South because she rejected the beliefs of her heritage. In fact, they openly called her a traitor. She was often the subject of newspaper articles, wherein she was accused of having undue influence on her husband's decisions and she was actually blamed for causing the President's health to deteriorate, making him develop a gaunt frame and very hollow cheeks, which grew more noticeable with each passing year. More likely, his haggard appearance was due to a wasting condition, known as Marfan's Disease, as well as the burden of governing a country at war with itself. But it suited some to believe otherwise.

Truth to tell, he himself had to spend a lot of time watching over his wife, who was becoming more paranoid with each passing day and whose behaviour was quite erratic and unpredictable. It was suggested that she suffered from a severe depression and to top it all, her dear son Willie died at age 13, having contracted typhoid fever. The same fever was also contracted by his brother Tad in the year 1862 but Tad survived and lived a reasonably happy life. The harshness of losing this son must have severely affected both Mary and Abrahams' lives—it should be remembered they'd already lost their second born Eddie just before his fourth birthday. He died of Tuberculosis and with the loss of two sons, Mary just couldn't bring herself to attend Willie's funeral—she was inconsolable and her other son, Tad, was still lying in the room next to Willie's— also suffering from the same Typhoid Fever. No one knew if he would live or die.

Willie's father, often called 'Honest Abe', did attend his son's funeral and gave him a magnificent ceremony. The last time he'd seen Willie was lying desperately ill in a huge rosewood bed, now known as 'The Lincoln Bed'. February 20th 1862 at 5.pm was the moment of William Wallace Lincoln's death and his father's last words to him were: "My poor boy, he was too good for this life, God has called him home. I know that he is much better off in heaven, but then we loved him so. It is hard, hard to have him die."

Elizabeth Keckley, a former slave who now designed and made Mary's dresses, stood at the bottom of the bed, waiting to wash and prepare Willie for his funeral. She saw Lincoln in a terrible state, crying and with his head in his hands, and she wondered how he could bear all the problems he had to face. He left the room and went towards his office, passing his secretary in the corridor and saying, "Well Nicolay, my boy is gone—he is actually gone." He was sobbing as he closed his office door.

The day of the funeral was 24th February when the family gathered in the Green Room and said a private and final goodbye to the boy. Mary of course wasn't there—she was unable to attend even this and lay on her bed upstairs, listening to one of the worst storms the city had seen for many years—so much rain, thunder and lightning and high winds. It was as if the world was weeping for Willie. The huge gilt mirrors in the White House were draped in mourning, with black fabric covering the frames and white covering the glass.

Lincoln and his son Robert sat within a circle in the room—a circle of family, members of the Cabinet and of Congress, of soldiers and invited people from foreign countries. They regarded Lincoln as their brother, and some could be seen shedding a genuine tear for the loss of his child. Willie was laid to rest in Oakhill Cemetery in Georgetown but was subsequently moved to lie beside his brother Eddie at Oakridge Cemetery, Springfield, Illinois. This was where the Lincoln family vault stood.

It was a time of great sadness in the White House—two dear sons now dead—and the American Civil war continuing with more deaths than any war that country had ever seen before. The pressure on Lincoln must have been colossal—the war, the deaths of his sons, his beloved wife's increasing depression and his own health issues which were visible for all to see. He was more gaunt and haggard each day but still gave full attention to the needs of the war and the people.

There was little easement for Lincoln—he was pulled in two directions—one by the North and one by the South. His wish was for a united country, but the time hadn't yet arrived. He couldn't appease both and so he chose a policy of silence, hoping and believing that the Southern Unionists, who were against the Confederate war with the North would carry the day and bring the South back into the Union again. It never happened of course but there were many committees and meetings to try to agree the way forward—there was one negotiation after the other but all through them, Lincoln remained emphatic that he was absolutely opposed to anything which would allow the expansion of slavery into any new states or territories. He would have gone along with the South's need for slavery, but he was against its expansion into further parts of America.

However, in mid-December 1860, the Crittenden Compromise was proposed. It meant that slavery would be protected in the federal states of the South and above a fixed line in the North, slavery would be forbidden. Congress could not interfere with the domestic slave trade in the South and newly admitted states could decide on the status of slavery within their borders. Lincoln did not like this proposal and asked his republican Senators to oppose it—and it was therefore never adopted by Congress.

Abraham Lincoln actually believed the South's threats of secession were mere bluster and the whole situation would inevitably be defused—but he was wrong in this and by February 1861, seven states had seceded from the Union and the Confederated States of America (CSA) was formed with Jefferson Davis as the appointed provisional president. The North and South were established as firm opponents now.

It must have been an incredibly worrying time for Lincoln—a new President whose country was heading for Civil War. It could be argued that his adamant refusal to accept the South's secession from the Union was the main cog in the wheel—but he believed in the unity of the American states and would not support the possibility of their breaking away from each other. He was called upon to handle both the political and military aspects of the war, both of which presented him with many challenging decisions. It was a frantic time for him and as Commander in Chief, he was forced to work his way through several different military commanders, finally settling on General Ulysses S. Grant as the best contender. Grant's opponent in the Confederate Army was General Robert E. Lee—two men, whom history will never forget.

Command of the Union Army was offered to Robert E Lee at the start of the war, because of his reputation as a great leader of men and for his tactical skills, but he refused it, saying that as a Virginian, he couldn't bring himself to fight against his own.

He was a very popular leader, loved by his countrymen and hero-worshipped by his troops. He was not only a great tactical commander, but a man with a warm personality. His pride in and respect of his men was absolute. A story some of his men told after the conflict, was about a Virginian farmer, who gave him a flock of chickens, which he immediately gave to his men to subsidise their rations. One cunning chicken escaped however and roosted in a tree that stood right beside the General's tent. The chicken became his friend and he ended by adopting her as a pet, opening wide the flap of his tent so she could come in and out freely—to visit him.

After a short while, she began to lay an egg almost every day beneath Lee's cot. She became a well-known figure in the camp, but on the evening before the Battle of the Wilderness, Lee invited several Generals to dine with him. His slave cook couldn't find sufficient meat to feed them all, so William Mack Lee caught the unsuspecting chicken and to save the General's day, he killed it and stuffed it with bread stuffing and butter.

That was apparently the one time in 4 years that Lee admonished his slave and William Mack told people afterwards, "It made Massa Robert awful sad to think of anythin' being killed, whether t'was one of his soldiers or his little black hen." A tough and brave leader but with a soft and sentimental heart. He'd lived in Washington before the Civil War began and when he and his wife left it to go to war, he told her, "We'll be back when this is all over." But it never happened—his house and land were at Arlington which the Union confiscated and used as a cemetery for their war dead.

After the Civil War, his son sued the Government for their 'taking' of his family home and lands and they gave them back to him. It proved to be a pointless gesture as, by that time, the grounds were covered by servicemen's gravestones and is now the cemetery used for all military personnel who died for their country. In the end, he sold the house and land back to the US Government—as it was of no use to him.

After a short story about the leader of the Confederate Army in the Civil War, it seems only right that we record something about General Ulysses S. Grant, the leader of the Unionist Army. The first thing that should be mentioned is that the 'S.' in the middle of his name stands for nothing. It was an error made in his young life by an administrator and it stuck with him thereafter and in the end, he decided to keep it. His true name was Hiram Ulysses Grant, and he was a notoriously bad businessman, who'd worked at various jobs, even selling firewood in the street.

At the Battle of Tennessee's Fort Donelson, he forced 15000 Confederates to surrender, using his famous command, 'No terms except complete and unconditional surrender can be accepted.' This was the first time in the war that an entire Confederate force was captured—and grateful Union sympathisers inundated the General with cigars when the story of his liking cigars got around. He also became known by his men as 'Unconditional Surrender Grant' and it was said that he'd smoked a huge cigar all the way throughout 'the surrender'. This was the story that won him so many cigars from grateful well-wishers.

He had a drink problem and was often drunk before and during battles. A group of Congressmen once reported his drunkenness to Abraham Lincoln, who reportedly said, "Please find out for me what Whisky he drinks so I can get some for my other Generals—if it produces fighting Generals like Grant, I must get some."

For a general, he was a scruffy man, who chose to wear the lowest ranking soldier's coat rather than that of a General. He was obviously not a vain man, but he **was** a brilliant strategist. When he accepted the surrender from Robert E. Lee's Army in North Virginia, he offered generous terms and allowed the

Confederates to return home to their families. He was furious when a Federal Grand Jury later negated his terms of surrender and attempted to charge Robert E. Lee with treason. Ulysses told President Johnson, who was in office at the time, that he would resign the command of the army, if he was ever ordered to arrest either Lee or any of his generals for treason. President Johnson capitulated on hearing this.

He eventually became President of the United States himself and was responsible for controlling and almost wiping out the Ku Klux Klan during his term of office and Mark Twain urged him to write his memoirs. The book was a best seller, but he was diagnosed with Cancer at the time and the royalties from the book went to his widow, Julia—all $450,000 of them.

These were the men known well to Abraham Lincoln, a President who not only had a Civil War to oversee but also to deal with the sadness in his own family. His first decree as President had been to call for 75,000 volunteers from the Union states to deal with the Confederate Army's attack on Fort Sumter—and he got his volunteers. He 'd been astute enough to ensure that the South fired the first shot in the Civil War but also that the North was ready to meet the challenge.

Brothers fought against brothers, uncles against uncles, even fathers against sons—families were split, their loyalty sometimes falling on different sides and doing what they thought was the right thing. The slogan 'Brother against Brother' was often used during the Civil war. A story lives on about a young Union soldier who came upon a Confederate and fired his rifle at the enemy—only to discover that he'd shot his own father. True? Most probably and more than once!

As President—and although it didn't seem right—Lincoln couldn't dictate the rules incorporated in the company of The American Banknote Company, an independent printing business. They were responsible for the production of the US Dollar bill which because of the green coloured signature on the back, became commonly known as 'Greenbacks.' As the Civil War had in effect wiped out at least half of their normal workload, the company began printing the Confederate States of America Dollar Bills for the South and they became known as the 'Greybacks'. Needless to say, they were worthless by the end of the war!

Of course, the government soon passed a bill that stopped the American Banknote Company from producing bills for both the North and South—so the company moved part of their company to New Orleans. A new company was formed there, called the Southern Banknote Company and the production of both currencies continued as before. In addition to dealing with family problems at home and to the overseeing of the Civil War, this is typical of the kind of domestic issue with which the President had to deal.

One day in the White House, Mary was having a quiet afternoon and was stitching a sampler. She was sitting comfortably on the sofa. Her husband was in a small study just off the sitting room and had left the door ajar so he could keep an eye on her. She suddenly stopped what she was doing and called out, "Mr Lincoln, have you heard about General Daniel Sickles shooting the man Philip Key—he was having an affair with his wife?"

Abraham sighed and said, "No, my dear, I have not but I'm sure you're going to tell me." He went on shuffling copious papers around his desk and waited for the rest of her story.

"Well, he found Philip Key with his wife and shot him dead. He pleaded temporary insanity in the Court and was acquitted by the Judge. It was accepted that he'd killed the man in a crime of passion, when he was quite out of his mind with anger. What do you think of that, Mr Lincoln—do you think it was right?" She'd begun stitching again but seemed quite irritated by her own story.

"Well, without knowing all the facts of the case, I can't really give an opinion, but that is the lawyer in me—as a husband, I can understand Sickles' anger—but I can't condone his killing an unarmed man. By the way, wasn't Philip Key the son of the man who wrote *The Star-Spangled Banner*—my favourite song?"

Mary tutted and said, "The song is not the point of my story—I'm really asking if you think Sickles is sane enough to fight in your army?"

"I am grateful to all my Generals, my dear—as I think you should be as well. They are all brave men, fighting for a cause in which they believe." Changing the subject deliberately, he asked, "How is Tad just now, my dear?" He was aware that Robert, his eldest son, was doing well at Harvard and caused his father no concern. Strangely enough Robert, his eldest son had never been particularly close to his father, even as a child.

"He is well, Husband, and despite his problems, still the happy-go-lucky boy he always was." She began to concentrate on her work again and Abraham knew he should not engage her in any further conversation. He understood his wife very well. She'd been even more excitable of late, following a carriage accident when she suffered a head injury and the doctors now decided she suffered from severe depression and anxiety. Her repeated migraines never went away, and she had to learn to live with them. Also, with the deaths of two of her sons, she developed a leaning towards a spiritualist philosophy, which seemed to bring her comfort. She believed the living could communicate with the dead. It seemed to calm her down, so her husband decided to support this indulgence.

"Willie visited me again last night and do you know, he surprised me by bringing Little Eddie with him—both my boys come to see their mama. They stood at the bottom of my bed like two good little men, which I'm sure they would have become, had God not chosen them early." She reached for a different coloured skein of silk, which she dropped on the floor. Abraham picked it up for her.

"Thank you, Husband, you'll be pleased to hear your sons looked well and happy—mind you, they probably did that to give me some cheer. I told them we miss them dreadfully. I could see Willie understood how we felt, but Little Eddie looked quite confused. He probably wondered why I looked so sad." Mary went on chatting to Abraham, but really to herself. She often talked about seeing the boys and having little chats with them and, as it did her no harm, he chose to indulge her beliefs. She'd always believed she could commune with the dead— and if it made her happy, who was he to say she was wrong?

As President, Abraham Lincoln was personally involved in making tactical decisions about the war—he was determined to re-unite the country—that was his over-arching goal. He averted potential British involvement in America's troubles, by defusing the Trent Affair in late 1861 and he was personally involved in the selection of his army Generals, especially of Ulysses S. Grant. He decided on a naval blockade that shut down the South's normal trade and river system. He was also intent on capturing the Confederate capital of Richmond but several and repeated Generals had failed to take the town—until his own choice of General Grant finally succeeded in winning the prize.

At this time in late 1862, Lincoln was also dealing with 'The Dakota Conflict' or 'Little Crow's Uprising' when several bands of Dakota Indians fought with the United States government. At the start of the conflict, a young Dakota Indian was on a hunting party with three fellow Indians, when for whatever reason, they attacked a string of settlements along the Minnesota River valley—the attacks were intended to chase all 'White Men' from the area.

Throughout the next few months, there was much conflict between the Indians and the settlers and in the end, the US Army became involved to protect the settlers and after that, most of the Indians surrendered. There was more than a thousand Dakota Indians interred in Minnesota and after trials and judgement, 38 of them were hanged on the same day. It was the largest one-day execution ever carried out on American soil. The other Dakotas were expelled from Minnesota and sent to Nebraska and South Dakota—to remain there for ever. The Government then set about clearing and abolishing all the Indian's reservations wherever possible.

Despite his significant involvement in the Civil War and many of the skirmishes that took place regularly, Abraham Lincoln still fought for the fairest way to bring about the eventual abolition of slavery. He persuaded the US Government to agree to compensation payments to the emancipated slaves. He believed in a slower and fairer way to free slaves—one that could persuade both North and South to agree. He knew full well that, if the slaves were suddenly told they were free they would be confused and unsure—where would they go and how would they live? He wanted to be fair to all the people.

The South used their slaves to cultivate the land and make their masters rich in the process—they were used to support the men who went to war by managing the home front and doing anything and everything to cover the inadequacies left by the fighting men. In effect, they used the slaves to support and help in their war effort. An immoral thing? Abraham Lincoln thought so and he arranged for 'The Emancipation Proclamation' to be issued, claiming it to be 'a fit and necessary war measure' so that the Confederate use of slaves to support their war effort, could be declared an immoral act. Lincoln used a lot of his natural political savvy to think this out and bring it about.

Still the Civil War dragged on, and Abraham Lincoln grew more and more haggard with each passing day but his appetite for work was insatiable and he seemed to need no sleep at all—but he still kept going. The year was 1865 and the month April, when unknown to the President, a very significant battle had taken place in Virginia—the Battle of Appomattox Court House, which was a continuation of an earlier battle fought at Lewis Farm. There, the 'The Siege of Petersburg' had been on-going since June 1864 through to April 1865 and General Lee's army was 60,000 men as opposed to 100,000 Union troops. Grant was able to circle the besieged town and Lee was eventually forced to evacuate. Troop desertion was rampant amongst the starving and exhausted soldiers—and who could blame them when facing such a situation?

General Lee's men moved forward in an attempt to escape and break through the Federal line of cavalry, hoping to reach North Carolina. General Grant however anticipated Lee's movements and ordered two battalions to march through the night and stop the exodus of troops. The Union soldiers marched all night and were ready and waiting for the exhausted Rebels to attack.

"There is nothing left for me to do but to go and see General Grant, and yet I would rather die a thousand deaths." Robert E. Lee spoke the last words he'd ever wanted to utter. Some of his officers tried to convince him to do otherwise, but Lee knew what his men would become if they fought on—thieves, marauders with no rations and no control by the officers. "If I were to take your advice, we would bring on a state of affairs it would take the country years to recover from." He knew a guerrilla war would soon develop.

In the early afternoon of 9 April 1865, Generals Lee and Grant met in the McLean house in the middle of the battlefields. It was a solemn affair with many officers from both sides present—terms of surrender were then discussed. Grant was fair in what he allowed—all troops could return home after giving up their weapons, the officers, cavalrymen and artillerymen would be allowed to keep their swords and horses if they agreed to lay down their weapons and abide by Federal Law. He also gave the Rebels rations as they were starving. He also saved the 'rebels' the humiliation of having their weapons taken by his men and allowed them to pile them on the ground in surrender. The whole business was was dignified and respectful on each side!

When both sides finally heard the news that the war was over, they cried and cheered—happy and sad at the same time. The Union soldiers felt very emotional when the Confederates came forward to lay down their weapons and flags and the Union Officer in charge ordered his men to salute their defeated foes as a gesture of respect. It was reported later that the immediate interaction between Yankees and Rebels was kind and friendly. The concept of 'Brother Against Brother' was finally over.

"Well, Mr Lincoln, I hear it's over at last—is there truth in that?" Mary was relieved for her husband but found it difficult to believe the American Civil War was really over. The previous 4 years had been challenging and had dominated their very existence, not just with the war, but because of all the issues they'd had to deal with—both personal and political. Mary was not the woman she used to be—now she was very much into spiritualism, and it seemed always on the verge of a nervous breakdown. Her dementia getting even worse.

Abraham was both mentally and physically exhausted and yet he had put his name forward for another, and second, term in office. He believed a second term could not be so demanding as the first had been—hopefully this time, there would be no war and he could concentrate on bringing the country together once again.

"Are you almost ready, mother—and yes, I am assured by despatches from General Grant that the massive Virginian army has surrendered and have completely laid down their arms." He was folding a rather elaborate cravat around his neck and pocketing a few cigars for after the performance at the theatre. He was very smart and suitably attired for a social evening. "I'm glad to see you in that wonderful purple colour Mother—it suits you well."

He felt as if a great weight had been lifted from his shoulders—as it had—and he handed Mary her lace fan. Ford's Theatre would inevitably be very warm, and she would welcome the use of her fan. He was laughing to himself and on being asked what was so funny, he said, "I was accused in the Senate today by a very moral gentleman of being two-faced so I came right back at him, 'If I had two faces, Sir, why would I be showing you this one?'" Abe liked jokes and funny stories and loved when he could say something funny in the Senate. Even with all the problems he had to face, he was known for his humour and ability to laugh in diversity.

One month before this night, a certain actor was planning with 6 conspirators to kidnap the President—also the Vice-President Andrew Johnson and the Secretary of State William S Seward. They believed the assassination of these senior and influential figures would throw the Government into disarray. In the actor's eyes, the Civil War had not come to a satisfactory end—the rebels should have defeated the Yankees. John Wilkes Booth had remained in Washington throughout the entire war, never taking a positive part on either side. He was however an ardent supporter of the Confederates and of course, of General Robert E. Lee. He came from a family of actors and had often tread the boards himself—a known actor, but not a very well-known one.

A couple of weeks earlier, he and his fellow-conspirators had waited at a spot where Lincoln was expected but for whatever reason, the President never appeared, and the plot was foiled. Richmond fell 2 weeks later, and it was then that General Lee surrendered to Grant—so causing Booth to come up with an even more audacious and sinister plan, although he must have realised there was little he could do to help the Confederate cause now—but he could still make big problems for the Federal Government.

The night of 14 April saw Booth attend Ford's Theatre in Washington D.C.—the play was a comedy performed by the well-known actress, Laura Keene and was called 'Our American Cousin.' Abraham and Mary occupied a private box and were accompanied by a young army officer, Henry Rathbone and his fiancé, Clara Harris. The party—especially the President, who had arrived late—laughed heartily at the production. At 10.15 pm precisely, Booth slipped easily into the box and with his 44-calibre single-shot pistol, fired into the back of Lincoln's head. He quickly stabbed Rathbone in the shoulder, leapt down onto the stage and shouted 'Sic semper tyrannis', which was one of the Virginian State Motto, meaning 'Thus ever to tyrants!'

Lincoln had come to the theatre on a high note—the Civil War was over, and the Union had won and he was laughing and enjoying a comedy. He was feeling positive about the future of the country, and he was happy—but he was stopped in his tracks by a man, not even brave enough to fight alongside the Confederates whom he claimed to admire so much.

At the moment when Booth swept into the President's box, gun in hand, the bodyguard who should have been there was nowhere to be seen. It was reported later that he'd been seen in the salon next door to the theatre. Was he in the pay of the conspirators, or was it just plain negligence of duty? No one would ever know!

The audience thought at first it was part of the drama on stage but when they heard Mary Todd scream, they knew otherwise. Booth broke his leg when he jumped from the box but managed to escape from Washington on horseback, helped by one of his fellow-conspirators. One of them—a man called David Herald had been waiting outside the theatre with a ready horse and then both rode into the night. They weren't brave men and obviously not willing to die for their cause as their get-away horses had been ready and waiting. They'd wanted to survive their treasonous act.

In the theatre, a young doctor—Charles Leale—was in the audience enjoying the play but on hearing the pistol shot and the First Lady's scream, he leapt to his feet and made his way to the President's box. Lincoln was slumped in his chair with the young, wounded officer trying to help him. He couldn't move and seemed paralysed and had great difficulty in breathing. Several soldiers carried their President across the street to a boarding house and the Surgeon General arrived quickly at his side, but only to say there was no saving him and he would probably die in the night.

Around his bed, Vice President Johnson, members of the Cabinet and some of Lincoln's closest friends stood in a vigil. The young man from the theatre—Doctor Leale—was still in attendance as was the young officer who'd been stabbed. His fiancée, Miss Harris was still by his side. As was her usual practice, Mary Todd couldn't face what had just happened and had taken to a bed in the adjacent room. Her eldest son Robert was with her.

Clearly heard by all those in the room, Lincoln said, "We will visit the Holy Land and see those places hallowed by the footsteps of the Saviour."

His wife Mary slowly entered the room on hearing his voice and sat beside his bed, taking his hand in her own. She bent forward and whispered, "What would Miss Harris think of my hanging on to you so?"

He replied faintly, "She won't think anything about it." And those were his last words. Miss Harris's was sobbing loudly.

When news of Lincoln's death reached General Ulysses S. Grant, he was devastated. He'd been invited to go to the theatre that night but had declined because he and his wife had made plans to visit their children in New Jersey. He formed the opinion—and wouldn't budge from it—that, had he been at the President's side, he would have been able to stop Booth from firing his pistol. His thoughts were only of Lincoln, even though he'd probably have been a target himself. He described the news of the assassination as being the 'darkest day of my life' and never got over the fact that he'd declined an invitation to be there at Lincoln's side.

News of the popular President's death spread quickly through the city, then the country. By the afternoon, flags were flying at half-mast on all main buildings and businesses and shops had put up their shutters, plunging the city into deep mourning. It was the same people who'd recently been rejoicing at the end of the Civil War. On 18 April, the President's body was carried to the Capitol Rotunda to lie in state and 3 days later, his body was boarded onto a train to return him to Springfield, Illinois. Travelling with him was his son Willie's hastily re-interred body and they were both laid to rest at Oak Ridge Cemetery on 4 May 1865, alongside the youngest Lincoln, Eddie. As was usual, Mary took to her bed for weeks—she was devastated by the whole thing—and she missed the funeral of both her husband and son. Elegant society ostracised her for her self-indulgence and this put another nail in the coffin of her increasing mental disorder.

Following her husband's death, Mary wasn't sure which way to turn for financial support and in the end, she had to petition Congress for a widow's pension, which was granted to her sometime later, but only after she'd produced evidence that proved she merited it. Many people thought it should have been granted automatically, but that's how things were.

In the year 1871, Mary lost her second son, Thomas (Tad), whom it was thought had died of Tuberculosis—a condition that seemed to run in the family. After all this, she was finally pushed over the edge towards insanity and had to spend some time in a mental institution—the decision for this was taken by her eldest son Robert, following his mother's two attempts to commit suicide. She was released into the custody of her sister Elizabeth and so, returned to Springfield where her husband and sons were buried. She lived until 1882, when at the age of 63, she died—but only after travelling to both, Great Britain, and Germany for holidays. Despite her health issues, she was obviously quite a feisty woman.

There must have been periods of normality in her young life, and she found her sister's presence reassuring, certainly enough to allow her to travel to other countries. Her son Robert outlived her and in so doing, experienced a rather strange incident. He was involved in an almost fatal accident on a train platform. He was travelling from Harvard University to Washington and was standing on a busy platform being jostled and bumped by people eager to buy tickets for sleeping compartments. Behind him, someone gave him an almighty push and he lost his balance—the train jolted slightly and Robert, who was leaning against the carriage, fell between the platform and the train into the existing gap. His legs were dangling in the gap, and he found he was trapped and unable to move. Suddenly, he felt someone grab his coat collar and haul him to safety. Shaken, he turned to thank the gentleman and recognised him as the famous, Shakespearian actor, Edwin Booth.

"Sir, I am most sincerely grateful for your assistance and can't thank you enough." Robert was infusive in his thanks. "I really thought I was a 'goner'—the train kept moving and I was unable to save myself."

"Think nothing of it, Sir—you would have done the same had the situation been reversed." And so, in the very year when his brother, John, had assassinated the President of the United States, Edwin Booth saved Robert Lincoln. The amazing thing was that Edwin was an ardent Unionist and admired the President greatly—in fact, when he told his brother John Wilkes that he'd voted for Lincoln for his second term of office, the younger man's anger was so great, he looked as though he was going to explode. But he didn't. He shot and killed the President instead. So, John Booth's brother saved the President's son. Some things are obviously meant to be!

Whilst Lincoln's funeral was being arranged, John Wilkes Booth was on the run. The whole country was searching for him—he was the most wanted man in America. At the moment he shot the President, may people in the audience recognised him—he was a known actor after all—so the Union soldiers in hot pursuit, knew for whom they were looking. Booth and his colleague, David Herald made their way across Anacostia River heading for South Maryland, from where Booth originated. They stopped at the home of a Samuel Mudd who treated Booth's broken leg, for which action, he was given a life sentence. The sentence however was later commuted as he claimed he was full-filling his oath as a doctor—and aiding the sick. The authorities accepted this. After being with Mudd, the pair of conspirators sought refuge in the home of Thomas Jones, a known Confederate sympathiser, before setting off across the Potomac River into Virginia.

The two men were finally caught in a Virginian barn which the Union troops surrounded before setting it on fire. Herald escaped from the fire, but Booth remained inside. The fire intensified and a Sergeant shot his pistol at Booth, hitting him in the neck. He claimed that Booth had been aiming a gun at him, fully intending to fire. That Sergeant's name was Boston Corbett and he was thereafter seen as an American hero. Booth was carried out of the barn but lingered for 3 hours before gazing down into his hands, and muttering, "Useless! Useless!" Was he talking about his hands that had now failed him or was he regretting the assassination of the President of the United States? His last words were meaningless!

He died then in a merciful relief as the hangman's noose was all he could expect after what he had done. Out of his fellow conspirators, 4 were convicted for their part in the killing of Lincoln and were hanged on 7 July 1865. They included David Herald who'd run out of the burning barn and a woman called Mary Surratt, the first woman to be put to death by the Federal Government. It was at her boarding house, that Booth and his friends had often met to discuss their plans to finish the President, his ministers and so, destroy the Federal Government. She may have known nothing about the subject of their meetings— but it was decided that she had.

And so, such an insignificant and unimportant man changed history and not for the better. Booth wasn't even a good actor—nowhere close to his brother's brilliance—but he obviously wanted his 5 minutes of fame, which he certainly got—but at what a price. What great things would Abraham Lincoln have done had he lived and served out the rest of his presidency? For what he did in his life, the world should be grateful. Many clever and illustrious people have described him as the liberator of the slaves, as the man who saved the Union in America and who ended up being a martyr for freedom. His political astuteness and his tactical decisions in war were astounding and his character could only be described as kind, generous and reassuring in times of crisis. He supported and was loyal to a wife who must have been a challenge and the loss of his children could have broken a lesser man. Whether a Unionist or a Confederate, whether you're for the North or the South, you can't deny he handled things well and gave the people hope for the future.

Not bad for a man from such humble beginnings and surely enough to claim for any mortal man?

But I can't leave this story without quoting the opening lines from President Lincoln's famous Gettysburg Address, which refer to a document written almost a century before and known as The Declaration of Independence—it contained George Washington's own signature:

Four score and seven years ago, our fathers brought forth on this Continent, a new nation conceived in Liberty and dedicated to the proposition that all men are created equal.

Surely Honest Abe's own sentiments exactly?

The Bells! The Bells!

He was a waif and a stray and now an orphan—he knew it but didn't like it. He was fourteen years old, and he'd never been to school. He'd had no learning of any kind, but he knew what was what—at least he thought he did—until now. He'd lived in a one-roomed cottage—some might call it a hovel—but he wouldn't. He'd lived there till last week when the landlord told him he had to leave, now that both his mother and father were dead. They'd died together from the plague that was spreading throughout the home counties and probably further than that. There were many children such as he, with no one to care and no place to live.

Some people called it the Black Death but mostly, it was just referred to as the plague. It was proving to be the scourge of England and some villages were left decimated—most families had lost one or more from around its fireside. For some reason, young Dick hadn't caught the plague from either of his parents, but the landlord said he still had to go as he had no money to pay the rent.

The neighbours had given him scraps of food but they were poor as well and didn't have much. The whole village was a different place and people stayed indoors more than before and kept their doors closed. It was once an open and friendly place where everyone knew everyone else—but now out in the streets, people kept their eyes lowered and their noses and mouths covered. The news had come from London that the killer disease was being spread by rats that arrived on merchant ships coming into all England's ports. They had travelled along the coasts of Europe, spreading it in every place they visited.

As the human population decreased, the rat population increased. It was a nightmare and people knew it, even in the village communities, although the towns were even worse. The apothecaries couldn't control it and once a person had caught it, they had very little time to live. Everyone was afraid of everyone else and especially of those whose front doors were painted with a red cross. It meant the plague was visiting that house—so 'Keep Away.'

Dick couldn't understand how he'd managed to avoid the disease, especially as he'd lived with his parents. He'd never been out of the village in his life, but he knew he'd have to go now. With a heavy heart, he fetched a sheet from the cupboard, avoiding the one from his parents' bed—and laid it on the floor. It had a few holes here and there but it would do. He began to lay his belongings on it, his very few belongings, and tied the four corners together. Using a long stick as a shoulder pole, he left the house for the last time, carrying all his worldly possessions. No one waved him off, no one even came out of their house as he set off down the road, not with anticipation but with trepidation.

A boy on his own with nowhere to go, but going nonetheless. He walked over the Kent hills and as he walked, he began to feel better. He'd brought one crust of bread the old widow next door had slipped into his hand. It tasted mouldy and quite unpleasant but at least it was sustenance. He climbed towards a group of trees where he found a pool of water filled with the dew still dripping from the trees' branches. That felt better, he lied to himself.

The month was September and it was still quite warm—Autumn had not yet arrived. His cloak was the best piece of clothing he possessed—it had belonged to his father who had no use for it now. That night, he slept under a hedgerow and in the morning, was amazed to find he was close to a bush of brambles— they were just right for the time of the year and he carefully pulled them from the hedge. At first—it tasted unbelievable—then he began to pull off as many as he could. The meal was wonderful and he put as many as he'd already eaten, into his bundle for later. As he started to walk again, he realised his feet were hurting—and he could feel the odd sharp stone cutting into them. He tried to avoid the stones, but they found him nonetheless and he was pleased to see a more smoothly packed road ahead, bordering the fields at first and then going off in another direction.

He knew he was on the right road as he passed a helpful milestone—and so he walked on, not coming across anyone at all. The day slowly passed, and he kept his eyes open for any other berries ripened in anticipation of autumn—but there weren't many of those. He'd already eaten the fruit from the bramble bush—and his sheet of bits and pieces seemed to getting heavier every minute. He lay down to rest under a tree once the sun had fallen low in the sky—and he soon fell sleep.

He jumped up, thinking someone had touched him—fortunately it wasn't that. Someone must have silently and stealthily walked past him and lifted his bag from his side. The contents were scattered over the road and at least half of them were missing, although nothing was valuable—but it was all he had. Whoever stole them must have had even less than Dick because they took such worthless bits and pieces. Now he felt as low as he possibly could. He was a homeless down-and-out and yet someone had stolen from him. It sort of made him feel like a man of property. Luckily, they'd left him with an old locket that had belonged to his mother—actually, they 'd probably not seen it as he'd wrapped it in a sock. Thank God for that, he thought. That was all he had to remind him of his parents. And his mother had always said it was a valuable piece—but then she would say that—she'd always had a vivid imagination.

Putting his bits back into the sheet, he tied it to his pole and walked onwards into the coolness of the evening. His shoes were so tatty now, that even the stony road felt like sharp burning on the soles of his feet. But there was another milestone ahead and that cheered him—he was getting closer to London—what he'd do there once he reached it, he didn't know, but he'd heard the streets were paved with gold. Imagine that! When he reached the milestone, he crossed a bridge which suddenly appeared. He'd been on the road two days and two nights and his stomach hurt with a gnawing pain—he'd been hungry before, but not as bad as this.

The third day on the road dawned with grey clouds promising heavy showers and he pulled his father's cloak tighter around his shoulders. He listened carefully and could hear the rumbling sound of cartwheels and there it was coming up behind him. He stopped and waited hopefully. The cart was laden with boxes and the driver was bowed low under an oilskin cover. The rain was torrential now. Dick stepped in front of the cart which had to stop suddenly, "Please Sir—can you give a poor boy a lift on your cart?" The driver ignored him and started up the cart again, but Dick jumped in front of it again. "Sir, have some pity—I've been walking for days and I'm exhausted and hungry."

The driver peered at him and looked thoughtful for a moment. He asked, "How do I know you won't rob me?"

Dick assured him he wouldn't do anything like that, "I'm an honest boy—I really am—and if you let me climb aboard, I'll help you unload the boxes when we reach your destination." It worked and he let the young boy climb aboard.

They rode in silence for a few hours until the driver suddenly pulled the cart to the side of the road and reached behind for a package. He had cheese and bread wrapped in a checked cloth and he also had a flagon of mead. Dick's stomach rumbled and he licked his lips at the smell, but he knew he daren't ask for a share—it would be like begging and he knew the man wouldn't like that. The driver munched his way through two halves of bread and swallowed a cup of mead, then he held out the last chunk of bread to Dick and gave him a cup of mead as well. Dick took them gratefully and tugged his forelock to the driver, "You're a kind man—and I won't forget you." He gobbled down the food as fast as he could, in case the driver changed his mind.

"There it be—there's Lunnin ahead. Is that where ye're headin then? Hope so, 'cause that's as far as I go." The road was very busy now—carts, sheep, geese, and pigs seemed to be roaming around and poking their noses into everyone's business. No one appeared to own any of them. Dich said this to the driver, who replied, "Ye couldna be more wrong—just try touchin' one o' 'em and ye'll soon see the owners."

Dick was learning about London already. The cart stopped at a busy tavern and the driver jumped down, "Well, ye said ye'd 'elp unload." And Dick did help, in fact it seemed that he did most of the work while the driver went inside the tavern, not to return for at least an hour.

"Right lad, ye be on yer way now—we're done wi' each other." And he as good as shooed the boy away. Dick said goodbye and wandered off on his own, he knew not where. London was not particularly friendly and no one spoke to the strange-looking boy in his crumpled clothes… Dick was hungry again but had no money for food. He sidled up to a woman selling apples from a stall. "Ma'am, would you have any fruit that might have gone off? I'm ravenously hungry and would be happy to work for it."

She looked him up and down before saying, "Take this pail and trowel and scrape the rottin' fruit scattered beneath the stall. If you do a good job, I'll see what I can find for you." That was as good as he was going to get from her, so he set about the chore—and made a good job of it. She was as good as her word and rewarded him with an apple—and not a rotten one either, but then she chased him away and told him to get home.

He was still soaked to the skin—the rain had been unrelenting all day and he looked like a drowned rat. And then one real rat appeared—a large one—it nosed around in the pail he'd filled with dead apple skin and cores. He kept well away from it—he knew they had sharp teeth and also what disease they could bring.

He wandered along the streets, not knowing where he was going. It was getting dark and he knew he'd have to find some place to sleep. But where? The streets were becoming quieter as the people returned to their own sleeping places and he found himself in a street of more attractive houses than those near the market. The candle lights were beginning to show at the windows of some of the quality houses. It looked so appealing to the beggar boy and he suddenly missed his mother and father. He had to get himself out of the rain, which was falling more heavily than ever, so he looked for a house with a canopy over the front door and eventually found one. It even had candles in the downstairs windows and looked so inviting. He used his bag of odds and ends as a pillow and settled down on the doorstep, pulling his cloak tightly around his frail body. He soon fell asleep from exhaustion.

He woke up to someone kicking him—gently kicking, "Come on, boy, get up, you can't sleep there. Move yourself, the gentleman wants to cross his own front door." A moon-shaped face glared into Dick's wakening eyes. It was the butler from inside the house, leaning down from the top stair. In the street, a gentleman stood in the rain, waiting patiently to get inside.

Dick stuttered, "Sorry Sir—I was just sheltering from the rain—I must have fallen asleep."

"I don't want to hear none of your excuses, just get up and begone." The butler spoke even more harshly than before. He pushed the boy's shoulder and dislodged him from the stair. Dick sat on the wet pavement, arms akimbo and shook his head—his cloak was dripping—and still the rain came down.

The gentleman suddenly spoke in tones gentler than that of the butler. "Now, now, Henderson, don't bully the boy—help him up. What's your name, boy, and why are you sleeping on my doorstep?"

Dick could hear the kindness in the voice and replied hopefully, "Dick, Sir—my name is Dick. I've come to London 'cause my parents died and I had nowhere else to go. I've come to make my fortune, you know."

"Have you indeed—that's a big plan—but first I think we should find you someplace dry to sleep, don't you?" He turned to the butler, "Take him inside Henderson and get cook to give him a bowl of hot soup. Don't argue, my mind's made up—we can't leave this drowned rat here." And he brushed past Dick and swept into the house.

Henderson was not happy—the master was always helping waifs and strays, but he knew he'd best do as he was told. "Come on boy, you've landed on your feet this time."

Dick was taken into the kitchen where the cook was fast asleep beside the fireplace. "Come on Molly, you'll have to get up. The master has taken in another beggar—you've to give him a bowl of hot soup and then let him dry off by the fire. Put him in the small room at the end of the corridor. I don't want to do it, but you know what the master's like."

And that was how Dick found a place to sleep in London. The room they gave him was really just a big cupboard, but it did have a little bed that felt like heaven to Dick. The first night, his belly full of good broth and his clothes dry at last, he fell onto the bed and gratefully fell asleep. He didn't wake at first light, and everyone had probably forgotten he was even there, but when the sun managed to come through the bars on the window, he sat up, remembering where he was. Creeping along the corridor, he found his way to the kitchen, which seemed full of people. Cook was there bustling around the room, banging pots and pans and shouting orders to a little maid who was busy, scrubbing the hearth with a wire brush.

Cook spotted him, "Ah, there you are—sit yourself down and eat that crust of bread left over from supper—you'll get a mug of tea to wash it down. You'd better be on your way after that—there's nothing more we can do for you." She didn't even look at him as she spoke, just got on with filling a tray that was probably the master's breakfast.

Henderson appeared in the doorway, "Breakfast tray ready yet, Cook—the master's waiting in the dining room." He looked across at Dick, "And he wants to see you boy, but not until after he's finished his breakfast. You're lucky, he doesn't often remember if he's taken in a beggar." And he disappeared, carrying the splendid tray Cook had prepared.

Dick flattened down his hair with some water and quietly crept along the corridor towards the room cook had indicated. "Remember to knock the door loudly—sometimes the master doesn't hear too well," she told him. He knocked three times and waited. The master was sitting back in his chair, obviously replete after breakfast.

"Well, young man—Dick, isn't it? You see, I do remember some things—sit down opposite me—there's a couple of questions I'd like to ask." He lit an ornately carved clay pipe and puffed on it several times to get it going, then he leaned forward and looked into Dick's eyes, "Tell me your story boy and leave nothing out."

Dick told the gentleman his story and left nothing out. He told him he'd had no schooling but that he was a quick learner and willing to work hard. "I can turn my hand to anything, Sir—and once I find a job, I'll be sure to repay your kindness to me."

Mr Fitzwarren liked what he heard—he believed the boy to be honest—just fallen on hard times. He was an orphan with no one to help him. The gentleman was a philanthropist and known for his charitable deeds in the city. He was a merchant and owned two great ships and made his money by sailing them all over the world, delivering and collecting goods from foreign places. It was a lucrative occupation and looking around his home, it could be easily seen how well he did in his trade. He didn't make the journeys himself of course but had a captain and crew for each ship. He did however recoup the profits.

"Tell you what Dick, I'll set you up with a shoe-cleaning kit and a little stool for your customers to sit on. If you've succeeded at that after a month, I'll think again of what I can do for you. Is that a deal? Do you think you can do that?" Mr Fitzwarren was well aware how life-saving his offer was.

Dick collected his shoe-shine kit and stool and made his way to the local marketplace, where many people gathered. He charged a farthing to clean the shoes and he went to the same spot every day, so that people began to come looking for him, rather than his having to drum up custom from around the streets. One day as it was nearing Christmas, he dared to use one of his hard-earned farthings to buy a bag of roasted chestnuts. My goodness, they were delicious, but he limited himself to spending one farthing only. The rest was for the master—although the master himself wasn't aware it was coming. He was indeed an honest boy and meant to repay Mr Fitzwarren for his kindness—without him, he'd probably be dead by now. His pile of farthings under the pillow in his box room was growing fast but he'd had to use some of it to replenish his cleaning materials.

He was tired however of cleaning shoes and one day he realised he missed the village that he used to know so well. Also Henderson the butler, had never really taken to him—he was jealous of the way the master favoured the down-and-out. Usually, the master's 'pets' were only passing through—this one seemed to be staying! Perhaps it was time for Dick to visit his old home. He wouldn't say goodbye to the household though, as he would probably return to the city one day. One morning very early, he set off on the road—it reminded him of the journey he'd made in the opposite direction—but that was months ago now. He passed a milestone as he struggled up the hill out of London—he'd only come a few miles and already he was tired. He rested on a wall and realised how tired he was, so he decided to lie down by the side of the road to rest—just for a while, until he got his breath back. As he lay there, he wondered if he was doing the right thing—he wasn't sure. Soon his eyes closed and he dropped off to sleep.

Somewhere in the distance, he could hear a faint ringing of bells—then it became louder. Could that be coming from London still—could the sound of bells really travel that far? And it seemed it could—after all he was at the top of a hill and the city lay in the valley below, so the sound would drift upwards. In fact, with working so much in the market, he recognised the peel of the bells— it was the sound of the Bow Bells. In fact, it was as though they were trying to give him a message. But that was just stupid—how could bells give him a message? And yet, there it was again—he could make out some words now…

'Turn again! Turn again! Dick Whittington, you must turn and go back to London.' They kept pealing the words, 'Turn—Turn again.' The bells now spoke quite clearly. 'London will reward you—make no mistake. Retrace your steps— go back.' The sounds were slowly growing faint and then, they were gone altogether. Their message had been clear however and at one point, he thought he'd heard the words 'Lord Mayor'—but that couldn't be—it made no sense— the Lord Mayor of London would have no time for the likes of him. He must have misheard.

He was properly awake now. In fact, he hadn't known he'd even fallen asleep—but he obviously had. It couldn't have been a dream, could it? He sat up and shook his head. It was still the middle of the night and dark. Standing, he realised if he turned back now and re-traced his steps, he'd be back at the house before anyone knew he'd even gone. What to do? Had he really heard the Bow Bells ringing or had it been a dream? Did it matter anyhow? It had made him think again about what he was doing—he stood up and wiped the dust from his knees. If he set off now and with some luck, he'd get back before anyone in the house was awake. He had to look twice but in front of him stood two shadowy figures. Both had bowed heads. What on earth was going on? Where had they come from?

Although he couldn't quite see their faces, he soon realised it was his late mother and father—but they were dead. Where on earth had they come from? He reached out his hand towards them, but he touched nothing—he knew they were ghosts come to tell him something important. He couldn't see them properly but he could hear them 'Don't return to our village, Son—there's only a few people there now and many more have died of the plague and the houses have become derelict very fast.' Their words were quite clear, 'Stay where you are in London—there's good things there for you. You heard the bells, didn't you—do as they told you.'

The two misty figures disappeared into the darkness before the dawn and he was left alone. What a strange experience—first the bells with the message and then his parents with the same message. Dick made up his mind and immediately set off back to London and no one there was any the wiser that he'd even left.

The month had become three months before the master remembered his agreement with Dick—and so, one morning, he sent for a shoeshine of his own. Dick did his best job and looked up, pleased with his work. Mr Fitzwarren held out a farthing, but Dick declined saying, "Oh no, Sir, I couldn't possibly take money from you."

The master insisted however, "I always pay my debts, Dick—and you should remember that as you go through life." Dick accepted the coin and put it in his pocket with pride. He wouldn't spend that coin, it was special. "Dick, I have a gentleman visiting me today and I'd like you to meet him. He is the captain of one of my ships and he is preparing now to make a journey across the sea. Come here at 4 o'clock and you'll meet him."

Before leaving the house, he returned to his room to feed his cat. He'd found the cat in the market, thin and scrawny and for some reason, the animal adopted him and followed him everywhere. Of course, it could have been the little tit-bits Dick gave him—from the bread and ham Cook wrapped up for him every day. He just called it 'Cat' and it always answered to the name. "See you later, Cat— and try to catch as many rats as you can around the house today—Henderson is always grateful to you and it'll put him in a good mood for when I get home."

And so, Dick met Captain Stewart, who one day, would become his friend. The two men were having a glass of wine when he arrived. They'd been discussing the imminent voyage Stewart was about to make. Dick listened in silence, mesmerised by the men's plans. The ship would leave half full of English goods, it would call in at various foreign ports—sell some of the goods and take on board many local items which future stops along the coast would welcome. It was a trip that had proved most profitable in the past and the two men were sure it would prove so again. Henderson the butler came into the room and asked,

"Sir, will the gentleman be staying for dinner—Cook would like to know so she can make sufficient food."

The master looked at Captain Stewart and raised one eyebrow questioningly. Stewart nodded his head. "Yes Henderson, please tell Cook Captain Stewart will be staying for dinner and can you tell her to prepare the meal for three people—Dick will stay with us to talk over our plans." Henderson looked most put out, his mind jumping back to where he'd first seen the wet, bedraggled boy on the doorstep—and now he was to dine at the master's table. He couldn't wait to get back to tell Cook. She would be equally affronted.

"Well, I never," she said, "whatever next? Mind you, I must say he's been of some use to us—do you know, since he brought that cat to live here, I've not seen one rat about the house. You've got to agree with that, Mr Henderson."

"I suppose so—but it's the cat that's the hero—not the boy," he mumbled and went to the cellar to get some more wine.

"Well Dick, have you worked out yet what I plan for you? Especially now you've given me this enormous amount of money," and he indicated the two little piles of farthings on the table, "I'm more convinced now that my plan is a good one. How would you like to set sail with Captain Stewart as his midshipman, which really means that you do whatever he tells you? What do you think, young man?"

And that's how Dick found himself boarding the 'Northern Wind' two weeks later. He'd said goodbye to the house servants as he didn't know when he'd be coming back and he'd also said goodbye to the master's young granddaughter Alice, whom he'd only seen a very few times. She was a lovely girl in his eyes and he sometimes dreamt of marrying her, but he knew that was very unlikely—but he could dream, couldn't he? The servants weren't happy that he'd taken his cat with him on board the ship, but he explained, "I couldn't leave him behind—he's my friend and you can always find another cat." And so, Cat also went on board the 'Northern Wind'. Funnily enough, he took to the moving ship as easily as a duck takes to water and he was quite happy still to be with Dick—and his titbits. And of course, there were always plenty of rats there.

Ultimately, the ship was headed for Jamaica where the best plantations in the world were, but it would stop at West Africa en-route—to buy and sell to those countries. The North Atlantic Ocean could be a dangerous place with sudden storms and gales. Captain Stewart however, was an experienced and careful sailor and knew the wisdom of fearing the sea and treating it with respect. Dick learned a great deal on the journey and did everything he was told. Within a couple of weeks, Cat had almost rid the ship of all the hated rats. There were still some around but he would soon deal with them. Captain Stewart was delighted—his ship was a much better place without the pesky rodents. He thanked Dick profusely for bringing Cat on the journey.

"That cat is a Godsend, Dick—there's no other word for it—he's a Godsend." The ship was on the point of entering the area of the Barbary Coast so had to be careful of privateers, who didn't mind who they stole from—as long as they could steal. "We're going to go ashore in West Africa—I know a port there and it's usually where I sell most of what I have on board. We'll pick up things from the merchants there and make our way to Jamaica afterwards. I have a regular contact there where I can pick up things to take back to England. I don't deal in slaves however although there's good money to be made with them, but my ship is not well enough equipped to accommodate human beings."

And this is what they did—the event went quite smoothly and the captain sold nearly everything he had on board, making plenty of room for new things to take to Jamaica, where he would continue to buy and sell.

"Have you ever heard of the Maroons, Jack? They're a black people who originated from Africa and were sold as slaves in Jamaica to work on the fields and produce the sugar beet—and that's what we'll fill the ship with, to take back to England—and make a good profit into the bargain. I know the head man of the maroons—he's called Queen Nanny Maroon and I'm sure you'll like him." The ship was pulling out of the harbour into the Atlantic Ocean and luck was keeping on their side as no attacks had been made on the 'Northern Wind'—so far!

They reached Jamaica after a few days and dropped anchor just outside Kingston Harbour. It was the safest and easiest harbour in Jamaica, although there were actually 21 harbours in all. They requested the help of the men on the wharf who were working there and of course, paid them for their labours. The 'Northern Wind' was soon empty of everything she had in the hold and piles of goods sat on the wharf. Dick had played his part and helped the men unload the items—now he was to go with the captain to meet Queen Nanny Maroon, the main man. Negotiations would take place then, hopefully to both side's satisfaction. Dick remembered to feed Cat before leaving the ship—although there had been so many rats, the cat was becoming quite choosy over what Dick gave him.

"Be prepared for Queen Nanny to talk your ears off about the Maroons. He's very proud of his history and of what his people have achieved on the island. They were all slaves once, abducted from Africa, and taken to Jamaica where they had to work as slaves for the plantation owners—but they managed to escape in great numbers—up high into the mountains. This was when Spain owned and controlled the island. The Spaniards couldn't do anything to stop the Maroons from escaping and in the end, they gave up the island itself and the British took over. The escaped slaves formed refugee communities in the mountains and the slaves in the downtown part of Jamaica continued to revolt—this time against the British—until the British agreed to free all slaves, but only if the revolutionaries agreed to stop their attacks on the British. This is what happened, and the slaves were freed, so now you know how the Maroons came about in Jamaica. And that's their history in a nutshell but no doubt you'll hear more where we're going."

Dick was exhausted after that speech and was looking forward to a drink from Queen Nanny. *My God*, Dick thought, *you're learning something new every day*.

Queen Nanny's bamboo house was large with several rooms and he welcomed the captain and Dick as though they were royalty. He clapped his hands and a servant appeared carrying a glass jug of Coconut juice and Jamaican Run. It was delicious and Dick wolfed his down whilst Queen Nanny told him the history of the Maroons, of all the fighting there'd been throughout the years—first with the Spanish and then, with the British. "We had to live in the mountains in our communities—it was sometimes hard to get enough food but in the old days, we would raid the rich plantation owners and steal what we needed. It may have been dishonest, but it was necessary for us to live. After many fights, the Maroons were at last accepted by the British, as long as we stopped our people from revolting against them."

As Queen Nanny was talking, Dick saw a large rat cross the room behind his chair—and then another following. He mentioned the presence of the rats and was told they were everywhere in the house—in fact, in most peoples' houses on the island—there was nothing could be done about them. Dick thought quickly and tentatively suggested that he return to the ship and fetch Cat. He didn't brag about the cat but thought it best to let the Maroons see for themselves. Jamaica had only two cats at the time—both having been left behind by a visiting ship and both being female. They could catch some rats but what the maroons needed was a male cat, so they could breed and have enough cats to deal with the rat problem. "Well, my cat is definitely a male cat—so perhaps he could mate with the cats you have already."

And that was how it all panned out. Cat was treated by the Maroons as a special visitor and was fed only the best of meats—but not too often or he wouldn't be hungry enough to chase the rats. "Young Dick, if you will sell me your cat, I will give you what you want for him. He will be the start of a new population of cats in Jamaica and your name will never be forgotten here. What would you like for your cat?" Queen Nanny was almost pleading with the boy and Dick felt sorry for him.

Captain Stewart took him aside however and told him he must think of a value for the cat and then quadruple it. "The Maroons are a very rich people, especially Queen Nanny himself."

Dick did as he was advised and said that Cat was a very valuable animal and he would need a great deal of money before he could part with him. He was offered a sum beyond his wildest expectations—and Dick accepted it, although he was sad to leave Cat behind when the 'Northern Wind' set sail for England the next week. The ship's hold was crammed with sugar and with many valuable and locally made items from the island. The Maroons were also grateful to Captain Stewart for coming to the island and bringing Dick and his cat with him. Believing themselves to be very lucky, they showed their generosity to the captain as well and he was well pleased with the deals he'd struck with the maroon merchants.

Perhaps it was because he worked hard at everything, Dick did well. He suddenly had plenty of money both in the bank and in his pocket. Back in London, he paid a private tutor to teach him to read and write—and most important of all—to know how to work with figures. He began working for a merchant in the city and was soon promoted. After a while, he was clever enough to ask the merchant if he could become a partner if he invested some of his money in the business. Of course, the merchant knew Dick would be an asset and agreed. Dick was in his twenties now and whilst working with the merchant, he also studied the law, something he thought would benefit him should he rise even higher in the city. And he fully intended to do that.

He paid a visit to Mr Fitzwarren one day and when he rang the doorbell, he was pleased to see Henderson was still the butler. It made him feel good to have Henderson—who'd always been a bit of a bully—wait on him and serve him tea in the drawing room. Mr Fitzwarren was delighted to see his old protégé and shook his hand warmly.

"Now then, Dick, and what have you been up to since last I saw you? Sold any more cats, have you?" he asked with a smile.

"No, but I've done something I think is more daring than selling my cat." He laughed at Mr Fitzwarren's expression. The old man didn't know what the young man was talking about.

"Well, I've made so much money in my profession and now I'm a practising lawyer, I've won a few important cases, and been paid handsomely into the bargain. So—I've become a lender of money to the King himself. Because of that, I've been a visitor at the court several times. What do you think of that, Mr Fitzwarren? And I owe it all to you—you gave me my chance."

"I think that's wonderful, Dick—I had no idea you'd prospered quite so well, but I wish you luck—you deserve it, what with the terrible start you had in life. I'm pleased you think I had a hand in it." Mr Fitzwarren was still as nice as he'd always been, but Dick could see that perhaps he'd fallen on hard times lately. There was only Henderson left in the house—no cook nor maids—in fact, the old butler seemed to have to do everything himself. But how could he broach such a subject with his old master—his pride might be hurt.

"Mr Fitzwarren, I am on the point of buying a house for myself—most of my business is in London, so it would be a good idea. I don't suppose you've ever considered selling this house—or better still, could I buy your house but you and Henderson continue to live here with me? I'm out at work most days, sometimes well into the evenings—so you'd not really notice anything different." Dick hoped he'd said all the right things as the old man looked rather perplexed. He sat quietly and said nothing for a while.

"Will you let me think about that, Dick? My thoughts don't come as quickly as they used to—and I must weigh up the pros and cons of what you suggest before I commit myself. You may remember—I have my granddaughter Alice to think about as well."

Dick knew it was time to leave and he stood up. "I'll come back in one week, Sir—and you can give me your decision then. Will that be all right? There is something else I'd like you to think about, if you would. I've always been fond of your Alice—even when I used to do shoe-shining for a living—and I'd be grateful if you'd consider this too in your deliberations. I would like to ask for the honour of your granddaughter's hand in marriage—I know we don't love each other yet, but I'm sure that will come eventually."

Mr Fitzwarren nodded his head, "You've given me much to think about, Dick, haven't you? Let's leave things for now and I'll see you in a week. Obviously, I need to talk to Alice."

There was a messenger waiting for Dick at his office. He was an important messenger as he'd come from the Treasury Department and specifically from the King himself. Henry IV had deposed Richard II but none of that had affected Dick's highly successful deals in silks, cloth and textiles, all of which he imported into England and then exported to other parts of Europe. Three different kings had sat on the throne during Dick's lifetime, but it seemed Dick's luck just never ran out. He also owned two ships of his own now which travelled across the Atlantic Ocean buying and selling in Africa—both ships had a cat aboard and so, there were only few rodents to annoy the crew.

Dick had learned this lesson well and it made getting a crew easier than for those ships that were overrun with rats. Dick's reputation was good amongst those with whom he shared business and his varied projects were successful. He seemed to make money even when he wasn't trying very hard. It was as though whatever he touched, was an immediate success—and turned to gold. Not bad for a waif and stray who'd run away from a deserted village when he was fourteen and couldn't read or write. Maybe the streets of London really were paved with gold after all.

The King's servant had come to invite Dick to come to court—the King wanted to discuss some matters with him. The matters were to do with money of course. The Crown's coffers were rather empty and Henry IV was always looking for people to invest in the running of the country. Dick did attend the King and left the palace with his pockets very much lighter. The money was never repaid but it did gain Dick a powerful say in local council matters and few people ever again gainsaid what he proposed—he was a friend of the King after all and that meant a lot. Dick considered the investments he made to Royalty a good deal and he always benefitted from the association.

This time—as recompense for his generous donation—King Henry asked him if he would like the office of the Lord Mayor of London. Could he fit it in with his other commitments? Would it perhaps be too much for him? "I would personally welcome your acceptance of the position and I hope very much that you will accept." Dick did accept the position with alacrity—such status could only help in his business affairs—and it might serve to make his proposal to Alice Fitzwarren more attractive.

And so, the message from Bow Bells all those years ago was proven to be right and Dick became the Lord Mayor of London and he married Alice the same year. They all lived in one house and got on very well together. Mr Fitzwarren however hadn't much time left and a year after the wedding, he died, leaving Henderson as the only original in the house—but he too, was much older and was now quite frail. He continued as butler however—and no one would ever dare criticise anything he did. He was referred to as Cantacterous Henderson'. But it was a happy home and those in it, were happy too—as Dick had predicted, he and Alice soon fell in love with one another. The amazing thing was that they both accepted the many visits from Mr Fitzwarren—although he'd been dead for some time, the old man chose to hang around his house and would often pop up out of the blue—but no one minded and he certainly didn't scare anyone.

"Grandfather, you're here again. Honestly, you're certainly not going to 'shuffle off this mortal coil' any time soon, are you? It's not that you're not welcome—you are—but I wish you'd give me some notice when you're going to appear—you really do startle me. And Dick never knows when you're going to jump out on him—especially when he has important visitors in the house."

Alice couldn't tell him off properly—she'd loved him so when he was alive, and Dick didn't seem to mind that he had to share his home with someone who'd been dead for some time.

So, they all lived happily together—the Lord Mayor of London, his wife Alice, the previous dead owner of the house, the decrepit old bossy Henderson who acted as though it was he, who owned the house—and of course, several cats.

Dick and Alice worked together throughout the years, striving to create many of the Charities needed in London. They were well suited to each other, but the sad thing was they had no children, although both would have welcomed them. This arrangement however gave them more time for each other and Dick continued to be very successful in business. When his term of office was over, the people of London elected him for a second time—and then, miraculously for a third and final time. He had been Lord Mayor of London three times and the Bow Bells had been right all along. But they hadn't mentioned that he'd become a Member of Parliament for the city—maybe even they hadn't known that.

Alice was dying—she was still a young woman—but her time on earth was over and Dick was broken-hearted. He sat by her bedside and held her hand, "What'll I do without you, my treasure? How will I live in this house if you're not here beside me?" But his words couldn't make Alice any stronger and just as he was about to begin his third term as Lord Mayor, he had to attend to his wife's funeral. He knew however that he wasn't alone in the house—on occasion, he saw Mr Fitzwarren and Henderson the butler, who'd recently joined his old master—but he also saw his dear Alice—who obviously just couldn't bear to leave him on his own. He couldn't possibly have felt alone in the big house.

Dick Whittington, Lord Mayor of London, went on with his work and became a very well-known and well-loved figure. He eventually died of course, leaving no family to inherit his great wealth but the many charities he'd created, received a great deal. So many people benefitted from the waif and stray's generosity and Dick Whittington's name would never be forgotten by the people. In fact, he lived on in the minds of generation after generation, right up to the present day, especially in popular children's stories. His lifetime teaches children how hard work and loyalty can result in great rewards and happiness. He'd been someone they could look up to and marvel at his success story.

Thank God for the Bow Bells of London and their message in the middle of the night—without it, a great many people would not have benefitted from Dick's many charities.

'Turn again, Dick Whittington. Turn again, thrice Lord Mayor of London.'

And he did—and he was!

Be Careful What You Wish For

'I wish! I wish! Please make it happen!' Harry crossed his fingers tightly and waited. His eyelids drooped and he felt strangely dizzy. 'What's happening?' He didn't say the words aloud but he thought them. He'd managed it somehow—he just knew he had. His head cleared and he tried to stand up. Looking around, he saw only stone walls and he knew he'd arrived in Hampton Court itself. But what year was it? He'd wanted sometime in the sixteenth century and looking around the room, he thought he'd been successful. He shrank back into a corner until he'd got his bearings and because he didn't want to have to talk to anyone yet.

There were lots of people in the room, all rushing about and getting in each other's way. The air was steamy and the smell of cooking meat strong—'I'm in a kitchen—but what a size of kitchen—it's huge—and along the full length of one wall, there were many bronze-coloured pots and pans on shelves.'

"Hey, you, boy—get your backside over here and take over turning the spit. What do you think you're here for—I'm not doing your job." A big man with an even bigger belly stood looking at him—he wore a sackcloth apron which was covered in stains, some which looked remarkably like blood. He was one of the cooks in charge and Harry knew he had to obey him, so he reached for the spit handle and began to turn it. The heat was unbearable but he knew he had to persevere.

The big man went off across the room, wiping his brow with a dish cloth—the sweat was running freely down his face and he hit out at a young lad who'd fallen asleep on a wooden block. "Wake up, Boy—you're not here to sleep, but to work!" He was one tough man and a bully to boot!

Harry's face was on fire and he knew it must be very red. This wasn't how he'd pictured his life at the great palace—but then he hadn't really imagined how it would be. Harry came from the 21st century and had asked his lucky stone if he could visit a time 500 years before he was born—and the stone had agreed, it seemed. Luckily, he didn't look too out of place in his large, loose shirt and tight jeans. His hair was rather long, in fact he needed a haircut—but it helped him merge into his surroundings.

He'd known his lucky stone was special and could probably do some amazing things. He'd found it at the very deepest point in a cave by the shore— he'd had to wrestle it from the natural stone, but after a couple of minutes, it came out quite easily. Something had been scratched on its surface, some sort of symbol or letters. He'd taken the stone home and had it ever since, but this was the first time he'd really tested its powers. And boy, had it worked! He felt in his back pocket to make sure it was still there and he hadn't lost it in his time travel. Relieved, he found it was there.

"Come on son, you've been turning that spit for long enough—you're almost on fire yourself." Another man wearing a sackcloth apron, pulled Harry out of the gigantic fireplace. "Go outside and cool down—Cuthbert here will take over for a while," and he pushed Harry towards an exit. Cuthbert didn't look too pleased, but Harry obeyed with great speed and stepped outside into a yard that seemed to be covered with fish of all sorts. It was called Fish Court, he learned later.

He was scared. He'd wished for this but now his wish had been granted, he was scared. What was going to happen to him next? He'd always been fascinated with the time of Henry VIII of England and how he'd executed several of his wives—and also a great number of his acquaintances. He must have been quite a dictator, rather than a King. The monarch in Harry's own time was a perfect lady and she'd never ordered anyone to lose their head—or any other part of their anatomy either. He felt better in the fresh air and walked carefully around the wall of the enclosed courtyard.

A huge clock was built into a tower—in fact, it might not have been a clock at all, but rather a huge sun dial or something to predict the weather. It didn't matter he decided because it couldn't have been the right time anyway. To the side of the grand building, there was a garden full of roses and lots of low privet hedges turning and twisting around in pattern. Was it a maze? It might be. Then he saw a young woman, in fact, she might still have been a girl. She had reddish hair that hung all the way down her back right to her waist. She was scolding an older woman who was walking behind her, telling her not to be so nosey, but the woman wasn't in the least bothered by the reprimand and told the girl again, she must go back and fetch a cloak—it was too chilly an afternoon.

"Don't be silly, Cat—it's a lovely day—stop being such an old fuss-pot." The girl laughed and ran forward to meet another lady. The lady was older—but not old—and looked to be heavily pregnant. If he was right, she must be Queen Jane Seymour, Henry VIII's third wife. He'd once seen a painting of her—a rather pale and delicate woman.

"Madame, I hope you are not tiring yourself—you should be resting now that your time is near." The red-headed girl kissed the lady's cheek.

"Who's being a fusspot now?" Queen Jane laughed at Princess Elizabeth's concerned expression. "A short walk in the rose garden can only do me good."

My God, Harry thought, *that must be Princess Elizabeth and her servant, Cat. That woman was her nursemaid at birth and stayed with her until she died.* He was amazed by what he was seeing—but still, very scared. The women turned and walked together towards the open door—Cat staying well behind. He returned to Fish Court as it was the only place he knew. My God, the smell of fish was overpowering! He felt something grab him from behind—a beefy hand went around his neck and he was picked up into the air.

"Come on, young fellow-me-lad, what are you doing out here? Get back to the kitchen and turn the spit some more—the haunch of deer is almost ready." He pushed Henry inside the building and dragged him by the collar over to the spit. The kitchen was even more mad than before—with bustling cooks, maids and waiters running in all directions. Great mounds of food were piled on silver serving dishes, towering stands with prongs held cooked chickens, and in the biggest dish, a crowned swan sat in the middle of the other plates, looking as though it was still alive. It had obviously been cooked then stuffed with its head stuck back on top of its long neck.

On the other table, there were cakes, jellies, blancmanges, and lots of jugs of wine and ale. Harry knew it was a feast fit for a king and that king must be Henry VIII. Licking his lips, Harry remembered he hadn't eaten since he'd left his house that morning. He knew however he'd be offered none of the amazing food—not a spit-turner like him.

The dishes were carried from the kitchen by a long line of servants and suddenly the kitchen was quiet except for the cooks. Surreptitiously he slipped out of the door and hid in Fish Court—it seemed safer than in the kitchen. He knew he should be trying to get back home and searched for the magic stone— his time travel stone. It seemed to have stopped working however so he rubbed it furiously again, using his shirt tail. Nothing happened—now he was really scared. What had he done—wishing to return to the past—with no idea how he could get bac? What a prat he was!

He went out of the court and climbed a long staircase covered in a deep red carpet. It looked rather posh to be so close to Fish Alley—but did lead into a separate building from where Harry could hear a lot of laughing and shouting. *Must be a party*, he thought. A door stood open at the top of the stairs, and he went in—looking both ways first—it was empty. The room looked like an office of sorts with papers and parchment spread all over a desk. Pots of ink and quills stood ready for whichever scribe next arrived. Through a second door, he found he was looking over a banister—down into a large hall full of people. He knew he had to be careful as the hall was a long way down and the people were quite small—everyone sat around 3 great tables, eating the food that had come from the kitchen. There was only half a swan now—*poor creature*, Harry thought.

"Who is that watching us from above—is it a boy?" A man's booming voice bellowed through the air and he knew it was the king himself who had spotted the intruder. "Guards, go fetch that boy—he could be up to no good." He turned to the man next to him, "Thomas, is that one of your spies? Starting them a bit young, I think." The man he spoke to was Thomas Cromwell—his first Minister and a very important person. Harry knew that from his history books.

The king got on with his meal and ripped a chicken apart with his bare hands, eating only the juiciest and plumpest parts, before discarding the carcass onto the floor. The guard found Harry and pushed him forward with his pike. The king looked up from his meal, "Ah, he is a boy, I see—well, what were you doing in the scribes' office, watching us have our meal?" Harry couldn't answer and Henry went on, "I'll have to think about what to do with you." He turned to the guard, "Take him away Guard and lock him up overnight—I'll see him again tomorrow." He waved a drumstick in the air and Harry was dragged from his presence.

In the darkness of the small room, Harry fumbled in his pocket and brought out his stone, rubbing it as hard as he could. He opened his eyes and found himself still in the dark room—the stone seemed to have lost its magic. As dawn approached and the sky began to lighten, he could make out the shapes around him—he'd been put back in the scribes' room where he'd been the night before. Somehow, it reassured him—at least they hadn't put him in the dungeon, although they probably would still cut off his head—that seemed to be the answer to most things at the Court of Henry VIII.

At the crack of dawn, he could see things more clearly and he leaned over the banister, as he'd done the previous night, and saw the king there again. This time, he was sitting in a large chair on a dais at the centre of the room and he was holding his head in both hands. A dejected figure if ever Harry had seen one. There was no one else there and the boy leaned further over the banister and grabbed hold of the heavy brocade curtain which fell from the ceiling to the floor. At that moment, he was grateful for all the hours he'd spent in the gym. He knew he could climb down the curtain if he had to. In the meantime, the king looked sad and Harry felt for him.

"Sire? Excuse me, Sire, is there something I can do for you?" Luckily, from his life in the 21st century, he wasn't in such awe of the king as he might have been—and he genuinely felt sorry for 'Bluff King Hal' who looked near to tears. He said again, "Sire, can I help you—you're obviously upset about something?"

The King looked up and his face took on a quizzical look. "You're the boy from last night, aren't you? How did you get here—I thought you'd been locked up?"

"I was, Sire—but you looked as though you needed someone to talk to. Tell me your problem—you see, I'm not an ordinary boy—I've come from the future and I'm only here for a short time. I may even have been sent here to help you—I'm not sure." He knew how mad his words sounded but he stood his ground.

"Sit down at my feet, young man, and I'll tell you—what have I got to lose?" Harry shimmied down the curtain and settled on the floor.

"My father began a dynasty—a Tudor dynasty—and it's my responsibility to protect the Tudor line by producing a male heir." The King told him how he'd had two wives already and there was no male heir. "Oh, I've got two daughters but that's no use, no woman can inherit my throne." He explained how he should never have married his first wife, Katherine—as it was a sin against God, she having already been married to his older brother who'd since died. His second wife Anne had never managed to produce a live baby boy and she had not been loyal in her marriage—she'd chosen other men and behaved badly with them.

"My present Queen Jane is an exceptional wife and I believe I love her more than the other two. I have just heard she has gone into labour and the birth of her child is imminent—I am afraid, young man—I am sorely afraid that something bad is about to happen—either to her or to the baby. I am desperate for a son—but there's nothing I can do to help her. The women are with her, as we speak." And he dropped his head into his hands again.

"Sire, do you believe I've come from the future—and I know now I've been sent here to help you." Harry knew he had the power to put the king out of his misery.

The big man stood up. *My God, he was tall*. Harry instinctively shrank back.

"I'll believe anything you tell me if you're going to help me. I know there's many a thing in this world of which we have no understanding. You help me now and I'll give you a valuable reward—well, what can you do for me?"

"I can tell you emphatically that you're just about to have your long-awaited son—your wife is about to give birth to a male child—just give her some time. The pregnancy is difficult, but she will deliver the baby safely." Harry felt as though he was talking out of turn, but history had taught him he was telling the truth.

"I must go, Boy—but thank you for giving me news of good cheer—I only hope you're right. I won't have you locked up again—but you should remain here until I go to see my wife. She has been in labour for some time now, so I'll go and ask her ladies how she is." And he was gone—the great King Henry VIII had listened to a stranger whom he'd considered a ragamuffin.

Hours later, Harry heard a loud clanging of bells and then the sound of trumpets, as though heralding something wonderful. Suddenly, courtiers were pushing their way into the room, jostling each other, and shouting happily. They ignored the boy sitting at the foot of the King's chair and called for the servants to bring wine and more wine. Henry himself rushed into the room, laughing, and crying both at once. "Well, boy—you were right—you see before you, a happy king who now has a male heir—a male heir who will secure the Tudor dynasty." He danced around the room, playfully punching his friends' shoulders. Harry thought, *A king isn't any different from other people after all*.

He felt the sweaty hands of the king touch his neck and turned around to face him. He pressed a small object into the boy's hands and said, "This is what I promised you, boy—I promised you a reward if you proved to be right about the Queen's baby and you have certainly done that. I wish it could be more, but I have had to deal with some insurrections in the north of the country and the Royal purse is rather empty just now. But look, it is a handsome gift, is it not?" He looked strangely humble as he spoke. It was a look he seldom showed but the birth of his son had made him more emotional than usual.

Harry looked at what the king had pressed into his hand and was delighted to see it was a small square-shaped box, obviously made of gold and with a very large ruby as the lid. It must have been worth a fortune. He looked into the king's eyes and for a moment, saw a kindness there that not many people ever saw. "Sire, you are kind—and I appreciate your generosity." It must have been the right thing to say as the King smiled before turning away to join his drunken cronies.

At King Henry's command, two gentlemen took Harry from the room and marched him down a long corridor, where they exchanged his clothes for a doublet and hose—and hung a sort of medallion around his neck. Now he really looked the part of a sixteenth century upper-class nobleman. He made sure however that he was also given a pouch to wear around his middle so he could keep his magic stone and gold box close by. He'd need that stone later, he hoped.

"Well, Young Man, that's more like it." The King welcomed the 'new boy' into the court. He was sitting on a great chair on the raised dais, surrounded by many ladies and gentlemen of his court. He motioned to Harry to join him—making some of the courtiers raise their eyebrows questioningly and snigger behind their closed fists. What was the king doing?

"Who was this—where did he come from?" the words spread around the room and the ladies soon joined the gossip. The Princess Elizabeth came forward, followed by an older woman—still young though—but older than her sister. It was the Princess Mary.

My God, that's Bloody Mary who burned all those people and tried to change the religion of the country back to Catholicism. Harry was in awe of her and her rather severe face. He remembered that she'd done this, even after her father had done his utmost to make England Protestant. These were real people—not just characters from the pages of history!

"These are my daughters, Young Man—this is Elizabeth and this Mary—you must bow to them both." The king understood the boy had no knowledge of how to behave at court—he didn't mind helping him, especially after he'd predicted the birth of his son.

"That Princess's mother was Katherine of Aragon and that one's was Anne Boleyn." Harry couldn't stop himself showing his knowledge of the royal family.

The King looked surprised and none too happy at the mention of his other wives, "I thought you said you'd come from the future—how can you know so much about my family—tell me, if you know so much, which daughter will make me most proud?" He looked at the two young women.

Harry hesitated, realising his knowledge might get him into hot water but he had to tell the truth, "The Princess Elizabeth will become a great queen one day and look after England for you—and she'll ensure the religion you've chosen will survive into the future of England."

The King jumped up, "You say that, but what about my son just born? He is destined to be the king." Bluff King Hal looked crestfallen for a moment and stared angrily at Harry.

"Oh, don't misunderstand me, Sire—your son will be king one day—but not for many years. You will still be on the throne for many years to come." He was learning the diplomacy of the court ways and how important it was to be careful with what he said to the King. Too much knowledge was perhaps a dangerous thing.

The mood changed in the room and some of the ladies asked about Queen Jane's health—and that of the baby. Whilst they were chatting, Harry took the opportunity to look around the room. The walls were hung with the most elaborate tapestries—mainly of gold thread, but with a rich ruby colour interwoven here and there. They were Flemish works, Harry recalled—and around the edges of the room stood thick candles on platforms, spaced a few feet apart. What a rich room it was.

"Have you seen the beautiful emblem the queen has chosen as her own? It's a Phoenix rising from the ashes—apparently it represents the end of the two previous Queens and a better time ahead for her—it's surrounded by red and white Tudor roses, representing the children she and the king will one day have." The ladies gushed and congratulated the Henry on his clever wife. On this occasion, Harry knew to hold his tongue. He knew Jane Seymour's life was in the balance but only he knew that.

King Henry looked at his daughter, Mary, and to mend bridges, he told her she was to be one of his son's Godmothers—if she signed a document swearing that his marriage with her mother was illegal and that she herself had been born outside of wedlock. It was a great favour to be a Godmother but such an insult to Mary's mother, Katherine. She did sign the document however—she was wise enough to know her head remaining on her shoulders was dependant on it. A little voice however inside her head said 'wait'—I will be queen one day and then I'll make sure the sparks fly. And of course, as Harry knew, this she did!

The baby's christening was in two days and Henry insisted his Queen rose from her sick bed—where she had remained since the child was born—she was to attend the christening ceremony. Jane was not a well woman—she'd developed a fever and had a high temperature—but Henry was insistent that she attend. Queen Jane did attend her son's christening but retired immediately after the service as she was too weak to stand. She'd developed Child Bed Fever and her frail body couldn't deal with it.

Thoughts rushed through her mind as her head rested on the silk pillow—she'd managed to change the French style of dress at court, the one Anne Boleyn had brought from France: she'd encouraged the King to make peace with his estranged daughters—but she knew there'd be more challenges ahead. The King and Jane had been married just over a year—in fact, they'd married only 11 days after Anne Boleyn had lost her head: the King was now the Head of the Church of England, and no longer dependent upon the Pope in Rome, so he was content. Jane of course followed the Protestant faith and had also persuaded her husband to promote her brother Edward, to the elevated position of Protector of England. Despite her quiet and unassuming demeaner, Jane had achieved much in a short time and the Seymour family was on the rise because of her. She rested her head on the pillow and was pleased she'd played a part in bringing this about, but her greatest achievement had just happened—she'd presented Henry with a living son and heir, something he'd always wanted. As she lay there in high fever, she thought of all that had happened over the past year and yes, she'd made quite a difference.

The year was 1537 and Jane was not yet 30 but it was to be the year of her death. Nine days after the birth of her son, Jane died and left a grief-stricken king behind. The whole court went into mourning—and Harry found himself in mourning too. He now had several changes of outfit and slept in a cot in the room next to the king's own—at the sovereign's request. He'd become very privileged at the court of King Henry VIII. His presence seemed to give comfort to the now—broken-hearted king—whether or not it was believed he came from the future was another question—but he was liked and been made welcome at the court. He felt very special, which was a good thing, as his magic stone still didn't work. It was in his pouch and although he'd rubbed it many times and wished as hard as he could, it didn't seem able to take him back to his own time. He began to worry about what his family was thinking but he was stuck in the past for the time being and despite attempts to make the stonework—he couldn't do it.

Then the question he'd been dreading, "If you're from the future, why didn't you tell me my dear wife was not long for this world—you predicted the birth of my son—yet you never forewarned me about Jane." The King was feeling bad that day and wanted to blame someone for his sadness, so he picked on Harry who'd proven he had the gift of seeing into the future—but who'd failed to tell him about his wife's imminent death. The boy felt he was being unjustly accused of something and felt inclined to defend himself—but he reminded himself where he was and that he was afraid of the King—and rightly so!

"My dear, sweet Jane has been taken from me—I loved her more than my other two wives—I absolutely worshipped her. She should have been more insistent that she was ill—she should have spoken up—I'm not a mind reader, am I?" He was crying into his unusually sombre clothes and as always, managed to blame Jane was not insisting she was too ill to attend Edward's christening—although he knew she'd left her sick bed at his insistence. But then, that was Henry's ways!

Harry could take no more—he though the King was indulging himself in maudlin thoughts—although his tears seemed genuine. He stared into the big man's eyes and blurted out, "Perhaps if you'd listened to her when she told you she was too ill to attend the prince's christening, she might still be alive. You didn't listen though, did you?" A stillness filled the air and no one moved.

Harry then heard the words dreaded by the whole court, "Take him away, Guards—and throw him into the dungeon—I'll decide later if he's to lose his head. A traitor if ever I've seen one!" The king didn't mince his words—it was much easier to fall from his good opinion, than it was to gain it. The boy was dragged away by the guards—and this time, thrown into a dark and dank small room in the dungeon.

'My God, he was imprisoned in a cell in the Middle Ages, and he'd earned Henry VIII's wrath. Why did he speak up? He knew the answer to that however, the king always blamed everyone else for the bad situations he, himself had created. But to blame Queen Jane for bringing about her own death was just too much! Harry just had to speak out!

His cell had one tiny window at the top of the wall. It didn't allow much light inside and there was no chair to sit on. He lay on the stone floor which was covered by a thin layer of straw—a very thin layer that gave no softness for the body. There were rats too—two at any one time—they scuttled around the floor, obviously hungry and looking for food. Harry hoped they wouldn't mistake him for the latter. Strangely enough, the rats gave him some comfort—he wasn't alone in the cell, which seemed to belong to them as well. He didn't know how long he'd been there when a guard appeared and threw a chunk of bread through a gap in the door—he placed a cup of water inside on the ground.

He told the prisoner, "That's all you'll get today—make the most of it—it'll keep you alive until the King decides what to do with you." What a threat! But he did eat the bread although it was mouldy and smelly. Despite his fear, he managed to fall asleep on the floor. Before closing his eyes however, words came uninvited into his mind, 'Careful what you wish for '– and he had wished for the magic stone to bring him here and into this freezing, dark dungeon. If only he'd known!

A glow in the corner suddenly appeared—it had awoken him from an uneasy sleep and it scared him. What could it be? He recognised the court ladies from paintings and books—they both held a candle and were dressed in very fashionable dresses. The older one stepped forward, "Do you know who I am?" she asked.

"No, Madame, I do not, although your face seems familiar. Will you tell me your name?" He was even more scared now but knew he mustn't show it.

"I am Queen Katherine of Aragon, mother of the Princess Mary—and this is Queen Anne Boleyn, mother of the Princess Elizabeth. We know you have incurred the King's wrath, something that is easy to do. You defended Queen Jane, did you not—and accused the king of hypocrisy? Very brave but I fear not very wise." Anne Boleyn stepped forward too and raised her candle above her head.

"I am very honoured to meet you both—but why do you favour me with your presence?" he felt brave enough to ask. He realised he was actually becoming quite good at courtly language.

"We've come to ask you to use your influence on the King—we have seen how he likes you and he does believe you're from the future. Although he's aggressive and has a foul temper, he can be persuaded to do certain things—and now he's lost Jane Seymour—you know, she was never actually crowned queen, unlike both of us. (She couldn't resist saying this)—he'll be looking around for his next wife. That's the kind of man he is—shallow in the extreme. You could be very important at this time and influence him in his choice of bride." *What a responsibility! Harry thought—a poisoned chalice to be sure!*

Anne took over the conversation at this point and added, "Believe it or not, he has already sent Thomas Cromwell to Germany to investigate the possibility of a lady of rank who lives there. Oh, he'll mourn Jane for a few weeks but being

Henry, he'll soon be looking around. What Queen Katherine and I want you to do, is to remind him you are from the future and you know that marriage to the Cleves woman from Germany, would be his best marriage to date. He will no doubt send for a miniature portrait of her and you must ask to see it and tell him she's the most beautiful woman you've ever seen. Do you think you could do that for us?"

"But Ladies, Anne of Cleves will not be his favourite—I know that because I am from the future and I already know what will happen to her."

"We're aware of that—but that's why he must be encouraged to do it. We are more aware of what is still to come, now that we have passed to the other side. His unhappiness is the only thing that gives us pleasure. You know how he treated each of us and now that Jane Seymour is to be buried at Windsor—he is a free man again." Queen Katherine couldn't conceal her dislike of Henry—and yet she'd loved him once. "You should know that Jane was not the innocent, sweet woman she pretended to be—she was first my lady in waiting and then the same for Anne Boleyn—she just patiently waited until we were both gone—and then she pounced."

Harry thought about the proposition. He'd come to terms with ghosts visiting him in this place, strange though it was. He was already in an unreal situation being a boy from the future, living at the Tudor Court, albeit now in a freezing cell—he'd even been threatened with his head being removed and it could still happen—so what did he have to lose—but there should be something in it for him. *Harry had never been slow and realised he might have an advantage here.*

"Tell you what, Ladies—you persuade the King to release me from here and take me back under his protection and I'll do what you ask." He couldn't believe he was actually negotiating with two dead queens—*life could be funny!*

"No sooner said than done." Both ghosts disappeared at once, leaving a gentle misty glow behind—but only for a few seconds. The very next day, he was taken before the King, who remained in deep mourning for his wife and still dressed in unusually sombre clothes. Normally, the powerful king favoured more flamboyant attire.

"Well, Boy from the future, have you decided to show me more respect? Do you want to keep your head on your shoulders? If not, I can easily arrange for it to be removed." The King was gloating—he loved the power he had over everyone.

"I do respect you, Sire—I want you to know I am your friend—and always will be." Harry chose his words carefully—the King was so temperamental, he could blow up at the smallest thing. But he was also susceptible to flattery—he liked people to admire him as much as he admired himself.

"Accompany me to Windsor Castle then—today my Jane is to be interred in the chapel there. There are horses ready for us outside—and a retinue of soldiers to accompany us. Come!"

In the chapel, Jane had already been laid to rest in the vault and on her tombstone, the words had already been carved:

Here lies Jane, a Phoenix who died giving another Phoenix life
Let her be mourned, for birds like these, are rare indeed.

Harry knelt in prayer at the side of the King and helped the big man to his feet afterwards. Henry's legs still troubled him since his fall from a horse years before. The castle had been made ready for them to rest the night—and Harry was impressed by, not only having lived at Hampton Court, but now at Windsor Castle as well. The Princesses Mary and Elizabeth were in attendance and joined their father to dine in the great hall. The meal was not as flamboyant as normal and the mood was sombre, but the hall was decorated by a great many candles and there was a huge fire in the hearth, around which the lesser courtiers sat to enjoy their meal.

"She is gone—but my son is safe. Daughter Mary, what do you think of your Godson? And you, Lady Elizabeth, is he not a handsome fellow?" The King was obviously feeling melancholic and needed some cheer from his daughters.

Mary spoke up first, reassuring her father that the child was exceptional for one so young. "I believe he already knows people as individuals—it's the way he follows one around the room with his eyes. Obviously, a bright child!" She kept her eyes lowered as most people did when they spoke to the King—he took offence so easily.

The feistier Princess Elizabeth said, "At least he's good and healthy—and that's what we want, is it not Father?" Her red hair shone in the candlelight as she picked her way through a chicken carcass, choosing only the leanest parts. "I am also pleased that he was baptised in the true religion—in the Protestant faith!" She looked provocatively at her catholic sister, Mary. Outwardly Mary was a Protestant but secretly, she remained an ardent Catholic, Again, Mary kept her eyes lowered.

"Aye, that is true, Elizabeth—after all, his father is the Head of the Church of England, with no need for interference from the Church of Rome." He watched Mary closely from narrowed, shrewd eyes, almost begging her to differ. However, she did not—she would bide her time for the present—she felt sure her time would come. And as Harry knew, it did just that—and with what venom!

Once the court had settled again at Hampton Court, Thomas Cromwell returned from Germany with a miniature of Anne of Cleves, painted by the famous Holbein artist. She looked a beautiful woman and Cromwell sang her praises to the King. She was a lady of good education and well experienced in the way of royal courts, having lived with her relatives in several palaces. She had been betrothed whilst still young—and that to a gentleman of nobility—but it had fallen through and no one ever knew why. She was at an age ripe for marriage and had already accepted the offer from King Henry VIII of England to become his wife and Queen of his country.

It had taken some time to arrange and after some months, the lady set sail for the English east coast where she disembarked with several of her ladies in waiting. The drawback was that none of them knew how to speak English and the guttural tones of their own language were difficult to understand.

"Come with me, boy—come to Kent—to Deal, to meet the Lady Anne. I would value your opinion of her." It wasn't an invitation but an order and of course, Harry agreed. On the ride to Deal, Harry hung on to the horse's bridle as best he could, but he hadn't been brought up around horses, so he wasn't too happy. They arrived at the house where the German newcomers were temporarily living—they'd left the ship and they'd only been on land for two days.

The King disguised himself as a common traveller and burst into the room where his intended was—Harry at his back—and grabbed hold of the Lady Anne. She drew back and ran to her ladies in waiting. She burst into tears as she thought she had been assaulted by a brigand. The king was very embarrassed and displeased as he didn't know what he'd done wrong—it was quite usual for a groom to surprise his intended in this way—but unfortunately not in Germany.

At that very moment, the King formed an unfounded dislike of Anne of Cleves and immediately rode back to Hampton Court, leaving her in Kent. "What a stupid woman, boy—and she is to be my wife! Also, she is not nearly as beautiful as the lady Holbein painted in the miniature. Do you agree, young Harry?" He was whipping his horse impatiently and his companions found it difficult to keep up with him.

Harry knew he must hang on to the horse and stay by the king's side—but it wasn't easy. "I agree she is quite unusual, Sire—but she is still a pretty woman, don't you think?"

"No, I do not, boy—I am betrothed to her however and there's nothing I can do to change that. Wait till I see Thomas Cromwell—and his lies!" And he galloped off quickly into the distance, as though the Hounds of Hell were after him.

The couple did marry however, but the King made no secret of how repulsive he found her. He said she was ugly, smelt badly, had rotten teeth, and dressed like a peasant. He tried to get a divorce, but he had no reason for it and couldn't go down that avenue. She had done no wrong—and her character was unblemished—it seemed she was his wife after all.

That night, the king's three dead wives visited Harry as he slept in his bedchamber. Jane Seymour had joined the other two Queens, although she had no real reason to hate the King—he had done nothing bad to her—but then he hadn't had time to get around to that before she upped and died. In fact, he still told whoever would listen to him, that he'd loved her more than anyone else. She was still a dead wife however and had obviously found her place in the afterlife, so here she was! The three queens stood together in a line and waited until Harry woke up properly.

"I've done as you asked and he is now married to the lady—what more do you want? He really doesn't like her, you know—and yet she is really a nice person. She means well and is kind—she can even speak English now, although still badly—but he hates her. You probably know this, but he is planning to have his marriage annulled and to make her his sister—if she doesn't object to his plans." Harry was fully awake now.

Katherine spoke up first. "Yes, we know what he plans to do—the man really is a monster. You are aware he already has his eye on a girl young enough to be his daughter—Catherine Howard—how we pity the child—for that's all she is. It will not end well for her, whereas if Anne of Cleves goes on playing her cards right, she should do very well out of the arrangement he wants."

Anne Boleyn broke into the conversation which Katherine was hogging too much. "We need to ask you for one more favour—and if you do it well, we'll help you get back to your own time. What do you think of that?"

Jane Seymour smiled at the boy, "You must miss your own life and family—and they'd be so please to see you again." She really was the gentlest of the three. It was a shame she'd died so suddenly.

"What is the favour—I swear, if it's in my power, I'll do it—if you help me return to my own time." He was wide awake now and needed to go home and see his family again. "Tell me what you want!"

It was Anne Boleyn's turn to speak, "You must seek out the young girl Catherine Howard and warn her that the King has his eye on her and will seek to marry her, once he rids himself of Anne of Cleves. He always gets what he wants in the end. She should be afraid—very afraid—but she is young and simple and probably doesn't realise how cruel the man can be."

"Tell me why you continue to watch what he does—and need to involve yourselves in his life? He can't mean much to you now—I don't understand why you watch him so closely." Harry was genuinely confused.

More than one Queen started to talk but Katherine was louder than the others. "What do you see in front of you, boy? Do you see just ghosts of dead women?" Harry waited, his mouth agape, unsure of what to say. He could only see three ghosts, what did she mean?

"What you see are three anxious, worried mothers—not just ghosts of who we once were. My daughter Mary has never been a favourite of her father and I worry about her future. She will never forgive him for making her sign a paper, denying me as his Queen and making her turn her back on her chosen Catholic faith. I fear if he marries the child Catherine Howard, Mary will be even more pushed out into the cold—with no prospect of any happiness." Could a ghost cry—Harry could swear he saw tears run down her cheeks. *But surely not!*

Anne Boleyn broke into the conversation, "What about my daughter, the Princess Elizabeth? Her future beggars the question—what position will she have at court when a younger whippersnapper comes along and pushes her aside. I am aware she will one day be a great queen if the line of succession remains as it is now—there should be no more children born to Henry. Catherine is also my cousin and I would not want her to suffer as I did at the hands of the king. Do you understand what I'm saying, boy?" She didn't cry though; she was made of sterner stuff.

Then it was Jane Seymour's turn to answer his question, "I had to leave my precious baby in the arms of strangers when God called me to his side. Although I accept that his father loves him—I fear he loves himself more. If he marries this young girl, the need to care for his son will be forgotten and she would not be a good mother for the boy—in years and in outlook, she is barely older than he is. It is a marriage that will not work and the girl herself will suffer the consequences. Please listen to the others and persuade the King not to wed Catherine Howard." Jane was such a gentle person with such a soft, soothing voice, that Harry took more notice of her than of the others.

"I'll make sure the next time I have the King's ear; I'll warn him of the girl's frivolous nature and her disregard for his position in the country. You must leave it with me—I'll do my best—but don't forget your promise to help me get back to my own time. I've have been away far too long now and my family will be really concerned."

It was several days later before Harry had an opportunity to talk with the king. A group of courtiers, including the Lady Catherine Howard, had come in from the gardens where they'd been practising archery—and where she had been dancing around and laughing at everyone's wit—especially at the kings. She seemed to love being the centre of attention and enjoyed the way Henry's eyes followed her wherever she went. She was a very pretty girl but for her age, she seemed too comfortable in the company of gentlemen—there was an awareness about her and a maturity that belied her young age. It seemed to suggest she'd already led a colourful life before coming to court. There was nothing demure about her! The king however, saw none of this—he just saw a young, vivacious girl, not afraid to enjoy herself.

Harry knew it was now or never and he worked his way through the group until he stood at the king's side. "Sire, you look at that lady with great admiration in your eyes."

"I do that, boy—I do that. Is she not quaint and very pretty? I think I would like to share my life with her—especially after the ugly Anne of Cleves—what do you think of that?" The King never seemed surprised by Harry's remarks— in fact, he allowed the boy from the future greater freedom than he allowed many others.

Harry took advantage of this, and remembering how the three ghosts had promised to help him, he felt he had to be brave, "Sire, do you not think the Lady Catherine is just a little too frivolous for someone as dignified as you—and could she really hold the position of queen at the court and command the respect of the nobility and of the people? I'm sorry if I appear forward but you know I care only for your safety and happiness." He really had learned the language of the court. *He almost made himself feel sick at his sycophancy!*

The great bear of a man stood up and roared his annoyance at what Harry had just said, "Who do you think you are, Boy from the Future, you are nothing but a guttersnipe—you've been allowed in my court at my pleasure. Now I have only displeasure for you and I wish you gone from my sight. Guards! Guards! Where are you? Take this wretch and throw him again into the dungeons where he can be left to rot for all I care."

He turned his back on Harry as the guards grabbed the boy and dragged him from the king's presence. He must have bashed his head against the as he was dragged away as he felt drowsy in the cell before passing out completely. He did manage to shout to the three ghosts however, hoping they could hear, 'Don't forget your promise.' And then all went black!

He turned and twisted and felt as though he was buried beneath something heavy. He kicked out and managed to free his legs. Where was he? It didn't feel like the smelly, musty walls of the cell where he'd been thrown. His head was swimming as he sat up and the dizziness made him fall backwards. Funny, there was something soft beneath him and there was no sound of any rats. He could hear someone calling his name. He thrust what turned out to be a quilt onto the floor.

"Harry—Harry—you've got to get up now. Tea's almost ready and Grandma and Grandpa are already here." He recognised the voice—it was his mother.

My God, had the three ghosts kept their word after all?

He sat up and realised he was in his own bed, and in his own time. Oh My God, what was happening? He remembered he'd upset the King Henry and felt afraid again of what was going to happen to him. The king could be absolutely ruthless when he wanted to be, and Harry knew he'd crossed the line with him when he criticised the young Catherine Howard. Still, it looked as though the three dead Queens had kept their word. Boy-oh-boy, that whole thing had been scary!

He looked down and was surprised to see he was dressed in his normal clothes—not those of the Tudor court—but unsurprisingly he felt very strange. If Mother was calling him down for tea, she mustn't have missed him from the house and yet, he knew he'd been gone for several months. There was a soft knock on his bedroom door and it opened slowly to show his mother, still with her pinny on—except his mother looked exactly like Anne Boleyn—in fact, to Harry, she was Anne Boleyn in modern clothes.

"Come on sleepyhead, you've had a good long sleep—people are waiting downstairs, ready for their tea." She closed the door on a confused Harry. How could his mother look like that? Had she always looked that way? He followed her downstairs and went into the dining room where he found another two people whom he recognised. King Henry VIII sitting at the table with Katherine of Aragon by his side—both were dressed in modern clothes—but it still looked like the king and his first wife—the oldest one—Katherine.

"Come on, Boy, we've been waiting for you and I, for one, am starving. Look what's waiting for you—freshly baked scones with jam and cream and one of your mother's famous Victoria Sponges." It really was Bluff King Hal—except it wasn't. He looked just as greedy as the king, but it was just Grandpa, always ready with a joke and a smile. Even the way he called him 'Boy' was just like the King did.

"Be still, Harry, and stop teasing your namesake." Katherine of Aragon looked at the boy and held out her hand. "Come on darling, don't mind silly, old Grandpa, you know what he's like. When he's hungry, he starts talking gibberish." It was both his grandparents and now they looked remarkably like the Tudor King and his first wife.

His mother came into the room saying, "Daddy's going to be late tonight—he's got an unexpected meeting—but Jane and Lizzie have arrived." She went to hang up the new arrivals' coats. Harry watched them come through the door and his mouth again fell open in amazement. Bursting into the room amidst giggles, came Jane Seymour and the Princess Elizabeth—this time, they were mother and daughter, his aunt and his cousin. What was happening to the world?

Lizzie's hair was as red as the Princess Elizabeth's had been and her sweet face was just as pretty. Aunt Jane was livelier than Jane Seymour had been—but she was the image of the young queen.

Led by Grandpa, everyone delved into the delicious food and soon, his mother noticed how quiet her son was. "What's wrong, Harry—has something happened?"

"Mother, how long was I asleep upstairs?" He played with his cake rather than eating it.

"For two whole hours, Harry—I had no idea you were so tired—but that's why I let you sleep on. By the way, before I forget, have you finished the essay you need for first lesson tomorrow. It was about Tudor times in England, I think."

"That's right, Mum—it is about Tudor times—and I still have some work to do on it." He spotted his magic stone on the mantlepiece and asked if it had been there all the time. Apparently it had, so how had he travelled back to his own time without its magic? There was no answer. He felt in his pocket in case there was a second one—but there wasn't—but what there was instead, was a small gold box with a large red ruby top. How could that be? And how had the magic stone come out of his pocket and onto the mantlepiece?

Grandpa reached across the table and took the box from Harry. "Where on earth did you get this, boy?" He looked just like the greedy Bluff King Hal! *Did he recognise the gift he'd once given Harry?*

"I found it in the woods, Grandpa, and brought it back for Mum. Do you like it, Mum?" he asked her—just a little white lie, that's all.

"I do indeed, Harry, very much—but we'll have to hand it in to the police to see if anyone claims it." She looked closely at the box. "This is real gold, and the ruby is probably real as well. It must be worth a great deal of money." She looked thoughtful. "Mind you if no one claims it in an agreed time, I believe it reverts to the finder—and that was you, Harry. I'll hand it in to the police station tomorrow if you like—and fingers crossed, no one will come looking for it. Maybe it's lain in the woods for hundreds of years, you never know."

"Okay Mum, you do that, will you—and I'll go upstairs and finish my essay." He turned around at the door and looked at the Tudor King, three of his wives and his daughter. He knew he'd have no problem finishing his essay now—he knew exactly what he was going to say. He'd met and understood the problems of the queens—and strangely enough, even those of the king.

"Bye everyone, safe journey home—and Mum, don't worry about the real owner of the box coming along to claim it—I'm pretty sure that's not going to happen." *Especially after 500 years*, he said to himself. *But please Mum, don't let me sleep so long again—I don't think I could bear it!*

The Foundling

Gertie crept along the side of the hedge and stopped when she could see the garden gate. Any minute now, the gardener would come out, untie the strings tied around his trouser legs to keep them out of the dirt and wash his hands under the tap on the water butt. And sure enough, there he was! George Cameron had been working in the kitchen garden since 6 o'clock that morning and he was ready for his dinner. In his usual way, he walked the length of the walled garden and on towards the kitchen door of the big house.

All was quiet, just the sounds of the birds singing and twittering, and jostling each other out of the way to get at the worms George had disturbed by his digging. It was a feast and no mistake! Gertie crept along the hedge and pushed open the gate, dragging her sack cloth behind her. My, but the plants were looking good—all healthy, and thrusting through the earth, begging to be picked!

It would be rude not to show my appreciation, so I'll just help myself to as much as I can—she told herself. She began to fill the sack—a couple of cabbages and cauliflowers, carrots, leeks, potatoes, turnips and beetroot. She left the sack on the ground and moved towards the greenhouse where she picked a few tomatoes and carried them back in her apron to add to the sack. That was as much as she could manage to drag carry—and anyway if she was too greedy, George would notice things were missing and begin to keep his eye open for thieves. She hurried through the grounds and reached the edge of the estate without being seen by anyone. On through the woods she went—woods she knew very well.

"Mrs Cratchit, are you there? It's only me—it's Gertie—come with some bits for your belly." The cottage was quiet, and Gertie took her sack around to the back. And there she was, old Mrs Cratchit sitting on a basket chair, sound asleep and with her old moggy Cat on her knee.

"Oh Gertie, you did give me a fright—where have you come from, girl?" and the old woman staggered to her feet, forcing Cat to run off into the trees. "You do pop up at some strange times." She was a sweet, old woman with white hair and rosy cheeks. She must have been about 70 years of age and couldn't walk very well, but she loved it when visitors popped up at her cottage.

"Come on girl—come into the kitchen and I'll boil some water—I've still got a little nip of tea leaves and I'll share them with you."

Gertie followed her indoors. "Where on earth did you get tea, Mrs Cratchit—you must be a richer woman than I thought." She laughed at the old lady's expression.

"Cook at the big house sometimes sends a little bit across to me—and I'm grateful. Sometimes, I give her a few herbs for her stews and she's quite happy with that." She filled the teapot that Gertie had always loved—it was covered with tiny blue flowers and its lid covered the chip on the edge quite nicely.

The two friends enjoyed each other's company—one so young and one so old—yet both alike in many ways. Gertie worked as a maid in the local vicarage and felt no guilt in stealing vegetables for elderly people in the village, like the old lady—in fact, she thought it was only right. The people at the big house had so much and some of the villagers so little, so she considered it was her duty to help them—and if doing so cost her nothing, then all the better, as she had no money of her own. She was just 14 years old, and she and Mrs Cratchit had the same sense of humour and similar outlooks on life. Both were nice people, at least they thought so.

Gertie had been a foundling who'd been left on the doorstep of the church vicarage with nothing more than an embroidered shawl to cover her. She was lucky however as she was taken into the vicar's own home where she was brought up by the servants who worked there. She was not part of his family however and had to work hard—even as a child—taking on some of the household chores, just like the others. She couldn't complain though as she'd always had a full belly and the odd, sweet crumb from the table. There was a cook too, who took a shine to the young girl and taught her all the basics of baking and cooking. In fact, she'd also brought Mrs Cratchit a small loaf she'd baked herself and she reached into her deep pocket to produce it.

"Oh, you are a good girl, Gertie." And she hid the loaf under a tea towel for later. "Let me pour you another cup of tea." And the two cronies spent the next hour changing stories and laughing at each other's tales. Gertie took half the contents of her sack and gave them to her friend. "Are these stolen, girl? Now, tell me the truth—did you come by them honestly?"

"Of course, I did—George Cameron himself told me to take them—so I did." She was a good liar was Gertie, but her smile gave her away.

"I'll believe your fibs this time because it suits me and I benefit from your naughtiness—but you'd better be careful or they'll catch you. Right, that's my scold for today—now off you go—but thank you for thinking of me—you're my good, little friend." Mrs Cratchit waved her off at the door. "Come and see me again soon now."

Gertie took her sack and left, heading straight for old Mr Parkinson's house. The rest of the vegetables were for him—she knew she couldn't take any back to the vicarage—and he was one of her village favourites. He was an abrupt old man who was obsessed with the comb-over of his hair which was folded over his bald head. If it fell out of place even just a little, he panicked and had to go indoors to re-arrange it.

"Bless you, child—you'll get your rewards in Heaven. Unfortunately, I have no rewards to give you now—but I'm sure your Guardian Angel will watch over you." He took the vegetables inside and returned her empty sack, hoping she'd fill it up again on another day. "Have you seen your Guardian Angel lately, Gertie—last time you visited me, you'd just come from her?" he asked the girl.

"Oh, I see her regularly, Mr Parkinson—she's never very far away. I can't stop and chat today I'm afraid—I spent too long talking with Mrs Cratchit. See you soon!" And she was gone, running quickly back to the vicarage.

"Where have you been, Gertie?" Cook was on the warpath and needed help preparing the dinner, so she hurried to help and asked if a nice cup of tea would go down well. Cook thought it a good idea and sat down, waiting for the little maid to make it. Gertie knew how to get around the woman—who was actually a very kind person—but she did love her tea.

Potatoes peeled and mutton on the boil, Gertie sat down for a few moments and as she often did in moments of relaxation, she played with her wrist bangle. She'd had it since she was a baby and was always amazed the way, John, the stable boy, could move the clasp to make it bigger as she grew. She wouldn't have been able to wear it for so long if he wasn't so clever. She fingered the tiny padlock attached to the band and again wondered who had locked it—the key must have been very small. It had often been suggested that it was snapped off—secateurs would have done the job easily, but she always shied away from that, as it was the only contact she'd ever had with her natural mother—at least that's what she liked to believe.

Somehow, it made her feel less lonely, and she'd been told it had been wrapped inside her baby shawl when she was left outside the vicarage. It was said that mothers who deserted their babies always left an item for remembrance with the child, so that, if she ever came back to claim her baby, she would be able to describe the token. In her own case, she liked to believe her mother might have the key to the wrist band. She might even come back one day to claim her child. It was a good story and quite true in many cases—so Gertie waited for that day when her mother would turn up. She often pictured their reunion in her mind, and it brought her comfort.

"Get up, Gertie, time to set the dinner table. Now remember which sides the knives and forks go—and don't embarrass the mistress again." Gertie had always had a difficulty knowing her left from her right—even her shoes needed different marks to show her how to put them on. People would often laugh at her, but not unkindly but to Gertie, it wasn't really funny and frequently got her into trouble.

"I know—I know, Cook—don't you worry." And she whisked the cutlery basket from the kitchen cupboard, first putting on a clean apron. The mistress could be very fussy sometimes especially when there were guests, like tonight. There weren't many dinner parties at the vicarage as the Vicar was quite poor, but when they did have one, it was always done properly.

"No, no Gertie—use my mother's lace napkins, they look so much better that the plain ones." Mistress Barbara was hovering nervously in the dining room. She liked to oversee the preparations and make sure that only the best of everything was being used. "The antique candelabra please—the silver ones— and the best candles, we don't want the ones that splutter and fill the room with an unpleasant odour." Gertie was moving as fast as she could but was happy when the mistress finally left the room and she felt as if she could breathe again. Mistress Barbara was usually a kind woman but when she was entertaining guests, she became a bit of an ogre.

Back in the kitchen, her nose began to twitch—the smells were lovely and filled the warm kitchen. "Mmm…Cookie, it all smells great—will we be having the leftovers?" Gertie had a healthy appetite and looked forward to the meal she and the other servants would often have when the guests had left. As usual, it was a lovely meal, and the mistress came down to the kitchen to say thank you for everyone's efforts. Gertie knew she'd been a lucky girl to have been left at the vicarage and not someplace else, where they might not have been so kind.

Mind you, she had to work hard for her keep—but she didn't mind—it was only right.

The Master and Mistress from the big house arrived at 8'clock—a fashionable time to dine. The Vicar and Mistress Barbara met them as they climbed out of their carriage and escorted them into the house. The mistress looked very handsome in the candlelight and the lady from the big house looked exquisite, with her jewels shining brightly in the soft light. The ladies began with a glass of champagne, but the men opted for some claret. It all looked so beautiful with the crystal goblets sparkling and tinkling, the ladies laughing and the maid servant, helped by Gertie, acting as the go-between from the dining room to the kitchen. Unlike the big house, the vicarage didn't have many servants—one maidservant, one under-maidservant (Gertie), one stable boy (part-time) and one cook. It was all that was needed to keep the house in good running order.

The Master from the big house was watching the maid servants closely and he suddenly moved closer to the table, "I don't know this little maid, do I?" he asked the others. "I don't know her, yet she looks familiar. I know I haven't visited you in a long time, but I don't remember ever seeing her." He seemed more interested in the girl than was warranted.

Mistress Barbara waved her hand in the air rather dismissively and said, "Oh, that's our Gertie—she helps around the house and is the under maid. She can turn her hand to most things—and I don't think Cook could survive without her." She immediately lost interest in the servants and continued chatting with her other guest. Sir Jeremy the Master kept right on staring at the young girl, until his wife broke the silence by saying how ready she was for dinner.

The evening passed pleasantly, and the meal was a success. Mistress Barbara was pleased and called for Cook after the guests had left for home. "Bessie, that was a very nice meal—you surpassed yourself with the choice of puddings and the lamb was cooked to perfection. Thank you very much—now you and the others enjoy the leftovers—I hope there's plenty for everyone."

"Oh yes, Ma'am, there's enough vittles' left for us, and I'm pleased your evening was a success. But then, you always lay on a good meal. Goodnight, Ma'am—and you, Sir." She glanced at the Vicar who was already falling asleep in his chair. She always thought it funny the way the mistress always called the mutton, lamb—she supposed it must sound better. She'd always known it as mutton and it tasted nice whatever it was called!

"Night Bessie," the vicar lifted his hand in a salute. When Bessie had gone, he turned to his wife, "Barbara dear, didn't you find Sir Jeremy's interest in our Gertie rather more than is acceptable? Did you notice the way his eyes followed her around when she was clearing the table?"

"I did actually—most unusual, but then he is a bit odd, isn't he?" Barbara wasn't really interested, but she did say, "Well, our Gertie is growing up Dear— and some men will notice her—he's just one of those kinds of men, I'm afraid."

He answered, "I suppose so—but it was rather odd. By the way, is Gertie still stealing vegetables from the big house kitchen garden?" he laughed as he asked the question. "She really does think we don't know—and that George Cameron doesn't know either. He's always known but she never takes too much, and she always gives it to the poorest in the village, so he has no problem in turning a blind eye to what she gets up to." He lit his pipe and would have his last smoke before bed. It was the best part of the day as far as he was concerned.

"Cook, would it be all right if I baked a cake for Mrs Allison? She does have a sweet tooth—but rarely gets anything sweet." Gertie was planning one of her visits to the village and hoped Bessie was in a good mood, which luckily, she was—and even offered to help if necessary. "No Bessie, this is your afternoon for resting—I must do it all by myself." She reached for the big bowl from the top shelf and raided the cool larder for sugar and butter. The eggs she collected fresh from the hens and then she was all set.

"Hello Mrs Allison, I've come to see you, if that's all right?" and she put the fresh cake on the kitchen table. The old woman licked her lips and nodded her head approvingly. She wasn't quite as old as Mrs Cratchit, but she was more unsteady on her legs, and Gertie liked looking after her.

"You get your little self in here, Gertie, and sit yourself on that chair. My, I reckon you're getting prettier every time I see you—you're quite the young lady now, aren't you? Do you know, as you get older, you remind me of someone I used to know, but I can't think who it is!" She put her fingers to her chin and pursed her lips, lost in thought.

They had a glass of milk and a slice of Gertie's cake. '*Not bad*, she thought, *but Bessie's are better*. Next time, she'd accept Cook's offer of help. After the feast, Mrs Allison took her embroidery over to the chair by the window, "Pick me out some skeins of yellow and blue, will you, Gertie, so I can get on with this? The Devil makes work for idle hands, doesn't he—so I must keep busy,"

118

and she laughed at her own little joke. The old lady was as far as could be from any Devil.

Gertie picked out the colours. "It's odd that you should say I remind you of someone you used to know, the same thing happened to me the other night. Sir Jeremy from the big house said I reminded him of someone he used to know as well—but he couldn't put his finger on who it was. Strange, isn't it?"

Mrs Allison looked up and clicked her finger, jabbing her flesh as she did. "I think I know who you remind me of—it's your kindly ways and how you like to look after everyone. Sir Jeremy used to have a sister when he was a young man and it was said he was very fond of her, but she died, I'm afraid. I never knew what she died of but one day she was there, and the next she'd gone. The villagers said he was broken hearted for a long time—he missed her so."

Embroidery dropped to the floor as Mrs Allison was more interested in her story, so she went on, "She used to come from the big house and visit the old folk in the village, bringing them provisions—just as you do now. I wasn't one of the oldies then—but I remember her. You do have a look of her, but I suppose it's just your hair colour and the way you walk." Her memory was fading with the years, and she knew Gertie had nothing to do with the young mistress, but she enjoyed telling her stories.

"I'm off, Mrs Allison—Bessie will be looking for me. Now, you enjoy the rest of the cake and next time, I'll bring you something different." She left the cottage and started to walk through the woods. There were wildflowers all around, mostly pink and blue. She wasn't sure of their names, but they were pretty and smelt lovely—she must take a bunch home for Bessie. She breathed deeply—*it felt good to be alive today*, she thought.

The sun was still quite high in the sky, although evening was fast approaching, when she heard a soft voice singing a song she recognised as Barbara Allen. Now who could that be? She could hear the voice coming through the trees—it was quite clear, but she couldn't see anyone:

'Twas in the merry month of May
And green buds all were swelling
Sweet William on his death bed lay
For love of Barbara Allen.

It was a young voice,

and it sang in perfect tune. Gertie knew the song—she'd been taught it at Sunday school. She started to move on, towards home, when she heard it again:

He sent his servant to the town
To the place where she was dwelling
Saying, you must come to my master dear
If your name be Barbara Allen

So, slowly slowly she got up
And slowly she drew nigh him
And the only words to him did say
Young man, I think you're dying.

It was so melancholy that Gertie felt tears coming to her eyes, but she still could see no one around. Where was that voice coming from—she still could see no one. She went home then—rather quickly, as she suddenly felt afraid. She wasn't alone, she knew that—but where was the girl's voice coming from? The silence gave no answer.

"Oh Bessie—the oddest thing happened." And she told the bewildered cook about the sweet singing in the woods.

Bessie turned around, wooden spoon in hand and said, "I know that song, Gertie—it's very old. It came from Scotland but crossed the sea with the emigrants and became a great success in America. It's so sad! Now young lady, get on with shellin' the peas and slicin' the rhubarb—that's your chores for the next hour. By the way, I should tell you, the young Master from the big house is comin' home tomorrow—a break from his college—it won't affect you, but you might be needed to help with some chores at the big house—they'll let you know."

"Oh, I like Master Tom—it'll be nice to see him again—I don't think I've seen him for almost 2 years. He was always kind to me—he'd give me jellybeans which I loved. Yes, it'll be good to see him again," and she went on shelling the peas and thinking, *Poor Sweet William, he must have loved Barbara Allen a lot.*

Cook tut-tutted again and said, "Well, just you make sure you don't look for jelly sweets this time—you're not the child you used to be."

120

Tom arrived next morning and before going home, he popped into the vicarage just to say 'hello.' "Hello there, young Gertie—my, how you've grown. You'll soon be a lady!" Tom handed her a paper bag full of jellybeans. "But don't eat them all at once or you'll be sick—and I'll get the blame."

"It's good to see you, Master Tom—the house has been very quiet since you went away." He was 18 now and really a man, but he was still just Master Tom to Gertie. He'd always been kind to her, probably because he knew she was an orphan, in fact he could just about remember when she'd come to live at the vicarage and how she'd been left outside the front door of the church. He'd taken pity on her then and throughout the years had always made a point of being nice to the little girl.

The vicarage was only about a mile from the big house, so he reached home very quickly and threw the reins of his horse to Michael, "Give her a good rubdown, Michael—she's pretty sweaty."

"Tom dear," the Mistress came out from the hall, "You're a sight for sore eyes and no mistake—I believe you've grown another foot since you went away. Father is in the study, but we'll get you some breakfast first and then we can all eat together." And she swept her one and only son off to find Sir Jeremy, first calling out over her shoulder to some invisible servant, "Tell Cook the young Master has arrived and he's famished for one of her excellent breakfasts."

Cook was already preparing breakfast and she told the maid to go to the cow shed and bring back a pail of fresh milk. "The boy should have finished the milking by now." Mrs Jefferies was Cook's name and she and Bessie at the vicarage were always exchanging recipes—and of course, gossip. They enjoyed their chats and visited each other's kitchen regularly.

Sauntering across the yard at the vicarage, Gertie thought she could hear singing again. *'You're imagining things, girl—there's no one singing.'*

She'd been sent on the same errand as the maid at the big house and she waited by the cow shed—the stable boy had almost finished, and the pail was already three quarters full. "Can you hear that, Michael? Can you hear someone singing?"

"No Gert, I can't hear nuthin'—you're a strange 'un an no mistake!" Michael wasn't just a stable boy who looked after the single horse—he could turn his hand to most things that needed doing—everyone in the vicarage thought he was invaluable. The only problem was, he knew it and was known to swank around the place showing off. He'd even tried to kiss Gertie a couple of times, but she soon sent him off with a flea in his ear. She took the pail to the kitchen, splashing some as she went. There it was again, only this time it seemed to be coming from inside the house: –

He turned his face unto the wall
And death was in him welling
Good-bye, good-bye to my friends all
Be good to Barbara Allen.

This time, it was just a snatch of a song, but the sweet tone was unmistakable—it was the same voice as before. Gertie felt goose pimples rise on her arms and quickly plopped the pail at Cook's feet. "There you are Cook— now you must have heard the singing that time. You did, didn't you?"

"Don't know what you're blabbin' on about—I heard nothin'." And she bent to scoop a couple of ladles of frothy milk from the pail.

Late that same morning, Gertie did her usual trick and went to the hedge outside the big house's kitchen garden and sure enough, George Cameron was just coming out of the gate, washing his hands, taking the strings off his trousers, and making his way to the kitchen. He never knew which day Gertie would choose to strike again, but he'd left an old sack just inside the gate, in case she needed it. *Shouldn't really be encouragin' her, I know—but Sir Jeremy knows all about it and he says it's okay.*

Gertie did her usual and collected whichever vegetables were ripe and ready for cooking. Only a couple of this and a couple of that—never take too much! She delivered the 'stolen goods' to her favourite pensioners and then folded the sack under her arm. She started to make her way home and came to the woods where she'd first heard the singing. It was deathly quiet though, no sound of that sweet voice—but she did hear a horse ambling through the trees and before she knew it, Sir Jeremy was in front of her, sitting aloft his stallion. She was startled but he wasn't—it was almost as though he'd expected to meet her.

"It's young Gertie, isn't it? What have you been up to today?" He smiled and it was a kind smile. She reached up to touch the horse's face and he suddenly grabbed her wrist.

"I'm sorry, Sir—I meant no harm—I love horses, you see." Gertie could feel her lower lip begin to tremble.

He dismounted and said, "I know you meant no harm, but where did you get that bracelet you're wearing—it's most unusual. Is that a padlock hanging from it? Ah yes, I can see it is." And he bent down to have a closer look.

Gertie backed away quickly and said again, "I'm sorry—I really am."

"It's perfectly alright, Gertie, I just wanted to have a closer look at your bracelet. You know, someone I used to know had one just like it—and I wondered where you got that one from."

"I never stole it, Sir. I don't steal—the Vicar always told me to be honest and I am." She felt indignant now.

"And yet, you often help yourself from my kitchen garden, do you not? Isn't that stealing?" Sir Jeremy was beginning to enjoy the conversation and he knew now, for definite, that she reminded him of someone. Gertie said nothing—there was nothing she could say. It was true but she wasn't aware that he knew.

He sat straight on his horse again and waved his hand in goodbye, "We'll talk again, young Gertie—but just now I have some business with the Vicar, so I must be off." And he disappeared through the trees—then she heard it quite clearly:

When he was dead and laid in grave
She heard the death bells knelling
And every stroke to her did say
Hard-hearted Barbara Allen.

She hitched up her skirt and ran all the way home. She crushed the pretty blue and pink flowers under foot—she was in a hurry and would have stopped for no one. The song was beginning to haunt her. Sir Jeremy had of course beaten her to the vicarage—his horse was tethered by the railings but there was no sign of him. She peeped in at the window and there sat the two men in the sitting room, enjoying a dish of coffee. They were in deep conversation, so Gertie avoided the front of the house.

"I'm back, Cook—is there something you'd like me to do? Clean the silver perhaps—or work on the copper saucepans? I feel like working hard at something." Gertie had slipped around the side and come in the back door. Bessie was making some fresh scones for afternoon tea, so was preoccupied and covered in flour. She turned around suddenly and realised Gertie had come back.

"I wasn't expecting you just yet—you gave me quite a start!" and for some reason, she continued to stare at the girl. "My God, Gertie, you do look familiar—you actually have a look of young Mistress Jennifer, who must have died 10 or 15 years ago—no, 15 years it has to be." Bessie looked a bit perplexed and turned back to the scones in haste. "I suppose it's because you've reached the age when a girl becomes a young lady—you look quite grown up. Funny I've never noticed it before."

"I've never seen the young lady, I'm afraid—she died about the time I was born," Gertie replied wistfully. "When Sir Jeremy leaves, I'm going to ask the Vicar if he has a likeness of Mistress Jennifer—he may have one—and people keep telling me I look like someone—I'm becoming more and more curious—and now you say I look like Sir Jeremy's sister." Even Master Tom had looked at her strangely the other day. She was sure of it! This was becoming a bit of a mystery, she decided.

The day was very warm, and she tied her long hair in a plat and fastened it to the top of her head, before going to the dining room to fetch the silver. Sir Jeremy was just leaving, and the Vicar was seeing him to the front door. He paused when he saw Gertie cross the hall, "You look more grown up with your hair like that—quite the young lady." And he was gone—obviously in a hurry.

He reached the big house quickly and gave the reins to the stable boy before running upstairs into his study. He had a special bureau where he kept the precious heirlooms that had belonged to his sister Jennifer. He had loved her and still missed her although she'd been dead for many years. He lifted a small chest onto the desk and opened the top. My God, he could smell her still—he believed smells were the strongest jog to a memory and he could almost feel her presence in the room.

He looked through some of her jewellery and small, personal ornaments she'd loved and then, in the corner under a lace handkerchief, he saw what he was looking for. It was a tiny key—a tiny key that could easily be overlooked. Attached to it however, was a tiny scrap of paper on which Jennifer had written the words: 'Mustn't loose this.' He touched it with his finger before slipping it into a piece of tissue paper which he slipped into his waistcoat pocket. He closed the chest and put it back in its place. He'd really have to give this some thought before he decided what to do.

Meanwhile, at the vicarage, Gertie had almost finished cleaning the silver. Bessie had fallen asleep in her rocking chair with the sun shining on her rosy face. She looked so at peace; Gertie knew she mustn't wake her. Then it happened, the lovely young voice floated in through the open windows and hung in the warm air of the kitchen. She realised she was being told the story of Barbara Allen—bit by bit—and she was looking forward to hearing the end.

Oh mother, oh mother go dig my grave
Make it both long and narrow
Sweet William died of love for me
And I will die of sorrow.

And father, of father, go dig my grave
Make it both long and narrow
Sweet William died on yesterday
And I will die tomorrow.

Gertie could feel the tears running down her cheeks. The voice was so wistful and soft—the words so beautiful and sad, but Bessie never heard them. She didn't even stir.

Michael, the stable boy, came to the kitchen door to ask for a drink and because Cook was asleep, she invited him inside and poured him a cup of cool lemonade. "You are a kind lass, Gert—but you always were. In fact, I've been told you're like the lady who used to live at the big house—you know, because of the way you look after the old folk in the village—takin' them gifts an' food an' other stuff. Mind you, they say too that one day she seemed hale and hearty, then the next day they heard she'd died. I was only a young boy and my parents were servants at the big house—but I can remember her. She was kind, you see, and you never forget the kind people, do you?" He was very talkative that day and Gertie listened with interest.

Bessie jumped up and told the lad to get lost—"There must be some horse needin' care. Get you gone, Michael."

Following dinner that night, Gertie asked the Vicar if she could have a few words alone with him. Rather surprised, he invited her to come to his study at 8 pm.

"Well Gertie, do you have a problem and if so, I'll be happy to help." He couldn't stop staring at her—Sir Jeremy was right—she did resemble his late sister, but that could only have been a coincidence. She explained to the Vicar how several people had begun mentioning her resemblance to someone they knew—but they couldn't put their finger on who it was.

"I'm beginning to worry, Reverend—I can't imagine who it must be, and I've been experiencing strange, ghostly voices lately, as though someone's trying to tell me something. I hear a young woman's voice singing verses of a song called 'Barbara Allen'. It's a very sad song and makes me want to cry."

"Now, that is most odd, Gertie. I know that song well, in fact I remember teaching it to one young lady I used to know. We would sing it together sitting at the church organ—she had the sweetest voice I've ever heard. Now, I've never kept anything hidden from you—you know that, don't you? I've always told you how you came to us as a foundling—a tiny, little baby wrapped in a shawl. The shawl was of very good quality and hidden in it, was a small silver bangle with the tiniest of padlocks hanging from it. That was all you had—underneath the shawl, you wore no baby clothes." He paused and reached out to take her hand. "I know I'm a man of few words, but you should know you've been a Godsend to us, and I haven't told you that enough."

Gertie bowed her head and her fair hair fell about her shoulders. She looked very young and at the same time, like the woman she would soon. He went on, "Let me show you something—I wouldn't be doing this if Sir Jeremy hadn't visited me to talk about the way you look—he sees a strong resemblance to someone he once knew, and who was very dear to him—his late sister, Jennifer." And he produced a small miniature of a young, fair-haired girl. She was dressed in blue and had eyes the identical colour of her gown. "That's young Mistress Jennifer not long before she died—she sat for a painter, and he captured her beautifully. Jennifer herself gave it to me as a token of affection and I've kept it ever since."

She held the miniature and gazed into the face. "She does look a bit like me, I suppose—but it can't be anything other than coincidence. It's always been said that I was left on your doorstep by one of the village maids who worked for the Squire at the time. Isn't that so?"

"It's certainly what we've always thought—but now you're turning into a young lady, your looks are changing, and I have to agree with Sir Jeremy that you look very much like Jennifer." It was all too much for Gertie and she returned the miniature to the Vicar. She excused herself and thanked him for his honesty, but she needed fresh air—she suddenly felt she couldn't breathe—and so she headed for the meadow beyond the trees. *Was she about to discover who her mother was? She'd imagined this moment since she was a child, but it had never been this way.*

Sitting on a gnarled tree trunk, she listened to the birds' song. It was sweet and lovely, like the actual sound of the evening itself. The birds suddenly fell uncannily quiet, and she knew what was coming. The song was crystal clear but again no one was around. The voice didn't sing at first but spoke the words instead.

It said, *the two star-crossed lovers lay in graves side by side in the old kirkyard and with the passing years, one beautiful red rose bush grew where Sweet William lay and on Barbara's grave, a thorny rose came from the earth. They represented the natures of the couple. The shrubs grew towards each other until they touched and became intertwined.*

She started to sing then and to complete her sad tale:

They grew and grew in the old churchyard
Till they could grow no higher
At the end, they formed a true lover's knot
And the rose grew round the briar. Sweet William had his own true love

at last.

The soft lilt disappeared with the evening breeze and Gertie felt alone again. The voice had obviously been trying to tell her something. *Who were Sweet William and his love, Barbara Allen? Was it somehow linked to herself—and if so, how? Was it happening because of the uneasiness she was feeling about her birth? She didn't know the answer.*

The next day, Sir Jeremy and his son, Tom, came to the vicarage. At first, they sat with the Vicar and Mistress Barbara, his wife. It was a long conversation and the two men from the big house kept walking round the room in an agitated manner.

"Was her death really mysterious, Father? No one has ever discussed it with me—what did Jennifer die of?" Tom could remember his Aunt Jennifer as a nice, kind lady, who liked to hug him. "What I do remember is that she died at about the same time Gertie was abandoned on the church doorstep. I remember because everyone was grieving for Jennifer, but Gertie's arrival seemed to change their mood." He looked at the Vicar and his wife, "That's right, isn't it?"

They both nodded their heads in agreement and Mistress Barbara added, "Wasn't Jennifer about to become engaged to the Squire's son, Matthew, at the time? Squire Jennings in the next county, I mean?"

There was a deathly hush in the room, and everyone stopped talking. "Have I said something amiss?" the woman asked. "I'm sorry if I have—but that's the way I remember it."

Sir Jeremy stood up and the Vicar fetched a bottle of Claret—it seemed they all needed something to sustain them. Tom spoke up again, "Another thing I remember is hearing the servants whisper and one of them saying, 'She bled to death, they do say!'—I was only a child, and I didn't understand, but it was a horrible thing to hear. Was it true, Father—did Aunt Jennifer bleed to death—had she had a bad accident or something?"

"No, boy, she'd had no accident, but everything makes sense now. She loved that Matthew Jennings and he pretended to love her—but he obviously didn't—he deserted her and married an older but very wealthy woman instead. Now it all begins to make sense. She must have told him she was with child and so he wanted nothing to do with her. The wealthy woman was much more attractive." Everyone in the room sat with bowed heads, except for Tom who couldn't keep still and kept walking up and down the room.

Sir Jeremy went on, "Nothing could have been worse—she was a shamed woman, and she didn't tell a soul about the child—not even me. For months, she must have been hiding her swelling belly beneath shawls and loose clothing—I remember how strangely she dressed at the time—but no one guessed and she never told a living soul that she was carrying that wicked man's baby. My own mother didn't even suspect anything was amiss."

He looked suddenly old and haggard—and so very sad. "I'm ashamed to remember how I used to tease her about getting fat. My God, I was being cruel and I didn't know. She was a lovely sister and there's not a day passes but I miss her afresh—I particularly miss her lovely singing voice—she used to sing that old ballad about Barbara Allen and some young man." The Vicar's wife added sadly, "That would be Sweet William I believe." But no one seemed to hear.

"So, my poor sister must have had the baby in secret and all on her own, struggled the mile to the vicarage to leave it by the church—what a terrible journey that must have been—even the return home must have been difficult. No wonder she lost so much blood and I, like the fool I was, could only tease her about getting fatter. What a good brother I was!"

Mistress Barbara was very distressed and realised they still hadn't mentioned young Gertie. She was a practical woman and said, "But are we just assuming that Gertie is that child—just because she resembles Jennifer? Lots of girls have fair hair you know, and Gertie only has a look of her—that's all. What evidence do we have?"

Sir Jeremy took the tiny key from his waistcoat pocket, "This will be all the evidence I need—the bracelet she's been wearing since her abandonment at the church—it's the same as the one Jennifer always wore—in fact, it just doesn't look like it, it is it—and I have the key to open its padlock. Jennifer must have left it for her baby because she wanted the child to know she was loved—she had nothing else to give."

The Vicar reminded them all that it was something pregnant women did when they were abandoning their child as a foundling—they left a keepsake within its shawl, so that if and when they return one day to claim the child—they could prove ownership by describing the keepsake. Everyone already knew about the practice and said nothing.

"So, Aunt Jennifer left the bracelet with the foundling and took the tiny key with her to prove the child belonged to her? Don't you see, that proves she meant to come back one day and claim the child as her own—she wasn't abandoning it forever. If your key opens the padlock on the bracelet, does it mean that Gertie is your niece and my aunt—my God, she'll be younger than her uncle!"

"I think you should fetch Gertie, Tom—she's comfortable with you—and always has been." Sir Jeremy sat back in his chair and waited, key in hand.

Young Gertie came into the room with Tom. She looked rather sheepish as she thought she'd done something wrong. "Hold out your hand to Father, Gertie—he just wants to see if he's found the other part of your bracelet." Surprised, Gertie did as she was told, and the tiny key slipped into the lock as though it had been specially oiled for the purpose. The bracelet clasp fell open and the padlock fell to the ground at her feet.

Gertie looked puzzled and everyone began talking at once. Tom was the first to jump in with both feet, "You're my aunt, Gertie—I know I'm older—but it sometimes happens like that. My Father is your uncle—Jennifer's brother—and you are her daughter. It may sound bad that she abandoned you when you were a baby—but wait until you hear the whole story—then you'll understand."

Mistress Barbara made the girl sit on the sofa by her side, which made Gertie feel awkward—she'd never been allowed to sit in such people's presence before—it all felt very odd.

Slowly they began to fill in the gaps for her and soon she understood. "Now I know who that lovely voice belongs to—it belongs to my mother, Jennifer. She's been letting me know how sad she was to be deserted by the Squire's son and how dejected she felt when she had to give me up. So, that's what the bracelet and key is about—she meant to come back to get me one day, so she must have loved me, mustn't she? She didn't know she was going to bleed to death and die so young. Poor girl—all alone and scared."

Sir Jeremy put his hands on her shoulders and bent down to look into her eyes—the same eyes as his sister's, "You'll have to move into the big house now—that's where you belong—and we'll be your real family. Tom will take care of you and teach you the ropes—I'm just sorry we've missed so many years of your life. But then, you've been in excellent hands." He kissed her lightly on the cheek and beamed his gratitude to the Vicar and his wife.

"Please may I stay here with the Vicar until I get used to the idea? This has always been my home and I've been treated so well here—I've been trained to do so many things, I've been educated and taught the need for good morals. I do understand what I must do in due course but would love it if you just gave me some time. I promise I'll be ready soon." She suddenly felt more grown up than when she'd first come into the room. She was her own person with a place in society and she had a real surname at last. She had relatives and good friends, she loved the village folk and the big house, including Mr Cameron, who'd always turned a blind eye to her pilfering of his vegetables.

She had a real mother, who had abandoned her because she had to and not because she chose to—and now she was on the threshold of womanhood herself, her mother had come back to make sure she knew exactly who she was. It was like a dream. Her mother had made sure she'd inherit her true place in the community, and she'd waited until Gertie was able to understand all that had happened.

The whole group calmed down and went their separate ways—Gertie to her own small bed she shared with the other maid. She would have to visit the woods next day to see if her mother was happy now and could enjoy her rest at last.

Next morning, she knew Cook was looking at her strangely—it was amazing how quickly the servants learned what had happened the previous night. "Are you going to have some porridge, Gertie? There's plenty in the pot. I need fresh milk, but I don't know whether I'm allowed to tell you to fetch it." It was rare to see Bessie embarrassed but she certainly had rosy cheeks today.

"Don't be silly Cook—of course, I'll fetch the milk. Michael should have finished by now." She knew she should be skipping across the yard—she should be so happy—but there was still a lingering sadness in her heart, and she didn't know why. Everything was so familiar, and the vicarage had been good for her—she could read, do her sums, sew and bake—and everyone had always treated her well. *I've been a servant though*, she told herself, *and been at everyone's beck and call—but I've loved all of it. Now, I'm not an orphan anymore, I have a mother and a family at the big house.*

"Well, Miss Hoity-Toity, how are you today? Do you feel you're better than the rest of us?" Michel had filled the pail and it was waiting for her at the door of the shed.

"No, I do not, Michael—I'm still Gertie—and I hope still your friend." She stood there, arms akimbo with fists resting on either hip. "It's true my fortune has changed and I have a Mama all of my own, but I'm still the little baby found on the doorstep. You should be glad for me—you've always had a mother of your own whereas I've not—and even now, I know I'll never be able to hug her, but at least I know who she was, and I know her name, and that makes me feel so much better."

Michael shuffled his feet and looked at the ground, "I am glad for you, Gert, you know I am. You've always been my friend and I wish you well. Can I come and visit you at the big house—I'll always call at the back door?"

"Of course, you can Michael—in fact, I'll be disappointed if you don't." She lifted the pail and as was usual, splashed some onto the courtyard.

Later in the day, she walked to the woods and was amazed to see how the wildflowers had changed in colour. Now, everything was mostly yellow and the pink had faded away—Summer was well and truly here. She sat on her usual tree stump and held her face up to the sun. Her hair hung to her shoulders, and she spoke words aloud as though someone was there to hear. "Mama dear, I wish I'd known you. Everyone talks of you with such love, and I want you to know I truly understand why you left me at the church—you couldn't have chosen better for me." She wasn't really surprised to sense a sudden change in the atmosphere and to hear the gentle singing come to her through the breeze:

'Twas in the merry month of May
When green buds all were swelling
Sweet William on his deathbed lay
For love of Barbara Allen.

She spoke then and said how much she loved her and of how proud she was to be her daughter. She told her not to feel sad any longer—she understood everything. "Please rest in peace, Mother—I am happy with the family you've given me—and I'm proud to bear your name, something I've never had before."

Her mother's words were more of a whisper now, '*Goodbye Sweet Child—I will rest now and always remember that I love you.*'

Everything was bright yellow again and the birds began to sing. The sky was even bluer with only one or two white clouds floating past, as she wandered back through the trees towards the vicarage. She knew she wouldn't hear the sweet singing ever again—her mother was at peace now.

In the vicarage garden, there seemed to be some sort of party going on. Everyone was there, gathered around a table, spread with lovely things to eat and drink. The Vicar and Mistress Barbara were there, Sir Jeremy and his wife and son, Bessie the cook, George Cameron the gardener, all the servants from both the vicarage and the big house—and lastly, but certainly not least, many of the old people from the village, including Mrs Cratchit, Mrs Allison, and old Mr Parkinson. What a party of people it was, and Tom ran forward shouting, "And here she is, the guest of honour—our Gertie—or Gertrude to give her proper name." And he pulled her into the circle of people, who'd all come to welcome her for who she really was.

Mrs Cratchit cheered and shouted, "She'll always be our Gertie, so she will—a kinder and more generous girl you'll never find."

Gertie was the foundling no longer—but she was still their Gertie. As she sipped at her cordial, she didn't know what to say. After a moment's thought, she managed, "I know I'm guilty of pilfering a few vegetables from the big house garden now and then—do you think it would be all right if I went on doing it? I love seeing my old friends' eyes light up when I bring them the goodies. I know I'm being cheeky, but do you think I could go on doing it?"

Sir Jeremy held up an imperious hand and the party quietened, Not a sound could be heard. "Niece—you have my permission to do so." And he looked at the gardener, Mr Cameron, his eyebrows raised in question.

"Yep Gertie, ye can steal from my vegetable patch any time ye like! I promise I won't be tellin' on ye!"

Benedict Arnold—Saint or Sinner?

Was he a villain or a hero? Was he a traitor or a loyalist? Was he an American or a British supporter—was he perhaps both? These are questions the reader must answer for himself, but first, read this story and only then can you decide.

Benedict Arnold was born in Norwich, Connecticut on 14 January 1741 and came from a well-off family. His father was a prosperous trader, who married a wealthy widow called Hannah and between them they had eleven children, but only two of whom survived to adulthood, the rest dying of Yellow Fever—a common occurrence at the time. One of the survivors was Benedict Arnold, who had been very close to his mother, but she unfortunately died of the same Yellow Fever as did her children. Benedict had one sister—he was only thirteen years of age. He had joined a Cadet Force and was on a training course when he heard his mother was seriously ill, so he deserted his post and hurried home to see her. He was however too late, and she'd already passed on—in her room however, he could still sense her lingering spirit.

"I'm sorry, Mother, I tried to get here in time, but I was too late." Young Benedict was in tears, but he could hear his mother's voice.

"Don't worry my boy, you did your best and I love you for it. You'll always do your best in life but sometimes, you'll find your best might not be quite good enough. I'll always watch over you—stay strong and look after your father and your sister." And he could hear her no more—she was finally gone and although the body still lay on the bed, the room was quite empty.

"Father, what are we going to do now mother has gone. Will we be all right, do you think?" Benedict asked his father when his younger sister was out of ear shot. "I am old enough to know we lived mainly on Mother's money—will your trading company be enough to support all of us?"

"Of course, we'll survive, son—I am in complete control." His father answered and reached for the whisky decanter from off the sideboard. "Why do you ask? Do you doubt me?" The man was already slurring his speech. "I will see us through our present predicament, just you wait and see."

"It's just that I know how much you miss Mother—but do remember, you have me and I'm ready to help. I'll finish school and find some work. I have studied medicine and feel confident enough to become a Pharmacist. I am almost fourteen and ready to take on more responsibility." He had attended a local Public School and had received a good education, but it had been costly, and lack of funds brought it to an end. However, he felt well equipped to look for work.

His father filled his glass again and Benedict could see the tears gather in his eyes. "I do miss Hannah and I'll not stop doing so. Your mother was a very exceptional lady. Don't look at me like that Benedict, I know I'm drinking too much but I plan to stop—see if I don't."

"But he didn't stop—he couldn't and soon, he went too far and was found dead in his bed not long after Hannah had gone. He had died of misery, alcoholism, and a failed business—in that order."

"Oh father," Benedict and his sister stood by their father's grave and cried. He put his arm around her shoulder, "Don't you worry, Sis—I'll look after you— you're my responsibility now." He felt angry at how things had turned out and swore to himself that he would make a good life for both of them. At least, they'd been left with a roof over their heads, but very little money.

His family had always believed in retaining strong links with Great Britain— and were known to be loyalist sympathisers. However, they also knew they must support their own country and support 'The Sons of Liberty' whose strength was growing by the day. It was a time of indecision, but Benedict chose to join the local militia and the Sons of Liberty—it made him feel he was playing his part. He was a natural soldier and soon attained the rank of Captain—quite an achievement for one so young and with no military background.

It took him all of eight years to complete his apprenticeship, but he did emerge a fully-fledged Pharmacist and ready to practice. Before he opened for business, he volunteered and fought alongside the local militia in the French— British war being fought on American soil. He showed himself to be eager and ambitious in his support of the Continental Revolutionary Army, but evidence of his quick temper soon emerged, something that would prove to be a hindrance for the rest of his life.

When he returned to New Haven, he first traded as a merchant with Canada and the West Indies. For a time, the Pharmacist chose to be a sea Captain, but he took his hot-headed nature to sea with him and was known for fighting at least two duels on trading voyages. His fiery temper was alive and well it seemed and those who knew him, said 'That temper will get the better of him one day.' Little did they know how right they were. He was good at what he did though and repeatedly proved he was an entrepreneur and unafraid to tackle new ventures—but that temper would be his undoing!

Back on dry land, he settled down in New Haven and soon, acquired not only a Pharmacy, but also a General Store—both of which proved successful. However, the Sugar and Stamp Act in the 1760s imposed by the British, pushed many traders to change their way of thinking and to keep making money, Benedict had to turn to smuggling and to flout the Law. He had no option but to do this as he couldn't afford to pay the unfair and heavy taxes—and he'd learned a lot about smuggling when he was on his sea voyages, so he was a successful smuggler. He began to believe that Britain was pushing her luck as far as the Colonies were concerned and he felt very strongly that America should have the right to vote on decisions that affected his country and its finances.

His sister came to see him one day, "Benedict, I heard you took a whip to a man in public and beat him soundly. Surely, you've not become that kind of man. Surely, it can't be true Brother." She was shocked at what she'd heard.

"He was going to report me to the Authorities, my dear sister—I had to teach him a lesson—if you were a man, you'd have done the same." Benedict was not troubled by her criticism, "We must defend ourselves against unjust laws imposed by the British—and smuggling is all that's left. It's a dictatorship, that's what it is!" Although at heart he was a patriot and loved his country, he didn't actually hate the British as much as some others did, and he believed having the protection of King George III was worth a lot—but these additional taxes were proving too much for any hard-working Americans.

"Why did you want to leave Norwich—you were doing pretty well there?" his sister continued. She was obviously concerned that he'd moved his businesses to a different town—and she'd been left alone in Norwich.

"Newhaven is hardly the end of the world. And you can come visit, you know. I'm not going to change—you'll always be my sister and Norwich the place I was born." He was moving some barrels of brandy around the floor—they were probably smuggled, but he had to make money somehow. The British were determined to put an end to the smuggling however, it was losing people a fortune in revenue. In fact, the taxes—including those imposed by the infamous

Tea Act—was what sparked off the Boston Tea Party when shiploads of tea were thrown into Boston Harbour. It was a protest against Britain's decision to change and introduce many new tax laws for the Colonies. However, things were due for a change, and something was about to happen. The Colonies were beginning to waken up at last!

News of the battles of Lexington and Concord in Massachusetts—the first battles of the Revolution—reached Benedict in 1775 and he immediately gathered together a company of Connecticut Militia, and rode at their head. They set out for Cambridge, in the same state where George Washington was waiting at the head of the Continental Army, ready to fight the British. In his usual headstrong way, he had marched to Massachusetts with no orders to do so but even then, his ability as a military man ,was soon recognised and he was given an official mission to attack Fort Ticonderoga near New York—currently held by the British. The attack was successful, but he was given little credit for his part in the operation—the credit actually went to the well-known troops, the Green Mountain Boys, whose reputation grew on a daily basis.

George Washington told him, "I want you to lead an attack into Canada—Quebec, to be exact—it'll be through snow and storms and rough countryside, but I have every confidence that you can do it and you will be taking many of my best men." Washington obviously thought highly of the man, although he was aware early on of Benedict's impulsive and arrogant nature. That however, didn't make him a bad leader—in fact, the opposite in Washington's opinion. Benedict accepted the mission with enthusiasm and started to prepare for the journey immediately.

On arrival, he met up with the other General and together, they led an assault on Quebec—the date was 31 December 1775. The attack failed and the other General lost his life, whilst Benedict suffered a severe leg wound. The wound was deep and shattered the bone and thereafter, his left leg was always to be a problem. Although with a bad limp, he immediately fought in two further sea battles which helped delay the British from reaching New York from Canada. He played a large part in this and in recognition of his bravery and leadership skills, Congress awarded him the rank of Brigadier General. A very good rank for someone who started off his military career as a corporal.

In the following few months however, he was the subject of several accusations—thirteen charges in fact, with misconduct and incompetence being only two of them. His bad temper and impulsive behaviour cast serious doubts as to his reliability under pressure—something that affected his entire military career. He made some careless and dishonest mistakes by abusing his position as a Brigadier General and so, lining his own pockets. He was however found innocent of some of the charges. In 1777, Congress promoted five Brigadier Generals to the rank of Major General—they were all junior to him in seniority and this absolutely infuriated him.

"I must resign my commission in the army Sir—I am left with no choice. The insult of Congress is damning to my name and reputation." Benedict Arnold was speaking with George Washington. Washington had always admired Benedict Arnold, but that didn't mean he was unaware of the man's defects.

"Nay Sir—this will not do. I know you to be an excellent soldier and a good leader of men." George Washington needed him to stay around. He knew all his failings but knew too, it was better to have him on side, rather than on the side of the enemy. "Stay Benedict—your country needs you." Those words did it, after all he was an American. born in Connecticut—and he greatly admired General Washington, so he took his advice and returned to his home in New Haven for a well-earned rest and where he could calm down.

Whilst resting in New Haven, he heard of a British attack on an American supply station in Danbury, Connecticut, so he quickly gathered the local militia and raced to stop the attack. It was too late to stop the destruction of the supplies, but they did succeed in chasing away the British and causing them to flee the area. In recognition of this action. Congress promoted him to Major General—but instead of gratitude, all he could think of, was that the other five Major Generals had more seniority in the rank, and he couldn't forgive the American Congress for causing that. He continued to nurse that insult for many years to come.

Straight after his promotion he had to face a formal charge of stealing goods and property from Canadian merchants during the recent campaign near Montreal. Again, he was accused of misusing his military status to take advantage of the civilian merchants. Subsequently, he was cleared of the charge, but the accusation so angered him that again he was tempted to resign from the army. It could have been a case of 'the lady doth protest too much' as it was quite likely he was guilty—but we'll never know. George Washington managed to talk him out of resigning yet again.

"I need you, General Arnold—one of our spies has reported having seen a British plan of how they are planning to attack North New York, intending to split New England from the other colonies. As you understand, this would be a huge catastrophe for our revolution and must be avoided at all costs." Washington had deep lines of tiredness and worry on his face and looked pleadingly at his General, who of course succumbed in the end.

However, the British did send General John Burgoyne from Fort Ticonderoga down the Hudson River intending to reach the centre of New York. They failed in the mission and Burgoyne lost his whole complement of men when he surrendered in 1777 at Saratoga New York. In the final battle of Saratoga, Benedict Arnold was again badly wounded. His wounds must have caused him great pain, but he was a soldier—and soldiers fought!

There had been two major battles in which General Arnold played a major part in bringing about the British defeat. In fact, his actions so annoyed Burgoyne, that the British General said of him, 'It was his doing!'—pointing directly at a picture of Arnold. His reward for his part in the attack was Congress's award of raising his status above the other five Major Generals and making him their superior. This at last satisfied him! However, the new wound he'd recently received when he caught another bullet had been to the already—damaged leg. Now, he walked with an even more distinct limp and had difficulty in walking.

Four years after the death of Margaret, his first wife, he married again and this time to another Margaret, but this time, she was one 'Peggy' Shippen. She was just eighteen years of age, pretty and vivacious as well as educated and her father was a well-respected and wealthy Philadelphian gentleman, who moved in the highest social circles in Philadelphia. Peggy enjoyed her life and knew many officers and officials from both the Revolutionary and British armies. The family were known to lean towards the British and Peggy was to become known as 'the highest paid spy on the British side.'

No one actually knows what rewards she received but they must have been substantial to have earned her that title. Her father, being a Judge and a member of the Provincial Council of Pennsylvania, knew many important men from both sides of the conflict and therefore so did Peggy. She had two brothers, but both had died. Her father made sure his daughter was well educated and understood the political forces that drove the American Revolution. However, Peggy sided with her father and shared his opinion that breaking away from Great Britain entirely would be a bad thing. She was to learn this was an opinion she would share with her future husband.

The British captured Philadelphia and the Shippen house became a place for social gatherings for many British officers. A gentleman called John Andre was a frequent visitor at the house and Peggy and he became good friends—but Andre had to leave Philadelphia when in 1778, the French entered the war, and the British withdrew from the city. Peggy and John Andre however, stayed in contact with each other. She then met Benedict Arnold who was the Continental Military Commander of Philadelphia, a position which showed Congress's faith in him. The couple were attracted to each other, and Benedict asked her father for her hand in marriage.

For some time, he refused to entertain this—as Arnold's repeated involvements in several court cases caused him concern as to the man's reliability. Such opinions seemed to follow Benedict around and he always seemed to be defending his reputation—but Peggy's father did eventually agree to the wedding. They married and immediately set about accruing massive debts by socialising and entertaining way above their means. Much of the Philadelphian hierarchy dined and partied in their home at the Arnold's expense. They were spendthrifts beyond comprehension. 'Live for today and tomorrow will take care of itself' seemed to be their motto. It was certainly their belief.

One night, Benedict was awakened from his sleep by a sound he didn't recognise. He could sense her presence however and slowly got out of bed— Peggy was sound asleep. He saw Margaret Mansfield standing at the foot of the bed and she was dressed in one of the beautiful gowns she'd worn when they were husband and wife.

"Why, Margaret, how come you here? I have never seen you in death before." He was scared but knew she could mean him no harm. They had had three sons together in their short marriage until the day the Yellow Fever took her away. "Why are you here now, Margaret?"

"Husband," her voice was low and he had to strain to hear her, "I have come to warn you if you don't mend your ways—and be loyal to either the Continental Army or the British Army, you will suffer severe consequences. I am concerned at the way you are behaving at present—and about how you may suffer in the future." She was as beautiful as he remembered her but looked soft and fragile in the half light—a very ghostly figure.

"Why, Margaret, what can you mean? Yes, I am struggling over my decision as to whom I should favour, but my own conscience will guide me in the end." He felt a degree of impatience with the spirit and felt she was wrong in approaching him on such a matter. She was just a woman after all. He made a movement towards her and waved his hand dismissively—she seemed to shiver and fade away.

As she slowly disappeared into the greyness of dawn, she whispered, "Remember this night, Husband—I come to you out of love and concern for your future. Your recklessness will lead you down the wrong path and I fear for the days ahead."

And she was gone—the bedroom returned to normality. It felt differently from before however, and he crept back into bed and forced himself to fall asleep. *Nothing but a dream*, he thought, *nothing but a dream!* But sleep was slow to come that night.

"We are husband and wife now, my dear." At breakfast next morning, the newly-weds were happy in each other's company and Benedict was very much in love with Peggy and believed he had a treasure in her. He'd led a rather 'up and down' existence and promised her he would settle down and not become involved in any more financial deals that often turned out to be 'dodgy.' They did share an interest in political affairs however and if anything, she was the keener of the two to see the American revolution fail.

The incident with Margaret Mansfield had never happened, he told himself and he certainly didn't mention it to his wife. It prayed on his mind however.

"I believe you, husband, but don't settle down too much—I like you as you are, and I respect and love you. Our future life together will be good, I have no doubt of that—after all, don't we believe in the same things?" Pretty, vivacious Peggy gave him hope for the future and he adored her. Everything was rosy in the garden.

Peggy however, still kept in contact with her 'Dear Friend'—Major John Andre, who was one of the spies employed by the British. Inevitably, she introduced her husband to Andre and the seal was set for 'Benedict Arnold to become one of the most detested figures in American history.' The Arnolds were a very sociable pair and Benedict bought a grand house—Mount Pleasant— which he put completely in Peggy's name—for her and any future children they might have. They didn't live in the property, but rented it out to secure an income and took their family home at his Military Headquarters.

"My dearest, I am very pleased to have met your friend, Major John Andre— he clearly thinks as we do and is very loyal to the British cause. By the way, how long have you been corresponding with the British and passing them information about the Revolutionary forces." He asked her the question on impulse, hoping he'd surprise her, and she'd give him a straight answer. He was resting in the sitting room of their home, and she was busy arranging some blooms, freshly picked from the garden.

"Oh, long before we married." She answered him outright with no hesitation. "I have always followed my father's advice and played to both sides of the conflict. It seems the wisest thing to do and allows me to learn so many secrets—after all, one never knows who will be victorious in the end." For one so young, Peggy was a very cunning woman and wrote regular letters to Andre—all about the weather, the servants and the fact that she was with child. In effect, about trivial things to cover the real messages. Her letters were cleverly worded to allow her to share secrets with Andre.

Benedict then took to including his own messages in her letters using code and invisible ink. The couple mixed regularly with a circle of British sympathisers who didn't believe in the Colonies' actions and Arnold had only recently hired one Joseph Stansbury to initiate communications with the British and offer his services to them—he used the loyalist Stansbury as an intermediary.

"I would greatly appreciate being given the Command at West Point—I understand its position on the highlands of the Hudson River is of paramount importance to our cause. As you know, I am an experienced soldier and strategist who would give his absolute loyalty to our great cause." He spoke with a representative of Congress who took his request to the Party Headquarters. His arrogance and confidence did win him the Command at West Point and he and Peggy settled there after the birth of their son, Edward. The year was 1780 and they were living on the Hudson River, just two miles south of the Point itself and close to New York city.

From the moment he assumed the Command, Benedict Arnold began to collate information for the British. He also began to systematically weaken the defences of the important West Point—his intention being that this would make it easier for the British to capture it. At this same time, he maintained his contact with Major John Andre and continued to pass on any information that came his way. He informed the British of American troop locations and of supply depots—the knowledge of which helped the British to achieve many defeats against the Continental Army.

He also began to move his personal possessions to England, so there'd be a comfortable home for him there, should he have to leave America quickly. He contacted the British military to offer to help them achieve the conquest of West Point itself. For this help, he asked £20,000 and an officer's commission in the British army. This was agreed and so he believed he was sitting pretty, with a solid foot in each camp—that is until he was ready to leave one of them.

Arnold and Andre met on the banks of the Hudson River on an arranged date and time—this was Thursday, 21 September 1780. "Well Major," Arnold spoke first, "I believe we are making progress with our cause. I fear the revolutionaries are no match for the British and this war will soon be over and we'll be free to show our loyalty openly to King George." Benedict was at his most pompous when mentioning British royalty.

Andre actually didn't think very highly of the man—after all he'd stolen a lady on whom he was once sweet—but he knew the value of the information he could provide for the cause—he pretended a false admiration of Arnold, who lapped it up.

"Yes Sir—I feel strongly that the end might be in sight. You are correct—this will all be over one day, and we can all live our normal lives. Now, what have you brought me today?" The Major liked to play a humble and junior officer when talking to Arnold—the man reacted well to flattery.

Maps and documents describing the fortifications at West Point exchanged hands, something that would make it easy for the British to capture the Point. It gave precise measurements and security points. The two men said goodbye and Arnold returned to his wife and son, feeling very positive that he was doing his part for the British cause. And so, the American was!

"Well done, Husband—things are going to plan and I'm sure we'll soon hear the phrase 'The British are coming'—only this time, it will be for good. Once we hold West Point, the Colonists will have to accept that their cause is lost." She reached up and kissed his cheek—she really was fond of him—but only in a limited way—after all she still had a hankering for her 'Dear Major'.

Two days later, Andre was on his way to British-held territory when he was arrested. Of course, the treasonous maps and documents were discovered, and the plot was exposed. Benedict Arnold received a message, telling him what had happened. He lost no time and dashed upstairs to Peggy, who was dressing for a celebration breakfast which they were hosting for General Washington and his immediate officers. Their hypocrisy was amazing! The group of riders were already on their way, riding towards West Point. After a brief discussion with Peggy, Benedict fled the area and was lucky enough to reach HMS Vulture on the Hudson River, where he was welcomed on board and helped to reach safety. It was apparent to everyone, from where and from whom the documents had come.

Meanwhile, Washington's party had arrived at West Point and Peggy welcomed them at the door—but strangely, she was having a fit of the vapours and was completely hysterical. She used her hysteria as a delaying tactic to allow her husband's escape, but also to convince the General and his men that she'd had nothing to do with any treason and was as shocked as he was, at what Benedict had done. The 'poor, pathetic woman' played her part well and she and her son were allowed to leave West Point to join her family in Philadelphia. She continued to play the part of an innocent and when asked if she knew where her husband was, she replied that she did not.

Unfortunately for her, a letter from Andre to her was discovered and it was seized as proof that she'd been an accomplice in her husband's treachery. The Supreme Executive Council of Philadelphia banished her from the city and she and her son, Edward were escorted by her father to the shores of the Hudson River, where she was put on board a ship bound for New York. She was allowed to seek her husband there.

When the two eventually met, the first thing she asked was, "What will happen to Major Andre?"

And he answered, "What does it matter to you what his fate is? I thought you were not interested in him, you Jezebel." He was very annoyed at how things had turned out and felt that Andre could have done a better job of delivering the documents.

"No Husband, you are wrong—I have no care about what happens to him, but he was a friend after all, wasn't he?" She knew she'd gone too far in showing her true feelings, and desperately needed to appease him.

"He will be hanged as a traitor, what do you think? And that's what will happen to me—and perhaps to you—if the Revolutionary Militia ever catch us." And he was right in his prediction as Major John Andre was condemned to death as a common spy and hanged at Tappan in New York.

General Washington sent men to New York to seek out and kidnap Benedict Arnold, but it was to no avail, as he and his family had already escaped to New Brunswick in Canada. They lived there for a while but of course, the adventurer Arnold had itchy feet and he joined and fought for the British, becoming involved in some minor skirmishes. He actually put on the uniform of the British, whilst his American one was probably still in the closet. The skirmishes may have been judged as minor at the time, but they were not so judged by the Americans who suffered from them—Americans who soon learned of Arnold's duplicity.

He'd been very much involved in the incidents and actually led raids against Richmond, Virginia and New England in Connecticut, all of which were sacked and burned. However, the American Revolution was nearing its end and in 1781, following the surrender by the British Cornwallis at Yorktown, the Arnold family travelled and settled in London on 15 December 1781. His earlier plan of sending personal possessions ahead to London had at last paid off.

At first the city of London welcomed both Benedict and his wife and they were even presented at Court by Lady Amherst. George 111's wife, Queen Charlotte also awarded Peggy an annuity of £100 sterling a year, for the maintenance of her children and for those yet to be born. King George too awarded her £350, as reward for her services to Britain. At first, they were treated as heroes and the Arnolds lapped it up, but details of his past soon spread throughout society and the welcome turned chilly with many people thinking of him as an unprincipled mercenary, who had helped bring about the death of a real hero, Major John Andre.

One evening whilst attending a theatre performance, the Arnolds were greeted by hisses and boos from the audience. The National Press too wrote only negative and accusing reports about him and blocked his being offered positions with the British Military or with the East India Company. It had soon become an unhappy time in the Arnold's lives—as they fell from grace in the city, Peggy unfortunately also lost two children in the time spent in London—William and George in 1783 and in 1784. Not a happy time! Benedict too, had reason to feel frustration as he only ever received £6,000 from the British Government, instead of the agreed £20,000. In effect, he switched sides for a lot less money than he'd wanted—and needed. And there was no sign either of the officer's post he'd been promised.

To meet his need for adventure, Benedict took up a new business opportunity and sailed for Saint John in New Brunswick, where he arranged for his eldest sons Benedict, Richard and Henry to join him. These were the children of his first marriage and they were eager to join him. Whilst he was in New Brunswick, Peggy gave birth to a third child, Sophia Matilda. After the birth, she sailed to join her husband and left two of her other children in the care of a private family in London. New Brunswick must have seemed like a new start for the whole family and the trading venture with the West Indies resulted in healthy revenue.

"Husband, I would very much like to visit my family in Philadelphia—do you have any objection to my doing that? I feel if I don't do it now, then I never shall." She was feeling rather tearful, following the birth of another boy child, and desperately needed something to lift her mood.

"You must do as you wish, my dear—I only wish I could accompany you—but you know I cannot." Benedict would genuinely have liked to pay a visit to her father, but of course, he knew that Philadelphia would not welcome him.

Going to Philadelphia was perhaps not the best idea in the world as the good people of that city treated her with coldness and contempt—to them she was still very much a traitor. Although her father was a prosperous and well-to-do citizen, Peggy didn't share in his limelight. It was a miserable visit and she quickly returned to New Brunswick with her new baby, George. The year was 1790 when she crossed the Channel to be with her husband—arriving back in England in 1791. Departure from their home in New Brunswick had resulted in more misery for the family, as friends and neighbours there gathered in mobs and pelted the family home with stones, calling out the word 'Traitor' as loudly as they could. Arnold must have felt like a man with no country—something for which he'd worked hard.

The family home of the Arnolds was now Great Britain, specifically London, and Benedict and Peggy lived out the rest of their lives there. He continued to dabble in trading however, in both the West Indies and in Canada, but as he'd done all his life, he overspent and accrued huge debts. A fifth child was born—their last—and this was at least a welcome event.

Margaret Mansfield paid Benedict a second and last visit. She appeared by his side as he lay on his death bed. Her first words were. "You stupid man, I told you to change your ways, but as usual, you wouldn't listen." He opened his eyes and almost smiled before realising she was telling him off. She was angry with the dying man and stood there, tapping her feet. "Man, you could have had a wonderful life and died in glory as a hero—but Oh No—you had to do things your way and disappoint us all."

As with the last time, she began to fade away but not before he heard her last, faint words, "You'll be joining me soon, I fear—but it's only what you deserve." He closed his eyes again and wondered if it was just his conscience talking or whether Margaret really had visited him. Ah well, he'd soon find out.

On 14 June 1801, Benedict Arnold died of gout—a rather ignominious end for a man who had done some incredibly brave acts and some treacherous ones. He left a wife and five children and died penniless and in considerable debt. He was buried at St Mary's Church in Battersea, London. Peggy had first to auction the contents of their house and then the house itself, in order to clear her husband's debts—and also to afford to bury him.

She died just four short years after he did—she was aged only 44 years and left several small children with no one to look after them. She was buried alongside her husband, and both lie together until this day.

Benedict Arnold was buried with no military honours, something that would have been quite usual for a man who had reached the military ranks he had—but in his case, he reached those ranks by fighting on both sides of a great war. He wore both uniforms with pride and fought hard, as much for the American Revolution as for the British Militia. He took slights very badly, if indeed they were slights—but that was how he saw them, and it was something that had plagued him since he was young. Remember how he couldn't get over the seniority of his Major General rank. It would have upset him considerably had he known that the British Government disinterred Major John Andre and reburied him in Westminster Abbey. He'd died and spied for the British after all, but luckily, Benedict Arnold never knew that Andre had been re-buried as a hero.

Some of the things he did made significant strides forward for both sides of the conflict, significant of course, depending on which uniform he wore at the time. Greed and the love of high living were his downfall as was his ever-present quick temper which caused him to make a great many wrong decisions. He was not a believer in false modesty and resented the fact that promotions didn't come fast enough—from either side—and that honour and awards were too slow in being heaped upon him.

He was nonetheless a very clever man and a brilliant strategist. His mother and fathers' deaths forced him, still a child himself, to take on responsibility for his sister, something he had done willingly. His life was full of ups and downs—very high ups and very deep downs. His great love for money ruined his life—he liked spending it but also spending what he didn't have. Debts always hung around his neck and money ran through his fingers like water.

When the American Revolution was over, the name of Benedict Arnold was removed from all Military records at West Point and the fact that he'd once been in command there made it all the more shocking. In fact, his name was removed from many official records in other States and his plaque at West Point was torn down—plaques had been erected there in honour of all the great names who figured in the War of Independence and although his name had actually been there originally, it was quickly removed.

The Saratoga battlefield has a monument to his leg however but there is no name on it, nor mention of the man to whom it had once belonged—no mention of the positive differences he made to the Continental Army of America. It is merely known as 'The Boot Monument' and was erected to honour his twice wounded leg—but only his leg. The 'leg' monument has been allowed to remain there because at the start of his military life, he did some miraculous deeds—but of course in his own eyes, he was never given the recognition for them. On the stone, it does however mention 'a brilliant soldier' who was 'desperately wounded' but it avoids mentioning the name of Benedict Arnold. The actual inscription says:

In memory of the most brilliant soldier of the Continental Army who was desperately wounded on this spot, challenging the BORGOYNES GREAT WESTERN REDOUBT—7 October 1777, winning for his countrymen the decisive battle of the American Revolution and for himself, the rank of Major General.

However—the residents of Philadelphia paraded a 'two-faced' effigy of him down the streets in the city, newspapers compared him with Lucifer and Judas, and the Continental Congress passed a resolution permanently erasing hi name from the Army Register.

For a man who loved to be the centre of attention, he would have been shocked by how America actually remembers him to this day and of how his name has become synonymous with the word 'Traitor' in all English-speaking countries the world over. No one ever wants to be known as 'a Benedict Arnold.'

Read all of this story and decide for yourself what kind of man he was. Was he a Saint or was he a Sinner? The decision is yours!

Sawney Bean and Black Agnes, His Wife

*Reader—read this story at your peril. There's no doubt it will disturb you and may give you bad dreams. History tells us the characters did exist in a part of Scotland, but as only scant records were kept at the time—actual evidence is hard to find. **YOU HAVE BEEN WARNED.***

He was born in an Ayrshire village in East Lothian, Scotland. It wasn't a great distance from Edinburgh, the capital of Scotland. He was a lazy man, and although his father had found him work as a hedger and ditcher, he didn't like the work. He tried his hand at training as a tanner, but he didn't like the smells of the trade.

"I'm not a natural hedger, Father. I find the work plays havoc with my hands and I lose the skin regularly." He said and tried to look pitiful—as he was dependant on his father's support.

"Well, Sawney, that's too bad—but if you persevere, your skin will soon toughen up." Mr Bean Senior was made of sterner stuff and told his son to get on with the job. He turned his back on his only son, who had repeatedly disappointed him.

"You're too hard on the boy, Sandy—if the work's too much for him, he'll just have to find something else." His mother had always cossetted her only son and always stood up for him. "Come away now, Boy and have your supper—it's your favourite, mince and tatties. You always like a bit of meat, don't you?"

Sawney, whose proper name was Alexander after his father and grandfather tried to get on with the hedging and the digging of ditches, but it was no good— his hands were suffering too much. He was courting a woman in the next village—her name was Agnes Douglas and they'd been fond of each other for a while. She was sympathetic with Sawney's problem and suggested it might be easier if they ran away together—away from their families—and he found different work somewhere else.

"Your father can't follow you everywhere, can he—and at least you'll not be under his thumb." She was a cunning woman who was not liked by many people and was called 'Black Agnes Douglas'—she was reputed to be a witch and a woman of ill repute. Sawney didn't mind however.

In fact, the local people had threatened her with burning at the stake, if she didn't mend her ways—and Black Agnes had no intention of changing anything about herself.

She often had talks with the Devil and liked to think he was giving her instructions on what she should do. She also had friends who were goblins and she was proud of them. Goblins were ugly, mysterious creatures who lived in the trees. When they manifested themselves, they were about 3 feet high and weighed 50 lbs. Pointed ears and a large nose on a flat face gave them an odd look and they differed from each other in colour—some being red, yellow or orange. Agnes had been given them by the Devil and they helped her with her spells and potions.

"Come, my friends," she spoke with them, "I need you to persuade Sawney Bean to do as I want. He's a rather weak man and needs someone to control him, so between us, we can do that, I'm sure." Agnes called two goblins to come down from the trees and go with her to meet Sawney. The creepy little figures waddled beside her—no one else could see them, until they wanted to be seen. "There he is, Goblins—resting against that barn door. I'll go talk to him first and then you join us. You just must agree with me and look as ferocious as you can—he'll be scared and do what I tell him. Okay?" And Black Agnes crossed the yard towards Sawney.

"Sawney, I could teach you so much if you join forces with me. The Devil is on my side—but I'm not a witch." She said it quickly as she saw the fear enter his eyes, when she mentioned the Devil. "I do have little friends however sent to me by the Devil and they've always helped me in the past. You and I—and the goblins—should go away from here—no one really likes us, and we could be free to do whatever we wanted. I want you to meet my little friends—don't be afraid by their appearance, they're different from other folk, but they have special skills that could help us." She beckoned the two goblins to come over.

Whatever they did and said to Sawney, it worked. They persuaded him that his parents were bad for him, and the village people hated Black Agnes—a fresh start would be just the thing for both of them. It was amazing how their frightening appearance and wild, staring eyes worked on people—they could hypnotise whoever they were talking to. It was the eyes; they were completely overpowering—and very scary.

As Sawney didn't like any type of work, the couple eventually ran away together with the goblins at their heels and the first place they chose to settle was Ballantrae—not that far away but far enough to be able to steer clear of people who knew them. They left with great speed and the goblins showed them where to hide in the deep and well-hidden cave at Bennane Head. It was a scary place but ideal for what they wanted. They made the cave their home and as it turned out, their 'place of business' for many years to come. They were fond of each other and happy to live in the cave—as some people did at that time in Scotland. It was about 200 yards deep, and the entrance disappeared completely at high tide. Quite deep inside, the floor divided into two paths—one was quite short and seemed to lead nowhere, but the other one went much deeper into the safety of the darkness. They felt safe there and the goblins were always close by and quite a comfort although they were so ugly.

Agnes was pregnant with their first child who was born with no problem, but they needed money to buy some home comforts, so, one night sitting around the fire in the middle of the earthen floor, they hatched together a plan to get what was needed. The goblins were sitting staring at the flames—it felt cosy, and they listened closely to the conversation.

"At low tide, Sawney, we'll wait on the road above the hill—it's not a big road, but it's quite a busy one, going a distance from one village to another. And it's the through path to the town beyond—many people will be travelling there. We'll hide until some lone traveller comes along and then we'll jump out and one of us will hit him over the head. They're bound to be carrying some valuables and we'll help ourselves." Agnes was more of a leader than Sawney, but she'd expect him to do any necessary killing. The goblins were dribbling in anticipation—they'd be sure to help their mistress, Agnes.

Sawney was cutting his own hair and she leaned across to help him. "Good plan, Agnes. But what about food—we need sustenance as well. I can catch plenty fish and the odd rabbit or two—but it won't be enough to keep us both alive." He felt better now that his long hair wasn't covering his face quite so much. "Where can we get meat? Could we go into one of the villages, or even the town, and buy some provisions?" As he said it however, he knew it would be too dangerous and people were always nervous of strangers. Especially if there were robberies in the area.

"Tell me, Sawney, have you ever tasted human flesh? I have—and it tastes just like chicken—not unpleasant at all—in fact actually very tasty." Agnes could tell by his face that he was startled and quickly added, "It's a solution to our problem. Whoever we rob, we'll kill and make sure he's dead. Dragging the body back to the cave at low tide won't be difficult and we can then cut it up, keeping the best fleshy bits for our bellies and discarding bones and what we don't want, into the high waves—and the bits will float further down the coast, well away from here. If we're going to live on what we steal from people, we'll soon get caught—unless we leave no clues and murder them all—just make them completely disappear. They'll just be missing persons then. That way, we could survive. What do you think?"

Sawney wasn't the brightest pebble on the beach, and it sounded like an excellent plan. "Let's do it, Agnes—I'm in!" And he could hear the goblins giggling in the dark, but he still had difficulty seeing them—anything to do with evil and the goblins were right there. They were not nice creatures and thrived on evil deeds, so the Beans' plan really appealed to them.

And that was how 'their business' took off and became very lucrative, as well as filling their stomachs. The first time they did it was nerve-wracking and both were very nervous. They'd left the baby in the cave after giving her a good meal of Agnes's milk—so she was sound asleep. The coast was clear, and they hid behind dense shrubbery at the side of the road and waited patiently.

"Excuse me, Sir—but could you help me please?"

The young man walked towards the woman who was bent double. "Are you in pain—what's wrong?"

Sawney came up behind him and grabbed him around the neck. "You've already helped, young man—let me help you with that heavy bag you're carrying." He drew a sharp knife across the man's throat and laughed as the blood spurted onto the grass. 'I'm good at this,' he thought—and was already looking forward to doing it again next time.

"Well done, Sawney, now let's get him back to the cave—the tide is on the turn and we haven't got much time." Between them they hauled the body down the track towards the beach and on into the cave entrance. It was there they completed their first butchery of a human being. They had several knives they'd brought from his hedging work—all lengths and with very sharp blades. It was easier than they'd thought and soon, they'd successfully amputated both legs and arms, leaving a nice, meaty torso which they cut into pieces and wrapped in seaweed, straight from the ocean.

In due course, they taught themselves to pickle the choicest pieces of meat in barrels they'd found when the tide went out—it was quite amazing how easy it was to improvise when needs must. Their butchery skills were limited but they learned as they went along.

The whole experience exhausted them, and the baby had started to cry. Agnes fed the child with the same bloodstained fingers she'd used to cut up the man. She wrapped the child in its shawl and cuddled its little body, the blood staining the baby's skin, but that would soon become the normal state of affairs. Sawney wrapped the amputated legs and arms in an old piece of sackcloth which he left at the door of the cave—until tomorrow when he'd walk down the coast and throw them into deep water. Hopefully, none of the limbs would come ashore again until well washed out of the area.

Whilst Agnes was feeding the baby, Sawney cut two pieces of flesh which he laid on the hot stones around the fire. It worked beautifully and the appetising smell filled the cave. They ate ravenously that night and fell into a comatose sleep—they hadn't eaten anything so solid for quite a while and the young man's flesh was like manna from heaven. They felt replete and languished on the floor of the cave, with neither one showing any guilt or remorse. It was something that had to be done and, truth to tell, they'd enjoyed the excitement. The man's heavy bag had proved fruitful as well as he'd been delivering some silver plate to the jewellers' two towns away.

Of course, a search party came from the man's village and scoured the countryside but no trace of him was ever found. As his journey was quite lengthy, he'd planned to spend the night at the inn in the village, but for obvious reasons, he never reached it. The search for the young man was conducted thoroughly— primarily because what he'd been carrying had belonged to one of the town's most influential merchants—and he wanted his belongings back. Despite scouring the road several times more, the young man was never seen again, and the search was eventually abandoned.

The pattern was set, and Sawney and Agnes were never hungry—or poor— again. With the passage of time and the successful attacks on travellers, the couple settled down to live in the hidden cave. They only came out at low tide when it was safe to do so. In fact, they thought it was a perfect solution to the unhappiness they'd both felt at home. Running away had been a good idea and as Agnes said, "The Lord will provide, Sawney—and he certainly has for us. We know carriages have begun to travel much more than they used to and there could soon be some even richer pickings. I think it's time to branch out and keep watch for the carriages and carts. We can just watch their coming and going for a while until we know when to expect them. In fact, I could innocently go into the villages and check on the travel times—I could find out find out how many passengers the carriages usually carry. It would be good information to have."

Agnes was the planner and enjoyed her work. Sawney was the obedient one and did as he was told. Now and again, the two goblins would accompany them on their climb and would hold down the victims and kick their shins. It was fun and they really liked to see how the victims were horrified by their twisted faces—and they liked to help Agnes of course. She'd noticed recently how the skin of the goblins had changed and was no longer orange—now it was red. From her conversations with the Devil, she knew this was because they were getting older and would soon need replacing, something Agnes was perfectly willing to do. They were fonder of her than she was of them—and of course, she had no conscience whatsoever. How else could she do what she did?

The Sawneys followed their plan and soon they had to build racks in the cave for hanging the meat and limbs. It was the easiest way to store them. The contents in the trunks they dragged from the carriages helped to make the home more comfortable and were useful for storing the valuables they'd prised from their victims' hands. On a very odd occasion, one of them—but never both—would venture into the town if anything was needed—something they couldn't steal or lay their hands on.

On occasion, Sawney travelled to far away towns to sell some of the valuables—then he could load up his cart with provisions and travel back under the darkness of night. The cart had been a good buy and was easy to hide in the cave. Their plans were laid with military precision, which was the reason they managed to avoid capture. For two relatively simple people, their murderous trait was their protection, and leaving no sign of those they robbed and killed was the best protection of all.

Years soon passed and a couple of times, they did come close to being captured by those searching for lost relatives and friends. The Bean couple were cunning however and, although initially they'd started out as just thieves and robbers only, their murder and consumption of the victims served as the best protection they could have. After all, as Agnes often pointed out, "The best way to rid themselves of corpses, was to eat them."

A scary atmosphere began to settle around the area on the hill and people began to avoid it if they could, but of course this wasn't always possible—it was a through road after all. Sawney and Agnes continued to reap the rewards of their work and life passed pleasantly as far as they were concerned. Not so, of course, for their victims. Their family grew and after 5 years, they had 5 children who knew no better than to eat what they were given by their loving parents—and they thrived on the human flesh diet—it being full of protein.

The whole Bean family were confirmed cannibals and continued to live in the cave, only seeing the light of day when it was low tide. The children and the goblins were happy to help string up the bits of bodies around the cave walls and used fresh, strong seaweed as ropes. They actually kept some arms and legs from the sea and hung them up too—the plumper they were, the better.

Twenty-five years passed, the children grew up and with the incestuous mating of brothers and sisters, there now were grandchildren to feed and clothe as well. Some of the children were 'lacking' in the brain's department, but what did that matter? The attack on travellers was even more necessary than ever with all the mouths to feed. Sawney and Agnes themselves also continued to breed more offspring of their own and so it continued until there were enough of them to be called a Clan—Clan Bean, in fact, as they liked to call themselves.

The couple's children had produced a high number of births themselves and many of the babies were born with disabilities, some of them were badly disfigured and some had mental disorders. The incestuously mixed genes produced many impaired sons and daughters and overall, the Clan Bean was considerably lacking in intelligence, but they had no idea about inter-breeding and the problems it brought. Although there were no records to confirm dates of births, deaths, etc, it was said the Bean family had produced 8 sons, 6 daughters, 18 grandsons and 14 granddaughters. How many were completely normal has never been established—if indeed there were any.

As well as eating their victims and so leaving no evidence of the crimes, avoiding capture was mainly because of their hiding place in the cave. It reached a mile underground and could hide all their sins. The people in the coastal villages were regularly alarmed by what they found on the shores and eventually stopped going near the beach all together. The whole area was undergoing changes and all because of Sawney and Agnes Bean.

Agnes made sure she kept in touch with the Devil and always obeyed his instructions. She was regularly goaded by him, and she could hear him speak to her quite clearly. Sawney had never seen him but believed everything his wife told him and after all, he did allow them to have his friends the goblins, who were like servants to the Beans.

One night at low tide, Sawney and two of his older sons set off along the road and walked some distance before concealing themselves behind big rocks and trees at the side of the road. They'd heard there was a fair in the nearby town and so there would probably be some people passing along the road. They waited patiently and soon heard the clip-clop of a horse's hooves, plodding along the road—the horse bore two riders on its back—a man and a woman.

As it neared the ambush where the Beans were waiting, the brigands attacked the couple furiously, first dragging the woman off the horse and cruelly stabbing her several times, almost before her husband could even dismount. He had a sword however and he knew how to use it. The brigands quickly cut her throat and ripped open her stomach, pulling her entrails out and discarding them on the ground. They were behaving like wild animals and actually began drinking her blood when it was still warm. They acted as though it was the best of wines. The goblins were prancing around and kicking the man's legs whilst the horse shied away in fear. The husband couldn't believe his eyes and was stricken to the spot with the horror of the scene.

Luckily, a large group of people who'd been at the fair arrived on the road and started shouting at the brigands. The man jumped in front of his wife's body and waved his sword high in the air—the Beans hadn't expected a defence—and they all ran off together, not stopping until they reached the cave. Some of the men chased after them but the Beans were more sure-footed and knew the area well—there was no chance of their being caught. The shaken man gathered his wife into his arms, but of course, there was nothing he could do—the Beans had made sure of that.

He took some moments to pull himself together and to satisfy himself that the brigands really had gone, before he rounded up the horse and lifted her body onto the saddle. The passers-by helped him, and then followed him, "We're your witnesses if you need us." They all moved off together and rode straight to Edinburgh where they sought the local Magistrate, who called for officials to come help the travellers. Behind them on the road, they left a pool of blood from the woman's wounds.

This was a really bad break for the Beans—the man had escaped, and the crowd had seen them—something that had never happened before. Now, the authorities would have something to go on and knew from the witnesses that the attackers lived in the local area.

The court listened to his story and to that of the witnesses before a couple of officials spoke up, saying, "That's the spot on the road where people keep disappearing, never to be found again." Two and two were quickly put together and it was agreed to search the whole area, right down to the shoreline—it was high time, these culprits were finally found and made to stand trial. No one had been safe for twenty-odd years, and it was high time it was brought to an end. The number of people who went 'missing' was unbelievable and now the reason why, was known—the people were actually being robbed, murdered and removed from the place of the attack. The location was widespread and difficult to search, and the sea could be wild and dangerous, hiding a multitude of sins.

The Edinburgh Magistrate reported what had happened—and how it had been happening for a long time—he reported straight to King James V1 himself, who was present in Edinburgh at the time. The King immediately took a great interest in the case. He had always had a personal interest in the paranormal and was very curious by all the disappearances from one spot. Attempts had been made to discover the culprits but with little luck—and blame for the disappearances was often laid on men such as local Innkeepers—after all they'd usually been the last person to see the 'missing' person alive. This of course was because any victim probably called at the inn for a last drink before going home and not for anything more sinister than that. But still it was the inn keepers who saw the missing people for the last time, before they disappeared for ever.

Unfortunately, there were also several hangings of innocent people because the villagers were so afraid and desperately wanted to find the guilty party—it somehow made them feel safer if they thought they had. But of course, the attacks continued. The villages along the coast were alarmed at the number of limbs that washed up at low tide. It was a horrific sight and changed the whole area for everyone who lived there. In fact, the actual population began to decline as people moved away to safer parts of the country. Local searches for the culprits had found nothing—the cave was always ignored as no one could believe any human beings could live or hide there—so the cave was never searched. No one would venture into that deep, dark place—and anyway, the high tides made their searches almost impossible.

King James VI sat on the throne of Scotland and the suspicious disappearances of people in Ayrshire soon reached his ears. The Magistrate himself had reported the crimes, and the King now felt a personal involvement. His interest came about by the story about the man with the sword, who'd managed to chase off the brigands. The king vowed to do something about it and sent a message to the bereaved man saying this. He would very shortly inherit the throne of England as well as Scotland and he desperately wanted to stop the horrendous crimes before moving his seat to England. He owed it to his people, and he didn't want the English to think of the Scots as barbarous killers— something they already suspected.

His fears were founded however, and the English Broadsheets now began to print regular tales of the strange disappearances in Scotland. There were already considerable anti-Jacobite feelings amongst the English population and having a Scottish King would not be welcomed south of the border, especially following someone like Good Queen Bess,

Therefore, King James gathered and led a force of 400 men with a team of Bloodhounds to travel to the Ayrshire coast. Their intention was to solve the riddle once and for all. Having just lost their illustrious Queen, the English already though of James as an upstart Scot who was being handed their country on a plate—so they resented him and all Scots at the time. He wanted to do something great in their eyes. The two countries had been enemies for centuries and it was common thought that areas in Scotland were completely off-limits to honest, decent people.

The English Press in their broadsheets took every chance it could to criticise the Scots and until the guilty party was caught in Scotland, they'd go right on doing it and damaging James' reputation. The story of the attacks sold papers and the more horrendous the crimes, the better—everyone liked a superstitious and murderous story—and these were certainly that. King James therefore knew what he had to do. His dream was to bring together the two old enemies and he had it fixed in his mind that to catch and punish the perpetrators of such horrific crimes in Ayrshire would help his own image. It would quieten the English Press and allow him to dabble in witchcraft and devilry, things that had always fascinated him.

James, his chief knights, and many soldiers were camped near Edinburgh. They'd been riding up and down the coastline for several days but could find nothing suspicious, except the way people regularly reported finding limbs, hands, feet and skulls that sometimes washed up along the coast.

"Where will we search tomorrow, Sire? We've covered the whole area and found nothing untoward. What can be happening here? Where are the people disappearing to—and why are there limbs turning up along the coastline?" one of men asked, not expecting a reply. "Do you know that local gossip says there's been about a thousand disappearances from this area over the past twenty years?"

"We'll back-track tomorrow, that's what we'll do—we must have missed something—something obvious. I must discover what's happening here—my future depends on it." James was genuinely desperate to solve the mystery and of late, had begun to believe the supernatural was certainly playing a part in the whole business. Was the Devil himself involved? The darkness of the crimes was evil, and no one was more evil than the Devil. Was the supernatural involved? He felt sure it had to be so. A weary King retired for the night, fearful of what the morning would bring.

Next day, the army again began their search of the area. Obviously, it had been searched many times before—by local people and magistrate's men—and even the King's own but this time, but this time the army was accompanied by several hungry bloodhounds and, as it turned out, the smell of blood around the cave entrance was like a beacon to the dogs. They were not afraid to go deep into the cave—and they did, one reappearing with a foot hanging from his mouth. The Beans' hideout in Bennane Head had been discovered at last.

The goblins were seated close beside the Beans—not a good omen, as they rarely came into the semi-light. Something bad was coming and Sawney and Black Agnes were afraid. They huddled together for comfort—but it was too late for them. The King's men entered the cave by torchlight and the Bean family surrendered to the well-armed soldiers without a struggle. They were so startled when the soldiers and dogs invaded their home that they found they couldn't move.

The soldiers were disgusted to find body parts hanging around the walls of the cave and barrels full of pickled limbs—arms and legs stood out from the chunks of human flesh and the smell of blood and rotting meat was overpowering. Several men vomited on the spot—and added to the filthy conditions in the cave. Some of the barrels were filled with piles of valuables and heirlooms, stolen from the victims and there was a lot of loose jewellery which had been wrenched from many necks and fingers. In fact, there were even some rotting fingers still wearing the owner's rings. The Beans hadn't minded that. It couldn't have looked more disgusting and yet, the Bean family had lived with this every day. The riches were amazing and yet, the thieves had never used much of it, only to barter for supplies in the towns—the human flesh was more valuable to them.

There were 45 members of the Bean family, and they were all there when the soldiers arrived—except for one daughter who'd run away from the cave when she was 18. Something had told her this was no way to live, and she'd helped herself to a few jewels from the barrel, and left one night, never to return. She was someone without an addled brain. The Beans didn't miss her—it was one less mouth to feed—and they had plenty other children anyway. The escaped daughter settled in Girvan which was not very far from the macabre location where the scenes of murder and debauchery were carried out.

Unfortunately for her, angry local people discovered who she was and hanged her with no trial—from a tree that became known as The Hairy Tree. She had allegedly grown the tree herself, from a single seed—probably not true but it added to the tale. The goblins turned up at the foot of the tree and watched the whole thing. They were dark red now in colour and watched the girl struggle—their red, twisted and ugly faces enjoying the spectacle. She had deserted the Bean family and had gotten what she deserved. They would report back to Agnes.

"We don't have enough chains for all of them, Sire—we'll have to go and see the local Magistrate and get more from him." The Captain of the Guard reported to the King, who had refrained from entering the cave—of course at his men's insistence. He'd remained outside but the smell filled his nostrils and made him feel sick. "There is such depravity in that dark hole, Sire—it would offend your eyes to see what men are capable of. In fact, I think the name of man is too good for them. Where would you like to go now, Sire—we have enough men here to deal with the atrocities? You have done your part by bringing us here—the local people will be very pleased." James would make sure the English Broadsheets printed this!

He travelled to his castle in Stirling and settled there for the time being. Extra chains were collected from the nearby town and the soldiers attached them to each of the Beans—even the children It was obvious that they were cannibals too—and it wouldn't be safe to allow them to roam free. The army escorted the whole family to Edinburgh and there, they were imprisoned in the famous

Tolbooth Jail in the middle of the city. The grandchildren were separated from the rest of the family and whilst the others were then transported to Leith, the children remained in the Tolbooth.

"What do we do with them, Sire? The people around this area are baying for blood and we mustn't be seen to be lenient—the Beans are no better than wild animals. And why should we waste money on a trial, they'll be found guilty anyway. Caught in the act, they were, surrounded by the limbs of their victims—I have never seen a more horrendous sight in my life—and it'll never leave me till the day I die." The officer was not just upset, he was furious. "We must be seen to be ready to stamp out such atrocities. What do you want us to do, Sire?"

"I want it to be brought to a speedy end—I want the people to see us act as those in authority should act—and stamp out the family as a whole. My throne is in a precarious position and England especially must see me as a strong King—the people of Scotland will see it for themselves when we—are you ready for this?" and he paused for effect—"when we take them to a place of execution and disembowel the males, cut off their hands and feet and let them bleed to death? It is a death they deserve after what they did to all those innocent people.

"The females, including the children will then be burned at the stake—but only after they've been witness to their men's torture and deaths." He spoke with great anger—it was the way the Beans had behaved all their lives—and it was only right that they be treated the same way themselves—inhumanly and barbarously. The King had spoken and when the people heard his decision, they were well pleased.

The Beans were considered to be sub-human and so, were not given a trial. Their crimes over the years were so heinous and the evidence collected in the cave so atrocious, their immediate execution was the only option the officials had. After all, a clear instruction had come from the King himself. It was what the people wanted—in truth what they demanded.

Sawney and the other family males had their genitalia cut off and thrown into a fire. This was done right before their own eyes. Their hands and feet were then cut off and they were then left to bleed to death. Many dogs began to gather around the execution and had to be shooed away. Sawney's last words were shouted into the crowd, "It isn't over. It will never be over."

His meaning wasn't clear, and no one understood. The people asked each other, 'What did the mad man mean? What would never be over? He won't come back, will he?'

The children were brought from the Tolbooth Jail and Black Agnes with all the Bean females were tied to stakes and burned alive—even the children. The country needed to get completely free of the Beans and it was the only way to bring the family line to an end. No one could be allowed to live and pass on the family genes to other generations. It was too terrible to contemplate.

Strangely enough, Agnes saw the Devil standing in the crowd of onlookers and by his side were the two goblins. Agnes thought he'd come to save her and held out her hands pleadingly. He just laughed in her face and lifted the goblins—one in each hand—and threw them into the fire, calling out, "We'll all be together soon, My lovelies!" It seemed he wasn't her friend after all.

What Sawney had shouted into the crowd was never understood and the crowd who had witnessed the executions found the words odd—they had sounded like a threat but hopefully not a promise. They often discussed the matter in small groups, but no one could come fathom it out. However, they did at least feel reassured, now that the horror was over and done with and the Beans were gone. Afterwards, there was talk in the markets and in the inns about what Sawney's last words had meant. 'What wasn't over—what did he mean? Was there more evil to come?' His words are probably still discussed today in Ayrshire in Scotland.

Many of the people in Scotland were and still are superstitious and scared of the unknown—they couldn't believe what the Beans had done—it was an unimaginable horror.

It was a sad thing when the word 'Sawney', or 'Sawneys' was taken into the English language—particularly by the English people themselves. It was used when referring to a Scot—a rather rough, uneducated Scot, perhaps the worse for drink—or just someone who had completely lost control in an argument, but definitely not to describe a decent man!

Sawney had bequeathed a new word to the world—but for all the wrong reasons!

Now, I would like you to decide if you believe Sawney Bean and his family ever existed. There are no official records, so it's difficult to provide dates of births or deaths which could prove their existence. They were so evil and cruel and committed such dreadful crimes, that the country of Scotland just wanted them to be washed away—wiped from the earth. There are no records of their trial because there was no trial—their story has been handed down by word of mouth and often used to frighten children who wouldn't go to bed when they were told.

The use of the word 'Sawney' was however taken up and used in every-day language and we all know the power of the word of mouth. The story has lasted this long and there's no sign of it going away—could a man and woman really have done the things the Beans did? Could they have raised a family of retards and cripples who ate nothing but human flesh? What do you think?

And don't forget the goblins! Should you meet such beings during your lifetime, and believe me, you will—ask them about Sawney and his strange family! They'll tell you the truth because they're proud of their good friends, the Beans!

Bartholomew Quelch

Bartholomew Quelch, son of Talimar (at least that's what he had always been told), lived and worked in one of those underground cellars beneath grand Victorian houses in London, the kind whose one window was covered in iron bars and was at street height. He could easily see anyone walking past and, if they bent over, they could see into his shop. Over the window, he'd put up a sign, saying ***Want something old, strange, or funny? Come on down to Bartholomew Quelch's Emporium.*** Unfortunately, some of the letters had fallen off through time and people would stand in the street trying to decipher the meaning of the words—but then his reputation was already widespread and when people wanted something cheap and unusual, they'd regularly find their way to his emporium. Actually, it was nothing as grand as an emporium, but the word sounded better than shop and promised all sorts of wonderful, interesting things.

"Come in—come in—Bartholomew Quelch at your service—how may I help you today?" and he'd begin to tell them stories about the objects he had for sale. If he didn't know anything, he'd just make it up—better an interesting lie than a boring one and it helped him sell more goods that way. A mother and two young boys had just come down the outside stairs and cautiously pushed open the door—the 'jingle-jangle' bell rang out clearly and brought Bartholomew from the back of the shop.

"Hello Madam. Hello boys—how are you today? A fine day, isn't it? Are you looking for something in particular or would you prefer just to browse? Whatever you want, just remember I'm here and always ready to serve you."

The boys were looking around and examining bits and pieces. The little lad had lifted a small sailing boat and was holding it up to the sparse light of the window.

Bartholomew couldn't resist saying, "That there boat has come from the bottom of the deepest sea—it was found by a diver on the ocean bed in the wreck of The Titanic. You know about the Titanic, don't you—the newest, fastest and biggest ship of its time but it hit an iceberg one night and within just over 2 hours, it sank beneath the waves of the Atlantic ocean with more than a thousand people losing their lives. It's still on the seabed in two halves, but the sea is stealing it and soon there won't be anything left." He was warming to the subject and loved to see the lad's eyes shine with excitement.

"I know about the Titanic," the older boy added to the conversation, "but I never knew divers had been able to go down to such a depth."

Bartholomew ignored him and drew his attention to a pile of old comics lying on a table. "Have a look at these son—they're really old and probably worth a lot of money—or will be one day." He zoned in on the younger boy—a better prospect, he thought.

"Mum, is it okay if I buy this boat—it's only £5 and it's in very good condition?"

"It's your pocket money Sweetheart, you can buy it if you like." His mother was more interested in a rather battered brass coal shuttle, resting against the wall.

Bartholomew moved closer to her. "That very shuttle came from the kitchens of Buckingham Palace—a maid who worked there, found it at the back of a cupboard and knew it was really old. She brought it to me—in fact, she's brought me a few things over the years, but I think that's the most special. Just think, Queen Victoria's fire could have been fuelled by coal from that very shuttle." He'd told a few people that story before, but she seemed to be the most receptive.

Bartholomew looked like a gypsy with his gold hooped earrings and black, pointed beard, now with white edges that showed his advancing years. He also dressed like a gypsy with corduroy trousers, lilac shirt, and purple waistcoat—a veritable dandy if ever there was one. Yes, his hair was quite grey now but he believed he looked the part, and acted the part as well. He sometimes wore a cap at a jaunty angle but today, he was bare headed.

"If I, were you, madam, I would grab that item while you can—as I won't have it for long—it seems to catch everyone's eye." Contrary to how he looked and what he said, he was a poor man, usually living right on the bread line—the shop didn't make much money so he had to try very hard to make a sale when he could. The items he picked up from here and there never cost him much money as he picked them up from some 'down-at-heel' places. So, he was trying very hard to sell to these customers—they seemed reasonably gullible.

165

When they finally left, he deposited £20 in the cash register—it had been a very successful afternoon and all he'd lost was a cheap, half broken boat and an old, battered scuttle that he'd picked up for 50 pence and a half dozen tattered and well-thumbed comics. Life was good when customers were so easily impressed. He felt the stories he made up added to the mystique of the load of tat he sold. He moved to the back of the shop and settled down in an old armchair that had seen better days—time for a little nap after all that selling. He was soon asleep.

A booming voice woke him up. "Bartholomew, what did we discuss about your selling style?" He knew it was God's voice, so he pretended to be still asleep for a while until the voice boomed again "Bartholomew—I know you're not asleep. Look at me."

"Yes Lord, how nice to hear your voice—you've not visited me for a while." He rubbed his eyes and sat bolt upright—may as well get this over. "What's brought you here this time—although I should say it's always a pleasure to see you." Bartholomew's silver tongue had gotten him out of scrapes before—but God was an altogether different matter. He was smarter than the gypsy.

"I can hardly move in here—your shop is so full of rubbish. Where on earth do you get it all?" God sounded exasperated, but then he'd spoken with this man so many times. Bartholomew loved to tell lies although he always threw in a little truth for good measure—but it was the bits he took from his own head that he enjoyed the most.

"But Lord, the people like my stories—you can't deny that—and some of them even come back for more." Bartholomew went back to his comfortable chair, leaving God tutting loudly.

The doorbell jingled again, awaking the shop owner, who jumped up out of his sleep, shook his head and walked down the shop. Had God been there again, or had he been dreaming? He often dreamt of God but only because his conscience pricked him from time to time. He shrugged off the feeling and walked towards his customer. Four customers in one day—that wasn't bad.

"Ah Sir, well spotted! I believe those playing cards belonged to the Count D'Artagnan, the French soldier and friend of the Musketeers. I picked them up on a visit to Paris where I visited the local markets. You can see from the designs that they're very old and have been well used, maybe even by the Man in the Iron Mask. Who can tell—card playing was a popular pastime then, you know?"

Bartholomew knew he must stop gushing about the playing cards or the customer would become suspicious.

The young man asked, "Why aren't these cards kept in a museum if they're so special?"

"Ah, that's a secret I can't share with you—I have some friends in high places and if I get my hands on certain items first, they make sure I'm not bothered by any such things." He really did have an answer for everything. The lies fell freely from his lips. The customer wandered around the shop, picking up some things and examining others, but he kept going back to the playing cards. Bartholomew knew he was hooked but didn't rush him—in fact he went into the back behind a small curtain and made two cups of tea. He believed refreshments were always a sign of a classy establishment.

"D'Artagnan also became the Marshal of France and politically was a very important man—to own cards that belonged to him, would be a great honour." He handed the young man a cup and saucer and settled down on a spare chair at the front of the shop.

"I don't know if I believe you, but I find the cards intriguing and for the right price, I'll buy them—how much do you want?" he asked.

Bartholomew named a ridiculously high price and watched the man's face fall. *Too much*, he thought, so added, "But for you, with so obvious an interest, I would charge half of that, but there can be no further negotiation after that."

The man finished his tea and reached for his wallet, "All right—I'll take them. My friends won't believe me but it's a good story and who can prove it's not true?" He handed the shop owner £25 and put the cards into his briefcase.

The shop was quiet again—but Bartholomew was not too concerned, after all he'd had a reasonable day so far. He sat there thinking things over, Was that little boat really from the bottom of the Atlantic Ocean? Did it matter—after all, the boy believed it was and that was what was important—his imagination could now run wild. And did the coal shuttle really come from Buckingham Palace? It might have—it could have—in fact, he was sure it did.' He looked around his shop—everything could have an interesting history and so what if he did help things along a bit—everyone left his shop happier than when they'd come in?

Yes, he did a good job in spreading cheer amongst strangers and God was the only person who seemed to mind. Was it God who minded, or was it himself? Drat that conscience—always reminding him he was telling lies. In fact, was he telling lies? He wanted to believe the stories he told—well damn it, he did believe them when he was telling them and that's what made them so convincing.

He reached across to his counter and picked up a rather tatty book lying there in a pile of others. It was written by Charles Dickens and if he squinted at the inside front page, he could just make out it was a First Edition. The words were rather scratched, but he was sure it said First Edition—in fact, he knew it did. Now where had he picked that up—he remembered the old shop beside Euston Railway Station that had been selling off old stock and he'd gone in for a look around. He'd actually spent £10 that day, which was a lot of money for him but he'd managed to get several books for the money—and this was one of them.

The book was *A Christmas Carol*, the most loved work Dickens ever produced and avidly he began the first chapter, although he already knew the story very well. Book still in hand, he soon fell asleep again and his arm dropped over the side of the chair. A little later, he spotted a glow coming from the back of the shop and, thinking it was the start of a fire, he woke himself up and rushed across the room. He rubbed his eyes and shook his head—he thought he was fully awake but doubted it now.

Sitting there at an old desk with 2 bright candles burning on either side of him, was Old Ebenezer Scrooge himself—scribbling some figures onto a scroll and scratching his head with a quill. *Now, don't be stupid, Bartholomew—there can't be anyone else in the shop—you're the only one here—and certainly not someone who looks like that*, he told himself.

Nonetheless, he tentatively asked, "Excuse me, Sir, who are you and what are you doing here?" He found he was still holding the book and he reverently laid it on a nearby table.

"Who am I? Who am I? You ask me who I am—I am Ebenezer Scrooge, and this is my office. I would say rather, who are you?" and he returned to his scribbling, wiping his inky quill with a piece of rag.

"Are you a figment of my imagination? Are you the result of a dodgy sausage I had for lunch—I knew it looked rather old when I ate it. Or perhaps the pint of ale I drank is sitting uncomfortably in my stomach? Well?" Bartholomew bent down and looked into the old man's face. He was using Scrooge's own words against him—when his old 'dead' friend Marley visited him in his house.

"Get away from me—are you a burglar—are you a thief? You're certainly no friend of mine." Scrooge raised his bushy eyes questioningly. "But then I have no friends anyway—nor have a need of them."

"Have you brought me a message, Ebenezer—is there something you want to tell me? Is that why you're here?" Bartholomew wondered if he was dreaming again but the old man seemed real enough.

"How dare you address me by my Christian name—I am Mr Scrooge to you. By the way, has Bob Cratchit turned up for work yet—he's always late?" He turned and snuffed out one of the candles—"Mustn't waste candles," he said before going on, "Actually, I've been asked to come here with a message for you and that is—you must mend your ways and stop telling your customers so many lies. Both you and I know that book you're holding isn't a First Edition—although I admit it's in such a terrible state, it might once have been. Now the fly page is torn and dirty." Ebenezer stood up and blew out the other candle.

Bartholomew stared into the old man's withered face and thought how lonely he looked. Scrooge could read his thoughts and said, "No lonelier than you—you have no friends, do you? You live alone and have never married—all you do is buy and sell old tat and tell lies every day." He began to back away into the corner, where in the blink of an eye, he disappeared. No more Scrooge—just two unlit candles, an inky quill, and a small bottle of ink.

Bartholomew's first thought was, "Well, I won't get much for those things! But at least, they prove he really was here—or do they—they might have been there all along, amongst all my other bits and pieces." *Have I been dreaming again?* And he looked at the book and picked it up.

There was an eerie atmosphere in the emporium—especially at night and it had become dark outside—he looked closely at the candlestick. It was quite unusual and might be worth a bob or two. He was always on the lookout for potential valuables. Locking the front door, he pulled back the curtain that hid his little bed—it was time to go to bed and tomorrow was another day and one never knew what that would bring. His last thought before he dropped off was about Count D'Artagnan's playing cards—had the Man in the Iron Mask played with them? *Yes, I think he had and I'm glad that young fellow went off happy when I told him. All I do is make people happy, but others might find fault with that—you just can't please some people.*

Next day, Bartholomew dressed in his best blue velvet jacket and corduroy trousers and walked smartly in the direction of the British Museum. He wasn't actually aiming for the museum itself but for a small book shop just off the main street. Unfortunately, it was the young girl assistant at the counter today—he wanted the balding, elderly man who really knew his stuff. *I mustn't be ageist*, he told himself.

"Good day, Mr Quelch, it's always nice to see you." She was always rather gushing but that was how she treated all the customers. "Buying or selling today?" She was a pretty, young woman about 30 years of age and was always dressed very smartly and in the latest fashion. She waited patiently for his reply.

"Is Mr Cruickshank not in store today?" She was so self-confident that he thought the question would put her in her place. He stroked his beard and then tapped the counter with impatient fingers.

"I am in charge today, Mr Quelch—how may I help you?" She really had a good opinion of herself.

He produced the small leather-bound book from his inside pocket. "I have brought a First Edition Dickens' novel of *A Christmas Carol*. I would appreciate an educated valuation of it." He handed it over to her, stressing the word educated first and then pretended an interest in other books whilst she studied the book.

"I will have to have a second opinion on this, Mr Quelch—as you can see, the flyleaf where publication information usually is, is quite scratched out. Would it be possible for you to leave the book with me so I can show it to Mr Cruikshank?"

"Of course," he replied. "I'd like a receipt if you please." And he left the shop, receipt in pocket. He walked around to the British Museum as he wouldn't dream of being this close to the wonderful building, without going inside.

"Ah Ginger—how do you feel today?" Bartholomew never visited the museum without going to the Egyptian Rooms, for there as usual, was Ginger— his 3,500-year-old friend, whom he'd visited many times before. The Egyptian mummy lay on his left side with his knees reaching up towards his chin—lying in the foetal position. He regarded Ginger as a friend and often stayed to have a chat. The age of the mummy was amazing, and it was incredible to think he wouldn't have been there without Napoleon Bonaparte's invasion of Egypt in the eighteenth century. Amazing how one incident brought about another! On Bonaparte's defeat by the British, Ginger was brought back to Britain to live, and be cared for, in the British Museum. Ginger seemed happy enough.

He liked to visit the Rosetta Stone as well—the inscribed stone which helped the experts to finally decipher hieroglyphics and learn more about Egypt and its culture than anyone had ever known before. He would also buy some postcards and a couple of small replicas of exhibits which he could sell in his shop—they always sold well—people were fascinated by anything Egyptian—and he could always make up stories to make them seem even better.

When he returned to the book shop next day, Mr Cruikshank was there, and the shop was empty so the two men had time for a chat.

"Mr Quelch, I won't make you wait—I'm afraid this is not a First Edition of *A Christmas Carol* but it is quite an old book and I'd be happy to buy it from you. I'm afraid I could only offer £20, which I assure you is a fair price."

Bartholomew looked at the man and then at the book before saying, "I'm sorry, Mr Cruikshank, but I couldn't let it go for that. Is there any room for negotiation?" He was used to bargaining and negotiating and was not daunted by the little man's first offer.

"I'm afraid not, Sir—that's the best I can do." He obviously wasn't going to budge, so Bartholomew pulled himself up to his full height of 5 feet 4 inches and left the shop with the book under his arm, thanking the shopkeeper as he went.

'Well, I tried to give him a bargain. His loss, not mine!' And he wandered back towards his own little shop, where two ladies were waiting for him. "Good afternoon, ladies—I hope you've not been waiting long—I had some important business to take care of. Do come inside and make yourselves comfortable." He really could charm the birds from the trees. Well, at least he thought he could!

"Would you care for some tea and whilst I'm making it, you can have a browse around the shop? There's lots of interesting finds here—any questions, just call out and I'll try to answer them."

The ladies wandered around, picking up different bits and pieces and one said. "Our friend Thelma told us about your shop—she found an old coal shuttle from Buckingham Palace the other day—and bought it for a song, she said." At that statement, he picked up his ears—that meant they weren't short of a bob or two, or so he surmised.

"She did indeed and hopefully we can find you something of equal value and history." He brought two cups of tea—with matching saucers—and found two chairs for the ladies. No mugs for these customers. "May I enquire if you're looking for something in particular?" he enquired politely.

"It's my husband's 60th birthday soon and I want to find something unusual for him. Not necessarily of great value, but of interest." She saw his face fall and added, "Not that I'm unwilling to pay as much as it takes, but the interest is more important." Bartholomew's expression perked up again.

"Strangely enough, Ladies, I've just picked up something of interest—near the British Museum, in fact. I bought this from a gentleman there and I believe I pulled off a veritable coup"—and he produced the 'First Edition' of *A Christmas Carol*.

Whilst sipping their tea, the ladies 'oohed and aahed' over the book. "Is it really a First Edition?" The more astute one asked.

"Well, the man I told you about at the British Museum said it was—and he should know." He cleared away the teacups and left them to discuss things. They went around the shop, investigating all they saw—a couple of fancy clay pipes, an old wooden box with shelves for letters and an inkwell and quill pen which was still covered in ink. However, they kept returning to the old book, looking thoughtful.

"By the way, whilst we're here, my son was very jealous of the small boat Thelma's son bought from you—apparently it was found on the seabed where the Titanic lies in the Atlantic Ocean. Is that true?" She looked sceptical.

He reassured her it had definitely come from there and added, "I have another piece which came from the sunken ship if you're interested, but I'll have to go to the back of the shop to have a rummage around—I put it there for safekeeping." And he disappeared, desperately thinking what he could produce. And produce something he did—emerging from behind the cloth curtain, he was carrying a metal box which contained a set of dominoes.

"This box was found alongside the toy boat that I sold the other day, but I have to be honest with you and tell you this is not the original box, but a duplicate of the original. When the diver brought the box to the surface, the air attacked the metal, I'm afraid and it deteriorated in the atmosphere. All that was left were these beautiful domino pieces. Look, they are made of ebony and ivory—and are absolutely unique."

And the sale was made! The ladies left the shop with both the 'First Edition' and the box of dominoes. The word 'unique' had done it—the precious items became desirable in just a few seconds. Bartholomew put £30 into his metal box—it wasn't as much as he'd wanted, but the ladies were more shrewd than he'd expected. In fact, in negotiating a price, one of them had the audacity to say, "Without any proof of provenance, how do we know what you say is true?" So, he let both items go for £30. Mind you, it made his day—he didn't often make £30 in one transaction.

He went to the market again next day to see what he could pick up and met an old acquaintance he'd not seen for several years. "Hello Bart," the old man said, "how you been keeping?"

"Not so bad, Charlie—but not so good either, still having to struggle to make ends meet. What about you, still digging up old things and trying to pass them on as valuable?" He remembered Old Charlie's ways as he did exactly the same thing himself—but then he did it with aplomb and excitement—old Charlie was just an old man, tired all the time and without much time left. He must have been about 90 years of age, but he'd worn well.

"I know what you're thinking, Bart—you're thinking Old Charlie doesn't have long to live—I look pretty haggard, don't I?"

Bartholomew reassured him he looked fine and offered to buy him a cup of tea. Gratefully received, the two old friends settled down in a café to talk over old times. They talked about what a laugh they used to have and mentioned names they hadn't thought about in years. Bartholomew crossed to the counter and bought the old man another cup of tea and said, "I'd best be off now Charlie—things to do and people to see." A lie of course, but it sounded better than, 'I'm bored with you now.'

"Just before you go, Bart—I've got something for you," and he fumbled in his pocket. "As we both know, I'm on my way out, so you can have this"—and he handed an old brownish coin to his friend.

"A penny, Charlie—you're giving me a penny. I won't get much with that now, will I?" He smiled inwardly, Charlie had obviously gone a bit gaga in his old age.

"Nae lad, it's not a penny—it's a very rare and unusual coin a mate of mine gave me. I did him a favour and he insisted I have it. Feel its weight, it's not an ordinary penny—I know it's pretty dirty, but that's because it's been around for a very long time."

Charlie was becoming indignant, and Bartholomew could see the rheumy eyes filling with tears, so he changed tactic. "I'm very grateful and I'll look after it. It's a kind thought and when I look at it, I'll think of you."

They parted company and Bartholomew didn't think he'd see his old friend again—not alive anyway. He put the 'penny' safely into his inside pocket and then wandered around the market looking for something saleable and cheap— preferably something he could spin a good story about. It always worked— people could be so gullible! And he found it—another old book by Charles

Dickens, this one was called *Oliver Twist* and he knew the story well. The other Dickens book had made him a few pennies, so this one was worth a try. He bought it for £3! A bargain, he thought, and went home quite happy.

The next couple of days were very quiet and he sold nothing, but he did meet a couple of new acquaintances—ones associated with his items, like the Judge's gavel he'd had for a long time. He told people it had belonged to Judge Jeffreys, the Hanging Judge from the seventeenth century.

That night he was awakened in the early hours by a lot of loud shouting, 'Guilty! Guilty! You Sir are Guilty and will hang by the neck until you are dead.' Bartholomew pulled the bedcovers from his face, but only a little, and peered into the darkness. There was a man dressed in Jacobean clothes and wearing a long, curly grey wig—he was banging a table with his gavel and sitting in the same chair as Ebenezer Scrooge had used when he'd visited.

"You're all guilty of the crimes recorded here and in defence of his Majesty King James, I sentence you to death—not only the men but the women too." He was known to be a bad-tempered man who'd attended Cambridge University, but left prematurely without getting his degree, something which couldn't have made him too happy. He then studied Law and King James promoted him and gave him a title. Folklore said he hanged 700 people just because they favoured Protestantism and not the old faith, Catholicism. He also punished many of those who'd been involved in the Monmouth Rebellion.

Right now, he was staring at Bartholomew with hatred in his eyes, "Well man, do you stand for or against the Catholic faith—speak up, I can't hear you."

Fully awake, Bartholomew told himself he was looking at a ghost—or at a figment of his own imagination. "Don't you come into my home and shout at me, you fleshless corpse—I am neither Catholic nor Protestant, nor have I any wish to be, so you can take your ugly face as far away from here as possible. You should be ashamed of yourself, hanging all those people for treason, when all they wanted was to be allowed to practice their chosen faith." Bartholomew was on his soapbox now and it worked—the Hanging Judge just disappeared and allowed Bartholomew to sleep again. *Good riddance to bad rubbish*, he whispered in his sleep and turned back onto his side, snoring loudly at once. It had been that gavel he'd been holding before getting into bed he knew—that's what made the judge appear, he was sure. He had a second dream that night, which did happen from time to time but usually when he'd had a little drink or two—which he'd certainly had the night before.

A very tall and rough looking man arrived beside Bartholomew's bed, shaking his shoulder and waking him up. He wore a strange cap and a muffler scarf and carried a wooden club, which looked dangerously threatening. He carried a pistol in his waistband and looked as if he knew how to use it. He looked strangely familiar and was very much from the time of Dickens—probably from one of his books. The big man held the club above his head as though he was going to strike and Bartholomew covered his face, but still managed to ask, "Who are you and what are you doing here—this is my home, not yours! Get you gone, get back to where you've come from."

"You know my Nancy, don't you?" The big man's voice was rough and uneducated. A jagged scar ran down the full length of one cheek and Bartholomew couldn't help picturing how he might have got it—from someone like himself, no doubt. He looked like a rogue, a thief and a murderer, and always had a bull terrier by his side. The dog looked as though he liked to collect pieces of flesh from peoples' shins.

"When did you see her last? I know she's been carrying on behind my back and I need to punish her. Where is she? Is she hiding here?" There was no doubt now as to who he was, it was Bill Sykes, looking for his sweetheart, Nancy.

Bartholomew knew he was dangerous and that he'd murdered Nancy, so he answered, "I've not seen your Nancy, so go look for her someplace else."

Bill Sykes grabbed hold of the bedcovers and sneered into the older man's face, "She needs a good beating, that's what she needs. Come to think of it, that's what you need too." And again, he raised the club as though to strike.

"You're nothing but a bully, Bill Sykes—oh yes, I know who you are, and I know what will happen to you before you're much older. You'll soon be dead, yes, that's what's going to happen. The police will soon be after you—they'll find that dear, sweet girl lying dead in her room. Everyone liked her because she was lovely and kind. You've closed your mind to it all now, but you've already done your worst and you'll keep seeing her every time you close your eyes. You'll see her lying on blood-soaked sheets in her attic room, where you've abandoned her. You're on the run now but you'll get your come-up-pence, Bill Sykes—and you'll get it soon."

The big, ugly man disappeared—he couldn't argue with this idiot any longer and Bartholomew told himself he must stop buying books by Charles Dickens, the characters were so lifelike. Sleep only escaped him for a few moments, but in that time, he wondered why the visitors from the past had increased of late—

was it because of his frequently made-up stories? What did it matter anyway? It helped him make a few pennies and that's what was important!

Next day the sun was shining, and he'd forgotten all about the night before, but he was disappointed to find he had another visit from God, who didn't come very often, but when he did, he really told him off.

"Your conscience is working overtime lately, that's what it is. What am I going to do with you? You're your own worst enemy—why do you tell so many lies and exaggerate everything?"

"I don't know Lord, I suppose it gives me pleasure—people always go away from here happy and delighted with what they've bought. I am offering a service to the public, you know—and keeping 'your people' contented. Is that so bad?" Bartholomew felt defensive today.

"I believe I'll soon have to make a decision about your place here on earth— it may be time to take you back with me." God had obviously reached the end of his tether.

"Not yet, Lord, give me more time—I'm not too old, you know." It was as if he was pleading for his life—as indeed he was. He shook his head and God disappeared, but Bartholomew knew he'd be back.

The doorbell jangled loudly and awoke Bartholomew from his afternoon nap. He recognised the boy who came in—it was the lad who'd been with his mum and brother—the one who'd bought the old comics. "Hello there, young man, how are you today. Come in for a browse, have you?" He hoped he'd come to buy as money was getting a bit short. The boy walked around the shop, picking up things and looking carefully at everything. Bartholomew noticed he was wearing football socks. "Come straight from the sports field, have you?"

"Yes, that's right—is it okay if I look around some more?" he asked politely.

"'Course it is—you take as much time as you like. I'll be at the back of the shop. If you need anything, just give me a call." He disappeared to give the boy some peace and lit up his pipe, still closely watching however. He didn't look like the sort of lad who would shoplift, but one had to be careful. A little later, he joined the boy and asked if he was looking for something specific.

"I'm looking for a birthday gift for one of my friends—he plays football too. I'm afraid I only have £10 to spend. Can you suggest anything?" he asked.

Yes, thought Bartholomew, *£10 would do nicely—get him out of a hole!* "Lookee here, what do you think of this? It's old and comes from the First World

War and have I got a story to tell you about it!" Bartholomew was eager to impress the lad.

"Have you ever heard the story about Christmas Eve and No-Man's-Land? No? Well, you just sit there, and I'll get us both a cup of tea and a Kit-Kat—this story's worth hearing." And he fetched the tea and biscuits before beginning…

"It was Christmas in 1914 and the turn of the British Forces to be on the front line in the trenches, fighting almost face to face with the Germans. The British began to hear singing coming from the German trenches and when they cautiously looked across, they saw the other side holding up lanterns and small Christmas trees. Within minutes, the British joined in with the carols and soon both sides began to shout messages to each other—across 'the top' of No-Man's-Land. It was Christmas Day and both Germans and British climbed out of their trenches and met in the middle. The different languages made little difference—it was amazing, but they managed to communicate very well. Both sides had received Christmas parcels from home, and they shared them with each other—plum pudding, chocolate, sausages and cigarettes all changed hands. One observer at the time said a German soldier first climbed out of his trench and held up his hands. He had some English and he shouted, "Don't shoot for today and we will also withhold our fire." And that's exactly what happened."

Bartholomew paused for breath and to gulp his tea, the boy was transfixed and was almost goading the shopkeeper to continue with the story. "What happened then?" he asked.

"Well, apparently, there was great jollification and a couple of Scotsmen fetched their bagpipes and so they even had music." They all said how tired they were with the war and how they wished it was over—little did they know it had only just begun. They admired each other's equipment, saying it was better than what they had—some of them were only boys and wanted to exchange things like knives. Someone fetched a football from his trench and both sides joined in the game. It didn't matter who won—it was just a friendly match.

"The officers were concerned that the friendliness would undermine the fighting spirit and a messenger from HQ Command arrived next day, to warn against any communications between the sides and that friendly intercourse must cease immediately. And it did stop—that small episode of humanity in the darkness and misery of hand-to-hand combat in war. It must have left both sides feeling very strange."

Bartholomew needed a rest after that story—he felt rather breathless and couldn't understand why—but then he wasn't getting any younger as God had pointed out to him only the day before.

"That was a brilliant story, Mr Quelch—absolutely brilliant. Did you remember it because I was looking at this football?"

"No Son, I didn't have to remember it—I never could have forgotten it. Have you sussed yet why I told you that story? No? Well, that is the actual football that was used in the 'Trench's Truce', as it became known. I bought it from a friend at the market—you can see how old it is, made from leather and laced up tightly. There is no doubt in my mind this is the original ball, obviously brought back from the war by a very lucky soldier, who managed to avoid even stray bullets."

"Is it really for sale?" the boy asked hesitantly.

"Of course it is—and because it's you—£10 is the price! Do you want it?" The boy gave him his £10 and shot out of the shop before the mad man could change his mind. £10 for such a treasure was incredible—he couldn't wait to tell his friends what he had—he'd just have to get something else for his friend now.

Bartholomew secreted the £10 in his metal box, feeling good. The boy was happy and he was happy—in fact, he thought he could have asked for more money, but the lad only had £10. So, all was well! The room however darkened suddenly, and he realised he wasn't alone. *Who was it this time? Was it someone who'd been listening into his conversation with the boy?* he wondered. The booming voice soon told him—God was paying another visit.

"Bartholomew Quelch, you've been up to your old tricks, haven't you? That lie must be the biggest for a while—I know you want to make a sale, but really! That boy believed every word you said and has gone off to tell all his friends, who won't believe his story—and may even ridicule the child. I hope you're proud of yourself, my man!" God was obviously in a dark mood and was in no state to hear Bartholomew's excuses, so the shopkeeper decided to keep quiet and take the rebuke on the chin.

He waited for what was to come next, but couldn't resist saying, "Why has it become so dark in here, Lord?"

"That's because it's your last day on earth—I've come to escort you from this world." The words were serious, and Bartholomew could tell God meant business.

"It's too soon, Lord—I'm not really an old man—I've just had my 72nd birthday." He began to plead.

"Ah well, you are already on borrowed time—three score years and ten is quite the usual, you know." Yes, he was adamant this time. "Come Bartholomew Quelch, settle yourself in your most comfortable chair—that will be a nice place for your friends to find you."

"Ah, that's the fly in the ointment—you see, I have no friends. I suppose that's my fault too and I should have tried harder to make friends. But then, I'm the way you made me—so indirectly, it's your fault, not mine." Bartholomew was going to go down fighting.

"And that's why you have no friends—you never tried to make any—but don't worry, I'll arrange for you to be found."

Bartholomew suddenly remembered the old penny he had in his pocket—the penny Old Charlie had given him. "I suppose I should pay the ferryman to take me across the River Stix." And he held out the coin to God. God however never got to take it as Bartholomew fell to the floor and passed away within a few seconds. No more lies would come from that mouth it was certain, and he never did reach his most comfortable chair, but lay there on the floor in all his finery— his purple shirt and denim jeans. A positive dandy!

God kept his word and arranged for the postman to find the body and to send for the ambulance. He was taken away from his little emporium, where all his stock was scattered all over the place—not done by some burglar, but by his own lazy carelessness. He'd believed the mess had made everything look more valuable and interesting. The doctor at the morgue examined the body and clutched tightly in the dead hand, found a coin that resembled an old Victorian penny. He gave it to the police saying, "That won't make much of a dent in his funeral costs, I fear."

The policeman looked closely at the penny and found it intriguing—he didn't recognise the design or inscription, except to know it was of American origin. Something drove him to record the coin and then to book it out temporarily from the station. He took it to a long-established coin shop near Piccadilly Circus, where the man there asked to keep it for a day or so, until he sought a second opinion.

"I don't recognise it myself but that's what makes me want to find out more about it—it's unusual for me not to know at least something about a coin." The policeman agreed and left, receipt in hand. He was called two days later by the shop and asked to come in as something needed to be discussed. "Can't you tell me over the phone?"

But no, the man was insistent—he wanted to see him in person. "What I have to tell you is not something that should be said on the telephone." And with that enigmatic reply, the policeman agreed to call the next day.

"Does the coin belong to you?" was the first question the man asked.

The policeman told him it didn't and explained the circumstances under which the coin had been found. "And that's the story—the man who died clutching it was quite poor, he lived in a damp cellar and ran a curiosity shop from there. He was renowned for his story-telling and amazed people on a regular basis."

"Well, I want to tell you a story now, if you have the time. In 1849, the Gold Rush took place in California and the area filled up very quickly with prospectors, looking to make themselves rich. America had just come out of a war with Mexico and the country was on the up-and-up. The US Government struck and issued a gold coin and named it 'The Liberty Head Double Eagle Dollar' and its value then was $20. There were only a certain number issued but one of them ended up, clutched in your gentleman's dead hand.

"And that's the story—your poor man who lived and died in such poverty, always on the lookout to make a quick 'buck', actually died with a solid gold coin in his hand—a gold coin worth $35,200—thirty-five thousand and two hundred dollars—at today's valuation. And it can only increase in value with the passing years."

The policeman had listened in silence and now had no words—the situation was unbelievable. "The poor old chap—what bad luck was that—he never knew what he had."

"Did he perhaps leave a will? Is there someone who will benefit from this find?" The man was genuinely moved and reluctantly handed the coin back. He looked even more sad when told there seemed to be no relatives and certainly no will. "I wonder why he was clutching the coin when he died—what was he planning to do with it? I'm surprised he didn't have the coin valued himself because it's a heavy coin, being solid gold." He looked thoughtful and added, "Perhaps it was to pay the ferryman to take him across the River Stix—over to the other side." The very words Bartholomew himself had used to God.

The policeman responded with, "Well I'm sad to say, that what the Ferryman lost, the Inland Revenue will gain. The Taxman wins again!" Even Bartholomew Quelch couldn't have made up that story!

America—It All Started at a Party

"Another meeting, Paul? Surely, you must be joking! You've been attending meetings every second night for months. What can need so much discussion!" His wife was tired with looking after their seven children and being pregnant with the eighth. "Some days I don't know how I'm going to face it all—and you just keep right on disappearing. What is it this time—the King of Great Britain or the colonies and their problems? Who exactly do you think you are, that you're needed to address such things?"

She knew she was just winding him up and that her questions only served to annoy him—but she couldn't help it. There had been considerable consternation amongst the people in the town—and she didn't really understand what it was all about. They had food and warmth and a roof over their heads—what more could they want? It certainly wasn't enough for Paul who was always troubled over the British question. She really didn't understand him—after all, they were British themselves, weren't they?

Sarah Orne married Paul Revere on 4 August 1757 when she was 21 years of age. She hadn't known she was marrying an ardent patriot who had always immersed himself in the politics of how Great Britain treated the colonies. Colonies which were all governed directly by the Parliament in London—a Parliament of members elected by the people in Great Britain, but not by the people in the colonies. They had no say in any of the decisions taken, although it affected them just as much.

Sarah was not particularly interested in politics, needing all her time to manage the upbringing of the 7 children she and her husband already had—6 daughters and a son. She was still a young woman but a very busy one and her husband's regular disappearances to meetings didn't lighten her load one bit. Paul however was dedicated to his beliefs and believed a close eye was needed to watch the British Prime Minister, Lord North, and on King George himself.

"I must go, my dear—I am expected and needed by my friends." He was adjusting his neckerchief and brushing imaginary pieces of fluff from his jacket. He was born in Boston on 1 January 1735 and his real name was Rivoire. He was one of 11 children, and his father was called Apollis Rivoire who'd changed his name to Paul Revere after a few years in Boston. His mother came from a local artisan family and was called Deborah Hitchborn. Between them, they had 11 children. Apollis had been an immigrant from France and came to Boston when he was only 13 years of age. Although born of a foreign father, Paul was a Bostonian through and through.

Apollis trained as a silversmith—and after a very long apprenticeship, he grew to be a very successful one—his good reputation in Boston was widespread for his elaborate and beautiful work. He opened a shop in the North End section of Boston and apprenticed his own son Paul in the craft and skills needed to succeed in life. Unfortunately, Apollis died when Paul was only 19, leaving his son to take on the responsibility of caring for the family (his mother and 6 siblings)—something the young man did willingly. Then he met Sarah Orne, married and his own young family began to grow. He was now 40 years old and a successful artisan in his own right.

That evening he left his home to walk to the secret meeting place where he met several similarly minded men. The members of the group were known as 'The Mechanics' and the name stuck with them for many years. In 1773, the British Government had passed the 'Tea Act', and it was this decision which infuriated the patriotic colonists. It was one Act too many and closely followed the 'Stamp Act' which had cost the colonies significantly. The colonists were not involved in passing these Acts. The meeting therefore was to agree on how to deal with the perceived injustices heaped on the country by King George. In reality, Great Britain's Tea Act was not intended to hurt the colonies but rather it offered a cheaper tax on the tea which came from the British East India Tea Company, who had the monopoly on all sales. The new rules were handed to America as a fait accompli.

Following the Act, the price paid for tea would be half the cost it had been—but it all had to be purchased from the company only—and from nowhere else. The Colonists had frequently bought their tea from other companies, especially from the Dutch, where it was much cheaper than Britain's—now it had to be smuggled into the Colonies and therefore, no taxes at all were being paid. The British had to put a stop to this as they were out of pocket and at the same time, it was done to help the British East India Company who were undergoing great financial problems at the time—and were facing bankruptcy.

Therefor who could blame the Colonists for taking exception to the changes—although it wasn't the Act itself that upset them so much, but rather the way Britain just imposed it on them. Even the locally elected Colonial officials, had no input—hence the well-known phrase associated with the times appeared: 'No taxation without Representation' was soon on everyone's lips. It was as simple as that, the colonists were tired of Britain making decisions in their Parliament in London that affected them—with no voice in Parliament, they had no control over any decisions made for them. They were not allowed to be elected to the British Parliament although allegedly they were British Citizens. Confusing or what?

This then is what Paul Revere, and many other Colonists were aggrieved about. It was said at the time that Lord North, the British Prime Minister had no understanding of what it meant to live in one of Britain's overseas colonies—and so many of his decisions were not wise. The Colonies had been the subjected to many other Acts imposed by the British, with no colonial representation—but the Tea Act seemed to be the last straw and so, the 'Mechanics' were meeting to discuss the future. The British East India Company was to be allowed to sell their tea to the colonies without having to pay tax—it was nothing but favouritism, even bordering on nepotism, and had been decided unanimously by the British. It was very unfair and gave a monopoly of sales to themselves only and nothing to the colonists.

At the Sons of Liberty meeting, Samuel Prescott was on his feet and speaking to a packed hall, "This is now very bad, gentlemen, and we must act. It's not too much to claim that our very lives depend on what we do next. The principle of self-government without the burden of higher taxes must be addressed at this time." There were shouts of 'Hear, Hear' around the hall.

Samuel's colleague, William Dawes, shouted, "I think we should take positive action and go down to Boston Harbour right now—it's the only way notice will be taken. There are 3 ships anchored there, full to the brim with the tea—something over which we have no say. Let's go there and empty the tea into the harbour—it might not seem much in the big picture, but it's a start. From little acorns, great oak trees will grow."

Paul Revere spoke out then, "And if any of you are thinking we are wrong—and that we shouldn't be doing this—cast your minds back a couple of years to the Boston Massacre. A few of our fellows were a bit drunk and started arguing with soldiers who were strolling around the streets." He paused and saw some of the dissenters drop their gaze and stare at their feet. He went on, "And do you remember troops arriving to settle the disagreement and turning their rifles on unarmed colonists. Six men were killed that night and we have the British to thank for that. My friend Billy died that night, and he didn't have a political bone in his body—but they still killed him, because he was an easy target."

He stood up and raised his fists above his head, "We've got to join each other and support each other. The British need to learn that they've treated us with contempt for the very last time. Are you with us, boys?" And he waved his arms in the air.

Cries of 'Let's do it' and 'Come on, what are we waiting for—let's get down to Griffin's Wharf'! The cries were loud and clear and there wasn't even a need to take a vote—it was unanimous. The Sons of Liberty therefore met on 16 December 1773 but also agreed they should disguise themselves as native red Indians—to avoid recognition. It was after all a crime they were planning—probably both criminal and civil and therefore serious—but it was a necessary crime. The three ships anchored in Boston Harbour were 'The Beaver', 'The Eleanor' and 'The Dartmouth', and each one had brought a hundred chests of tea—they were just waiting in the harbour until the unloading could be done.

When Paul Revere arrived home later that night, Sarah was waiting for him. "Well, and what has been decided tonight—or was it yet another meeting where no decisions were taken?" She was well into her pregnancy, tired all the time and had little sympathy with her husband's causes. She'd always known he was politically motivated, but he'd become worse of late. She was beginning to feel the initial pain of birthing and knew it wouldn't be long until the baby put in an appearance. She decided not to mention it yet—as Paul's head was obviously still full of Liberty matters.

"You'll be surprised soon, my dear, when you hear of our decisions." He lit his pipe and settled in the rocking chair where his old father had always sat. Being a successful Silversmith, his works were often purchased by the Boston upper classes. In fact, when he visited them in their homes, he often supped tea from his own designs. Yes, life was good for him—he was comfortable and proud of his young family. If only the British could be taught to behave fairly, all would be right with his world. But alas, that was still to be achieved. He looked around the room where he suddenly felt an icy chill in the air—the fire in the grate had dropped low as though dying—and he reached for the poker to stir up the burning logs. Then he saw him standing in the corner of the room, a worried look on his face. Paul jumped to his feet and made towards the figure.

"Come no closer, Son—I am not of this earth and if you touch me, it could cause me harm. I come to see you with a message about your political activities. It has become too much of late and you are bordering on treason towards your King." It was quite a speech from a ghost, and a ghost it must have been, as Apollis had been dead these many years.

"Father, is it you? Although I'm pleased to see you again, I am concerned as to why you've come. I am not too closely involved with the Sons of Liberty—well, only as much as is needed." Paul felt as though he'd entered another world, it was all so unreal and yet, there stood his father with a perturbed expression on his face and the two men were having a conversation.

"I am worried about your future—your skills are without question and God has given you this talent to use. However, you are more interested in what's going on in the British Parliament than here in Boston." The old man was shimmering in the light of the candles and Paul rubbed his eyes to see more clearly. Was the figure beginning to fade?

"Father, the problem with the colonists' rights does need addressing and I am not the only man who thinks so. This is a new country, yet Britain allows us no rights over our future—what are we supposed to do?" He began to feel angry at having to justify his beliefs.

"You must take care of your family my son—they are your first priority. Your wife, Sarah, needs you more than you know—her child is due to be born and she will need you more than ever. I am here to make you see Sarah's situation and to remind you that she must come first." The old man was slowly disappearing and in one sudden movement, he was gone completely, leaving Paul alone in the room. The fire suddenly burst into flames again and his pipe began to smoke. Had that really happened—had he seen his father's ghost?

He sat up straight in the rocking chair and walked over to the corner where his father had stood—but nothing remained. 'It must have been a dream,' he told himself and shook his head a few times to make himself more awake. 'Was it a dream, or a nightmare? Had he fallen asleep without knowing it?' He wasn't sure, but it made him put out his pipe and go upstairs to see if Sarah needed anything.

The next night Sarah went into labour and knew the baby was ready to be born. She sent the oldest child two houses down to ask her friend to come and help, "Tell her my pains are coming fast and they're pretty bad—and tell her that your father is at one of his meetings and I can't get hold of him." The girl did as she was told and soon the neighbour was leaning over the sweating Sarah and bathing her head with a cool cloth. She sent the girl back to bed, gathered some clean towels and boiled a kettle. Ironically, she also made a cup of hot, sweet tea—which Sarah just couldn't face.

The birth was long and agonising for Sarah—she knew things weren't going well—after all she'd had 7 children before. Her eighth child was born just after midnight, and it was another girl. Sarah looked and felt like a washed-out rag doll and even pushed away the sweet tea offered her for a second time. She was exhausted and lay back against the pillows, asking, "Where is Paul—hasn't he come home yet?" The little girl was named Isannah, and she was the last baby Sarah would have. She was a rather small child who would need a lot of nourishment and care. Wrapped tightly in a woollen shawl, she was laid on the pillow beside her mother, but Sarah was so exhausted, she could only turn her head away and close her eyes.

When Paul returned home that night, he was still excited and feeling good about what had been discussed. He crashed in the door and threw his coat on a chair. "Sarah, where are you? What a night I've had—you'll be amazed." But the house was silent, and his wife's friend appeared on the stairs, coming from the bedroom he shared with Sarah. "What's amiss, Maggie? Where's Sarah? I've something to tell her." He knew there was something wrong but didn't want to know what it was—it must be bad, judging by the expression on her face.

"It's not bad news, Paul," Maggie said, "but Sarah is very weak after the birth and will need a lot of caring. She had a long birthing and some difficulty in producing the child. You have another daughter—are you pleased?"

"I am pleased that it's all over for Sarah, although another boy would have been welcome." Paul felt crestfallen and not as happy as he should have. He went upstairs to see his wife and the baby and was shocked to see how pale and weak they both looked. In fact, they were positively grey in colour. He sat beside her on the bed and took her hand, "You'll soon feel better, my dear—just you wait and see. How clever you've been to give me another daughter."

But in the new year, Sarah was dead. She'd never recovered from the difficult birth and in the end, had died of a stroke. No amount of feeding or comforting had made any difference and she passed away, still a young woman. Paul was left with 8 children and had to find a wet nurse immediately to care for Isannah, his youngest. He did this and although life quietened down, it was never the same again and he involved himself even more with the Sons of Liberty. Times were difficult and needed changes to ensure the colonies were treated better by the British. Obviously, he grieved for his lovely Sarah—but too many births had taken their toll on the young woman.

He was in a contemplative mood and just puffed away quietly whilst his brain was working fast and planning the details of how their 'attack' on the ships would be carried out.

The children were all asleep and the house was unusually quiet. Sarah had never understood his beliefs nor how badly the colonists were being treated. There had been little point in trying to explain things to her—and anyway it was too late now.

Then the same thing happened as on the night his father had visited him. The fire went out and the room became icy cold just as before. He glanced into the corner and there stood his beloved Sarah. Not the Sarah as she had looked when she died, but a much younger version just as she'd looked when they first met. She looked young and healthy and vibrant with her long hair shining in the candlelight and her pretty face with rosy, red cheeks.

"Hello Wife, it is so wonderful to see you again." He made to move towards her, but she held up her hand to stop him.

"You mustn't touch me, Husband, or I'll just disappear." Sarah smiled and it was the same lovely smile he remembered so well.

"Have you come to see me with message? Not that it matters, it's just so lovely to see you. Tell me, are you at least happy where you are now? I couldn't bear to think you're not." He felt tears gathering in his eyes.

"I am as happy as I can be, Husband—so far away from you and the children. Is Isannah well—or is she suffering from the effects of her birth?" Sara obviously still missed her life, and the people on earth.

"Isannah passed way not long after you did—only months later. No matter how much we nourished her, she just couldn't gain any weight—our youngest child has been gone for some time, I'm afraid. She was not as robust as our other children—but I'm glad to tell you they're all fine." It still hurt him to speak of his little dead girl.

Sarah went on to explain that was why she was allowed to visit him. "Husband, everything must be different now and you need help to manage the home. I want you to know you are free from any loyalty to me and you must search for a suitable wife and mother. There must be someone in those you know. I understand you will find it difficult, but it's something you have to do—especially for the sake of the children. Do you understand what I am saying?" Without waiting for an answer, she too—as Apollis had done—began to shimmer and begin to disappear.

"Goodbye Husband, my time here is over, but I've given you my message and hope you will act on it." And she was gone and with her the icy air from the room. The fire was ablaze again, and Paul relaxed back into his chair. He was getting used now to these short visits from the dead—he knew they all meant him well—but he wished they'd forewarn him of their visit.

He had realised for some time now that he couldn't manage his large family without help, and so he did as Sarah told him and he found himself another wife—she was called Rachel and they were married in October 1773—just 5 months after Sarah's death. She was the daughter of a local artisan family and a very handsome woman. She was happy to be married at last as she was a little older and happy too, to inherit such a large family. Although he was unaware of it, Paul Revere, the successful Silversmith, was a very good catch as a husband. And so, his second marriage started off well.

Towards the end of the year, a large group of men—many of them members of the Sons of Liberty—met together and made their way to Boston Harbour. Nothing had changed in the colony and so it was time to take action. The crews onboard the ships were unsuspecting—this sort of things had never happened before—and all they saw were about a hundred men marching along the key side and getting into small boats, needed to reach the bigger ships anchored in the harbour. Most of the newcomers were covered in war paint and looked ferocious—real native Indians wearing feathered headdresses and carrying tomahawks in their belts. They were screaming and making loud noises. It was enough to scare anyone. The crews on board the ships kept well back and didn't attempt to stop the 'Indians'.

The men boarded the ships and were told to open the hatches and take out all the chests of tea and throw them overboard. It took some time, especially the splitting and cutting of the chests but their tomahawks soon made short work of that. Much of the tea floated on the water but most just sank out of sight—342 chests of the stuff—and although, the 'incident' was surrounded by armed British ships at the time, no attempt to stop the 'Indians' was taken. Their plan worked—and their demonstration was successful.

There was only one casualty on the night—at least it was a perceived casualty and it happened to one John Crane. He had been working hard with the other colonists to empty the ship's holds when a heavy arm of a cargo lift came down heavily on his head and appeared to crack his skull. His colleagues pulled his body from the ship and carried him across the harbour to an empty shed. They left him there—as there was much still to do on board—and covered him with mounds of straw to keep him warm.

Unfortunately, in the turmoil and chaos of the 'Party', he was forgotten, and no one returned to look for him. In the early hours of the morning however, John regained consciousness and for a moment, couldn't remember what had happened. Ducking his head in a nearby trough of water, he soon remembered and knew he had to get away as quickly as possible. Amazingly, he just sauntered off Griffin's Wharf and into the Boston streets, onwards to his home. No one else was even slightly hurt on the very eventful night.

On the morning of the Boston Tea Party, thousands of colonists had convened on the wharf and in the surrounding streets—they met at the Old South Meeting House where a great number of colonists voted to refuse to pay the taxes on tea or allow the tea to be unloaded, stored or used. (The strange fact was that the 3 ships had been built in the colonies and were owned by citizens of the colonies.) Governor Thomas Hutchison refused to allow the ships to return to Britain and ordered the Bostonians to pay the tea tariff, but the colonists refused to do it and that was the end of the matter as far as he was concerned. Why flog a dead horse?

The colonists had won the first challenge and would not allow Britain's East India Tea Company to be the only place tea could be bought. They fought the monopoly—and won.

Although it was known that the whole incident was led by Samuel Adams, John Prescott and a group of Sons of Liberty, the names of many of those involved were never known. Each man covered for each other. Only one was arrested for trespass and that was Francis Akeley but everyone else disappeared into the shadows with no further arrests. No one ever reported any of the men involved—even after America declared its independence. Although there was very little violence on the night, King George did not let the matter go unpunished and in retribution, the Coercive Acts (the Intolerable Acts) were passed, and these were:

1. The closure of Boston Harbour until all the lost tea was paid for.
2. Ended the Massachusetts Constitution so that no free elections of town officials could be held.
3. Moved judicial authority to Britain and to British Judges which resulted in martial law in Massachusetts.
4. Forced colonists to quarter British troops on demand, using their private homes if needed.
5. Extend Freedom of Worship to French Canadian Catholics under British Rule so angering most of the colonists who were of the Protestant faith.

The British Authority hoped these Acts would end the rebellions in New England and keep the rest of the colonies from uniting, but the opposite happened. The other colonies viewed the punitive law as further evidence of British tyranny and rallied to Massachusetts' aid, sending supplies, and arranging further resistance against Britain. In fact, there were several more 'Boston Tea Parties' across New England and beyond—but none as serious as in Boston.

Paul Revere was happily settled with his new wife, Rachel, who understood the problems experienced by the colonists and actively encouraged him to discuss matters with her. She was like chalk to Sarah's cheese. She loved to debate and discuss the issues that troubled her husband and actively encouraged him to attend his evening meetings.

"What will happen, Paul? What can the colonies do to rid themselves of British domination? I realise that many of 'The Intolerable Acts' passed by the British have been repealed—not the Tea Act of course—but they still will not allow us to have a say in the running of this country." She was angry at what was happening and knew Paul was deeply involved with the group of Sons of Liberty. In fact, if they'd allowed women to join, she would have been first in line. Alas however, such things were not allowed. Anyway, she was already pregnant with her first child and had to look after all the other children. She must have been very busy.

"Calm down my dear, things are happening. People won't take much more before something is done. Don't think we're taking all British decisions without asking questions—because we're not. At least throwing the tea into Boston

Harbour has had the desired effect of making people turn from tea drinking and having coffee instead—that must hurt the British pockets considerably—serves them right." He couldn't help smiling as he said this, then, "I'm afraid I have to attend another meeting tonight at the Old North Church—and this could be the 'make or break' meeting for our cause."

He sat down at the table with his young family—a table which was generously laden with food as his income was ever increasing. His own lot in life was very good and his family wanted for nothing—for this to continue however, Britain had to be made to understand the colonies had needs and plans of their own and they must have a say in how to introduce them and so develop their country.

Paul worked hard to maintain his healthy lifestyle and undertook dentistry work for the wealthy Boston people. In so doing, he became acknowledged as the very first to specialise in forensic science. His friend Joseph Warren (a well know revolutionary) had been killed but his body couldn't be identified. Nine months after his death, Paul Revere was asked about his friend and by examining the man's teeth, he was able to recognise wired dentistry work he'd performed when the man was alive. An amazing accomplishment in 1774 and one which added to the Revere ever increasing purse.

He really was a multi-talented man and whilst dabbling in dentistry work, he also created some astonishingly elaborate designs in copper plate engravings. His drawings appeared in books, magazines, political cartoons and tavern menus. His most famous work was a famous engraving of a sensationalised and propagandist depiction of the 1770 Boston Massacre—something he'd never forgotten. His artistry actually helped to fuel the growing resentment towards the British Army and Government, and this was something he welcomed.

In the Revere household, when the meal was over, Rachel put the children to bed and Paul left his home. The date was 18 April 1775, and it was to be the day all the colonists began to fight for their rights as an independent nation— independent from Great Britain at last—but they knew it was still a long way off.

Word was spreading fast around Boston that the British troops stationed there were getting ready to move—700 armed soldiers in all. Their intention was to march to Lexington and Concord where the main Revolutionary Leaders John Hancock and Samuel Adams were building a colonial militia to fight the British—when necessary. Paul Revere and two companions—William Dawes and Samuel Prescott—left Boston that night at 10 pm, first watching the British troops crossing the Charles River on their way to Lexington.

Two other Sons of Liberty went to the Old North Church which had the tallest tower in Boston and climbed to the highest point where they hung 2 lanterns. The agreed signal was, if one lantern shone out, the British troops were marching over land, but if 2 lanterns shone into the night, it meant they were crossing the Charles River to reach their goal. Two lanterns shone for one full minute only. Revere had suggested this means of warning the Revolutionary Militia that the British were on the move, their main intention being to arrest both Adams and Hancock—and so put an end to the entire colonies' disruptive thinking.

The riders stopped in every place along the way to warn people what was happening—and many colonists immediately armed themselves and waited—they'd been expecting this for some time. Word had to be spread discreetly and quietly—not by shouting 'The British are Coming' as has been suggested—but by silently spreading the word so that any locally billeted British troops wouldn't be aware of what was going on. The local people would not have understood such a message anyway as they still classed themselves as British, so as far as they were concerned, the British were already there.

As the 3 riders made their way towards Lexington, some troops caught up with them and they had to decide to split up—and so rode off in different directions. Although Revere was riding a good, solid horse named Brown Beauty, lent him by John Larkin of Charlestown, he was caught by the British and questioned—but was released a few hours later, there being nothing (yet) with which to charge him. He rode on to Lexington, but never reached Concord. Dawes unfortunately fell from his stumbling mount and never reached Concord but Samuel Prescott, a young doctor, did reach the colonial Militia leaders in that town. He told them the armed British were on their doorstep.

Although he was the one to reach the Revolutionary Militia, Revere's plan for the lanterns to be used to alert the Lexington/Concord Minutemen was equally important. So, Hancock and Adams were not arrested and escaped the danger. Although Prescott was the one to reach Concord, his name was lost in the annals of time, but the name Revere will live for ever. Much later, his name was made even more famous by the Longfellow poem which told of his midnight ride—but was obviously full of inaccurate facts. This didn't matter though as

Paul Revere was already an accepted hero and Longfellow's poem could always be put down to his own enthusiasm.

The opposing groups met on Lexington Green, each waiting for the other side to act. It was the British who fired first, and this was met by a retallying shot from the colonials. This became known as 'The shot that was heard around the World' and so the colonial fight for independence had begun. The battles at Lexington and Concord took place and would never be forgotten—they were hugely important, and both won by the colonies.

Paul Revere returned home to his wife and family where he continued with his silver and copper crafts. "I must continue with my business with the Sons of Liberty—you know that, don't you, Rachel? Nothing has yet changed and there is still much to do. King George will inevitably do something to punish us. We must be ready for that. Whilst waiting for our next action, I want to expand my business—it'll mean hard work and may put more pressure on you with the children and your pregnancy."

"I have no problem with that, Paul—you know I am totally behind our stance against the British. I can manage everything and the children as they grow, are becoming helpful, especially the older ones. You have nothing to worry about—I am here for you." She really was a Godsend and he appreciated it. His creative work expanded—and also his dentistry work—he sold many of his creations to the wealthy Bostonians and when visiting them at home, he now supped coffee rather than tea from his own, specially designed cups. He worked in gold as well as silver and his work was well known throughout New England.

Being a patriot, he decided to enlist in the Massachusetts Infantry and fight for his country's rights. He spent 4 years with the militia and fought in several skirmishes with the British. He was the Commander in the disastrous Penobscot Exhibition of 1779—in June of that year. British troops had begun to establish a fort in what is now Castine in Maine. Over the following few weeks, hundreds of the Revolutionary Militia converged on the outpost by land and by sea. Although the outnumbered British were initially prepared to surrender, the other side failed to attack in time and by August, enough British reinforcements had arrived and were able to force a Revolutionary retreat.

The leader of the Militia, Commander Revere, was charged with cowardice and insubordination and was court martialled and discharged from the Militia. It was claimed that, had he attacked sooner than he did, the colonials would have been victorious. Shattered with this injustice, he returned home to Boston and wouldn't speak of the incident to anyone. He was relieved however when the Authorities contacted him in 1782 and told him he was acquitted of the charge—but Paul never got over what had happened and to him of all people—the most ardent of patriots—and felt his reputation was tarnished for ever. He threw himself even more into his craft—not just in his silver and gold creations but in many other ventures as well.

Following the success of the American Revolution, he opened Boston's first Gunpowder Mill and also manufactured canons for the colonies' Militia, so still serving the American Cause in yet another and very important way. He also joined the Freemasons where he befriended similar activists such as James Otis and Dr Joseph Warren. Paul Revere never forgot the need to seek out and ensure the best for his country and he remained a pseudo-politician for the rest of his life, even becoming a spy for the Militia at one time, when he travelled all over the country as a courier—watching everything and everyone, especially anyone British and reporting back to his own side. He really was capable of almost anything.

His confidence grew with his increased abilities, and he took on even more challenges in the Boston area. He was so highly thought of that he was asked to print the first American money ever needed—and this too was to serve the brand-new country of America. The honour was huge.

"Rachel, my dear, I'm thinking of opening a copper rolling mill in the city. What do you think?"

"I think you should do it, Paul, but do you really want to take on more challenges when you are already so busy?" Rachel was having her fourth child and had her own hands very full.

"I don't think it would be too much—and I'm always at my best when working on a new business." He lit his pipe and rested back on the chair.

"Well then, you must do it, my dear—you know I'll always support you in whatever you do." She really was a most excellent wife for someone like him—nothing ever seemed to get her down.

"Well then, I shall." He beamed. "But I shall have to keep on running the hardware shop as well—it is so important to Boston." His foundry too was proving to be very successful, and he actually produced materials for the historic frigate USS Constitution, which played an important role in the War of 1812—and is now the world's oldest floating commissioned naval vessel. In the same foundry, he produced more than 900 church bells, one of which still rings every

Sunday in Boston's King's Chapel. His foundry remained in production for hundreds of years and his company—Revere Copper Products Inc—is still in operation today in Boston.

"We are a very rich family, Rachel." He couldn't help saying one day, as he cuddled his new-born baby on his knee. She crossed the room, placing 2 steaming cups of coffee on the side table. "You do know we're doing well, don't you?"

"I know you're a very successful businessman and that you take good care of your family." She took the baby and put her into the crib. She kissed her fingertips and placed them on the child's head. "Sometimes, I fear you're driving yourself too hard."

"I thrive on being busy, my dear, and I am very proud of the name Revere—Revoire, as it once was. You know my father came to Boston as an impoverished 13-year-old boy and he started his own business, ending up by opening his own shop. Also, he taught me all I know about my craft—without his input, I'd never have become the success I am. Do you know how old this house is, Wife?"

"How old is it—I like it, it's always been a good house and although there's so many of us, we all fit in nicely. I must tell the truth—at the beginning when we were first married—I wasn't sure if the shadow of your first wife would hang over me—but it has never happened and I'm very content living here. I know you sometimes think of moving, but I wish you wouldn't—I don't think we'd be as happy anywhere else." She finished her coffee and as the baby was sleeping soundly, she went upstairs to finish her chores.

Then he felt it—the icy air—and he couldn't draw on his pipe as it had gone out. There she was in the corner, just as before, except this time she had a small child in her arms. She was holding the child tightly and he knew it was Isannah. "How did you find her, Sarah?" Paul wasn't in the least perturbed as he had become used to these sudden visitations from spirits.

"Why have you come today, Sarah? Is there something wrong? Do you need me to do anything?" He felt anxious and he wasn't sure why.

"Your wife has never felt my presence in this house I know—but I have been here often—to watch over my children. You can't blame me for that, can you? I've come to draw your attention to something important—those unfortunates who've arrived in this country as immigrants—they need all the help they can get. I know you employ many of them in your works, but you need to do more, Paul. Can you do that—even if it's just for me—and Isannah—and for Apollis who came to this country as a penniless child. He was one of them once and could have done with some help at the time, I should think." She looked down at the frail little baby in her arms and knew that bringing her along had been a good idea. Paul was obviously listening.

And that was how it all started. He never knew if his father, his wife, and daughter had really visited him, or could it have been to do with his own conscience? He couldn't tell, but their visits had been timely, and they'd steered him in the right directions. Paul Revere became known as, not only the city's greatest entrepreneur, but its very own philanthropist. He was a most generous sponsor for several charities and his name was well known for doing good wherever he could—and he never had a visit from his dead loved-ones again. It seemed he'd done all he could.

This remarkable man lived until he was 83 years old and had continued to work until he was 76. He outlived both wives and 11 of his children survived to adulthood, and when he finally died, 5 of those children were still alive. He really had led an astonishing life and touched so many other lives in the process. He made a difference to the world and his existence certainly changed history itself.

He had been a talented silversmith, a designer and artist, as industrialist, a propogandist, a philanthropist, a hero and very importantly, a patriot. He really did love his country. He was also a loving husband and father. (16 children to his credit.) He sold his house in 1800 and his great grandson bought it, to ensure it would be preserved for posterity. And it has been. It still stands there today.

When you visit Boston, which I'm sure you will, go down to Griffin's Wharf in Boston Harbour and throw some tea chests into the water. (Don't worry, they're all attached to a rope these days and can easily be redeemed by the handler.) Everything is there, all set up for you to relive the Boston Tea Party itself. Feel what it must have been like on the night of December 1773. It's still very real to each visitor to the harbour. The tea party really was the start of it all.

After this, you should visit Paul Revere's own house at No. 19 North Square in downtown Boston—it's the city's oldest building still standing and dates from 1680—erected on the site after the Great Fire of 1676 when the original house was destroyed. This is where it all began for the Reveres—and for America itself.

The Man in the Iron Mask

Who was the Man in the Iron Mask? Many have asked this question and despite several suggestions, there is no definitive answer. What is known about him is that he was imprisoned in the Bastille in Paris on the orders of Louis XIII and then Louis XIV, Kings of France—he was also in several other prisons during the thirty years of his incarceration. The story of the Man in the Iron Mask was widely discussed at the time by the people of Paris, and many tried to investigate his background, but with little success. Initially, he was imprisoned on a tiny Mediterranean island off the coast of Cannes and then the fortresses of Pignerol and Exilles in the Alps—always accompanied by one of the King's very personal Musketeers. Both men, guard and prisoner were transferred to the Bastille in 1698 when the guard, Benigne de Saint-Mars, was appointed the new governor.

In the memoirs of a Bastille official, were the words, 'the new governor is accompanied by a man who is always masked and whose name is never pronounced. Whatever heinous crime this man committed, it must have been against someone very powerful.' The punishment was harsh, a living Hell in fact—no visitors, no contact with other inmates, no books and no exercise—and the added punishment of having to wear an iron mask.

King Louis's elite guards were called The Musketeers and their captain was Monsieur de Treville—a very important man to King Louis. The Musketeers were the King's own private guards, and they were originally formed under the king's father—Louis XIII. They were specially chosen and trained soldiers who were there whenever and for whatever the King or the country needed. Three of the elite had formed a friendship and defended each other whatever came their way. Their names were Athos, the leader; Porthos, the witty and amusing one; Aramis, the handsome and melodramatic one. They were excellent swordsmen and feared nothing.

The Captain of the Guard valued them greatly and asked for them personally if he had a problem. Privately and only within their group, the three men didn't think much of Louis X1V and believed him to be a weak king who had inherited the throne at the age of four, when his father died. His mother, Anne of Austria ran the country as Regent. The Musketeers respected her but not her son as he grew up. They bided their time however, knowing something would have to be done one day for the safety of the country, but they were unsure of what that would be.

Cardinal Richlieu was a minster of Louis XIII and then of his son, Louis XIV—he somehow had achieved great power over both monarchs. He was an ardent Catholic and hated the Huguenot movement that was growing in France. His project was to separate the King from his nobles and keep them well out of the governing of the country. The King was after all the Sun King and absolute ruler in France—and Richlieu was his close and trusted adviser. He suspected everyone and had a network of spies to support him. The Musketeers were not part of Richlieu's circle, and he watched them very closely. Richlieu was a dangerous and powerful man and the Musketeers made it their business to watch him closely.

One afternoon, a young man, called D'Artagnan arrived in Paris, eager to become a Musketeer. He carried with him a letter from his father and was to give it to the Captain of the Guard, recommending his son as brave, enthusiastic, and an excellent swordsman. Although only eighteen years of age, he was trustworthy and would be loyal to France. That day, as he was on his way to find the Captain of the Guard, he accidently bumped into a gentleman in the market. The man had been carrying some bales of cloth which spilled onto the ground. The man was furious and began to shout at D'Artagnan who shrugged off the incident and told the man not to make such a fuss. He even offered to help pick up the bales.

In the crowd, the three Musketeers had heard and saw what had happened and challenged the newcomer to be more careful. A scuffle broke out and D'Artagnan ended by inviting the three Musketeers to a duel—he drew his sword and began to fight all three of them. The fiasco got worse and other Musketeers joined the argument and they turned on the four troublemakers, whom they believed had begun the affray. The man with the bales of cloth was long gone by the time the fracas happened.

The group of four fought so well, they chased off the other Musketeers and afterwards, congratulated each other and D'Artagnan was invited to join their group. Once the Captain of the Guard had confirmed the newcomer could join the elite group, the four men went to a local tavern and became merry and very drunk. D'Artagnan was invited to take the oath by which all Musketeers stood— all for one and one for all—and loyal to the King. Over the brimming tankards, the conversation jumped from one subject to another. It soon reached the story that was going around Paris—who was the man in the Iron Mask? No one knew but several theories existed.

Innocently, D'Artagnan suggested that they visit the Bastille in their official uniforms and demand to be allowed to see the prisoner. The others laughed and said, "You obviously don't know how secure the Bastille is. We would have to be a Willow-the-Wisp to squeeze through their defences." So, that put paid to D'Artagnan's idea. But the seed of the idea had been sewn and none of them forgot it.

Anne of Austria, Queen of France, had an English favourite in the Duke of Buckingham. She was very fond of him but couldn't bring herself to love him. He was devasted and told her he was going to return to England as there was nothing for him in Paris. Because of her fondness for him, she made him a gift of twelve large diamond studs which she'd been given by her husband. Buckingham returned to England and unfortunately, Cardinal Richlieu knew of the diamond studs—spying at the court was rife and popular and he used his spies to keep him informed of everything that went on.

The minister was very powerful and very loyal to the King, whom people claimed 'he had in his pocket', but he was not fond of the Queen, in fact his plan was to shame her in the eyes of the court and of the King as well, so he sent one of his spies—a lady of the court—across the Channel to the London court and there, she was instructed to steal the diamond studs from Buckingham and bring them back to Paris—straight to Richlieu.

His plan was to ask Anne in an open and busy court to show everyone her diamond studs—a gift from Louis—and when Anne couldn't do it, he would expose her as a wanton trollop who favoured an Englishman. When Buckingham had returned to England, he'd needed the help of both the new Musketeer D'Artagnan and of Constance, Queen Anne's closest lady-in-waiting, in order to get safely out of Paris.

The spy followed Richlieu's instructions, but she wasn't an honest woman and she stole two of the diamonds, taking only ten back to the minister. He was furious to find two of the gems missing and shouted at the woman. So angry was he that it scared her, and she returned the stolen goods immediately—and so the

Cardinal now had in his possession, evidence of the Queen's adultery. When asked to produce the gems, which of course, she couldn't—he would produce them for all to see and her shame would be inevitable. The Duke of Buckingham in England was aware he'd been robbed of the diamonds and he wrote to the Queen, telling her—and having questioned the spy, she learned it had been Richlieu's plan to humiliate her. When the Cardinal eventually confronted her at court, when all the courtiers and their ladies were present, she turned the tables on him and said, "Why Your Eminence, don't you recall? I asked you to look after the twelve diamonds for me—they are very valuable—and I couldn't trust myself to take care of them safely.

Aghast, the lying Cardinal was lost for words. He couldn't accuse the Queen in front of everyone, of telling lies—and he was forced to produce the twelve stones from a purse he carried in his cassock pocket. There was such on-going espionage at the French court that no one could trust anyone else and were forever looking over their shoulders. Richlieu was determined however to disgrace the Regent Queen—he believed her power over her son was not healthy—he wanted it all for himself. The court was bursting with intrigue. King Louis XIV had taken the throne when he was only five years old—just after his father's death—and the situation fuelled the spies and intrigue that abounded at the French court.

Everyone was trying to pull the young king in all directions, but his mother kept a tight rein on her son and even chose his first mistress when he was fifteen years old. It was the start of an incredibly promiscuous life, and he went on to one mistress after another. As well as his six children by his wife, Marie Therese, he had many more illegitimate children by many different women. When Marie Therese died, he married again and had another six children.

Whilst this was going on, D'Artagnan was learning to become a Musketeer, helped by his three friends. He was of course very young and after only a few weeks in Paris, he believed he'd fallen in love with Constance who served Queen Anne. Porthos tried to talk him out of such stupidity and told him, "Don't get involved with the court ladies—they're full of intrigue and you can't trust them—anyway you're far too young to tie yourself down to one woman." Porthos was a bit of a lad himself and knew most of the ladies in question. "Come now, we've to meet the others in the tavern and my throat is dry as dust." Both Musketeers strolled across the town just in time to see their two friends disappear into the tavern.

"Good, you've got the drinks in already—D'Artagnan and I are gagging."
He banged one leather-clad boot on the table and asked, "What are we here to
discuss then?"

Athos wasn't in the mood for Porthos's humour and said, "We're here to talk
about the identity of the Man in the Iron Mask—it's unjust that anyone is treated
like that—more so when people don't know who he is or what he's accused of."
He spoke with authority and the others listened intently. He was the natural
leader of the group.

Aramis banged his tankard on the table and said, "I think we should visit the
governor of the Bastille and say we are there at the King's command—we can
say we must check the security arrangements around the prisoner." He turned to
Athos, "You know the governor, so you should approach him on our behalf."

"Right," Athos interrupted, "Let's get on with it. You never know what we
might find. Times are changing fast—Louis XIV is now settled on the throne
although his mother still has his ear—but the horrific conditions surrounding that
man remain unchanged. Let's see what we can do—but keep our mission close
to your heart—Richlieu has ears at every door and already knows we four are
not on his side."

Queen Anne was being waited on by Constance, the maid who helped the
Duke of Buckingham return to England. This had made her a particular enemy
of Richelieu's. The Queen spoke, "You must go to the convent outside Paris, so
you are safe from the Cardinal's clutches—you'll be protected there by the
Mother Superior." Queen Anne really cared for the woman's safety and gave her
a hand-written note to deliver—Constance in her turn, told D'Artagnan where
she was going, as she knew he would worry if she just disappeared—and
anyway, she knew he was completely trustworthy.

Richlieu's spy however was listening behind a screen and heard everything.
Her name was Milady de Winter and she too, was one of the ladies-in-waiting.
Of course, she went straight to Richlieu with the information. "She was the one
who destroyed our plan to thwart Queen Anne over the diamond studs—and
shouldn't be allowed to escape her punishment. Do you agree, Your Eminence?"
Richlieu nodded his head in thought. "You must go to the convent yourself and
give her a poisoned chalice to drink—you will be my instrument of death, it's
what she deserves."

In a few days, D'Artagnan and the three Musketeers, who'd been told of
Milady's instructions, also travelled to the convent outside the city and dashed

inside the building, thrusting some scared nuns out of their way. But they were too late, Milady had already given Constance the poisoned chalice and the unsuspecting girl had drunk the cup dry. She began to swoon and dropped slowly to the floor—Milady rushed from the convent just as the four Musketeers came into the room. D'Artagnan caught the girl in his arms but only in time to watch her die. He turned to his friends, "What can we do? Could there be an anecdote perhaps?" But he knew the answer—without knowing the poison used, no anecdote was possible. Porthos tried to comfort his friend but there was nothing to be done. D'Artagnan laid her reverently on a couch and set off with his companions in hot pursuit of the poisoner. She hadn't gone very far when they caught up with her and accused her of all the evil deeds for which she was known, including the murder of Constance. She showed no remorse and seemed proud of her accomplishments. The four Musketeers held their swords in a circle, the tips touching the same spot on the ground and sentenced Milady to death.

"You don't have the power to sentence me—and Richlieu will punish you if you do."

She spat at them and was shocked to hear Athos say, "Oh yes, we do have the power—as the King's henchmen—we are officers of the law and will take you back to Paris for your sentencing." He made towards her, meaning to tie her hands but she fooled him and pulled a knife from her bodice and, without hesitation, plunged it deep into her heart. A few seconds later, she was dead. Out of decency, they returned her body to the door of the convent and laid her there. She'd carried out her own sentence and there was nothing more they could do.

Back in Paris, when the Queen heard what had happened to Constance, she was devasted, "I thought I was sending her to safety—not to her death." She confronted the Cardinal but to no avail—he denied even knowing a Milady de Winter. "Your lady-in-waiting's death has nothing to do with me—do not try to involve me in your plots of intrigue. I will have to report this affront to your son, and we'll see what he has to say."

Richlieu stormed from the room. "Drat those Musketeers—they will have to be next on my list!"

They dressed in their most impressive uniforms, very smart and important and marched across the city towards the Bastille in perfect step. The Bastille was a depressing sight, with its reputation known all over Paris and local people kept well away. There was continued speculation about the Man made to wear the iron mask—the man with no name.

The Musketeers arrived at the Bastille and demanded to see the Governor on the King's business. Of course, they were immediately ushered into his office. Athos spoke first, "Sir, we are come to investigate the conditions under which you keep your prisoner, known only as the Man in the Iron Mask."

"Yes, that is what I understand. I suppose you already know I have safeguarded this prisoner for many years, and it has always been my duty to keep his identity secret—at the King's command." The Governor was suspicious of the Musketeers as there'd never before been an inspection such as this. "I will however allow you to see the prisoner, but you cannot do it alone—there must always be a guard present. Will that suffice?" They were accompanied by a big man with a set of keys hanging from his belt and they walked along several corridors, then down two flights of stairs. They were obviously in the bowels of the earth—in a deep, underground cellar.

The guard opened the cell door with a very large key and there sat against the wall, was a hooded figure. His head was bowed, and he held nothing in his hands. He didn't look up until the guard told him to stand up and pay attention to the gentlemen who'd come to visit him. He shuffled to his feet but kept staring at the floor.

Athos said, "Monsieur, we have come to see if you are being treated well. To see if there is anything we can do for you."

The man very slowly raised his head and looked through the eye-slits in the mask. His face was completely covered in iron but there was an opening for his mouth so he could feed himself. Athos could just see two eyes staring at him from the depths of the mask. The Man didn't speak—perhaps he couldn't—he may even have no voice after all the years he'd been like this. Even Porthos, the jovial one, couldn't lift the atmosphere and he asked, "Monsieur, can you tell us who you are, and do you know the reason you're being kept in these appalling conditions? We don't want you to tell us your secret—but we've come here at the command of the King to see how you are." *A little white lie wouldn't hurt, he thought.*

The Man tried to speak but the sound came out muffled. D'Artagnan strained to hear the words and looked at the others, "He's asking who the King is—which Louis is it?" And before anyone else spoke, he told the Man, "Why, he's King Louis XIV of France and he's been on the throne now for almost twenty years— have you ever met him?"

At the question, the guard stepped forward and indicated the visit was over. Porthos asked for just another few minutes and asked the Man, "Do you know how many years you've been imprisoned, Monsieur? Can you remember what you did to merit this treatment?"

Through the mouth slit, the Man suddenly spat and his saliva trickled down the mask. Porthos persisted, "Why do you spit at the name of the King? It is he who sent us here to check on your conditions." The man spat a second time and the big guard pushed all four Musketeers from the cell, escorting them back along the corridor and up the stairs until he brought them to the big front door of the prison. He opened the door and the four men found themselves evicted from the building into the street. Their visit was over and they hadn't learned much.

In the tavern, Aramis said, "Well, at least we know he has no love for the King—he couldn't have been more explicit, could he?" Aramis was quite upset and D'Artagnan looked sick, horrified by the whole incident.

Athos returned with the four tankards and said, "Well, I don't know how you all feel—but seeing what we did—has made me more determined to find out who he really is. He can't stay in that place for much longer. I think it's plain that he really is being kept there at the King's command—although why on earth should the King be so obsessed in keeping his identity a secret?"

The four military men fell silent, each thinking of that wretched man in the grotesque mask. "That poor face!" was all Porthos could say.

"I think we should ask for an audience with Queen Anne—if anyone can throw light on the situation, it'll be her. She must have been aware when her husband first imprisoned the man and sent him into exile—with no intention of ever releasing him. His imprisonment has spanned two reigning monarchs now—a very unusual situation, don't you think?" And of course, they did.

D'Artagnan was chosen as the one to request an audience with the old Queen—she knew him because of his relationship with her lady-in-waiting, Constance. She couldn't refuse to see him but she was wary when she found out it involved the Man in the Bastille. Richlieu heard what was going on and asked Queen Anne if she'd like him to be present as he didn't trust the Musketeers. She declined his offer as she trusted him even less.

Anne was getting on in years and she adored her son Louis. She'd been married twenty-two years before he was born and he was a healthy child, who had his brother Phillip join him just two years later. Phillip was called the 'Monsieur' as the second son and the name stuck with him into adulthood. The actual birthing of Louis had been a ceremonial affair with many important nobles present—this was quite usual at royal births. There were however, so many nobles and their ladies present that pandemonium ensued and the room had to be cleared so the Queen could get some air. This is how the whole procedure was later recorded but only the Queen's closest ladies-in-waiting were actually allowed near to the three-feet wide bed where the baby was born.

As was usual in the court of France, this scenario caused gossip amongst some courtiers and soon the gossip spread throughout the court. Whispers began to circulate—what did you see? I saw nothing. Did you see a baby? I didn't. Did you see the nurse leave the room carrying a bundle of linen? Yes, I did.

Queen Anne was now past sixty and her health was not good. Her son encouraged her to spend much of her time at Versailles—out of the clogged-up city, there, the air was fresher. Anne's son spent an enormous amount of money transforming what had once been his father's hunting lodge, into the greatest palace in Europe. Unfortunately, his morals were questionable and the place became known, not only for its beauty and luxury, but more for its debauchery and loose living.

King Louis XIV lived a long life (seventy-seven years), kept many mistresses, had many illegitimate children and was responsible for the neglect of his people which resulted in the Paris his great grandson inherited. Louis XV had to pay for his great grandfather's lack of care. When Louis XVI finally arrived, the people of the country had reached the end of their tether and both he and his wife, Marie Antoinette, lost their heads at the hands of the revolutionaries. Madame La Guillotine was also used to end the lives of many of the aristocrats who had cared only for themselves, allowing the people of France to starve— whilst the aristocracy enjoyed all the luxury money could buy.

Anne of course didn't suggest there was confusion around her son's birth— but it didn't take much to make the Musketeers consider the possibility. Of all the Musketeers, Aramis was closest to the Queen—he'd been a friend of hers for many years—in fact, it was common knowledge that they'd had a son together. It was all part of the court intrigue and it seemed that everybody had some hold on someone else and was not afraid to use the knowledge to blackmail. The son of Queen Anne and Aramis was immediately sent off to the country where a wet nurse raised him, receiving a pension from the Queen. Secrets were safe within the circle of the Musketeers and Aramis's own secret was quite safe.

Aramis's old relationship with the Queen allowed him to approach her about the man in the Bastille. He asked her if she knew who he was and what heinous crime had he committed to justify such a cruel punishment? Why couldn't he be released—and why was he forced to wear such a torturous and cruel mask? Why couldn't he be treated like the other prisoners in the Bastille? At first, the Queen decided to pretend an ignorance of the situation, but on being challenged, she admitted it had been her husband who first imprisoned the man. "I don't know what crime he committed," she explained, "but I only know it was important that no one ever knew who he was. And my son feels as his father did, having been made aware of the man's background. That's all I know, Aramis—I'm sorry but I can tell you nothing more." She gestured for her ladies to come into the room, so the conversation had to come to an end.

Unfortunately, she soon developed a condition which made her feel increasingly ill—she was told by the Physicians that she had a cancer in her breast and there was nothing could be done for her. She was at Versailles when death came and claimed her and for the first time, King Louis XIV felt completely free to rule. Since childhood, he had been under his mother's thumb—now he only had to contend with Cardinal Richlieu who frequently acted as though he was the King. The Musketeers knew they'd have to keep an even closer eye on Richlieu as they believed he'd never been the friend of the people of France—but only of himself.

Louis XIV was called the Sun King, a title spread initially from the court itself—and something of which the King approved. His emblem was the Sun itself and Louis believed he could do no wrong—he had been chosen by God. The Musketeers watched the King as they'd always found him to be a weak and self-indulgent ruler—and they hadn't given up on the Man in the Iron Mask, a subject they decided to speak the Cardinal about. With their responsibility to the country's Secret Service, Richlieu had to listen to them. However, he pretended no knowledge of the prisoner and he claimed he certainly didn't know what the man's crime had been.

"Leave the matter alone—I would not encourage you to get involved—it is a royal matter and nothing to do with the Musketeers. Should you persist with this line of enquiry, you may find you've bitten off more than you can chew—and then, I may have to become involved." His advice was cryptic and the friends left the palace none the wiser than they'd been before.

Athos was the most intellectual of the four friends and he set off on travels to visit the other prisons where the Man had been kept. He believed that this investigation would throw up some information and nothing was to be found at this point in time, so going back to the beginning might be useful. He visited the very first prison where the Man had been imprisoned—it was easy to find, as records had been kept and were accessible to such elevated figures as the Secret Service. It was a full month later that he finally reached the second prison, situated on a small island off the coast of Cannes—he'd found nothing at the first one—but had better hopes of the second. He was in luck and actually found an old guard who remembered the prisoner in the mask.

"Monsieur, can you remember him well? Did you ever speak with him? And did he tell you anything about himself?" Athos fired one question after another and then realised he should slow down as he was almost bullying the guard. "You are quite safe from me, Monsieur, I am part of the Government's Secret Service and I am sworn to an Act of Secrecy." The old guard did seem to relax at the news. His voice was rather croaky and Athos had to strain to hear his words.

"I remember him well, but of course, I never saw his face—even then he was forced to wear the iron mask—in fact, no one ever saw his face nor learned his name. I cannot tell you who the man was, I'm afraid." He'd obviously felt sorry for the prisoner and would have helped Athos if he could. "He was quite a young man, if I remember correctly—maybe even a teenager."

Out of politeness, the Musketeer spoke with the old man and passed an hour or so with him. When he stood up, the guard did the same and held out a shaky hand, "Goodbye Sir—it was nice to meet you. Safe journey to wherever you're going."

Athos thanked him and started for the door when the old guard called out, "As I said, I never learned his name—but we used to have a nickname for him—if that would help." Athos told him anything would help. "Vrajum, they used to call him—it was what he was called when he first came here and he always responded to it—but that's all I remember, I'm afraid. Vrajum—that was it."

Athos left and thanked him—at least it was something. He visited the next prison where the man had been kept—but he learned nothing new except the same nickname of 'Vrajum' which of course meant nothing to him. Back in Paris, his friends had been up to all kinds of mischief, led primarily by Porthos and D'Artagnan. They drank their fill almost every night—it was easy with Athos away. But the intellectual one was back and the first place he looked was

208

in the favoured tavern—and there they were, sprawled on chairs with a table covered in empty tankards.

Porthos was on his soapbox, "The people are starving and the King lives the life of Reilly at Versailles with all his mistresses and bastard children." Voices cheered him on and made him feel good, so he continued preaching until he spotted Athos.

Athos was welcomed—he had really been missed. "Have you heard the latest Brother—the King's wife has had a black baby? It was supposed to be a secret but you know the court, everything gets out eventually. Apparently, she had a black African pigmy who was a servant and he is the father of the black baby. The morals at Versailles are non-existent, wouldn't you agree? I have to say I am less enamoured of the Sun King than I used to be—maybe something should be done about it." D'Artagnan hushed him up quickly—he was talking out of turn and one never knew who was listening and who was in Richlieu's employ.

"Enough Gentlemen, your tongues are too loose—Richlieu's spies could be close." And he shepherded them out of the tavern where the night air hit them and made them unsteady on their feet. "Come Men—let's go to my lodgings, we have much to discuss, but first you'd all better sober up if I'm to get any sense out of you."

Much later, Aramis said, "Versailles has become a place of such debauchery and incest that it seems the King encourages everyone to behave as badly as they can—and of course, word leaks from the palace when servants return home to their families. Stories will soon spread. Louis believes himself to be an absolute monarch chosen by God himself—his every wish is carried out—he is a danger to himself, and to the country. Our reputation in Europe falls far short of good and France is losing its once-glorious name. The people are not well off although our country's getting bigger—Louis's overseas policies are adding to his wealth and land—but he pays little attention to the needs of the ordinary man. What can we do about it? Richlieu encourages him in everything he does and does not help the situation, I fear." The others agreed with all he said—but how does one deal with an absolute monarch such as Louis? The problem was huge.

"But tell us, Aramis, what did you discover in your travels? Anything that might help?" They were eager to hear his news, although things seemed hopeless at the time. And Athos filled them in on what he'd discovered which wasn't much.

The following week, the four friends—D'Artagnan was not yet a qualified Musketeer but was working on it—travelled out of the city to Versailles. They wanted to see for themselves how bad the place had become. It was bad—the smells and odours were foul—people sometimes used chamber pots and sometimes didn't bother. There was human faeces lying around some rooms and people would be eating in the midst of the filth. There was a gigantic hall where the King and Queen had thrones and held court—but it too was filthy and smelly. Not surprisingly, disease was prevalent there and people would sometimes take to their rooms and never be seen again. Many of the servants lived on the premises but many went home to their families, so stories about the place were soon all over Paris.

The Musketeers requested an audience with the King and were told that—for a fee—they could either watch him go to the toilet or eat his breakfast, the choice was theirs. Porthos joked, "I've seen men go to the toilet before so I'd rather pay to watch him eat. Perhaps he does tricks to entertain us, you never know." He gave one of his belly laughs and Athos told him to quieten down. The King dined late so they were still in time to join the fee-paying group who had already gathered.

Louis's intention was that Versailles would be the biggest and greatest place in the world and he poured vast wealth into it. When he married Marie Therese, he took her there to live. However, he also took the whole court and many aristocrats as well and that was one reason, caretaking in the palace was almost impossible. It was one of the busiest places on earth. He often referred to himself as the Sun King or the Great King—both titles he believed were correct. It was the terrible state of the palace that won him the third name people gave him—the Mad King. He may not have been mad but he was certainly eccentric—something he never believed for a moment.

His wife gave him six children but only one actually reached adulthood and that was another Louis. His wife died in her early forties and he was a bachelor again. He wasn't lonely for long as he had many mistresses but he did re-marry in secret—he married his children's governess—Francoise d'Aubigne, the Marquise de Maintenon. He spent most of his time hunting—he didn't care overmuch about the needs of his country. He used the phrase once 'L'Etait c'est moi' which means 'I am the State'—and the phrase was attributed to him thereafter.

He also chose this time in his reign to try to change the religion in France, which didn't help his popularity amongst many of the people. He was an ardent Catholic and one day, probably on a whim, he decided everyone In France should be Catholic too. At the time there were many Protestants in the country and it had been so for a long time. They were known as Huguenots and they'd been given freedom to practice by Louis's grandfather Henry, many years before in 1598. Louis decided this should now come to an end and that his own religion should be the sole one in France.

Following his decision, he ordered the prosecution of the Huguenots, and the taking away of their rights as citizens. He issued an Edict which ordered the destruction of Protestant Churches all over the land, the closure of Protestant schools and the forced baptism and education of children into the Catholic faith. His Edict forced more than 200,000 Huguenots to seek religious freedom in other European countries or in the new colonies in America. It's safe to say that this didn't bother Louis one little bit—his persecution of his own people was necessary in his eyes and that's all there was to it.

The fact that one of his explorers in 1682—Rene-Robert Cavelier Sieur de La Salle—claimed part of North America for King Louis XIV and named it Louisiana. In due course, Louisiana seceded to the United States of America—but that didn't deter from the glory Louis rewarded himself at the time. He was the Sun King after all.

On the day in question however, Athos, Aramis, Porthos and D'Artagnan had gathered with others to watch the King eat breakfast—and of course, pay for the privilege. When it was over, they asked a court official if they could have a private word with the King. The answer was no, they could not—but Richlieu suddenly appeared at the door and spotted the Musketeers. He crossed towards them, "What do you want of the King, gentlemen? He is not used to be bothered this early in the day. Perhaps I can help?" He was smiling but the humour never reached his eyes.

They knew they were not going to succeed in seeing the King, so Porthos blurted out, "I don't believe you can help us, unless you can tell us who is the Man in the Iron Mask."

Richlieu gave a quick intake of breath and almost panicked at the question. "I can tell you nothing about him and I assure you the King couldn't do so either. Now, before I leave you, is there anything else you want to ask?"

The friends knew they were beaten and turned to leave the palace. "Let's go, Friends—there's nothing for us here and I see the King is ready to set out on a hunt. We are left with the same problem we came with." And they returned to Paris and picked up their normal duties.

A month later, they again visited the Bastille and asked the Governor if they could see the man again. They were accompanied this time by a fifth man who followed them closely. This time, they were questioned more deeply as to why they wanted to see the prisoner. And who was that fifth man? They used the Secret Service again to put pressure on the Governor and ignored the question about the fifth man. In the end, they called for the same guard that they'd met before. This time, the Man in the Mask seemed older and more bent than before. He still kept his head bowed but grunted in recognition of his visitors. Athos indicated to the fifth man that he should move closer to the prisoner—he'd been brought along to examine the fastenings on the iron mask. He was a locksmith and good at his trade. He looked closely at the mask and just nodded his head to Athos before stepping back.

Before they left the cell, Athos asked the guard, "Monsieur, you've looked after the prisoner for some time now—is that correct?" The guard agreed that he had, "Well then, have you ever heard him called 'Vrajum'?" The guard said he had heard that name before and when the Man had first come, the name was used more than it was now. The Musketeers looked at each other meaningfully.

"Our plan could work, if we all play our parts well." D'Artagnan was eager to attempt the audacious plan. "You, of all of us, must try to be quiet—people can usually hear you approach from a distance." He chastised the loud Porthos.

"Don't know what you mean, Old Boy—are you trying to say I'm loud?" he laughed as D'Artagnan nodded his head vigorously. Porthos went on, "Well as long as we don't intend the plan to kick off until next week then I'll be fine. I have to go on a hunt tomorrow near Versailles and I can't get out of it, I'm afraid."

"Next week will be soon enough—don't worry. You go off on your hunt and enjoy yourself. We'll start work on what's needed and by next week, we'll be ready. We'll remove his mask and smuggle him out of the Bastille. As to what we'll do with him then—well, that's still to be decided." Aramis spoke with more confidence than he actually felt.

The news was all around the tavern the next night when Athos and Aramis arrived. "Have you heard what has happened to your friend? He was brought through the market this evening on a stretcher—he was dead as a doornail."

In an offhand way, Aramis asked who it was.

"Why, your friend—the big bloke with the belly laugh—don't know his name."

The two Musketeers looked at each other, "You don't mean Porthos, do you? No, of course, you don't." But he looked suddenly scared. "Where have they taken him?" Athos asked.

"To the mortuary at the Musketeers' Headquarters—where else would they take him? The Captain of the Guard is already there apparently." And the customer went off to the bar for another drink.

The two ran all the way through the market until they reached the mortuary. "Will you go in first, Athos—I don't think I can do this?" Athos was only gone for a few minutes when he reappeared with the Captain of the Guard. Both men were ashen and all Athos did was nod his head to Aramis.

"It is Porthos, I'm afraid. He was hunting and his legs suddenly folded under him. They wanted to bring him back to the city, but he insisted on going on with the hunt. His legs failed him a second time—and then he was dead—as simple as that."

D'Artagnan appeared behind them—he'd run all the way when he heard. "Too late, Old Man," the Captain told him, "I'm afraid your friend died before they even reached the city."

D'Artagnan began to cry—he was after all just nineteen—and he'd really liked Porthos.

"We've lost our cheerful friend—the one whose glass was always half full— it's like we've lost a limb." Was all Athos could say.

The Captain of the Guard stepped forward, "This may not be the right time— but I don't think there'll ever be one—so, listen to me." He looked at D'Artagnan as he spoke, "I hereby award you the status of Musketeer, I know how much you want it. Visit the staff room tomorrow and they'll give you a proper uniform." He looked then at both Athos and Aramis, "I realise you may think I am being callous—but I assure you I'm not—it's always been our policy to replace a lost man as quickly as possible. D'Artagnan will now be your colleague—is that clear?" And he walked back into the mortuary, leaving the three sad men alone.

"I'll try really hard—honest I will. I'll make you proud of me, see if I don't." He was still crying about Porthos. The two others drew their swords and pointed the tips to the ground, indicating that D'Artagnan should do the same. They all swore the oath, D'Artagnan loudest of all, "All for one and one for all." And they truly meant it as time would tell.

One week later, they met up with their friend, the locksmith, and explained what they wanted him to do. Athos spoke quietly, "We'll go to the Bastille during the night—don't worry about getting in—we'll take care of that. We'll then require you, using your special tools, to undo the locks that hold the iron mask in place. You will have to work gently and carefully, as we have no way of knowing how the skin will have been affected throughout the years. As explained before, you will be paid handsomely for your services but—and I can't stress this enough—you will never speak of your part in this matter. Remember who we are—the Secret Service will never stop searching for you, should you break your word to us."

The locksmith replied, "For the money you're going to pay me, why should I tell anyone what I've done? I presume we will be breaking the law, so all the more reason to keep my mouth shut." They had to be satisfied with that!

The night was dark with no moon and the stars were too far away to shed much light on the small group of men who walked towards the Bastille. The building was formidable and threatening as they reached the front door. Athos held his gloved finger to his lips, reminding the others that silence was all important. He inserted the large key in the lock and turned it slowly. It worked and they heard the lock's click—the door was open.

Athos gently pushed it further open and could feel on his face the damp cold of the interior. He beckoned the others to follow him and they all went silently into the main hall. They should meet no resistance—the place was deathly silent as they picked their way along the corridors and down the steep stairs towards the cellar. Athos had paid one of the other guards handsomely to put a sleeping drug in the big guard's last glass of wine at supper. He was the only one who looked after the 'special prisoner in the mask.'

They passed the huge body of the sleeping guard—he was snoring like a pig and his bunch of keys lay on the table by his side. Athos picked them up quietly. The men had to feel their way towards his cell, but they knew well where the Man in the Mask was. The walls were damp with a wet slime running to the floor—their fingers slipped on the surface and they were glad they'd worn

214

gloves. The door opened easily and Athos whispered, "Don't be afraid—we are friends come to help you and he brought a candle from the folds of his cloak and used his tinder box to light it." The Man in the Mask had stood up, obviously alarmed but he could hear the kindness in Athos's voice so he made no sound.

The locksmith moved towards the prisoner and opened a small case he'd brought with him. He beckoned for Athos to hold the candle flame closer to the mask and he brought out a long, sharp ruler-like instrument and a small mallet. He began to examine the screws that held the mask in place and carefully inserted the sharp instrument into the workings of the hideous covering. For some reason, he fell forwards and swore as the ruler slipped into the Man's neck.

D'Artagnan whispered, "Be careful, man—you'll hurt him." The blood was seeping from the wound and dripping down onto the man's shoulder.

Athos interrupted him, "Can I do something to help? We can't injure him in this way." The locksmith continued to work on his task, but even more blood appeared. There was nothing they could do—they had to finish what they'd started—so they watched the locksmith use his mallet to force the sharp ruler into the workings of the mask. The Man in the Mask suddenly fell forward, his head hanging downwards under the heavy weight of the iron. The mask fell to one side and the group of men saw a face for the first time. It was scarred and pock-marked but his features were quite visible.

The men fell back in amazement. Aramis spoke first, "It's the King—how can this be? My God, that face is the face of our King Louis, isn't it?" The mask fell to the floor and the man did likewise into a pool of his own blood.

Athos felt for a pulse and then put his ear to the Man's chest. "He's dead—My God—you've killed him." He turned towards the locksmith, who was returning his instruments to the box. He was quite cool and calm and not in the least bothered that he'd messed up the task he'd been set. The Man's death seemed of little importance to him.

"You meant to do that, didn't you? You came with us with the express purpose of killing him—it was no accident, was it?" But the locksmith was already on his way to the door, obviously intending to make a quick escape.

"Get him!" Aramis spoke louder than he intended. "Get him—he mustn't be allowed to leave here alive—or he'll carry the tale about our part in all this." He drew his sword and pointed it at the locksmith, "Who are you working for? Who told you to do this?"

"You'd better let me go," he said. "My master is Cardinal Richlieu himself and he will avenge me should you hurt me." He was pleading now. There were three of them after all.

"You!" said Athos. "Richlieu will do nothing to avenge you. He cares for no one but himself. We however, will avenge the Man lying there. You're nothing less than a murderer and we will be your executioner—not your murderer. Grab him, we'll take him outside." He looked down at the body of the Man they'd wanted to help—and made the sign of the cross on his head. "There's nothing more we can do here—we came to help him—and we failed."

All of them made their way back to the front door of the prison and pushed the locksmith outside.

"Well D'Artagnan, you wanted to be a Musketeer—just like us! We have killed many times in our lives, now it's your turn. You must run him through—he mustn't be allowed to leave this place tonight."

Without hesitation, D'Artagnan drew his sword and stuck it into the man who'd cheated them—he stuck it right up to the hilt.

"Let's go—leave him here! When they find the Man inside, they'll probably put two and two together and blame this liar for his murder." The three Musketeers disappeared into the night—each in a different direction, but at the corner of the street, they glimpsed back to the prison door and saw there, the upright figure of the Man in the Iron Mask. His head was held proudly and the marks had disappeared from his face. There was no mask in sight. He raised one arm in a goodbye gesture and slowly walked down the street towards the River Seine. At last he was free!

The three friends met up next day in their favourite tavern. At first, no one spoke, they were still upset from their failed attempt to release the Man in the Iron Mask. "I've been thinking—in fact I've been thinking all night about his nickname 'Vrajum. Why that name? It's nothing in our language so what could it mean?"

Athos, the thinker of the group, said hesitantly, "Vrajum may mean nothing but what about Vrai Jumeaux? Could that have been the name they used for him throughout the years? It could have just been shortened in use. Do either of you know what a 'Vrai Jumeaux' is?"

"It means Identical Twin which would explain the Man's looks—take away the scars and pock marks and it could have been King Louis XIV himself. When the King was born, there must have been two of them and one was made to disappear to the prison on the Island near Cannes. As the child grew, he would have looked just like the King and so the decision was made to cover his face permanently. Queen Anne, Louis XIII, Louis XIV and Richlieu must have known of the twins but also that one would have to disappear." Aramis spoke confidently—now they were getting somewhere.

"There couldn't be two heirs to the throne—that could have had disastrous implications and caused friction between the sons—so it was logical to remove one of them. I've actually heard this possibility spoken of before—but never gave it any credence." Aramis was more excited than the others had ever seen him before, "And that would explain the strange story about the Queen's birthing—when the court was cleared of everyone. There was one baby too many."

D'Artagnan and Aramis were listening in amazement, and Aramis said. "Do you mean to tell us that poor man was encased in that cruel mask and imprisoned for life—just because of his birth—something he couldn't help?"

The three men sat quietly and supped their ale. "The whole thing is too unbelievable for words," D'Artagnan felt really miserable. "And in the end, we didn't help much, did we?"

Aramis slapped him on the back, "Think of it another way, we helped put him out of his misery. Living to him must have been sheer hell. And do remember when we were walking away from the Bastille—when we all saw the ghost of the Man in the Iron Mask walk tall and straight out of the prison and go towards the river—and to his freedom—and wearing no iron mask. He looked like a happy man, didn't he? Anyway, aren't you glad to have finished off that butcher of a locksmith?"

"I most certainly am! Nothing has ever given me so much pleasure! How could he have killed that poor man with us all standing there?" He looked at the other two and asked, "What do we do now?"

"I'm afraid our days as Musketeers are over—we just wouldn't ever be safe in Paris. Richlieu would soon have us picked off one by one—we'd be sitting targets. You never know, he may even have had something to do with Porthos's death. But it is a great pity our plan to save the man failed. The King, who believes himself to be the Sun King, is not as popular as he once was. He spends money on lavish living and in increasing the size of Versailles. I can't help wonder if his twin brother would have made a better king—he couldn't have been worse, could he? In the meantime, the people of France continue to suffer with no money and no food." Aramis was saddened by his own words.

"When I saw him and the mask dropped off, I began to think we might be able to exchange him with King Louis and make France a better place, with a better King—but that's not to be now, I'm afraid." Athos was almost preaching to the others—everything had gone wrong. What he was suggesting would have been difficult, but not impossible. However, it certainly was now.

The three Musketeers left Paris—D'Artagnan returned home to Gascony where he worked for his father; Aramis too returned to the place he was born and settled there with a new wife. Athos found he couldn't stay away from the city where it was all happening and in 1642, when he heard Richlieu had died of tuberculosis, he went back to the Musketeers and was made Captain of the Guard—he did have exceptional experience of the organisation.

Well, that was Paris in the seventeenth century—full of great richness for those near to the King or full of poverty, if you were one of the people. As the author, I would like to ask you, the reader if you believe everything I've told you is the truth or is it just most of what I've told you? Was Louis XIV so in love with himself that he had no time for anyone else—in fact records show that the people stood in the streets as his coffin passed and hissed and booed? I think this answers that question, don't you? A good thing he never saw that or it would have shattered his illusions about himself. Were the Musketeers as chivalrous and honest as I've painted them? I believe they were, but I could be wrong of course.

And the biggest question—was the Man in the Iron Mask really the identical twin of King Louis XIV of France? It's up to you to make up your own mind but I can confirm that they did bury a man who died in the Bastille in 1703—he was about fifty years of age and his name was Eustache Dauger. There was speculation at the time that he had been a valet to Cardinal Mazarin, first minister to the King Louis XIII.

The story goes that he knew secrets about Mazarin and all the money and Estates he stole from the Crown—and he made the mistake of blabbing about it. That was almost the kiss of death for him but instead, he was imprisoned for life and made to wear an iron mask. But I think his crime would have been easier to deal with by just killing him and stop his blabbing—after all killing people was quite commonplace at the time. But instead, they chose to return his body to the small island off the coast of Cannes, where he'd begun his incredible journey.

Again, the decision about who the Man in the Iron Mask really was—is yours and yours alone—no one has ever proved anything definite about his identity. And many years have passed since it all happened—so no one can ever know for sure now.

Two Queens Meet at Last

"No, you were not—I was her. You're just trying to steal my thunder." Beth playfully pushed her friend's shoulder and reached for the last slice of pizza. Lizzie beat her to it however and tried to stuff it all into her mouth at one go.

"Greedy Pig—that was my slice." Still feeling hungry, Beth was seriously disgruntled and swore under her breath.

"I heard that and I'll tell your mother. Anyway, to get back to the subject in hand, I was Mary Queen of Scots in a previous life. You could never have been her—you don't have the dignity and queenly presence like what I do!" She laughed at her own bad grammar.

The two girls were 17 years of age and went to college where they both studied the same subjects, one being Psychology. They'd been friends for a couple of years and their similar characters and interests meant they also enjoyed the same things when not studying. They both believed strongly in re-incarnation and often shared their thoughts when one or the other experienced moments of Deja-vu. Of course, it didn't happen too often, but when it did—it was the most amazing thing in the world. Tonight, they were bickering about who had once been Mary Queen of Scots in an earlier life.

"You don't sound even the tiniest bit Scottish, you silly girl." Beth had found a bar of chocolate she'd hidden in her bag some time ago—but it was still edible—and staved off her hunger for a short time. She was feeling rather frightened however and knew something was coming—it always happened like this—the soul of the dead fighting to come alive in the body of their chosen mortal. Her head felt heavy and she could feel the usual numbness creep over her. It was the feeling of Deja-vu.

"Ach, awa' the 'noo Hen! Whit dae ye mean?" Lizzie's Scottish accent left a lot to be desired and Beth had to laugh despite her feelings of impending doom. She also pointed out that Mary had been brought up in France and her accent would have been French not Scottish, but that fell on deaf ears. "But I am serious,

Beth, when I claim to have lived in the sixteenth century—it may not have been as the Queen but I have felt this way for some time now."

Beth interrupted her, "Lizzie, I can actually see the ring around my neck where my head was cut off. Beat that, if you can!" She held up her long hair to show her friend the mark.

Lizzie admitted, "I can see a faint line around your neck but lots of people have those—they're called Venus Lines and have nothing to do with a beheading."

"I assure you this ring is the mark of a sharp axe. What really scares me is the executioner actually missed when he struck the Queen's neck and then missed a second and third time. It was a blood bath in the end. In fact, he was a rubbish executioner—and when he held her head aloft, it fell onto the floor and then rolled across it. And there was the Queen's head—not with glorious auburn hair, but with short, white hair—she'd been wearing a wig, you see. He shouted 'Long Live the Queen'—and he meant Queen Elizabeth of England and not poor Mary whom he'd just despatched."

Beth's face was ashen now and she looked pretty scared. "Are you taking me seriously?" She was getting angry now and Lizzie told her to calm down. In fact, both of them calmed down and didn't speak for at least 5 minutes.

They separated after that—things were getting too hot to handle—Beth left her friend's flat to go home. She sauntered along the road thinking about how great Lizzie's shared interest in re-incarnation was. Odd really, how quickly the two of them had become such close friends—like kindred spirits. She too had experienced similar bouts of Deja-vu when she seemed to be in another world and in a different time. Lizzie seemed equally convinced however about her spiritual feelings. Beth had read and researched the subject for over a year now—she was better informed than her friend about the effects of believing in re-incarnation could have on people—but Lizzie's feelings were obviously genuine as well.

Snuggling under the covers that night, her mind was still full of Mary Queen of Scots—and she was aware of what a sad life the woman had led. She had been born to wear the crown and was only 6 years old when her father died—so young a child that her French mother, Mary of Guise, had taken her to live at the French court until she grew up. This was to protect her from the many political factions always ready to use the little girl to steal the power of the monarchy. So from childhood, the Scottish Queen was destined not to grow up in the land of her birth, bonny Scotland.

Beth knew she would dream about the unfortunate Queen—but she knew too, it probably wouldn't be just a dream—it would seem like something very real. She believed that Lizzie too had such dreams, but that's all they were in her case—just dreams. Her own dreams were more like actual memories of the things the Scottish Queen had experienced in her life—and now they were invading Beth's own life.

Sleep was difficult that night and suddenly she felt the dampness and icy coldness of the walls all around her. She knew she was in a prison of sorts, in fact she knew she was in Fotheringhay Castle, awaiting the decision of her jailer and cousin, Queen Elizabeth 1 of England. She sat up and wrapped her woollen shawl around her trembling shoulders—what was that noise—was it just the scurrying of mice around the room, searching for crumbs of food. She didn't like the mice but then, they too were forced to live here with no escape.

She'd been imprisoned now for almost nineteen years and despite her pleas to Elizabeth, no positive reply was forthcoming. All she wanted was to be released into freedom and be the Queen of her own country—she had very few illusions about sitting on the English throne—that belonged to her cousin, the Virgin Queen, but there were still factions of people who wanted to make her Queen of two countries. Although tempted, she had made very little attempt to bring it about—but she had had to pay for other's audacity by being locked away in this prison.

She crossed the room and saw through the iron bars of the window, that dawn was fast approaching. Another day in captivity. She poured herself a beaker of water—even the water tasted rank—but at least it was wet and soothed her dry throat. At that thought, she clasped her slender neck and shuddered. She had no friends and even the Scottish government had forced her to abdicate in favour of her 1-year-old son, James. Even her own people had no use for her.

I'll write to Elizabeth again—and swear she has nothing to fear from me. I am but an old woman—and she touched her now white hair, pure white although she was only 44 years old—*I'll remind her again of our shared family blood line. Perhaps it may prick her conscience this time.* Even as she planned these words, she knew Elizabeth was stubborn and made of sterner stuff and had heard the same plea many times before.

"Your Majesty, Mary—are you yet awake?" She looked down at her frayed nightshirt and longed for the clothes she used to wear in better times. She was still vain although her beauty had faded with years of being denied the warmth of the sun on her face. God, her jailers kept a close eye on her.

"Bring me my writing things, Mary—I wish to write to my cousin again. maybe this time God will open her ears and her heart and make her listen to my pleas." Mary Seaton was the only lady-in-waiting she had left now—the other four Marys had left her for various reasons—but Mary Seaton had no wish to marry, and for this the Queen was grateful. Her fingers were very cold and she asked for her gloves to try and make her fingers move more easily, but it didn't always work, as they were covered in ever-increasing chilblains.

As Mary was writing, Beth finally slipped into a deep sleep and so, for the time being, she was no longer the unhappy Queen. It was a merciful release and although she twisted and turned, she was at least free from the impending doom that waited for her in the bitterly cold castle. She'd been there and she'd thought as the Queen thought—in fact, she'd physically been Mary and knew how much she was suffering. . Today was going to be odd because she still felt heavily depressed and in her mind, she was Mary, desperately writing to Queen Elizabeth again and begging for her freedom.

"Lizzie, will you be at home if I pop over to see you?" Beth telephoned her friend as she had to talk to someone about what was happening to her—and Lizzie was the only person who'd understand…

She arrived late afternoon and Lizzie called out for her to come in. "What's wrong—I thought we weren't going to see each other today?"

"I know—I know—but I had to talk to you. I believe even more now in my reincarnation. Lizzie—last night, I really was Mary Queen of Scots—in fact I still am." She sounded desperate and Lizzie quickly dashed into the kitchen to make them both a coffee.

As she disappeared, she shouted over her shoulder, "How strong is this feeling, Beth? And how can you be both? "

"It's the strongest I've felt for a long time. You do realise we both can't claim to be the Scottish Queen—only one of us could have inherited her soul. Were you serious when you said you were Mary—or were you just sending me up?" She was feeling quite desperate. She twisted her long hair round and round her fingers—something she always did when she felt confused and unsure.

"Well, yes, I was exaggerating a bit I suppose—but I do experience Deja-vu now and again—in fact, I think that's one of the reasons you and I ended up friends—because we feel the same things. Those feelings drew us together. I believe wholeheartedly that I've inherited a spirit from Elizabethan times—I'm not sure who it was—but I do feel close to Mary Queen of Scots and her problems. That's all I can tell you, I can't explain it."

"I think you're right but I don't know if I like it. Just now, I feel both heart broken and scared about what's going to happen to me—I know what 'they' do the Queen and I don't want to experience that. From my research, I've learned that the dead person's soul can do one of two things—either adopt and enter a new-born baby's body immediately at the moment of its birth—or let the soul lie dormant for periods of time in a sort of limbo, and then choose when to enter a new life. Some religions believe in it strongly and call it continuous rebirth of the soul. That's what they mean by eternal life, I suppose! Does any of that make sense, Lizzie?"

"Of course it does and it explains so much. So, if you believe you're Mary Queen of Scots, then her soul must have adopted you when you were born. Yet, it's only been recently that you've experienced her presence, isn't it? That's odd! I wonder why she waited all those centuries before choosing." Lizzie looked thoughtful. "Or—is it possible that she's been in and out of other people's bodies throughout the years between then and now? That makes sense, doesn't it?"

"We just don't know, do we? All I can tell you is that I am very afraid of what's still to come. Can I stay here tonight? I don't think I want to be alone just now. In fact, I think I can feel 'them' coming to get me." Beth was genuinely afraid.

"Where is my Lady Mary? I need her." Beth looked completely different all at once and Lizzie was suddenly afraid too.

"Who is Lady Mary, Beth?" she asked.

"Why do you call me Beth—my name is Mary, as is the name of my Lady-in-waiting—Mary Seaton." Beth was sitting upright in her chair and actually had the straight-backed bearing of a Queen. "Refrain from calling me Beth—that is a derivative of Elizabeth, my cousin—and I am most certainly not she or I would have shown mercy to such as myself by now." She even spoke like a Queen.

"Beth—Mary—look at me—it's Lizzie—I'm your friend. I want to help you." Her eyes felt as if they were bulging out of her head—she'd never actually witnessed such a thing before. Should she argue with Beth and try to bring her back to the present, or should she just agree with what was happening? She decided the latter was the wisest and easiest so she tentatively asked, "Where is your lady-in-waiting now, Your Majesty?"

"I do not know, the wicked girl has disappeared and is remiss in her neglect of me. I require her to dress my hair, something at which she is very good." Queen Mary indicated the hairbrush lying on the table. Lizzie picked it up and was grateful that she'd left it lying around in her untidy flat.

"Gentle, girl, my hair is very frail and may come out on the bristles." So, Lizzie brushed as gently as she could. Suddenly, Queen Mary turned her head, "Who are you? I do not think I recognise you. Have you come from the kitchen to help?"

"No, Your Majesty, I am not from the kitchens. I am just one of your friends." Lizzie's hands were shaking and she almost dropped the hairbrush, but she pulled herself together and got on with the job in hand.

"I know who you are now—you are my cousin, Elizabeth, and have been no friend of mine. Are you now responding to my letters, my prayers—and come to see me? Have you come to take me away from here—to offer me my freedom with England's protection?" Lizzie really didn't know how to answer, so she said nothing. She sat down on the chair opposite.

"How are you Cousin? Do you feel well?" Lizzie decided to play her part in Beth's drama.

"I am well, Elizabeth, but feel so much better for having seen you at last— all these years and we've never met, yet we share a bloodline." She sighed deeply and seemed to slump in the chair. "I have had a difficult life, cousin—I fear I have not always made the right decisions—but I love my country and my people. I want only the best for them. I know my son James has already taken on my crown and I shall never wear it again—but if I could live the rest of my life in peace and under your protection, I would be content."

Suddenly, Lizzie felt the spirit of the Virgin Queen, Elizabeth I of England invade her body. It was the strangest feeling but she knew without a doubt, whom she'd become. Perhaps it was the depth of feeling Mary was showing that made the whole situation possible—after all she truly believed her visitor was her cousin. Either way, she knew now why she was here and what she had to do— she realised she wasn't playing a part—she really was Elizabeth. She knew too that Mary blamed her for her present situation although much of it was her own doing. She'd made some stupid decisions in her time.

"Madam, the truth is as you say—your life has been an unfortunate one—but some of it has been your own fault." Queen Elizabeth felt it only fair to remind her cousin of the wrong choices she'd made in her life. She had long wanted to do that and she did it with gusto. Mary had indeed behaved impetuously and perhaps selfishly in her life, married badly and been involved in plots against Elizabeth—but she had paid for each one of them in the twists and turns of her life, the last nineteen years of imprisonment being part of her punishment.

Elizabeth knew full well that she hadn't come to see the Scottish Queen in order to take her away from Fotheringhay, but she didn't want to have to say it. Mary would prove too dangerous to Elizabeth's own future—after all she still claimed to have a better right to the English throne and had already been implicated in several attempts to sit on both the English and Scottish thrones. She had always claimed that Elizabeth was an illegitimate child of Henry VIII and should never have inherited it in the first place. In Mary's eyes, Elizabeth was a bastard.

No, Mary could never be rescued from here—in fact, Elizabeth had just signed her cousin's death warrant. She had signed the document that would send her ministers hot foot to this place and execute Mary immediately. This was something she would later deny of course, claiming to have been deluded into thinking she was signing something more trivial. (Yet, historic documents revealed she had actually signed three separate death warrants. Her subsequent denial of signing them was merely an attempt to disassociate herself from the decision. *Lizzie was glad she'd studied Psychology in university!*

Both Queens now sat in the dark, dank room, surrounded by bare stone walls—they stared into each other's eyes and neither spoke for a few minutes because neither knew what to say. Mary, because she feared her cousin had not come to help her—and Elizabeth, because she knew about the recently signed death warrant.

Mary suddenly raised both hands and held them out in front of her, "Do compare our hands, Cousin—they are identical, are they not?" And sure enough, both pairs of hands were long, slender and white.

"They are indeed." Elizabeth conceded. Although something small, at least they could agree on it.

The door opened quietly and Mary Seaton entered. She bowed before her mistress and fell to her knees. She didn't see or sense the Elizabeth's presence.

"May I do something for you, Majesty—is there anything you need?" Mary Seaton was devoted to her mistress and was the only one of the original 'Four Marys' who had served the Queen since she was a young girl. There had been 4 Marys and of course, Queen Mary herself. Five Marys was unusual!

"It is time, Your Majesty, and I have been sent to prepare you. Firstly, allow me to fix your best wig in place and help you dress. You still wish to wear the crimson petticoat beneath your gown, is that right?" Mary Seaton kept her eyes lowered in humility and in love.

"Oh yes Mary, I must. Dress me well—as I must look my best and show no fear. I have just enjoyed a conversation with my cousin, Elizabeth—the only conversation we've ever had. But at least, we've met at last and spoken. I feel better for that, although it seems she has not come to release me, just to say good-bye."

Mary Seaton believed her mistress was imagining things, but she was allowed to do this, if anyone ever did. She dressed the queen as gently as she could and stood back against the wall as a Priest entered the room. He blessed the Queen and heard her confession. Mary declared before God that she intended her cousin Elizabeth no harm and had only wanted to be released from Fotheringhay Castle and live a free life again. "I stand accused of being a traitor—but before God, I am no Traitor to the English Queen." These words were the most serious in her confession.

"Have you asked the ministers from England—those who have come to witness my death—if I can have a stay of execution for a while, so I can better prepare myself to meet my maker?" She looked at the priest hopefully but could see from his downcast eyes that there was no hope of this. She had only been told the previous day that she was to die on the 8 February 1587. The suddenness of it had and she felt suddenly panicked and confused her and she wasn't even sure which day it actually was.

"I did try, Your Majesty—but was told over and over again that 'You must die now.' They wouldn't listen to me and chose to ignore me, continuing to repeat their words over and over again. I am truly sorry to have failed you." She held out her hand to him and he bent to kiss her fingers.

Lizzie as Queen Elizabeth, was still watching the doomed Queen as she talked with the priest. Her persona was changing and she was only partly Queen Elizabeth now, with the other half being Lizzie herself. She watched the situation unfold, knowing that if she said the wrong thing now, it could hurt her friend whilst she was in this traumatic state. She was Mary Queen of Scots after all. The Scottish Queen stood up and stretched her stiff back—something she'd suffered from throughout the years—and the damp prisons hadn't helped. In fact, she was riddled with rheumatics—and always in pain. She was tall for a woman and stood six feet in height—she was elegant and graceful—but her height didn't always help with her back pain and caused her to stoop—yet still she maintained the pride and bearing of a true Queen.

"We must go now to the castle hall—I assume everything there has been made ready for me? I am glad it is to be inside the castle as the February chill would make me shiver—and I mustn't look afraid, must I?" Mary Seaton nodded and wiped the tears from her eyes. She really loved her mistress. Climbing onto the specially built platform, Mary looked around the room and was astonished by the number of people who'd come to see her lose her head. "See how many people have come to see me die?" she asked of no one in particular.

Lizzie also found herself in the castle hall watching the little tableau gather. She realised they'd only moved across her sitting room—but the bitterly cold atmosphere was that of a draughty castle. It was quite surreal. She had become just one of the spectators now—and waited 'till Mary climbed the stairs onto the wooden platform. Mary Seaton removed her mistress's headdress and her outer black gown.

As planned, Mary wore beneath the gown a bright crimson petticoat with long sleeves which would be recognised by the crowd as the colour worn by martyrs—something she wholeheartedly believed she was. She had not been involved with the very recent plot to assassinate her cousin—that had been some of her loyal countrymen—but she had not taken part. Her crimson petticoat claimed her as a martyr, dying for her beliefs in Catholicism and not for any treasonous act—and this despite her closeness in blood to the English Queen.

The executioner stepped forward and Mary turned to look at him—he asked her to forgive him for what he was about to do. Mary's voice didn't falter as she replied, "I thank you, Sir, and forgive you with all my heart—for now I hope you shall make an end of all my troubles."

Her eyes were covered with a silk blindfold and she knelt down, placing her head on the block—before stretching wide both arms to either side. Still with a strong voice and great dignity, she said clearly, "Into thy hands Oh Lord, I commend my soul." Words once spoken by Jesus himself as he died on the Cross.

The axe came down quickly but failed to achieve its objective. Although there was much blood, Mary's head was not severed from her body—and it took a second, then a third strike before her head finally fell to the ground—and rolled across the floor. A statesman grabbed the head by the hair but was shocked to find himself actually holding the lady's wig. Mary's close-cropped, white hair shocked everyone present—she had been only 44 years of age and prematurely old.

As blood seeped from the body, Mary's little pet dog crept from beneath her skirts and lay down at her shoulder—unwilling to move away from its loving mistress. Eventually, a servant took the dog away—it needed to be washed, its coat being covered with much of Mary's blood.

Lizzie had seen all of this as it happened. She was shaking with shock—but now she'd actually been part of it. She'd been Elizabeth 1, the Virgin Queen and witnessed the Scottish Queen's horrific death. Beth's crumpled form was lying against the room wall. She was pale and sweating, both at the same time. Lizzie brought a face flannel and a bowl of cool water from the bathroom—she used it to bathe her friend's face. Beth was out cold however and no matter how many times Lizzie called her name, the still figure on the carpet didn't move.

It was odd, but although she knew she was back in her own person and time, she still felt the misery and horror of what she'd just seen. So, this is what re-incarnation was all about—and yet, there were people who still didn't believe in it. Beth really had been Mary Queen of Scots at the point of her death and all she'd wanted more than anything else, was to be released from her imprisonment and allowed to live a free life again. Lizzie understood, now more than before, that those wishes could never have been granted—she had actually felt the suspicions and fear that the English Queen must have felt—fear that Mary would 'steal' the English throne from her.

She felt quite back to normal now—but still defiant in Elizabeth's cause— and knew it was Beth who'd experienced the trauma of the execution. She herself had just played a part in it all, but a very significant part, and was left with the strong belief that Elizabeth had had no choice. Mary had been her enemy and had to be dealt with. Lizzie was Queen Elizabeth for a time and now saw things more clearly.

Beth started to stir and raised herself onto her elbow. She stared at Lizzie and said, "Have you fed my little dog yet?"

"Don't worry, Beth, it's all been taken care of," Lizzie reassured her.

"Yes, I know who I am now—but for a time, I was Mary Queen of Scots, wasn't I?" She struggled onto her knees and clutched frantically at her neck. "The executioner made a hash of my beheading, didn't he? I already knew the history of what happened—but now I've actually experienced it—the fear and horror of everything. No one felt sorry for me—even my own cousin, Elizabeth." She shook herself and asked, "Can you please make me a cup of coffee—I need something to wake me up."

Strangely, Lizzie felt herself bristling as her friend's remarks—she knew what the English Queen had been up against—and why Mary's death had been inevitable. So, she said, "But my throne—I mean Elizabeth's throne—was in danger from the people who wanted to place the English crown on your head. I know you had a claim but so did Elizabeth and hers was the stronger."

"That's just your opinion. I don't agree with it. What kind of person sanctions the execution of her own cousin? Not a very nice or kind one. And you should remember my birth line is legitimate—she was a bastard." Beth was suddenly awake again and ready to argue.

"Before we fall out, tell me what you've just been through. How did you feel—were you aware at all of our present time, of this room? Or were you completely in the sixteenth century, involved only with what was happening there?" Lizzie waited expectantly for her friend's answer.

"This time didn't exist for me—I was in that dark, dank castle when Elizabeth came to visit me—and I thought maybe she'd come to release me. Walking towards the executioner and having my outer garments removed—that was all very real and I was so afraid." Beth knew she would never allow anyone to ridicule re-incarnation again. "But, what about you—you were definitely there and you were Queen Elizabeth. Didn't one part of you want to help me—or were you just as mean and selfish as the English Queen herself?"

"If that's how you see it—then yes, I was that mean, but you have to admit you were asking for what happened—you'd had your chance—you were the Queen of Scotland and you blew it. You were beautiful and men loved you but you chose the wrong men as your escorts. You even murdered the second one—and as for your first, the French Dauphin, he died after only one year of marriage to you. Did you perhaps help with that one too?" Lizzie knew she was going too far now—there had never been any suggestion that Mary's first young husband had died of anything but natural causes and of course, she'd always denied she had anything to do with Darnley's murder in Edinburgh.

The two girls were both fired up in argument. It was beginning to get dark outside and they both realised they were hungry. "I know, let's send out for pizzas, shall we?" The suggestion seemed to calm their feelings so Lizzie phoned in the order and Beth poured them both a glass of cider. Neither girl felt normal and even sending out for pizzas seemed wrong for two girls, who'd just been living in the sixteenth century. But whatever century they were now in—they were hungry.

Having finished off two pizzas, the girls were stretched out to recuperate— one on the floor and one on the sofa. There was an awkwardness in the room and the usually chatty friends were rather sombre. The evening passed in silence and they soon fell asleep—stuffed to the eyeballs and exhausted from their time at Fotheringhay Castle.

By next morning however, they'd both bounced back again and were laughing over the flipping of pancakes. "Honey or lemon?" Lizzie asked and passed both across the small table towards Beth. "Do you have a feeling of Deja-vu this morning? I do!"

"Strangely enough, I do too. Have we ever been in a similar situation before—I don't think so." Lizzie's forehead was creased, trying to think.

"Well, we did sit together at Fotheringhay Castle staring at each other, not knowing what to say—didn't we? Just like this now." Beth smiled and realised it was freshly painful to bring up the subject again.

"Yes, we did, didn't we? That was when you explained why I should have released you—even after the plots you were involved with—the plots to steal away my throne." Lizzie found she was ready for another argument.

"I wasn't involved in as many as you think, Lizzie. But you do agree that I did have a rightful claim to the English throne."

"Not as good a one as I had. The people loved me you know and history said I didn't make a bad job of ruling the country. You have to give me that one at least—I was known as the glorious and greatest Queen in history." Lizzie felt her heckles begin to rise.

"All right—all right—keep your hair on." Beth was equally roused by the disagreement.

"More than you managed to do—you lost your wig and were almost bald at the end." Lizzie knew she was being unkind but couldn't help herself.

"This is what the Deja-vu we both feel is about. Listen to us—we're still arguing as the two Queens. Are you telling me that you still condone the way I was treated—you don't think it was abominable to slash my neck three times and let my head roll across the floor? And what about my little dog—can you imagine him lying by my headless shoulders, crying for his mistress and refusing to leave me?"

"Of course that was terrible—but what did you want them to do with such a troublesome Queen as you?" The argument was getting out of hand and the girls were becoming more and more angry with each other. They really were arguing as the two Queens.

Beth jumped up and said, "Let's go for a walk so we can both cool down. What do you say?"

"Come on then, what are you waiting for—fetch your jacket." This was a good solution and both felt the need for a breath of fresh air.

It was a chilly but bright day and the girls headed for the park. There weren't many people around on this early Spring day but enough to make the girls realise how lovely the world was and how lucky both of them really were. There were a couple of small boats on the big lake and everything looked so pleasant and inviting that they decided hire one and take it out. Beth paid the money—she had a little more money—but Lizzie bought two ice creams covered in sprinkles.

"I'll row first—I'm tougher than you."

Beth held up her arm to show off her muscles and Lizzie laughed, saying, "You go ahead—I'm quite happy to lie back here and let you sweat—I am, after all, the glorious Queen Elizabeth of England."

"Are you going to start that again?" Beth had manoeuvred them along the edge of the lake and then rowed into the middle of the water.

"I only mentioned that I'm a Queen—but then, I suppose you are as well." She was trailing her fingers over the side of the boat, almost falling asleep in the early Spring warmth. Suddenly, she was dazzled by the light and found herself on a curtained barge sailing up the River Thames. She knew she was the Virgin Queen again and being rowed by one of her ladies-in-waiting for an hour of relaxation—the river was beautiful at this time of the year and she stared at the trees along the bank. They were covered in new buds and would soon be in full leaf. She leaned forward and stared at the woman sitting opposite—she recognised the face but couldn't remember the name. Then she remembered. It was Mary Queen of Scots, her cousin—what on earth was she doing here, she was in prison at Fotheringhay Castle?

"Why are you here, cousin—I know you shouldn't be, yet here you are, large as life. My ministers advised me that you had been executed and had your head cut off—yet here you are on my barge." Queen Elizabeth was dressed in a very lovely gown of blue velvet, covered in many embroidered silver stars. In contrast, Mary was dressed in her crimson petticoat she'd last worn on the 8 February. Again, both queens were staring into each other's eyes—the silence was awkward as neither knew what to say next—or why they were both there. The situation was surreal and they both felt it. Deja-vu was as real as before.

"Now that you've signed my death warrant, can you tell me why you decided to do it now? Did you ever consider allowing me to live in freedom—albeit under your protection—but as a free person? Nineteen long years I spent under close arrest and it made me an old woman before my time. Look at me cousin—look at what you did to me." And Mary tugged off her auburn wig to reveal her shorn head with just a light sprinkling of white hair. "I am only 44 years of age—nine years younger than you—and yet look at me. Life and you have done this to me—but mostly you." She donned her wig again and waited for Elizabeth to speak.

"Oh, you've had such a hard life, my heart bleeds for you. You have always been the undisputed Queen of your country—but what about me? I was called bastard for most of my young life, my mother was beheaded when I was a child and I was passed from pillar to post all my life—one minute recognised by my father Henry as his daughter and then rejected by him. My mother was beheaded as a traitor. Can you imagine what that did to my mind?" Elizabeth's eyes were shining with anger at the injustices of her own life.

Mary interrupted with, "Yes, I understand how terrible that must have been, but you could have treated me with more compassion—I do have a claim to your throne, but if you'd agreed to my release from prison, I would have lived quietly and would have supported you."

"I don't believe you'd have lived quietly—there would always have been attempts to usurp me and take all I had. You are that kind of person—you attract trouble! I couldn't take the chance that you'd be any different. My ministers kept on at me to sign your death warrant—and in the end, I did—but they fooled me by putting the warrant amongst several other papers awaiting my signature. I might have just left you in prison to die—perhaps not have had you executed—but who can tell? Anyway, it's over now and you are no more!"

Mary stood up suddenly and the boat began to shake from one side to the other—but she steadied herself and reached for one of the wooden oars. She stood there, looking neither to the right nor left but raising the oar high above her head. "You had it in your power to save me, but you chose not to do it. I've heard all your reasons for your decision but nothing that actually tied your hands from forgiving me and allowing my freedom."

She brought the oar down on Lizzie's head and smashed her skull as hard as she could—spitting out the words, "This is the justice you dealt to me—and I give it back to you wholeheartedly." With blood gushing from her scalp, her friend fell back into the boat. The oar was raised and slammed against the bloody wound a second time, raising the girl's body in the air and forcing it over the side into the water. Beth didn't see it happen because Mary had taken her over completely—and smiled, proud at what she'd just done.

Lizzie was still alive and held onto the side of the boat. It was a strange thing, but she was wondering whose body she would go into, if she were to die. What a bizarre thought at a time like this! The oar came crashing down again and was thrust into her weakened body, pushing her further away and down into the water. Lizzie managed to call out, "Beth, Beth—please stop." But her voice was fading as was her strength and she was slowly moving further away from the safety of the boat.

Using the oar again, Mary hit out at her friend and shouted, "Ah, sign my death warrant would you? Shame on you! This'll teach you—you could have helped me but you chose not to—so I'm returning the favour." And she smoothed down her crimson skirts and settled down again in the boat. In her eyes, she looked and felt every inch a Queen. Queen Mary had begun to sink under the water, too late for the rescue boat which was fast approaching.

Several people on the lake had seen everything that happened and one man had jumped into the lake to try to save the drowning girl. He and the rescue boat arrived together and together, they lifted the girl aboard. It was a struggle but between them, they managed it.

"What the bloody Hell did you do that for? You crazy bitch! You've killed her," the man shouted, whilst the rescue man rushed his boat back to the pontoon and gratefully handed the girl over to the police and ambulance men who'd just arrived. They tried their best but couldn't pump the water from Lizzie's lungs— and she just lay there, her face crumpled and white. They didn't stop working on her for ages but had to give up in the end.

All through this, Mary, Queen of Scots was still sitting in her boat and the police rowed across the lake to reach her. "You'd better come along with us, I think—many people saw exactly what you did—most of them can't believe their eyes. I think it'll be prison for you, young lady," the policeman couldn't help saying. After all, she was sitting there showing no remorse for what she'd done. They hooked up her boat with a rope and towed her to shore. She said nothing, just glanced at them with disdain.

"Speak to me with respect, Sir—or you may live to regret it. Are you aware of who I am—or are you ignorant as well as rude?"

The two policemen looked at each other and one couldn't help asking, "Who are you then?"

She drew herself up to an imagined six feet (Beth was only 5ft) and said imperiously, "I am Mary, Queen of Scots, Monarch of all Scotland and I've waited a long time to get my own back on my murderer—Queen Elizabeth I of England. That's her over there being carried away—she got her just desserts at last."

They bundled her into the police car and used heavy handcuffs to restrain her. She went willingly with them, and said, "You say you're taking me to prison—prison holds no fears for me, young man—I've spent most of my life in prison. I am ready—please lead the way!" And she managed to maintain her dignity right to the end when the hangman placed the rope around her neck—the same dignity she'd shown before, when the executioner botched his job and had to strike her three times.

He Really Did Love the Lassies

"I tell you, she's a right wee smasher. I wouldn't say 'no' to her, I tell you." Rabbie Burns was drinking with his cronies in the local tavern. "I could write a sonnet about her right now." And he started, "Ah Jeannie, my Jeannie, you have stolen my heart." But his drunken friends shut him up and laughed at his passion for the young woman who was known as one of the 'Belles of Mauchline'.

"She'll never look at ye twice—ye'r too poor—and her faither would kill ye." His friends knew how to wind him up and never missed an opportunity to do it.

"Well then, if you won't let me talk about Jean, then I'll change the subject to the 'immorality and dishonesty in the Church—or the injustices meted out by the 'Haves' to the 'Have Nots'." Robert Burns didn't like the orthodox and organised religions—or any of the politicians and local authorities of the day. He was always happy to criticise them when he had the chance. He loved to argue about the French Revolution and about how right the people were to act the way they did. Getting rid of the aristocracy was a good idea in his mind. He was never short of a subject to debate with his cronies.

Again, his friends, whose tongues were loosened by the drink, shouted him down. "Oh no—not those old chestnuts again." And two of them pretended to leave the pub, saying they'd only come back if he shut up. He knew when he was beaten and got up to order another drink. "You're nothing but a load of Philistines—you know nothing and you don't want to learn anything." He shouted over his shoulder.

Robert Burns was still a young man but had had a hard life. He'd watched his father William, struggle on his various farms and work himself into an early grave. Robert had been born in Ayrshire in 1759 and his father had moved the whole family, firstly to a farm at Mount Oliphant in 1766 and then again to a farm at Lochlea in 1777. Although William worked very hard on the land, he died in 1784, worn out and bankrupt. In fact, he'd had a dispute with his landlord who claimed he was owed rent. William Burness (name subsequently changed to Burns) disagreed with this, claiming improvements to his home had never been made as promised. In fact he actually took his landlord to court and won his case against him. He was obviously not afraid of the authorities—just like his son Robert.

Having watched his father's struggles, it made the son inclined to rebel against the social order of his day. Robert was a bitter satirist where all forms of religion and politics were concerned, believing that they condoned and perpetuated inhumanity to lesser and more ordinary folk. His background was clearly the basis for his character and beliefs. His great-great-grandfather, great-grandfather, grandfather and father had all been tenant farmers and, despite the hard and demanding work they did, they still failed to make much money during their lives—and they all suffered one generation after the other.

Many families—and the Burnesses were one, had been forced to leave the Highlands and move to the Lowlands in search of work. It was not a good time to be known as a Jacobite and this was what the Highlanders had to escape from.

When he was just a young boy, Rab or Robbie worked on his father's land—and he had to work hard with no questions asked. His father had leased 9 acres of land in Alloway and had built his own cottage there, which the Burness Family shared with their farm animals—it was divided in two.—one end a home and the other a stable. This couldn't have been the healthiest option for the family and could have been the beginning of the boy's weak chest, which became much worse as he grew. He started 'proper' work when he was twelve but continued to help out on the farm for many years after that.

A very important factor in his life was the old, widow woman who used to help his mother Agnes, on the farm. She could turn her hand to everything and anything and was of great help to her mistress. She worked mainly in the dairy however, where she would entertain young Robert with her eerie tales of the supernatural. She was a good story-teller and held the boy's attention every chance she had.

"Tell me more, Maggie—I love your stories." He would say to the old woman, as she fed the two cows and filled the bucket with creamy milk.

"They're not just stories, Master Robert—they're tales about real things and people, so don't you forget it. How about I tell the one about the witch's party, the one the Devil himself was invited to?" She knew he liked the scariest stories and she knew plenty of them, having listened to them at the knee of her own grandmother.

"Oh aye Maggie, that's a good one—the one about the witches' coven in the old Kirk down the road—although I still don't understand why the witches couldn't cross over the running water in the stream." He liked to know the 'ins and outs' of all her stories and this didn't seem logical to him.

She started to milk the first cow, sitting on the little, three-legged stool, her arms and legs akimbo. "Wheest now boy! Don't you go worryin' your wee head about things like that, just accept what I tell you, 'cause it's just what my Grandma told me."

Rabbie, as she liked to call him, knew he mustn't interrupt too much or she'd stop telling him the story. "What happened to the man on the horse—did he get home alright? It's odd that the horse had the same name as you, isn't it? You know Maggie, when I get older and learn my letters better, I'm going to write down your stories and show them to people—that's what I'm going to do."

"Haud yer wheest ma wee man and let me talk." And so, like a sponge, Rabbie soaked up and remembered the things he learned at the knee of Old Maggie. (It's almost certain that he built some of her tales into his future writings. Tam O'Shanter is a good example!)

William Burness had spent many years before farming, as Head Gardiner to the local dignitaries but in 1757 he married Agnes Brown, started a family, and opted to take a lease of land at a place called Mount Oliphant. The lease was for twelve years and William and Agnes stayed there and went on to have seven children, four boys and three girls. In 1777, the Burness family moved again to a leased farm at Lochlea in the parish of Tarbolton. By this time, Rabbie was about eighteen years of age and had already started 'scribbling' down some of his poems and songs. He'd had only scanty formal education but was tutored by an intelligent and good natured gentleman—John Murdoch—who was deeply interested in eighteenth century English literature—the knowledge of which he imparted to the eager the young man, who never tired of hearing him talk.

Rabbie and his younger brother Gilbert had been entered into the Alloway School and so started their education. Their father was a very religious man and rated education at the top of the boys' needs. Unfortunately, due to financial problems, the small school had to close. It was at this point that William managed to persuade the locals to appoint John Murdoch as teacher at the school—and so Rabbie again benefitted from John's great interest in literature. John himself, was only eighteen years of age when he was appointed to the school but he had been educated in the sophisticated city of Edinburgh. He gave the schoolchildren the foundation of a classical education, teaching them the Bible, and exposing them to the works of Shakespeare, Milton, Dryden and some of the finest writers of the day. Unfortunately, John was 'stolen' to teach in a private Edinburgh school and William sent his boys to another school in Dalrymple, but only one at a time as they both couldn't go to school at the same time—(a) because he couldn't afford to pay for both and (b) one of them was needed to help on the farm and so, they were educated on alternate weeks. John Murdoch returned to Ayrshire for a few weeks and in that time, Rabbie studied French, English and Latin with him. He would read the books written in pure French so as to make it more difficult for himself and to teach him more of the language. (Actually, when he died, a book written in French was laid, still half open, by his bedside.)

He was an avid reader from his time with John Murdoch and for the rest of his life. As a family, the Burns' boys could often be found in the evening, reading aloud to their father and mother. In one of his letters to a friend, he remarked that from these stories, he was inspired by tales of Hannibal and William Wallace. He wrote of Wallace 'who poured a Scottish prejudice into my veins which has boiled there in each and every one of my waking moments.' These were his own words! He was so enamoured of what Wallace had been and done that he would march along the road at the side of soldiers as they passed through the town—pretending he was the great man himself.

As he grew into his teenage years, the young Burns' eyes had settled on a young servant girl called Elizabeth Paton, who worked for his own mother. She lived in the village of Alloway and after a few months, gave birth to his first child. Sympathising with the young maid, and angry that her son would not 'do the decent thing' and marry the pregnant maid, his mother took the child into her own family and raised it as one of her own. His romance with Elizabeth was never serious and he soon abandoned her to her fate. It was said that she admired him much more than he ever did her.

Luckily for him, his mother was more caring and helped the girl. After a while, Elizabeth did marry a young local farmer—but not the one she had wanted! As it would prove in the future, his charm always got him out of difficult situations and on this occasion, he walked away scot-free. He hadn't cared for the girl and told her so, leaving her to whatever fate had in store for her.

"What about that little maid ye were courtin' last month? I saw her yesterday and she seems to have developed a swollen stomach—I wonder how that happened." Will, his drunken friend, laughed loudly at Rab's discomfort. Of course, he knew exactly what his friend had been up to but couldn't help admiring the rogue.

"Nothing to do with me, Will—more likely something to do with you!" Rabbie laughed at his own weak joke.

Will wasn't going to let him off with that one, "I heard she was related to the Campbells and that the Clan Chief is coming to see ye and to make ye do the right thing by his clanswoman. What will ye do when he comes? Ye're part of the Clan Campbell yerself and ye'll have to do as he says." He swallowed down the last of his ale and added, "Wasn't it the Campbells who murdered all the MacDonalds whilst they were sleepin' in their beds? My God, but yer clan's a dastardly lot!"

"Stop talking such nonsense—and I'm proud to belong to the Campbell Clan before you start about that. I am aware of what happened at Glencoe when the Campbells put them all to the sword—but it was the MacDonalds' own fault. They failed to meet the deadline set by the King and the killings could all have been avoided if the Clan Chief hadn't been so stubborn." Rabbie was angry and bit his lip to conceal his anger. He was tired of the accusations aimed at the Campbells and believed the MacDonalds brought on their own fate. He saw the whole Glenco incident as another example of the domination over Scotland by the monarchy in England. (His later poem of 'A Man's a Man for All That' clearly defined his way of thinking.). Although he didn't like the monarchy, he liked the MacDonals even less.

"I think you should get back to 'the wee smasher, Jean Armour'—don't you?" It was a much safer topic of conversation and Will knew he'd gone too far with his friend. He'd put Rabbie into his lecturing mood—once he began, he couldn't be stopped… The drink had dried up, their pockets were empty and so, the drunken men left the tavern and staggered their separate ways home.

Burns had started writing as young as fifteen and at the same time, he had to work on the farm—even harder than before. His family had only managed to scrape a living from the land what with poor soil and lack of money for modern equipment. Rabbie and his brother, Gilbert, had to work long, hard, tiring hours and it was thought this was what caused Burns to develop a slight stoop as he grew and to have questionable health all of his life. In fact, despite his reputation for drinking, he could never consume too much alcohol at any one time, as it would have aggravated his already delicate stomach. Despite the reputation he liked to have, he wasn't a heavy drinker at all.

To enhance his place in society—and to meet the 'right people', he became a member of the Freemasons at age twenty-two—he obviously always had ambitions above his status and meant to do as well as he could. This attitude of course was sometimes reflected in his written works—he knew and believed he was as good as any other man but being a Freemason, would help introduce him to cultural and hopefully wealthy people—when he finally got to live in Edinburgh, as was his long-term plan. At age twenty five, his father died and he became the head of the household with many responsibilities. On William Burness's deathbed, the old man was asked if he had any matters on his mind which caused him worry—and he motioned to Rabbie and said he was concerned for that lad's future! What did he see for his son at that moment of impending death?

There was never any question—Rabbie really did love the lassies—and sought out their company whenever he could. Having deserted the servant girl, he turned his attention to Jean Armour, whom he'd met at a local dance. Jean was known locally as one of the 'Mauchline Beautiful Belles' and was a very sought after. His courtship of her however, didn't prove easy as the lass's father didn't like 'the Burns boy' and told his daughter to have nothing to do with him. In fact when Jean told him she was seeing 'the Burns boy', he fainted clean away with shock and never got over it.

Burns and his family now lived in Mossgiel, a few miles from Alloway. In Mossgiel and in the nearby town of Mauchline, the charming and attractive Burns had many short-term love affairs. (In fact, it is a matter of record that in his relatively short life, he had twelve children by four different women. (Two sets of twins, of course, by Jean!)

When Jean fell pregnant, he wanted to marry her but her father was dead set against it—and Jean was sent to Paisley to conceal her pregnancy and to hide her shame.

Life was not going well for Burns at this time and he had reached a turning point. The farming was not going well, he had no money and the Church was pursuing him as a fornicator. He believed that Jean had deserted him voluntarily when she went to Paisley—and now he was alone. He really began to believe that the world was conspiring against him. Jean's father then took him to court and accused him of being a fornicator. Jean was called back to attend the court as a witness and she swore Robert Burns was the father of her child. James Armour repudiated him as a son-in-law and in turn, Jean had to do the same and was forced to repudiate him as well. The Kirk Assembly judged him and he had to attend church three consecutive times and stand before the congregation to admit he was a fornicator Burns was furious at having to do this but could only admit the claims were true.

Life was not going well for him and he knew he had to change direction. On the 22nd of July of that year, he had a lawyer draw up a Deed of Assignment which was lodged with the Sheriff-Clerk in the town of Ayr. This Deed transferred all of his assets to his brother, Gilbert—to include his share of the farm, all the profits from any books he published and it also made Gilbert responsible for the upbringing of Rabbie's illegitimate daughter, Elizabeth. Although he wouldn't marry the mother, he obviously loved the daughter and was concerned for her future.

At one of the worst points in his life, Rabbie received a 'Writ' issued from Jean Armour's father and in fear of arrest and imprisonment, he ran away and hid at his uncle's home near Kilmarnock. As luck would have it, the very next day—31 July 1786, his first book was finally published—it was called 'Poems Chiefly in the Scottish Dialect'—it went on sale and was an immediate success, selling over 600 copies and earning him more than enough for his trip to Jamaica—a plan he'd had for some time but now chose to reject it. His friends in the Freemasons had helped him achieve this by subscribing money for the book's publication in Kilmarnock. His decision to join the Freemasons had been a good one!

It was when he'd been working in Mauchline that he started to write poetry and songs. He loved to poke fun at the followers of Calvinism who believed in God's absolute power over all humans. He found this a naïve belief and showed it in his writings. His book was an immediate success and people loved it. He was only twenty seven and had by then, written many satirical works against the establishment. He wrote many of his well-known poems at this time, one being 'To a Mouse'—a little creature a farmer had just killed with his plough. His works were coming fast and furious and people loved them. In fact, it was said at the time that his works were 'unequalled in their combination of accurate local language and depth of feeling—and that not for centuries, had such fine poetry been written in the Scots tongue.'

Ordinary folk and Edinburgh socialites alike loved his published book. They loved 'The Cotter's Saturday Night' and 'To a Mountain Daisy'—just two of the works it contained.

Before she left for Paisley, Jean had actually helped him in his work. She loved to discuss the sentiments he wrote about and she instilled in him a strong morality that showed in many of his works. He still pursued his courtship of Jean and she eventually produced twin babies before returning to Mauchline. Her parents still refused to allow the couple to marry because of Burns' reputation as a critic of religion and because of his fast growing reputation for chasing the lassies.

"Oh my Jeannie, how can we persuade them to let us marry? We love each other and now have two bonny children to prove it." He was sentimental at the best of times,—and on this occasion, he was reduced to tears.

"They will not allow it, Rab—no matter how I plead. You know how hard I've tried." And Jean too was in tears. "But, look at our children, aren't they bonny?"

"They are that, my Love, but what am I to do without you as my wife?" He was miserable and also astute enough to realise how much he needed her. She was good for his thought processes and how he presented his best works.

He was a very emotional writer and knew how to appeal to all kinds of readers—the posh Edinburgh people loved the good Scot's tongue in which the works were written, but they also respected him for his 'alleged' and exaggerated' lack of education and for how he'd raised himself above it. He was a canny man and knew the value of playing the humble farmer who'd had but little education—yet had managed to produce some amazing works. On the other hand, ordinary folk loved his stories and 'the good Scot's tongue' he used, was the way spoke every day. The 'Cultural Thinkers' in Edinburgh were deeply involved with the 'Enlightenment' period at the time—Enlightenment was a newly emerging thinking of the 'intellectuals', and was spreading like wild fire throughout the whole of Europe. Everything had to be questioned—and Burns was the man to do it.

Jean Armour stayed in Paisley for a while after she'd had her first set of twins. He felt she had deserted him and left him for good—he was at a low ebb but strangely enough, his misery over Jean didn't stop him falling in love with another woman just after Jean had left the area. Her name was Mary Campbell and he wrote one of his most famous songs about her—'Highland Mary.'

Although she died very young, in Greenock, several letters were found in her home, all written to her by Rab. They were love letters and left no doubt as to how he felt about her. He really did love her and actually asked her to emigrate with him to Jamaica where they could start a new life together. Mary agreed this would be a good thing to do.

She was nursemaid to a member of the Greenock gentry, eventually moving and becoming a dairy maid in Mauchline, where she first met Burns. He saw her in church and made it his business to meet her and get to know her. They first agreed to meet each other on a country path now called 'Burns Thorn' or Mary's Tryst' and this was on the second Sunday in May. The young Highlander, had a strong Gaelic accent and her English was rather broken and difficult to follow—so she earned the name Highland Mary because of the strong accent. She was the daughter of a sailor, Archibald and his wife Mary, who lived in Auchnanore near Dunoon.

The couple met a few times more, but she was due to leave to take up employment with a prosperous Colonel McIvor in Glasgow—and so the couple met for one last time on the banks of Ayr to say goodbye. They'd only known each other for a few weeks—from 23 April to 14 May in 1786—but so deeply had they fallen in love, that they plighted their troth to each other and exchanged bibles over running water—which was a practice between couples to formally exchange their wedding vows when they were unable to marry in church. On that day, Mary exchanged her vows with Rab and must have loved him deeply to have done this. She was a tall woman of slight build with golden hair and blue eyes—she thought him the most handsome man she'd ever met—and certainly the most charming.

They agreed to meet in Greenock where she was to live with friends until Colonel McIvor sent for her to come to Glasgow. This is what they told people at the time but Rabbie still wanted to emigrate to Jamaica and wanted to take Mary with him. This could have been why they agreed to meet in Greenock, as it would have been easy to leave from the busy port there and sail to Jamaica. But no one will ever know what their plans actually were, as they never unfolded…

The odd thing was that she was just as much of a 'temptress' with the lads, as he was with the lassies. Whilst living in Greenock, she was reputed to have had an affair with a man there. She had come to Greenock straight from nursing her brother who had been very ill and it was thought she had caught the Typhoid fever from him. As said, she was rather frail and before Rabbie finally came to Greenock, Highland Mary had died and was buried in the town cemetery. He never met his lovely Mary again and he never knew what had killed her.

(Many years later—about 100—the graveyard where she was buried had to be closed down and the graves moved to a new location. When her grave was opened, the remainder of a baby's coffin was also found buried there, and for some years it was believed the baby had been Robert Burns' child. Having said that, however, there was serious doubt that the child had been buried with her— it was then thought that the grave had just been used for the purpose as the real mother had no other choice of a last resting place for her dead child. The reader must make up their own mind on this!)

In a letter to a friend, Burns wrote: 'She crossed the sea to meet me at Greenock where she had scarce landed when she was seized with a malignant fever which hurried my dear girl to the grave in a few days before I could even hear of her illness.'

Mary had been only 23 years of age when she died—she had loved and lost.

Back in the local pub, Rab was drinking with Will when he said, "I'm going to Edinburgh, Will. I've made my mind up—my book went down very well there and I want to strike while the iron's hot."

"Why do you want to go to that city of Nancy-boys? You're much better off here with us." Will would never understand his friend. He was always reaching out for something new but it had to be admitted his book had been a great success, so maybe he was right this time.

In the seventeenth century, books could be published by public subscription and through his association with the Freemasons, they pulled together and gathered the money needed to publish the book. It was apparent that his clever decision to join the organisation when he did, had paid off. The book was incredibly popular and Robert Burns was suddenly a successful writer, who was being spoken of throughout the length and breadth of the country. It seemed likely that he chose the subjects of his book with great care, after all everyone loved sentiment and sadness.

He knew the audience he wanted to reach—the genteel folk of Edinburgh who were the ones with the money—and he knew to play up to the contemporary, sentimental views about the 'natural man' and the 'noble peasant. As said before but can't be stressed enough, he also exaggerated his lack of education, pretending a false naivety and played 'a part' for his genteel audiences.

Considering his brazen actions throughout his life with regard to the women, it was rather surprising that he filled much of his works with an excess of naïve and sentimental moralising. It seemed however that he knew exactly what he was doing.

He borrowed a pony from a long-standing friend—one George Reid—and set off for Edinburgh. The journey took two full days. He had received a letter from an Edinburgh gentleman called Dr Thomas Blacklock who was famously known as The Blind Poet. His poetry was much respected and he was acquainted with such famous figures as Dr Samuel Johnson and his biographer, James Boswell, as well as the philosopher David Hume—and also one of the most famous Americans of the time—Benjamin Franklin.

Blacklock thought so highly of Burn's work that he invited him to come immediately to Edinburgh. He predicted that a second, larger edition of his book could be published. He told Burns that a second book would have a more universal circulation than anything that had been published within living memory. The encouragement from such a cultural and honourable gentleman easily swayed Burns and he knew journeying to Edinburgh must be his goal. He had already been considering publishing a second edition as the first had sold out so quickly and he had already written more material which he could include.

A banker in Ayr had offered to lend Burns the money for the second edition—and he advised the poet to find another publisher in Edinburgh as this would greatly enhance the popularity of the book. On his way to the capital Burns broke his journey at Covington Mains by Biggar—to rest both himself and the pony—and found his friend George had arranged a welcoming committee. All the farmers in the local area could come and personally meet their new hero—and they did. The sign of his arrival was a white sheet tied to a pitchfork placed on a corn stack and soon the house was full of farmers, eager to shake his hand and fill his glass every time it was empty. The party lasted into the early hours of the morning and after saying his goodbyes, Burns rode on to the next farm where he breakfasted with another large party, who'd also been gathered to meet him. After this, he said goodbye to the well-wishers and lunched at the Bank in Carnwath before travelling on to Edinburgh in the evening. A very eventful journey.

My God, he thought, *I really have arrived.* And patted the pony's head. He was welcomed into Edinburgh, the gates were thrown open for him and he was treated like a Prince. Wined and dined by all who met him, he settled very comfortably there. After a few, temporary addresses he lived at Baxter's Close and immediately set about publishing a second and enlarged edition of his poems. He met and worked with James Johnson who was a collector of Scottish songs and Rabbie worked with him in finding, editing, improving and re-writing many old works. A series of volumes of songs was produced and was a huge success.

Rabbie was very enthusiastic and worked as editor of Johnson's work 'The Scots Musical Museum.' He spent a long time in refining the works but refused payment for doing it, as he said 'he did it for the good of Scotland' and that was enough recompense for him. His attitude made many of his friends decide to make a collection of money to help support his many illegitimate children. A considerable sum was collected, which he did use to help his children.

In Edinburgh, he mixed with many folk well above his own social station in life. He conversed with them and wrote many letters to them. He was a great talker and debater and could hold his own in any company. Back home, he was still regarded as a tenant farmer and in Edinburgh, he was a social butterfly and impressed everyone he met.

He was however, still a philanderer where the women were concerned and he started romancing a young servant girl—Jenny Clow—who was sent to his home with letters from his friend, Clarinda. Clarinda was really Mrs Agnes Maclehose, a middle class Edinburgh lady whom Burns always called Clarinda. They formed a platonic and caring relationship, during which they wrote many letters to each other. Young Jenny would deliver her mistress's letters to Burns and of course, ended up pregnant with his child. Nothing had changed it seemed. When Clarinda found out about her maid, she was angry with Burns and told him so—but yet again, his charm got him out of the scrape. She wrote to him and told him the poor girl was ill—she'd been dismissed from her position and was almost destitute. She berated him and spoke of the shame he should be feeling because of his part in the girl's downfall.

Burns did write back and sent some money for Jenny, his letter saying that he 'shed tears of blood' over the poor girl's situation and did actually offer to take the baby when it was born. Jenny however, refused to give up her baby. No one ever knew what happened to Jenny and her son and it was assumed that, after a very short time, both of them died, perhaps in dire circumstances. His friend Agnes or Clarinda must have felt let down by her hero. He did write a poem for her however, but she was proving to be an upright, virtuous woman who could never stoop to his level of depravity where women were concerned. She insulted him by refusing to consummate their relationship.

Their friendship did continue however—but it was never more than platonic. She was separated from her husband who worked in Jamaica and said she couldn't be intimate with Burns until she'd tried once more to save her marriage. Burns offered to marry her when she returned from seeing him in Jamaica, should her trip there be unsuccessful. It never happened for Clarinda—or Nancy—as her friends called her—she went to Jamaica and met her husband there, but he had already taken up with a native woman and had a child by her—so Clarinda could do nothing else but return to Edinburgh. (The words 'Oh what a tangled web we weave' come easily to mind!) Clarinda was however, the reason he wrote one of his best-loved poems 'Ae Fond Kiss and then we parted…' It was so heartfelt and so sincere, it has to be repeated here:

> *Ae fond kiss, and then we sever;*
> *Ae fareweel and then forever!*
> *Deep in heart-rung tears—I'll pledge thee,*
> *Warring sighs and groans I'll wage thee,*
> *Who shall say that Fortune grieves him,*
> *While the star of hope she leaves him?*
> *Me, nae cheerful twinkle lights me;*
> *Dark despair around benights me.*
>
> *I'll ne'er blame my partial fancy,*
> *Naething could resist my Nancy;*
> *But to see her was to love her;*
> *Love but her, and love forever;*
> *Had we never lov'd sae kindly,*
> *Never met—or never parted—*
> *We had ne'er been broken-hearted.*
>
> *Fare thee weel, thou first and fairest!*
> *Fare thee weel, thou best and dearest!*
> *Thine be ilka joy and treasure,*
> *Peace, enjoyment, love, and pleasure!*
> *Ae fond kiss, and then we sever;*

Ae fareweel, alas forever!
Deep in heart-wrung tears I'll pledge thee,
Warring sighs and groans I'll wage thee!

It could also have been titled, 'The One that Got Away!' as the relationship came to an immediate and sudden end. Rab returned to Mauchline where he met up again with Jean Armour, who had just given him a second set of twins. Her father had obviously softened towards the poet (perhaps his writing success and popularity in Edinburgh made him more appealing?) The couple were allowed to marry and under Scottish Law, their 4 illegitimate children became legal as though conceived in wedlock. The marriage had taken some years but happened in the end.

He tried his hand at farming again and bought a farm at Ellisland where he, Jean, their 4 children and the illegitimate child of Elizabeth, the maidservant all lived together. Jean, of course, continued to have children and in the end, actually had 9 babies.

Working on the farm proved too much for him and when he was offered a position as an Exciseman in Dumfries, he accepted and eventually moved his whole family there. The year was 1790 and for the first few months, he frequently travelled between Ellisland and Dumfries and, when in town, he lived at the Globe Inn. Needless to say, he met a barmaid there called Ann Park for whom he wrote one of his greatly loved poems—'Yestreen I had a pint o' wine' and inevitably there was another illegitimate child on the horizon. Ann Park was sent to Leith to have her child and soon 'Little Betty' was born. No one ever knew what became of Ann after that, but it seemed likely that she died as a destitute. He really wasn't good news for his 'casual amours.'

When he told his wife, Jean what had happened, she offered to care for the new little girl and so, a second illegitimate child entered his home. Jean Armour must have been a long-suffering and benevolent woman to take on so much—but she did it for him. She obviously understood her husband well and was quoted as saying: 'Rab should have had two wives and that may have stopped his wandering eye.' His charm however, never faded and was to last all of his life.

For a few years, he continued to work, provide for his children and write more poetry, although not nearly so much as he had done in earlier years. He did write one very famous work at the time and that was 'Tam O'Shanter'—regarded by many as one of his best works. It was a masterpiece and should be sought out by anyone who reads this story. (It's much too long to record here!) In a way, it resembles the kind of stories told to him by the old widow woman at the Alloway Farm—not really surprising really—he always said he would do it. In 1795, Rabbie developed a tooth abscess which needed extraction—there was a suggestion that a piece of the broken tooth got into his bloodstream and settled in his heart. This caused delirium and fever and he became very ill—very ill indeed—and the illness lasted for several months.

In fact, in a letter to a friend, he described his situation as 'having to crawl across the floor of his room, because he couldn't manage to walk.' He also lost a much-loved daughter that same year which seemed to affect him very badly—he spoke of losing his 'only, dear 2-year-old daughter Elizabeth,' which was strange and may have been because of the delirium, because he actually had several daughters.

It was at this time Highland Mary came to visit. He was fevered and delirious but sitting upright in his rocking chair drinking a hot toddy (hot water, sugar and whisky). The afternoon was grey and misty but there was enough light from the candle on the mantlepiece. He rubbed his eyes and tried to clear his head. "Who is there—I can't quite see—it's not Jeannie, I know that. And yet, I know that bonny face from somewhere in my past. Who are you, fair maid?"

The tall, slim figure moved forward and was silhouetted in the dim light from the window.

"It's me, Rob—dae ye not know me? It's yer Highland Mary who once ye loved so sweetly—and I ye. What is it that ails ye, man? How can I help ye?" She was wearing the same blue gown as when he first saw her in church all those years before and she looked young, so very young.

"Mary, my dear, is it really you? But how can that be—I know you left this life many years ago and yet, I see you quite clearly, as beautiful as ever." Even at this time, he still used his charm on the lassies. He tried to rise from the chair but fell down again. "You see me poorly Mary—I've been ill for some time now—I canny shake off this damned fever. Where have you come from and why do you look so well?"

"I've come from my eternal rest to help if I can. Ye must pull yerself together and get back to yer writin' again. Ye can get over this, Rabbie—I know ye can."

She was so beautiful in the low light that he rubbed his tired eyes again and said in a low voice, "I'm very ill, Lassie—I don't think you can help me."

"Shake yerself, Man—and sit up straight. I know what ye've been through and I know of all the maids ye've loved and the children ye've begat—but I forgive ye 'cause I love ye. Ye were my best and only love, ye know." She moved back against the wall and tossed her long, golden curls with pride. "Now I need ye tae get up out o' that chair—find yer quill and write about our meetin' this day." She started to fade and he reached out for her but his hand found nothing. Then she was gone, but he could still smell the sweetness she left behind.

That day however, he did rise from the chair, searched and found his quill and some paper and started writing. He felt more positive than he'd done for years and all because of his Highland Mary.

Although now in reduced circumstances because of his illness and absence from work and his regular income as an Exciseman, he managed to visit the local tavern, the Globe Inn, on a frequent basis. One night in the month of January 1796, he stayed very late, well into the early hours of the morning and enjoyed a jolly, boisterous party. Leaving the tavern and only able to walk slowly, he spent too long in the open night air. Winding his way home, he fell asleep on a rather uncomfortable stone wall. The night air was bitterly cold and the ground covered in frost whilst he slept—a chill seeped into his frail bones. And that was when she came to him again—his Guardian Angel, Highland Mary. She hovered above the glints in the frost and put a gentle, ghostly hand to his freezing face.

"Rabbie—Rabbie Burns, wake up, my lad. Ye're in the bitter cold night air—it'll be the death o' ye!" The figure bent down and whispered in the drunk man's ear, "Get up man, or I'll gie ye the slappin' o' yer life."

He moved as though he'd heard her and raised his hand to brush her away. "Who is that botherin' me this night?"

"It's me, ya goon, an I'm no' goin' awa 'till ye wake up." And he did, sitting upright. Mary shrank away and watched him get off the stone wall. She'd done what she'd come for.

On finally reaching home, the beginnings of rheumatic fever had taken possession of his weakened body. The Globe Inn was only 15 minutes from where he lived but that night, it must have seemed a long way to Burns. He didn't remember Mary visiting him this time and thought how lucky he was not to sleep longer in the freezing cold.

The genteel narrow-minded classes decided that he'd drunk himself to death and despite confirmations and declarations by his friends that this was not so, the stuffy Edinburgh folk preferred to believe it was the demon drink that finished him off. They preferred to believe he'd brought about his own death as that suited the moral mood of society at the time. He did have a great friend in one Dr William Maxwell who tried to help him through his illness and also swore as to the good character of his friend. In early July 1791, he persuaded Burns to travel to Brow Hill near the Solway Firth, a well-known local Spa. Medicine had begun to believe in the healing power of taking the waters—and also of paddling in the cold water too. In desperation, Burns took his friend's advice and visited the Spa.

Having taken the waters, he then wrote a letter to another friend, Alexander Cunningham and told him:

'Alas! My Friend, I fear the voice of the Bard will soon be heard among you no more! For these eight or ten months, I have been ailing, sometimes bed-fast, sometimes not, but these last three months I have been tortured with an excruciating rheumatism which has reduced me to nearly the last stage of my life. You actually would not know me if you saw me. Pale, emaciated and so feeble as occasionally to need help from my chair—my spirits fled!—but I can no more on the subject—only the medical folks tell me that my last and only chance is bathing and country quarters and riding.'

After a few days at Brow Hill, Burns was so weak, he couldn't manage to ride a horse and had to borrow a carriage to get home. He now knew he was dying, but retained his humour. When he looked up from his sick bed and saw Dr Maxwell standing there, he said, "Alas! What has brought you here? I am but a poor crow and not worth plucking." Burns' home now presented a miserable and sad picture—the Bard dying, his wife on the point of giving birth and all the children hungry and thirsty with nothing in the house to sustain them. Rab wasn't lucid in his last two or three days—he couldn't talk and was delirious and confused. Rather than help him, Brow Hill had increased his fever and diminished his strength. He had one last lucid moment when he made a gift of his pistols to Dr Maxwell. His servant, James Maclure tells of his last moments and describes them thus:

'On the fourth day, James held a cordial to his master's lips and Burns swallowed it eagerly—then rose almost wholly up and spread out his hands—he then sprang forward nigh the whole length of the bed, fell forward onto his face and expired.'

The date was 21 July 1796 and the Bard was only 37 years of age.

On 26 July, the Bard's funeral was large and was complete with military honours. His brother Gilbert attended but Dr Maxwell was attending at Jean's confinement and couldn't be there. Many, many people attended his funeral , so making a lie of the claims by certain notable writers that the Bard had no friends and was badly thought of when he lived in Dumfries. Reality proved otherwise!

It is perhaps ironic but certainly not surprising that his wife was unable to leave her home on the big day. At the same time of her husband's funeral, Jean was being delivered of a boy—her ninth child. Rabbie would have been pleased as he'd always wanted a son! Jean honoured the doctor by naming her son Maxwell after him and was very sure that Rabbie would have approved!

Author's Note:

Robert Burns, to give him his true birth name, died 21 July 1796 in the town of Dumfries. As in his life, his death was not without incident. As has been mentioned before, his health was not good and this may have been caused by the heavy work he had to do when very young—and he had to work so hard on his father, William's farm in Alloway. He developed a chest condition then and suffered from rheumatism throughout the years, culminating in a heart weakness that probably killed him in the end. When in Edinburgh, he'd fallen from a coach and horse and dislocated his knee, culminating in a rheumatic arthritis, which gradually grew worse with the passing years. He actually died of Endocarditis, a disease of the substance and lining membrane of the heart and this had originated long before his taste for alcohol had.

It is possible however that his increasing consumption of spirits did hasten the spread of the disease. Subsequent statements from eminent physicians however declared that the undoing of Scotland's Traditional Poet and Bard, was rheumatism—it caused the initial damage to his heart in the early years, it's pain embittered his life and finally cut short his amazing career. How many works could he have produced had he been healthy—and lived for just a few more years? If only he'd not had to work so hard as a child, the rheumatism might have stayed at bay and we would have benefitted by having even more of his exceptional works.

Mirror, Mirror, on the Wall

She knew the mirror was watching her so she crept up the side of the bookcase and hid herself from its vision. She'd make her own mind up about what to wear—mirror didn't have the right to choose for her. She wasn't going to allow it to dictate to her, it wasn't even alive and she was.

"Yes, I hear you, but I've already chosen my clothes for today—and I'm ready to go out now, so you mustn't interfere like you usually do." Cautiously, she stepped in front of the mirror and stared at herself. She saw a pretty young woman with blond, bouncy curls framing her heart-shaped face and a little rosebud of a mouth. Her blue dress matched the blue of her eyes—and she couldn't help smiling at her perfect reflection.

"See Mirror, I look okay, don't I? I'm not going anywhere in particular—just up to Covent Garden to see what I can pick up. Don't worry, I'll make sure I find something for you too." And she was off, out into the sunny streets of London where excitement and opportunity awaited her. Her name was Margaret and she was on the prowl!

"Let me help you, Madame—the printing on these machines is so small—I can hardly see it myself." And the kind gentleman took her money from her trembling fingers and asked where she was going. He punched in her destination and handed her the ticket.

"Thank you, Sir, you're most kind." And the elderly woman moved on towards the platform to await the next tube. She had to be careful with the step, she knew that—she could be wobbly sometimes and getting onto the tube was the worst.

On the tube, she caught sight of herself in the glass window and felt reassured—her hair was in place and her dress was un-creased. She looked like just what she was—a young, pretty girl out for the day. On alighting from the tube, she made her way to the lift where two people stepped back to allow her to go first—manners really were everything she thought and smiled her thanks to the strangers. It was only a few steps from the station and she was soon in the middle of the stalls and all the bustling, happy shoppers. She loved the atmosphere of the market and wandered amongst the people, listening to their conversations and watching their children's antics. The day was so pleasant and the gentle music from the lower floor of the market drifted upwards—the violinist and cellist were busy that day.

'A cup of coffee and a piece of cake, that's what I need.' And she sat down in her favourite café and ordered from the young waitress who approached her. "Coffee and cake Madam—which cake would you prefer today?"

"Oh, something plain, I think—perhaps the madeira or seed cake please—whichever is the bigger slice!" She laughed at her obvious greed. Fumbling in her handbag for her purse she 'accidentally' knocked the bag onto the floor.

The man at the next table quickly bent down and lifted it up for her. "There you are Madam—be careful—I bet you've got the Crown Jewels in there." and he placed it on her table.

"Thank you, young man, most kind." And she delved into her seed cake—the waitress had brought an enormous slice.

Poor old lady, he thought, *bet she can't really afford that. A double slice, if I'm not mistaken but it won't bankrupt the café*. He felt generous but it was always easy to be generous with other people's property.

She wiped the corners of her mouth with a napkin and stood up to leave. The stalls looked interesting—she loved the way different stalls were there on different days—one never knew which ones would be there on any given day. She crossed to the section where the Jewish merchants had laid out their silver and gold items for sale. What pretty watches, bracelets, rings and necklaces, she looked at them longingly, nestling on the black velvet. The black clothed men with their large black hats watched customers closely—the items were very valuable as well as attractive.

"Would you like to sit on this chair for a while, Madam—you look rather tired?" a black-bearded man asked, moving a chair from his side of the counter to hers.

"Why, thank you, I would like that." And she propped her walking stick against the counter, "May I look at your stock whilst I sit here?"

"Most certainly, my dear and if something takes your eye, let me know and we'll see if we can do a deal for you." He turned away to help another customer.

"How much would you want for this little silver ring, Sir?" she asked in her most shaky voice.

"For you, dear lady, I'd let it go for £10—and that's half of what it's worth. You'd have a bargain there." And he found a small, velvet box for her and pushed it forward.

She hesitated for a moment, before saying, "Could you perhaps let it go for £8—it's really all I can afford."

He pursed his lips in thought and then smoothed his chin with his fingers, "Very well, but only because it's you." And the deal was done! She knew she'd got a good bargain—and even more of a bargain when the two pieces in her bag were included. She was very deft and slipped the two items into her bag with unflustered speed.

"Thank you for your chair and my bargain." And she left the stall and moved on across the market, stopping at a stall selling small paintings and old pictures. She hovered until the stall holder spotted her leaning on her walking stick and he too, offered her a chair to sit on. Two little oil paintings of flowers were tucked securely in her bag and she left his stall but bought nothing. "None of this would match the other things in my home," she explained, "but your stock is very beautiful."

Mustn't push my luck, she told herself, *I've not done badly for today—and there's always another day!*

Back home again, she turned the key in the lock and called out, "I'm home—wasn't too long, was I?" She went straight into the sitting room where Mirror was waiting. She fluffed her blond curls in front of the mirror and put on some fresh lipstick. Mustn't let herself go, just because she was at home.

"What shall we do this evening, Mirror? What's your pleasure? Oh, and by the way, I must show you what I picked up in the market today. I've brought you a little painting of a lovely rose—and I'll hang it just opposite you, so you can look at it easily." And she took her day's 'purchases' from her bag, looked at the two paintings but had already decided on the rose one for Mirror. However, she held the two paintings before the mirror and asked, "Well, what do you think? No, you can't have the other one, that's mine—yours is the rose—mine is the lily. Take what you're given and be grateful." She hung the painting on the wall and stood back to admire it. Yes, she'd done well—it looked beautiful there.

"Before we settle down for the evening, I'm going to go for a run. Yes, I do think it's a good idea—it has nothing to do with you. I am not too old, what on earth do you mean—too old?" And she disappeared into the bedroom to change into her leggings and tee-shirt. She stood in front of the second mirror in her room. "Oh, I look ridiculous, do I? Well, that's not for you to say. Ridiculous! You really want to hurt me, don't you—well I don't look ridiculous when I look at myself. I look like a vibrant, young and healthy woman—perfectly capable of going for a run."

She went outside and was relieved to see it was still so light—she didn't like to run in the dark. She went towards the park and started going along the path by the lake. She was certainly slower than she used to be, but could still manage it. After a few yards, she felt herself begin to stagger on her feet. 'Get a grip.' She told herself, you're a young woman! She'd only come a few yards and at a very slow pace.

"Wouldn't you like to sit on this park bench—just to get your breath back?" A young girl who was out running too, stopped and took Margaret's arm. "Let's sit together—just for five minutes." They both sat on the bench and the girl produced a water bottle, which she offered to the elderly woman in the track suit. "Have a sip, do—I think you need it."

Margaret eagerly took the bottle and drank deeply. That was better, she could breathe now—but only just. "What's your name, my dear?" she spoke hesitantly and looked into her new friend's eyes.

"My name is Jennifer and I often run this way in the evening. I work in an office during the day, so I like to stretch my legs when I can." She drank from the bottle herself. "If I leave you now, will you be able to get home all right?"

"I think so—but I'll just rest for a little while yet, before I try to get up. In fact, think I may have to get a taxi home—I've run further than I meant to." She thought for a moment and then added. "But I've come out with no money and London cabs are so expensive. Still, never mind—maybe I'll be okay in a little while."

Jennifer looked at the old lady and felt sorry for her. She shouldn't really have been running at her age—she looked so frail. She felt in her trouser pocket and produced a £20 note. "This is all I have—I bring it with me for emergencies—and I suppose this is an emergency, so please take it and get a taxi home." She looked at her money with a lingering look—she didn't really want to give it away—but she had no option, she couldn't go away and leave the woman on her own, with no money.

"You are a sweet and kind girl—and I won't forget your kindness." Margaret said, with tears in her rheumy eyes. She held out her hand to take the money. "If you meet me here tomorrow, I'll return your money. Would that be all right?"

"Yes, that'll be fine, I'll look forward to seeing you then." She stood up and hoped she wouldn't have any emergencies that night. "Goodbye—see you again." Margaret continued to rest on the bench however, her head in her hands.

She pulled the trick twice more that night and eventually returned home with almost £50.

"Look at this, Mirror—are you impressed—that's a week's groceries for me! How do I look by the way—I don't look like someone who's been running around a park, do I?" And she went upstairs to have a relaxing bath.

She woke up with a start in the middle of the night. She could hear the mirror calling for her and she quickly got out of bed and hurried downstairs. "What on earth is it, Mirror? Why are you calling me?" She stood squarely in front of the mirror and saw the sleepy, young girl with tousled hair looking back at her. She liked her new blue pyjamas. "Yes, I'm here now—tell me what you want."

She waited patiently at first and then shouted, "No, I won't do it—you've asked before and I've told you 'no way'. I don't want a child living with us— I've never looked after a child before, and I don't want to start now. If you want a child, then you must go out and get one—I'm not doing it for you." She stared into the mirror and pushed her hair back from her face. "I'm tired, Mirror—we'll talk about it more tomorrow, but don't think you can boss me about." She went back upstairs and the mirror remained quiet for the rest of the night.

Next morning, she dressed in her 'Mummy' twin set and black skirt. She even wore a string of pearls. "Right, I've thought about it Mirror, and the only way I'm going to shut you up is by doing what you want—I can't take any more of your complaining… So, I'm off out and I won't be back until I've got a child—but you'll have to look after it—I'm not that way inclined at all."

She donned a smart beret and went out into the street, opening the garage door and fetching a child's pushchair from the darkness—she usually used it for bringing heavy shopping home, but it really was a proper child's pushchair. She knew she looked her best and put her bag into the chair—it wouldn't look so empty and odd then—lots of people used them for their groceries. She walked slowly down the street towards Wimbledon Park but had to rest a couple of times to get her breath back. It was quite a steep hill.

"Hello my dear—you're a beauty and no mistake." And she stopped beside two or three mothers, having a picnic with their children. One baby in particular had caught her eye—it must have been a little girl because she was dressed all in pink. She sat down beside a tree a few feet away from the little group. The older children were playing tag and tumbling all over the grass. The day was lovely and everyone seemed in a good mood. Two of the children dragged their Mums into their circle and asked them, to play 'Blind Man's Bluff'. They all started laughing and the two babies lying on the grass gurgled with pleasure and watched the group, enjoying themselves.

The day was really warm and Margaret pulled her hair into a bun on top of her head. She moved closer to the group. She took her bag out of the pushchair to make more room. 'Blind Man's Bluff' was going well with a lot of screaming and giggling. No one paid any attention to the elderly woman who was talking to the babies. She was harmless and obviously liked babies. Very slowly and gently, she bent down and lifted the baby in pink—the baby just stared at her. She walked off calmly, carrying the child and no one even noticed her. The empty pushchair was waiting and she slipped the child inside and quickly walked away. The park was full of people—it was such a lovely day—and she soon managed to disappear into the crowd. It had been too simple—*it shouldn't have been that easy,* she thought. Those mothers were careless and hadn't been watching their children. The baby didn't even cry in the pushchair, but just sat there, watching the world go by.

"Come on baby, come and meet Mirror—she's looking forward to meeting you." And the old woman with the pushchair left the park and walked along the pavement. She may have looked like a frail, old woman but she could move pretty fast when she wanted to. Well, she thought it was fast anyway. What she looked like was one thing—what she felt like was quite another—and just now, she was a young girl, full of fun and energy. The baby was inspiring her.

"Mirror—Mirror! We're home and I've brought you a surprise. I hope you've got the room ready." And she closed the front door behind her. She left the pushchair in the hall and lifted the baby into her arms. Amazingly, she still didn't cry but watched Margaret curiously.

She held the baby up to the mirror. "Yes, I know she's pretty and she belongs to us now. Her stupid mother left her lying abandoned in the park whilst she ran off to play some silly game. I'm glad you approve, Mirror; you see, I can do as I'm told, but only when I want to. Now, I'm going to check the room—I hope you've laid out the deepest drawer for her to sleep in. I'm going to have to go to the shops to get some nappies and jars of food—you must look after her until I get back. I think we'll call her Sally—I've always thought that a nice, friendly name. Good—I'm glad you agree."

She took the baby to the upstairs room and placed her in the big, wooden drawer. She really was the most amazing child—the minute Margaret put a soft, woollen shawl under her, she fell fast asleep and sucked her thumb to show how contented she was. Margaret didn't take long at the shops and soon came back with the things she needed.

She was up and dressed next morning, even before the baby awoke—*no, strike that*, she told herself—before Sally awoke. But then she did wake up and her screams were loud enough to awaken the dead.

"Hush, Sally, hush—I've got you a nice, warm bottle of milk." And the child snuggled down in her arms and sucked greedily at the bottle.

"Yes Mirror, I hear you—I'll soon be downstairs—I just have to change *someone's* nappy." Sally had fallen asleep again after her feed. She looked very contented. She didn't seem to be missing her mother in the slightest.

Margaret's second mirror was in her bedroom and sometimes, she preferred to talk with that one. It wasn't quite so opinionated as the sitting room mirror.

"How do I look today, Second Mirror—do I look good?" And she admired herself by twirling her red skirt in a circle. She made herself dizzy though and had to lie down on the bed, to stop her head from spinning. It was odd but she found herself getting dizzy more often than she used to. *I wonder what that can be?* She thought and then dismissed the whole thing.

"Thank you for the compliment, Second Mirror—you're much nicer to me than that other one. It often judges me and finds me wanting. I'm off to take Sally for a walk now—she's due some fresh air." And she collected the baby and plonked her in the pushchair. However, she made sure she sidled past the mirror in the sitting room—as it would have found something negative to say.

They sauntered along the street in the direction of some local shops. She made sure she took the opposite direction from the park of yesterday. As they passed the post office-cum-general store, there was a gang of boys smoking at the corner and laughing at each other's jokes in an exaggerated way. *Just trying to catch people's attention*, but she'd ignore them. She couldn't do that however—they made sure they were blocking the pavement. She stopped the pushchair in front of them. "Could you excuse me please—I can't get past and I'm not going to endanger the baby by stepping off the kerb."

"Oh, hark at Grandma—you don't own the pavement, Granny—we've got as much right as you have to be here." One of the youths moved towards her in a threatening manner. He was dressed just like the other boys—black leather jacket and skin-tight jeans. *Funny!* she thought. *They don't realise they're actually in a uniform. Don't go to school any longer cause that's beneath them but still have to wear a uniform. They just didn't see the irony of that.*

"I realise you have every right to be here, but I thought good manners would mean you'd get out of the way for a mother and her baby." Margaret shook her blond curls in annoyance.

"You're never that kid's mother—you must be joking, you're far too old for that. Maybe you're the Granny—is that what you are, Mrs?" another young thug joined the conversation, "Are you the little un's Granny?"

"Why don't you just get out of my way, you hooligans—or I'll report you to the police!"

"Well, if you're going to claim you're the mother of that little un, maybe we'll report you to the police cause you're obviously lying." The first boy said.

Margaret turned the pushchair around and went back the way she'd come. The boys shouted 'Hooray!' and whistled after her. Their mention of the police made her remember the baby was stolen and the police were probably looking for her right now. She hurried home—where it was safe.

Inside, she put Sally on the rug to play with a couple of toys she'd bought for her—well, not actually bought, more acquired. She turned to the mirror. "What am I going to do, Mirror—people outside think I'm too old for Sally to be my baby; and some rude boys made fun of me and called me Granny. I'm just a girl—isn't that right, Mirror?"

She could hear Mirror's voice in her head, saying "Well, on a good day perhaps—but on most days, you're not." The mirror was being brutally frank today, so Margaret reached up and turned it to face the wall. *See how you like that! She could always use her second mirror—the forgiving one!*

In the bedroom she told the second mirror what had just happened. "So, I made her face the wall. I am just a girl, you know that but—if people outside don't believe it, what am I going to do? Sally needs walking every day really—but I don't think I can face such rude boys again."

She lay on the bed and then remembered she'd left the baby in the other room. Oh dear, she'd better go and get her—babies shouldn't be left on their own. She felt so tired though, she didn't want to have to get up again but she knew she had to. She stopped in front of the second mirror and said, "I know what you're thinking and you're probably right. I shouldn't keep Sally, should I? I don't really want to keep her, you know, she's too much trouble and I only stole her because the other mirror wanted a baby so much. What should I do now?"

"Yes, that's what I'll do—you're such a good friend. Where should I leave her though—it would have to be some place where there's lots of people, so she'll be found quickly? She mustn't get hurt, must she?" and Margaret collected Sally and left the house, not turning the mirror back from the wall. *Let her stay like that for a while—serves her right! And when I return without the baby, she'll be disappointed.*

She decided on one of the largest hospitals as a good place for Sally—lots of people around—someone would be sure to find her quickly. She left the pushchair by the side of the cafeteria and sidled off to the waiting room where there were several empty seats. She watched everything but pretended she wasn't interested, when a young girl bent to speak to the baby. She looked around but could see no one looking for a lost child, so she went to the reception desk—and Margaret knew it was time for her to leave.

She moved at her best speed but when she got outside, she found someone had run off with her handbag and purse. At least, that's what she'd claim when someone asked her what was wrong. She slumped onto a bench in the hospital carpark and cried quietly into a handkerchief.

"Now then, what's this all about?" A middle-aged woman sat down beside her and reached for her hand. "It can't be all that bad, can it? I'm sure we can fix it, whatever it is." She had a lovely kind face and Margaret knew she'd hooked a good one this time.

Half an hour later, when the woman had bought her a cup of sweet tea and a bun, she left the carpark with £20 in her hand and the good wishes of the middle-aged woman ringing in her ears. *Yes—that was using my wits, wasn't it?* And she hopped on a bus to go home and it only cost her tuppence. A bad day had ended well and when she got home, she turned Mirror back around again, so she could see what was going on. She couldn't stay mad at her for long.

"Yes, I know what you're going to say—but it's too late. Sally's not going to live here anymore. How do I look, Mirror, I feel lively and positively flirty. Yes, I thought you'd agree this time—it's always best to keep on my good side—or you could be looking at the wall again." She went into her room for a rest. What a full day it had been.

Going to the cinema was always good fun, especially if a comedy was being shown—and it was—at the Rialto they were showing a Morecambe and Wise film. She loved them and if she played her cards right, that nice man in the box office might let her in free. It was certainly worth a try. Pear Drops in hand and a cup of cola, she was lucky—it was the nice man who always felt sorry for her. "You go on inside, my love—it's nice to see you enjoying yourself." He seemed to really like her, but then she was such a pretty girl, she couldn't blame him.

The gardener called that week—he usually came once a month. She didn't have a large garden but she was finding the bending difficult lately and next door's gardener had offered to help—just a little work, to keep the small lawn neat and the weeds at bay. She was grateful and he was a nice man, who was always whistling. She opened the kitchen window and called out, "Cup of tea, Brian? The kettle's just boiled." And he was in like a shot.

They chatted about this and that and she cut him a slice of cake. "You spoil me, Margaret—but I do like your cake." Brian was munching as he spoke. "Are you going to the Tea Dance in the Community Hall tomorrow?" He asked.

"Well, I hadn't planned to, but if you're inviting me, then yes, I'd love to come with you." She just assumed he'd meant it as an invitation.

He looked embarrassed and coughed behind his hand. "I'm actually going with Teresa two houses along—she asked me this morning, when I was cutting her grass."

Margaret felt irritated—she thought she'd made a fool of herself—and without thinking, she said, "That woman's a slut—and always has been. You really shouldn't be going with her—people will talk."

"Now then, Margaret, there's no need to talk like that." Brian started to get up to leave—the conversation had taken a nasty turn and he didn't know what to say. "Teresa is a nice woman—not really unlike you in fact."

"Like me, you say—why, she's years older than I am and not nearly so pretty." She was well and truly on her high horse.

Brian quickly disappeared at that, even leaving a bit of uneaten cake behind, and Margaret immediately reached for her jacket. She told mirror, "I'll just pop along to see that Jezebel and tell her what I think of her." Her mind was quite made up, but before she left the house, she rummaged through the cutlery drawer and took out the sharpest knife she had. And she was off down the garden path, passing Brian as he trimmed the roses. He saw her go but didn't look up.

Teresa's house seemed quiet as Margaret peered through the sitting room window. Perhaps she was out or maybe taking an afternoon nap upstairs. Either way, it didn't matter, she'd just wait for her to appear. The back door was open and she let herself in. Still, only silence! She went into the sitting room and looked around. Teresa had some nice pieces dotted around—a couple of Royal Dolton figures of long-skirted ladies and a beautiful gold watch, just lying on the mantlepiece where it had been left. It was asking to be rescued! *Maybe I'll just have those before I leave*, she told herself and sat on the sofa, waiting for the lady herself to arrive. She heard the key turn in the lock and suddenly Teresa was standing in front of her.

"Who invited you in?" she asked and folded her arms provokingly across her chest.

Margaret stood up and started to say, "I came to tell you off for stealing Brian from me—but what the hell, it'd just be a waste of words." She rushed across the room and stuck the sharp knife into Teresa's stomach—right up to the hilt. The woman crumpled and fell forward, hitting her head on the coffee table. The blood gushed from the wound and she went a horrible shade of grey. She lay there, not moving and Margaret didn't even check to see if she was still breathing—she just rushed over to the mantlepiece and grabbed the gold watch. She also quickly picked up the two lovely figurines and stuffed one in each pocket. She left the house as quickly as her tired old legs would allow and crossed over the back gardens of the next two houses, reaching her own garden, where Brian was tidying up his tools, ready to leave.

As she went in the back door, she called over her shoulder, "Now don't you forget, Brian, if Teresa lets you down, I'm here for you." She closed the door and leaned against it, quite out of breath. Brian looked after her but didn't answer.

"Mirror, Mirror, on the wall—do you know what I just did? No of course you don't, but I'm going to tell you." She hung her jacket on the coat hook, placed the china ladies on the sideboard and clasped the gold watch around her own wrist. *That's better*, she thought, *everything's tickety-boo now!* And she then proceeded to tell the mirror everything.

"Oh, don't worry, Mirror—I didn't leave any traces. No one will ever know I was there." And she put the kettle on to boil. A nice piece of her cake would go down nicely. That night, she burned her jacket on the garden brazier with the help of some turpentine—that terrible, careless woman had splashed blood on it. The cheek!

A couple of days passed and Brian never contacted her about the dance—but she'd moved on from that and didn't care. There was a commotion outside in the street—police cars, sirens and even an ambulance. How the peace was shattered! She wondered what was going on and even went out into the street to investigate, but by the time she did, all the vehicles had gone. She had a quick conversation with the mirror, before settling down on the sofa with a bar of chocolate. The TV was going to be good tonight.

There was a ring at her doorbell and she jumped up. Who could it be and at this time of the evening? It had better not be those Jehovah Witnesses who were always calling about something. It wasn't the Jehovah Witnesses however—it was two men, one in a suit and one wearing uniform—a police constable. They'd come to enquire if she'd seen anything strange over the last couple of days. They explained that Teresa Watkins had been found murdered in her own home and they were searching for any clues that might help with finding the perpetrator.

"Officers, how dreadful—do take a seat and I'll fetch some tea. Oh my, what a shock! I knew Teresa of course, but not very well. We spoke in passing, but that was all. Poor, poor lady, who could have done such a terrible thing?" She emerged from the kitchen with tea and biscuits and placed them on the coffee table. She could see one of the men eying the biscuits hungrily and she moved the plate closer to him. She had seen nothing unusual and no suspicious people around—then she paused and seemed to be thinking.

"The only one I can think of who was here in the last couple of days is Brian, the gardener. He was here and I know he'd already been to Teresa's house, because he told me he had. He said she'd asked him to go to a Tea dance with her but he'd refused. But that couldn't have turned nasty, could it? No, of course not. What am I thinking?"

"Please go on thinking—anything you can tell us might help. Do you know where this Brian lives?" Margaret gave them his telephone number but she wasn't sure of his address.

"Not to worry, Ma'am, we'll find him." They rose to leave. "And thank you for your time and refreshments—much appreciated. We'll probably have to get in touch with you again—but we'll let you know in advance. Good evening."

"Well, Mirror, what do you make of that? Stop tutting at me; I only told a little white lie about the Tea dance. You're always so critical of everything I do." She looked closely into the mirror and checked there was nothing stuck between her teeth—such teeth as she still had. "Yes, I know I did it but I'm hardly going to tell them, am I? Teresa asked for it you know, she was trying to steal Brian from me." She was just about to walk away but was sure she heard the mirror say something. "Yes, he did so prefer me—what do you know about such things? Absolutely nothing." She changed into her old tracksuit and told the mirror she was going for a run.

"I need a few shillings—I'm running short. That baby took all my spare cash."

When she returned home, she waved three £10 notes at the mirror. "Not bad, eh? This was for two taxis that I never took. People can be so stupid, can't they?" She was tired after her run so she had an early night and slept as innocently as a baby. And why not?

A different policeman called the next day. He'd come to ask her about little Sally, who'd recently been found abandoned at the local hospital. "I know nothing about any baby, Officer. I've never had any children—and I've certainly never wanted any." Margaret didn't offer tea and biscuits this time. She sensed this man was accusing and it scared her. He produced a notebook and handed it to her.

"We've interviewed a group of boys who gave us a description of you and a baby. On the next page, there's another description given by some people who were at the hospital the day the baby was brought there. I think if you look at these, you'll see why I've come to you."

Margaret took his notebook and read the descriptions. She glanced up at him and had to laugh, "Why Officer, these are nothing like me—they're describing an old woman—a very old woman—not someone young and pretty like me." She tucked her hair behind her ears in a nervous gesture. "I'm sorry but I'll have to ask you to leave—you've tired me out."

"It's not up to you to ask me to leave, I want to question you more. I know my colleagues are interested in you as well—about the woman who was recently stabbed. I'll tell you what I'm going to do, I'm going to send a car for you

266

tomorrow and we'll continue our investigation at the station. Don't go anywhere until the car comes for you." He left her then and told his colleagues back at the station, "She's definitely not right—she thinks she's a young girl, not an old woman. She thinks the descriptions we've got are of someone else—a much older woman! Tomorrow should be interesting." They all laughed together.

"Mirror, help me please—what am I going to do? They're trying to blame me for all the bad things—and you know I'm innocent. What's that, I can't hear you? Go and change my clothes—why—what'll I put on? Okay, okay, I'll do it now." She went into her bedroom and said the same things to her Second Mirror, who told her to do exactly the same thing.

She pulled a mini skirt from her wardrobe and a matching tank top. The trouble was that she'd slowly become so thin of late, everything was too big for her and actually hung on her loosely. She pulled on a pair of white knee length boots, piled her long, blond curls on top of her head and applied fresh makeup— a bright, cherry red lipstick and light blue eyeshadow. She turned to the second mirror, "What do you think—they'll never take me for an old woman now— their witnesses will all be proven wrong, won't they? The descriptions they have are nothing like me." She knew she looked good.

"What's that you're saying? Come close to you—really close? Okay," and she did. She really looked closely at herself and cried out desperately, "What's wrong with me—I look pretty and colourful, don't I? I did what you told me to do. I am not a frail old woman who looks like mutton dressed as lamb. How dare you—I thought you were my friend." She reached up to the mirror and threw it against the wall, where it shattered into lots of pieces. The second mirror had been her friend—but no longer!

In the sitting room, she went up to her first mirror—her first friend. It wouldn't let her down. It would confirm how vitally young and beautiful she was—not the old haggard woman the police were looking for. She could see herself clearly in the mirror and liked what she saw. Now, first mirror tended to be honest with Margaret, but she really couldn't go along with the 'young and pretty' description. It didn't see the woman as she saw herself!

"You what? You can't see me as a young woman—only as the woman the police are looking for? How can you say that after all the years of telling me the opposite? I really thought you were my friend. All right, all right, I hear you— you think I look like a very old woman—I can accept you may be right about the years I've lived—but not about the way I look—and that's what will save me from the police accusations. If I can look as young as I feel, then they couldn't match me with the old woman who stole a baby or murdered Teresa. Do you understand?" She was beginning to feel frantic, her first friend was letting her down.

"Okay Mirror—I hear you! Can I not change your mind? Can you not show me as the pretty, young Margaret that I know I am?" Her anger was growing and she was exasperated, so she grabbed the mirror from the wall and smashed it on the wall—just as she'd done with the other one—hard against the wall, where it smashed into smithereens and scattered all over the floor. Her own temper had ended her long-standing friendships with both mirrors—and she was left feeling vulnerable and looking exactly like the old woman the police were looking for.

She fell onto her knees amongst the glass shards and reached for two of the larger pieces. She could see her reflection staring back at her and it was the face and the body of a very old and very haggard woman, who had almost no hair and very few teeth. Her face was deeply lined and the teeth she did have were quite black and cracked. In fact, she saw the person described by the police witnesses. There was no way out, she would be arrested and once Brian was questioned, he would tell them what she'd said about Teresa and how he'd seen her going out that day. It would be enough to hang her or at least send her to prison for a very long time, in fact until she was dead—which wouldn't be too long now.

She slashed one wrist—and then the other. The blood spurted out and splashed onto her red miniskirt and top—and down her white boots. It didn't take long before she felt a dizziness creep over her and she dropped the jagged shards onto the floor. She fell forward amongst the broken mirror—amongst her friend who'd let her down—and she knew Mirror had been right and just couldn't go on lying to her any longer.

And that was how the police driver found her next morning. From his colleagues' description, he wasn't what he'd expected to find. Lying amongst the shattered mirror was a pretty young girl with blond hair—she was dressed in a red miniskirt and wearing white knee-length boots. It looked as though she'd recently applied fresh makeup and used a very bright lipstick. There was no doubt that she'd used the broken mirror to slash her wrists as she was still holding a jagged shard. She was lying in a pool of her own blood which had soaked into the carpet and he thought she looked pitifully young and vulnerable. She could have been no more than 20 years old.

He checked around the house and even called out, but there was no sign of the old woman he'd come to collect. It was a strange sight and not one he'd forget in a hurry. He didn't touch anything but called the station for back-up and warned them they'd be needing forensics as well. "What I've found here is definitely not your guilty party," he reported. "For some reason, she'd broken mirrors all over the house and then used the glass to end her life."

What age had Margaret been? Was she eighty or twenty? We know there was no doubt that she'd committed the crimes and that she was good at persuading people to part with their money—but this couldn't have been her, could it? What age had she been? It seemed to depend on who was looking at her—but when she was the one doing the looking, there was no doubt she was a young pretty blond—until the last moments of her life, when the mirrors finally showed her the truth. And it was too much for her to bear—so she ended it all. But the dead body the police driver had found that morning was young and pretty and had blond curls.

They do say that 'Beauty is in the eye of the Beholder'—and all Margaret had ever seen was herself as beautiful and youthful! And why not?

Creagan Ruadh Castle

He lived in a small cottage about half a mile from a ruined castle in the West of Scotland. It was often described as a 'But and Ben' and could house not only the family, but several animals as well. He'd lived there with his parents since he was born and for many years, had worked as a member of staff at the castle, when it was fully functional and lived in. It proved too expensive for the owners to keep and, as no one wanted to buy it, they just had to abandon it. At least that was the story spread about at the time of their departure—a very speedy departure in the end.

The castle stood there now in all its glory, a reminder of its formal grandeur. Jimmy Bell loved it and liked to believe he was there to guard it and keep it safe. He now looked after his sheep and his dog and that kept him busy, but he often found the time to watch over the castle and build the occasional fallen stone back into its original place. 'Castle Ruin' he liked to call it—but its real name was Creagan Ruadh Castle—called so, because of the pinkish hue of the stone used in its build. Red rocks were commonly found along the shore lines in the area, and the surface of the local quarry reflected a true pink glow.

In the Gaelic tongue 'Ruadh' means red and 'Creagan' means rocks, hence its name—Creagan Ruadh or Red Rock Castle. The Bell family had long been associated with the MacMillan Clan—and the Bells had lived in the Castle for many centuries. The area around Ayr in Scotland had long been the home of the Bells and being a Bell himself, Jimmy always believed he had a duty to watch over his ancestry home.

"Come on, Billy Boy," he called to his collie, "let's get these sheep in the barn—it's getting colder." There were only 10 sheep, so it was easy to keep them under control. Billy ran around the sheep and gathered them all together—he was a good old dog and a Godsend to his master. Jimmy had been on his own now for almost ten years—his Ma and Pa had died when he was 40 and although there'd been a second son, no one ever mentioned his name—that was his brother, William. But William had up and left the area when he was a young man—he'd emigrated to America where he believed the streets were paved with gold—and where a man could make something of himself. After the day he left his home, his name was never mentioned again. Ma and Pa had not wanted him to go.

Jimmy had never been interested in making his fortune, he was reasonably content to stay at home with his mother and father and look after them—and the few animals they had. He did wonder sometimes what would had happened had he gone to America as well—he might be a millionaire by now—but then, what would he do with all that money? No, he liked looking after his sheep and that was that.

Early next morning, he and Billy walked across the hills to the castle. It was cold but bright and the two friends strode out, obviously on a mission. Jimmy carried his heavy stone hammer—*it was good exercise,* he thought. There always was work to be done on the walls around the castle. If he didn't keep on top of it, it would soon get out of his control. As he neared the building, he could hear the bagpipes' usual drone wafting over the fields and he quickened his steps to try and catch a glimpse of the piper. He always considered it lucky to see the ghostly figure dressed in his full set of the kilts. The tartan was that of the MacMillan Clan as this had been their seat in years gone by and they were the head of clans like the Bells. The piper had woken them up in the mornings by playing his bagpipes and he had never stopped. He made a lovely addition to the atmosphere of the castle.

"Yes, there he is, Billy—do you see him—just disappearing around the far side." And the sound of the pipes slowly disappeared leaving the old castle alone in its sad run-down state. The man and dog didn't trouble to follow the piper—they knew he wouldn't be there even if they did. He had done his early morning performance and wouldn't be back until the next day. Although a ghost, his beautiful music was heard at the same time every morning—but only by certain, privileged people and Jimmy was lucky enough to be one of them. Man and dog went inside the building just to make sure no one was hiding there and Billy ran from room to room, checking for strangers.

After a couple of hours work, he opened his bag and took out a cheese sandwich, which he halved with the dog. Then they heard it! Someone had taken over his hammering—but who would be hereabouts at this time of day?

Outside, there was a young man who was placing a board on a pole at the side of the castle drive. He lifted a large board and Jimmy could see words on it. In bold black letters, it said, 'FOR SALE—If interested, please contact the selling office in Ayr: Tel No herewith,' and a string of numbers followed.

"Hey young man, what do you think you're doing? Who told you this castle was for sale? I'm sure you're making a mistake. It was for sale many years ago, but no one was interested." Jimmy was quite agitated and the dog began to bark at the man, taking the lead from his master's tone.

"I'm sorry, Sir—the owners have decided to try to sell it again and my office has been instructed to advertise it as widely as possible. This sign is the first thing we've done so far." He gathered up his bits and pieces and walked to his van. "Goodbye, I'm sure we'll meet again." And he was gone, leaving a very confused Jimmy.

"They're going to sell our castle, Billy. Can you imagine that? To be honest, I don't even know who still owns it."

Man and dog returned home and in the living room, Jimmy found his parents in their usual chairs, either side of the fireplace. They weren't there every day—only some days—but Jimmy was glad to see them today. "You'll never guess, the castle's up for sale again. I just saw a man putting up a 'For Sale' board. What do you make of that?"

The old man spoke up first, "They'll never sell that place—it's been empty too long." He was puffing on his pipe—there was no smoke, the pipe had actually gone out 10 years before, on the day of his death. But he enjoyed the feel of it in his hands and in his mouth.

"Father—put out that smelly old thing—how many times do I have to tell you? Disgusting habit!" The old woman had made the same complaint all her married life, but to no effect, the old man just went right on smoking.

They looked exactly what they were—an old Victorian couple, born at the turn of the twentieth century and came through the First World War. Father had come home after fighting in Normandy in the Great War. Mother thought he came back a different man but it was only to be expected after seeing the things he'd seen. She'd worked in the Glasgow Mills throughout the war years and they'd married when it was all over and moved to live with her parents in the little cottage, next to Ruadh Castle, where they stayed all their lives. Primarily because they had nowhere else to live.

They'd had a decent life there, both eventually working in the castle as servants and when their two sons were born, the grandparents looked after the children whilst their parents went to work. School was in the town of Ayr and the boys helped out at the castle when needed. It was a good life until the owners decided to leave and emigrate to Australia. They never came back so things must have gone well for them. The grandparents in the cottage died and Jimmy's Mum and Dad inherited the house. And that's where Jimmy and William grew up.

Although they'd both been dead for almost 10 years, the old folks liked to come back now and again to keep an eye on the place—and on Jimmy. He, on the other hand, was quite happy without the old folks watching his every move. He lived his own life and did what he wanted, although he couldn't escape their irregular visits from beyond the grave—someone had to keep an eye on the boy. Having said that however, it was nice to see them now and again—like today, when he wanted someone to talk to. He enjoyed talking to them but always had to 'make up' their side of the conversation.

"They'll never get a buyer for that old place—not now, after all this time. The kitchen will be a wreck and as for utilities, there'll be none still working." Ma was nodding her head in agreement and her top-knot of silver hair was bobbing up and down in time with the words. "If anyone does come along, he's going to need a great deal of money to get even beyond the front door." Again, the head moved up and down.

"We'll just have to wait and see, won't we?" Jimmy filled the kettle and set it on the hob. "I'm going out for a pint tonight, so I won't be home—in case you're looking for me." He looked straight at his mother. "You can't tell me not to go, Ma—the way you always used to—one advantage of your dying, I suppose." And he laughed to himself. "Ah those were the days, weren't they, Ma?"

In the pub that night, Jimmy was talking to his usual cronies. Old Jock was on his soapbox, "Well, all I can say is I hope new owners at the castle don't change things around the area. That's if anyone comes forward to buy the place of course!" The others at the bar agreed with him—it might be an old ruined castle, but it was their old ruined castle.

The town's main estate agent happened to be in the pub that night and he listened to the conversation, but couldn't resist telling everyone that he already had an American gentleman interested in the property.

"A Yank! A Yank, you say—I damned well hope not. They spoil everything they touch! Always wanting to make things bigger and better!" Old Jock was obviously upset at the thought of an American buying Ruadh Castle, so he said to the Agent, "Does he know it's haunted? Have you told him that—I bet you haven't."

"Don't be silly, Jock—there's no ghosts up there. Who's been telling you porky-pies?" The estate agent was not amused. "Who are the ghosts then, Jock?"

Jock obliged, "It's the old Macmillan's who appear at the castle—it was their family estate after all, and they only left because they didn't have the money to keep it. They still appear from time to time—you'll see them, if you take the trouble to hang about. And don't forget the piper some people see and hear. Why don't you ask Jimmy there—he's bound to have seen them more than once." He turned to Jimmy and raised his bushy eyebrows questioningly. His one eye blinked a couple of times and Jimmy realised he was being winked at.

He coughed nervously and said, "Well, I've certainly seen some things that would make your hair stand on end." It was his way of getting out of telling a direct lie. He looked straight at the Agent. "The castle belonged to the MacMillan Clan, you know—and on the odd misty night, you can see them in their ancient mustard tartan kilts going from room to room inside. I've come upon them many a time." Old Jock smiled at the exaggeration and Jimmy crossed his fingers.

He watched the Agent gulp and swallow hard, before saying "Really?" in a high-pitched voice.

"Oh aye—you'd better tell your American man about that, hadn't you?" Jimmy was enjoying himself now and Old Jock was smiling into his pint. "And don't forget to tell him about the piper playing the bagpipes every morning. I know a lot of people say they've never seen him—but I certainly have." And that at least was the absolute truth!

It was almost a week before he went again to the castle with his heavy hammer. There were plenty stones that needed breaking up to fill in the gaps made by the wild weather and wild animals. He'd put the sheep out to graze and they'd soon spread themselves all across the field—but Billy would soon round them up when it was time. He was a good old sheepdog and the animals were used to obeying him.

The two had started out early as that was when they heard the piper. The sound of the bagpipes in the open air filled Jimmy with nostalgia for the old days. There it was, clear as could be, "Listen Billy, I swear he waits for us to arrive before he starts playing." He laughed at his own madness, "Imagine believing a ghost would wait for an audience!" But wait he did and the man and his dog caught a glimpse of him as he disappeared around the castle wall.

Jimmy noticed the tartan of his kilt was the Ancient Dress MacMillan, a light-coloured cloth of orange and yellow—very old in appearance.

"Goodbye, Sweet Piper," Jimmy called after him—and then felt foolish, calling after a ghost. But there was no one else there, so why shouldn't he? The breaking of the stones began and he used an old wheelbarrow he kept there to move the heavy stones about the place. As usual, the dog went nosing about, especially inside the building—it seemed fascinated with the great rooms. Jimmy called out to him to share his corned beef sandwich but the dog was obviously too busy to come right away.

"Okay Mut, I'll eat it all myself." But he knew he couldn't do that and he got up and went looking inside the castle. "Come on, Billy, where are you hiding this time—ah, there you are in your favourite place!" He threw the piece of sandwich to the dog and it was demolished in one gulp. "Why do you find this room so interesting—and that corner in particular? One day, I'm going to dig up around that spot and find out why you love it." He started to turn away and then stopped, grabbed his shovel from its usual place and started digging. "May as well do it now—I've been putting it off for years now and if that American is coming, I won't get the chance for much longer."

An hour later, the hole was vast and he stopped to fetch a drink from his bag. Whilst he was away, Billy started digging in the hole for himself. He couldn't wait for Jimmy to return. "For God's sake, dog, let me get a drink." And he put down a bowl of water for Billy. "Not that you deserve it, impatient hound—I'm the one doing all the work." He started digging again. And his spade hit something hard which sounded metallic. "Well, I never, Billy—what have we here?" And he eased a large box from the ground and lifted it out of the hole.

"We really had to dig deep for this, didn't we?" It looked old and was held shut by several leather straps wrapped all around it. It smelt very musty and earthy and it looked as though it had been buried there for a very long time. "How many years do you think it's been down there, Billy? A good many, I should think." He got out his knife and tried to snap one of the straps but the leather was too thick and he had to give up.

"Tell you what mut, I'll fetch my wheelbarrow from the front and we'll just take it home with us—and then we can investigate it at our leisure." And that's exactly what they did, but not before he filled in the hole again. "No point advertising the fact that something was there!" The ground didn't look quite as it had—but then, who was there to notice?

He didn't take it into the house as it smelt so bad—and anyhow, Ma and Pa would probably appear to see what he was doing and he didn't want that. They never came out into the barn, so he was quite safe. Anyway, they would have opinions as to what he should do with the contents. Best to keep them both out of it! He fetched his sharpest knife as it was the only way he could deal with the straps—the leather was old and dry and difficult to handle. He pulled open the top of the box after a lot of struggling.

Wrapped in an old piece of sack cloth, he lifted out a Sgian Dubh with an enormous jewel embedded into the hilt—it was made in the shape of a cross. The jewel was blue and shone as if it hadn't lain in the earth for what could have been centuries. There was a large round ball which seemed to be made of glass and deep inside, there was the recognisable Emblem of the MacMillan Clan—a strong fist holding a sword in the air—and there in the centre, was a blue stone just like the one in the Sgian Dubh. It must have been the colour favoured by the Macmillans.

Around the emblem was the motto of the Clan written in Latin, *MISTERIS SUCCURRERE DISCO*—and the glass globe was wrapped in a piece of tartan; in fact it was the Ancient Old MacMillan tartan itself—and looked quite beautiful. Jimmy knew the words by heart and repeated them quietly: ***I LEARN TO SUCCOUR THE DISTRESSED***. The caring sentiment made him feel proud of his heritage!

The Clan of MacMillan originally came from Lochnabar in the Scottish Highlands and their history goes back to the 12th century—and probably way beyond that. They had been staunch supporters of Robert the Bruce and made their name in many battles. They had always been known as 'The Tonsured Ones' and initially, had half shaved heads in the ecclesiastical style of monks of the day. They must have looked a fearsome lot as they ran towards the enemy in battle.

From the box, Jimmy took out a scroll, tied with ribbon. It was sepia coloured and very old with a great deal of writing in a beautiful and ancient style. He laid it to one side to read later and searched further in the box. He pulled out a black Balmoral bonnet adorned with three Eagle feathers—the feathers a sure sign of a Clan Chief, the bonnet must have been worn a very long time ago. He twirled it on his finger and whistled, "My, what a find!" There was an envelope inside it, which said in bold letters—*DINNA WEAR THIS WHEN YE'RE OOT AND ABOOT*. What an odd message to bury with the other things!

The box was not quite empty. He felt around inside and found a folded piece of tartan—it was a plaid—a length of material for wearing over the shoulder and this time, was of the Ancient Hunting MacMillan tartan. He unfolded it and swing it around his shoulders—my, it looked and felt good. What very strange bits and pieces to take the trouble to bury so deep in the ground. Ah well, he put everything back inside and hid the box under a loose floorboard in the barn. The sepia coloured scroll he took with him into the house. Maybe it would throw some light on the box.

He was feeling hungry, it had been a long, eventful day and even Billy was looking at him with hungry eyes. He opened the drawer of the wooden table and cut himself a square of porridge he'd made that morning—he always made it in bulk and kept it in the drawer to have when he wanted it without the fuss of cooking. He soaked it in hot milk—some for him and some for the dog. Billy liked porridge as much as he did and began scoffing it.

Jimmy sat at the table and spread out the scroll in front of him. It started off with a warning, which was a little disconcerting to say the least. It said, *Whoever reads this missive which I planted in the ground, had better be a MacMillan or an associate of that clan—it will help you to understand the significance of the contents—but be of no use to others.* It went on:

In the regions of Glen Urquhart and Glen Morriston, the Clan of McMillan was much associated with the folklore of the area. There was one female goblin or witch who haunted the clan perpetually. For whatever reason—and that is not known—she hated every one of the clan with great venom. She was well known and feared—her name was Cailleach a Chretnich and when she came across a MacMillan, she contrived to steal his bonnet without his knowledge.

Once in her hands, she began to rub and pick at the bonnet and wouldn't give it back to the owner, despite his pleading with her. She rubbed the bonnet hard and then harder still—and all the time, muttering some spell as she rubbed. The man became weak and had to sit down—she went on rubbing the bonnet until she'd made a hole in it. At that point, the unlucky MacMillan actually died and lay there prone on the ground. No one could ever discover the reason for his death—his body appeared unmarked. He was however dead as a doornail—and it was the hole in the bonnet that had done it.

There were several of the MacMillan Clan who came across Cailleach a Chretnich in this way and they were all found dead on the moors, with no mark of violence on their person and wearing no headgear. Their bonnets were often found some distance away from the body, completely rubbed into holes. No one ever knew what was going on but the men warned each other to keep an eye out for the witch or her companion, the goblin.

One day, she came across a young man of the hated clan, one Daniel MacMillan of Balmacaan—Balmacaan was a wild mountainous area between Corrimony and the Braes of Glen Morriston. As they passed, he greeted her and went on his way. He soon discovered she'd somehow taken his bonnet so he ran after her to get it back. She was already rubbing the bonnet as hard as she could and wouldn't give it back—but he struggled with her and managed to grab it from her. As he made to go away, she hissed at him and swore he would die— she would make sure of it—he would die on a certain date which she would predict—and at exactly the same time as he'd met her.

On the dreaded date, Daniel's family and friends sat with him, to protect him from the old witch's spell, but to no avail. At the same moment on the day she'd met him, he suddenly fell forward and lay there quite dead, head resting on the table. Somehow, she'd managed to reach him although physically, she was nowhere near him.

In the area, many believed in the power and wickedness of witches and it was common for wax dolls to be found, covered with pins stuck into their bodies— the chosen way to get rid of those you didn't like. This then, must have been how the witch managed to end Daniel MacMillan's—whilst she was nowhere near him.

So, beware any MacMillan—or associates of that clan—who reads the above. Guard your bonnet well as the Old Crone is probably still looking for you on the moor.

Jimmy rolled up the scroll again, feeling petrified of its contents. What might happen—after all, as a Bell, he was an associate of the MacMillan Clan.

"Ach, come on, Billy—time for bed, although I don't think I'll do much sleeping tonight. I'll be too busy listening for the Old Witch to come and get me." He went to bed, with the dog at his heels, and slept the whole night through with no visits from any wandering spirits—even his mother and father were quiet.

Next morning after putting out some food for the sheep, he actually shouted to his parents, something he rarely did as he really preferred not to see them too often. There they were, settled in their chairs, "What is it, son—do you need help with anything?" his mother asked. Before he could answer, she added, "If it's about that old scroll you were reading last night, then I can tell you that I do know of Cailleach a Chretnich and the stories about her. She was a bitter woman who had the Devil on her side. You must keep well away from her, Jimmy, my son!"

"Oh Mother, I'll be having nothing to do with her. Anyway, surely, she's not around any longer. It must have been a long time ago when she was doing her damage." Jimmy wasn't all that surprised that the old folks knew about his find at the castle. They always knew his business. "Don't you worry—I'll not be wearing the feathered Balmoral around here. I'm not that stupid! In fact, since you have to know everything I'm doing. I'm off into town to visit the estate agent to find out how much the castle is being sold for. Just out of curiosity—not because I have any money." And he laughed as he strode off over the hill.

In Ayr, he found the shop he was looking for and was told the Agent had taken a gentleman to see over the castle. "Not an American gentleman?" he asked.

"Why, yes Sir—he was an American." That called for a quick pint in the nearest pub although it was only lunchtime! He sat there, nursing his beer and just thinking about things in general, when in walked the Estate Agent himself, accompanied by a bald-headed man. He stared at the man, thinking he knew him, but he couldn't have, if this was the American. Drinks in hand, they moved over to a table and Jimmy watched them go.

He knew who the man was—older but still familiar. It was William his brother, whom he hadn't seen for more than 20 years. He drained his glass and crossed the room.

"Hello Will, I didn't expect to see you here. You're never 'the American' who's interested in Creagan Ruadh Castle?" He sat down at the table.

"I am that—and I didn't expect to see you either Jim." He stood up and held out his hand to the brother he hadn't seen for so long. They shook hands solemnly and the 20 years seemed to disappear all at once—they were brothers again.

"Have you really got the kind of money needed to buy a castle, Will?" He couldn't keep the surprise out of his voice.

The estate agent was watching the exchange with interest and felt he should say something. "Jimmy, is this your brother who left for America a long time ago?"

"It certainly is and it's the same man whose family heard nothing from him for all those years. Who said blood was thicker than water? They've got it wrong, I fear!"

Will intervened and said, "Now, that's not true, Brother—I wrote to Mum and Dad many times—even inviting them to come to America. They never answered any of my letters—not once. I even wrote to you, asking you to join me as I was doing so well—and you never answered either." The man was obviously angry and upset. "In the end, I gave up writing—all of you obviously wanted nothing to do with me." Truth to tell, he seemed genuinely hurt. Both brothers stood up and the agent offered to get some more drinks. It worked and broke the bad atmosphere.

"We've obviously got a lot to talk about, Will—why don't you come back home this evening and bring your things, you can stay with me, if you like." They all finished off their second drink and Jimmy left the pub to let the others talk about the price of the castle.

"Guess who's coming to supper, Ma—it's your firstborn, William? Would you believe he's the rich American who's interested in buying the castle?"

Ma and Pa appeared from goodness only knew where and Pa said, "No Jimmy—don't let him come here—he's not welcome." Pa looked very agitated and Ma was flustered and had tears in her eyes.

"I never thought we'd see him again," she said. "He's been no friend of yours, Jimmy—he left you to look after this place and us—he didn't care if we lived or died."

"Well, either way, life goes on—and he's coming here tonight, so I want you both to disappear and not bother us. He'll freak out if he sees you—he knows you're both dead." Jimmy got on with preparing the supper. At the knock on the door, Ma and Pa disappeared and Jimmy invited in his long-lost brother.

"Nothing's changed here, has it? After all these years, nothing's changed." Will looked around the room. "It looks just as it did the day I left." He seemed upset so Jimmy offered him a whisky. Both men gulped back their drinks and wiped their mouths with the back of their hands—an identical gesture which made them both laugh.

"You'll stay for a few days, I hope—we can get to know each other again. Tomorrow, I have to go to Glasgow to see the man who buys my wool. It'll soon be time to shear the sheep and sell their coats—so you'll have to excuse me. Is that okay?"

"That's fine, Brother—what is that wonderful smell? Hope it's my supper." And the two brothers settled down at the kitchen table—with Ma and Pa watching from the doorway—but only visible to Jimmy.

Next morning, Jimmy set off for Glasgow and told Will to have a good look around the place—see how much he could remember. And Will did just that— he even climbed the rickety ladder into the attic to see if there was anything from his childhood there. *Oh my God. What a lot of junk*, he thought. It was worth the effort however as in an old bureau under the window, he found a bundle of letters tied with string—they were tucked right at the back of the drawer and hidden under a cloth. The letters were the ones he'd sent from America all those years before—he found it all very upsetting. He took them back into the kitchen—they were the proof that he had tried to contact his folks and hopefully, to bring them to America to join him. He realised his parents must have kept them hidden from Jimmy—but couldn't understand the reason why on earth they'd do that.

When Jimmy returned that evening, Will had spread the letters across the table and didn't have to explain what he was doing. "There you are, Jim—proof that I did try to contact all of you—but Mother and Father obviously had different thoughts about that. Now, you must believe me—you see in that one…" and he singled out one particular letter, "…it's addressed to you and asking you to join me in America and that I had a good job for you and a place to live." Jimmy read the letter and looked at his brother.

"Why would Ma and Pa not have given me this—I don't understand." He fell back onto a chair, letter in hand.

"Oh, come on now, the answer is obvious—they didn't give it to you in case you took me up on the offer and came to America—they didn't want you to leave them. In my opinion, what they did was criminal—you could have been with me all these years and had a great life. They didn't even want to come for a holiday— why? I can't imagine. It wouldn't have hurt and I even offered to pay for them."

That night, they got through a whole bottle of whisky before falling into bed and sleeping the deepest sleep imaginable. The estate agent woke them next morning and a tousle-headed Jimmy opened the door just a crack—the sun was too bright—and he quickly invited him inside.

"I've come to see your brother, if I may," he dusted off a chair and sat down. "I need to know his intentions about the castle—I have another interested party who wants to come and view it."

Will came downstairs and started to boil the kettle. Boy, he needed a cup of coffee.

"Well Sir, I've had time to think about it now and I don't think I'll be putting in an offer. I hadn't realised how much of a ruin it had become—I suppose I still thought of it as it was before I emigrated. It was quite magnificent then."

The agent immediately rose from his chair. "Well, I won't trouble you any further. I think you're making a big mistake as the castle is still quite magnificent—but the decision is yours. Goodbye, gentlemen." And he saw himself out.

"So, you'll not be buying the castle, Will? What made you change your mind? Is it really the condition it's in? Sit yourself down, man, I've just made a pot of tea—but if you'd prefer coffee coming from across the water, then there's the jar—only instant, I'm afraid." They sat down in companionable silence.

"Will you come back to America with me, brother? I've plenty of room at home and I'm not short of a bob or two. I never married either, so you'd be my heir and get everything I have. You're a few years younger than I am, so you'd have plenty of time to enjoy it. Well, what do you say?" He waited patiently for an answer.

"Oh man, you'll have to let me think about that—although I must admit, I'm tempted. Tell me one thing though, would I be able to bring Billy with me—I could never leave him here on his own?"

Will reassured him that that was possible and smiled at his brother's main concern. Then he hesitated before asking, "Jim, tell me if I'm barking mad—but have you ever felt Ma and Pa's presence in the house—I feel quite strongly that they're here. In fact, I think I saw them when I was in the attic." He looked rather sheepish as he asked the question.

"Aye, they're always here, Will—I'm not surprised you've seen them, but they do no harm and I'm used to having them here. Does it scare you? Not that I can do much about it—you know Ma—she always liked to have her own way." The brothers smiled at the thought of Ma and Will cautiously looked around the room, in case they were listening. Jimmy added, "They'll come out when they're ready and probably engage you in conversation—they do with me—often. And I've thought about your proposal—I will come back to America with you—but I won't sell this place, until I know if I like the new country."

"That seems fair and if it wasn't only 10 o'clock in the morning, I'd suggest a drink to celebrate your decision."

Jimmy just slapped him on the shoulder and said, "Let's have a drink anyway—no matter the time." And they did.

That afternoon, Jim had walked into town with his dog to visit the bank manager, having some business to sort out. But he told Will he'd be coming back by way of the castle—as it was something he and Billy liked to do.

Will was resting in a chair at the back of the building, when all at once, he heard his Ma speaking. "You great, lazy lump, get up and make yourself useful—lying there like a bairn." He recognised his mother's dulcet tones.

Pa was there at her side, but he wasn't smiling. "Are you trying to take away our son from us, William? I fear that's exactly what you're doing." He obviously didn't like the thought.

"Come away into the house, son," Ma said, "there's something we want to show you." In a daze, Will followed them indoors, hardly able to believe he was having a conversation with his long dead parents, but he had no option. There on the kitchen table was the old box Jimmy had taken so much trouble to hide from his parents. Will looked at the box and asked what it was.

Ma answered, "You're a Bell, aren't you, and as such, part of the Macmillan Clan?"

"I am that, and proud of it. The MacMillan Clan are a great body of people—and always were. I'm proud to be a part of them." And he fingered the bits and pieces in the box, removing the Balmoral bonnet with the Eagle feathers and the long plaid of MacMillan tartan. "Where on earth did this come from?" He asked the ghosts, but not expecting an answer.

"They're for you, William, my son," Pa spoke up. "They're for you to wear at the castle. And now you've decided not to buy the old ruin but instead, to take our son back to America with you, I think you should wear the outfit and walk over the fields to meet Jimmy at the ruin. After all, it might be the last time you see the old building—and Jimmy will get a kick out of seeing you dressed as a true MacMillan."

"Aye son, you should do what your father says—you'll look the 'bee's-knees' in that outfit. Away and dress yourself and let us see you before you leave." She ushered him out of the kitchen door.

He stood in the doorway—a true Highlander! He wore the Balmoral bonnet at a jaunty angle and the long plaid over his shoulder; he'd even borrowed Jimmy's kilt which was in the same tartan and carried the Sgian Dubh in his long woollen sock. He could have stepped straight out of the pages of a history book. "Now I feel like a true Highlander off to defend his clan. I'll be seeing you two later." And he was off, his kilt swaying to either side as he went.

The ghosts looked at each other and Ma said, "Do you think it'll work, Pa?"

And he replied, "Aye, it'll work, Lassie—the goblin has never really gone away—she just sleeps throughout the centuries. My God, but he does look magnificent—unknowingly on his way to meet his fate!" Pa's voice was suddenly sad.

"It's his own fault—if only he wasn't trying to steal our Jimmy away from us, we'd just let him go safely back to America, but needs must, I'm afraid. We managed to put a stop to his plans for so long—but we can't let him win now." And both parents disappeared from their cottage home—for the time being, that is!

Strutting across the fields, Will felt better than he'd felt for years. He'd even found a strong stick to use as a crook and he hadn't gone very far when he saw a figure approaching. It looked like a woman, but a strangely stooped woman, who seemed to have trouble walking. She stopped in her tracks and waited for him to reach her.

Will nodded his head in salutation and made to walk on, but she held up her hand to stop him. "Do you know who I am—and what I want from you?"

"I don't know who you are and I don't think I have anything that you would want." Will felt instinctively that he should be aware of her.

"My name is Cailleach a Chretnich and I am your destiny." She quickly snatched his bonnet and ran away with it as fast as her crippled legs would allow. She was rubbing it furiously as she went. She was cackling like a witch and shouted over her shoulder as she sped away across the field, "A true MacMillan in his regalia—the three feathers in your bonnet signal you as part of the hierarchy of the clan. Another MacMillan hits the dust." And she started to chant a weird verse and laugh like the banshee she was.

Eventually, he did catch up with her and made to grab the bonnet, but she danced away and spun around in circles. "Ye cannae catch me, ye stupid man, I'm a will-o-the wisp and way beyond your grasp." And she continued rubbing the bonnet and laughing at his frustration.

"Did ye not know I hate the Clan MacMillan—naw, ye couldn't have—or ye'd never have come struttin' about dressed like that. I hate them and anyone whose name is associated with theirs."

In the end however, she was no match for Will and he caught up with her, snatching his bonnet from her grip. "Away you go, woman, you're obviously mad—what would you want my bonnet for?" He wasted no more time in talking but turned and ran away as fast as his legs would allow.

She didn't follow him but shouted in a strong voice that floated across the wind, "Aye, go on yer way but ye canna escape my wrath. Yer bonnet's been rubbed by my hands—and rubbed hard—so ye'll die now—ye'll die in one hour from this very moment."

He didn't look back but had to stop running to catch his breath. He headed in the direction of the castle where he hoped Jimmy had already arrived. What on earth had just happened? He was confused and even wondered if it had really happened at all, but he looked at his bonnet and saw the hole in the material. What on earth had been her intention? She'd said she hated the Clan MacMillan, but why? For the first time in his life, he wished his family name wasn't Bell—and a solid part of the Clan.

Jimmy was waiting for him, sitting on a broken wall at the front of the Castle. "Well, would you look at you? I take it you found the old box I dug up—you really look a true Highlander—but what made you dress up today? Have our parents had a hand in this by any chance—is that what happened—did they encourage you to try on the clothes?"

"They did that, Brother—in fact they almost insisted on it—and here I am in all my glory—Sgian Dubh and all." Will felt proud standing in front of the MacMillan home and kitted out in the MacMillan tartan. "But look at my bonnet! Have I got a strange tale to tell you!"

And he told Jimmy about the woman, whose name he couldn't remember—but Jimmy could and asked, "Was it Cailleach a Chretnich by any chance?" Before William could reply, he went on, "Come Brother, we must get you home right away." But before the brothers could leave the castle, they heard the sound of the bagpipes. But that couldn't be—the piper only came early in the mornings—not in the middle of the afternoon. Yet, there he was, marching up and down in front of the building. Will couldn't believe his eyes or ears—but there was the piper, large as life, although not really as large as life, being a ghost.

"Oh my God, this is a day of strange happenings. That is not a good sign—he must be warning someone. What else is still to come?" Jimmy grabbed his brother's arm and said, "We've got to get home now, Will! Come on and take off that bloomin' bonnet." Will obeyed and began to run as well—he knew his brother was being deadly serious.

Jimmy suddenly stopped and shouted loudly to no one in particular, "*Miseris Succurrere Disco*. Please God, let the Clan's ancestors hear him and help his brother." He was feeling anxious enough for both of them.

They reached the cottage in short time but not quickly enough to miss a sudden and heavy rain shower—they found Ma and Pa sitting on their chairs either side of the fireplace. The dog shook his wet coat and settled down by the fire, waiting for someone to light it. Will removed his tartan clothes and Jimmy put on the kettle for a hot brew. He chose to ignore his parents as he knew it had been them who had set Will up and put him in danger. Not that Will knew he was in danger but Jimmy knew all tight.

"Sit yourself down, Brother, and have this coffee. It'll soothe your nerves." He put the Sgian Dubh on the mantlepiece and hid the scroll back in the box. He didn't want Will to read the story—he was wise enough to know that sometimes the thought of impending doom could make it actually happen—and he didn't want the witch's curse to come true.

"Who do you think that old crone was, Jimmy? Was she just a mad woman, perhaps been released too soon from an asylum? She was dressed in clothes from long ago and had teeth like tombstones. You've heard of her before then—is she a witch or a goblin perhaps but that's a stupid question, isn't it? There are no such things, are there?" He laughed into his cup at his daft question. "We don't have such things in America, but I'm not in America now, am I? I'm in crazy old Scotland." He was beginning to feel weaker and slumped down in his chair. "Gosh, I thought coffee was supposed to revive you. I feel quite groggy."

"Have a wee dram, Brother, that'll perk you up!" Jimmy was getting more worried by the minute and looked angrily at Ma and Pa, who were obviously enjoying seeing their plan reach its conclusion.

"I feel really bad, Jimmy—I think I'm going to pass out—if I do, you'll find a list of my contacts in my wallet—including my lawyer. And remember, I've left everything to you." Will was ashen now and his eyes were closing. He'd been perfectly all right before, yet now he was fading away before Jimmy's eyes. He slumped forward, banging his head on the table and Jimmy grabbed hold of him, trying to support his head.

It was all for nothing; Will was dead. Just like that, he'd left this world for the next. A big, healthy man with no medical conditions. Cailleach had obviously lost none of her powers. He turned to Ma and Pa, "You two did this. You talked him into dressing up in that MacMillan outfit, knowing full well that wearing the feathered bonnet would seal his fate. How could you do that to your own son?" He lifted Will and placed him on the sofa.

"It was no bother at all," Ma said and Pa nodded his head in agreement, adding, "The lad asked for it—he got his just desserts in the end. He was trying to take you away from us—and we couldn't let that happen, could we, Mother?"

"No, we could not, Father." She was in complete agreement with him and showed no sympathy at all for the death of her firstborn. "You'll understand one day, my boy—just you wait and see."

The ambulance eventually arrived and the police too. Will was taken away and Jimmy was left on his own with two constables. They were quite kind and made him a cup of tea, before taking copious notes. They had difficulty in accepting that he'd been fine earlier in the day and then just died at the table. He hadn't a bad heart or anything serious—so what could have done it? Jimmy didn't tell them about Cailleach a Chretnich and the MacMillan bonnet—he didn't want to sound mad or stupid. And that story would certainly have done it.

Following a post-mortem of Will's body, it was declared he'd died from a complete collapse of his immune system, something not so far known to the medical experts. Ma and Pa Bell said nothing to Jimmy about what had happened. It was as though they just didn't care. Ma's voice filled the house, "Pull yourself together, son—you hardly knew him, although he was your brother. So, he's gone—learn to live with it."

"Oh, you're a hard woman with a wicked tongue. Not that you'll be interested, but I've arranged for Will to be buried in the old Kirk just outside the town of Ayr. In fact, in the same cemetery where you both lie, but don't worry, he won't be joining you—I wouldn't do that to him. He mustn't lie forever beside the ones who brought about his death. That's what you did, you know, you knew exactly what could happen if he roamed the fields, dressed in the full MacMillan regalia."

He was disgusted with his parents and also disappointed that he'd never now see America nor get to know his brother better. He burnt the old scroll, the plaid and the Balmoral bonnet, then he took the Sgian Dubh and the glass globe with the large blue stone to an antique dealer and asked him to sell them at auction. He wanted nothing more to do with the 'things' that had come from the ground.

The antique dealer was delighted and said he would have them examined and valued, something he did almost immediately. He suspected the gems embedded in the items were 'Blue Diamonds' and if he was correct, they would be worth a very large sum of money—a very large sum of money indeed. But, as he told Jimmy, 'Time will tell.'

As more time passed, Jimmy buried his brother and in due course, inherited an enormous fortune from him. The antique dealer came back and told him the gems were indeed 'Blue Diamonds'—one of the rarest gems in the world and worth a great deal of money. The two unexpected windfalls allowed Jimmy to do something he'd only dreamt of in the past. He bought Creagan Ruadh Castle and had it renovated. He designed the interiors himself, taken from original prints he found in the local library and furnished it in keeping with the décor. It was a huge undertaking but one he relished.

On the day when everything was completed, he'd gone to the cottage to say goodbye. He'd lived there since he was born and felt genuinely sorry to leave it, but he'd always been drawn to the castle since the time when he'd worked there as a boy. It was one of those opportunities in life that couldn't be ignored and he felt he owed it to Will—it was after all something he'd wanted to do himself.

He stood in the kitchen of the cottage and called on his Ma and Pa to join him. It wasn't just his parents who arrived however, the ghost of Will had joined them. The three spirits stood together and stared at Jimmy. "I've come to bid you goodbye and to warn you that you're not welcome at the castle—that is, you and Pa are not welcome," he said pointedly to his parents, who both shrugged their shoulders as if they didn't care. "And remember, if you dare to ignore what I say and come to the castle, I'll have an exorcist there so quickly and you'll be chased off to where you really belong—and I don't have to tell you where I believe that place to be!" He turned to Will, "You, brother, are more than welcome—although it can never be your earthly home, it can be your spiritual one—it's as much your castle as it is mine."

He opened the cottage door and Will joined him, ready to leave. Ma and Pa stood quite still but looked daggers at their youngest son. Jimmy stopped just outside the door, turned and said, "Oh, by the way, I meant to tell you before—I've rented this cottage to a man from Glasgow, so you'll not be alone. In fact, I doubt you'll ever be alone again because he has a wife and ten children—and I'm told they're a very lively family—so, all I can say is *goodbye and enjoy the noise*!"

Please Give Generously to the Poor

Walking quickly through the falling snow, the three nuns were in a hurry to get to their individual spots, where they would wait with their collection tins for as long as the cold would allow, but usually for no more than an hour. The park was their choice of location today—it had three gates, one for each nun and so they separated inside the main gate. The nuns were dressed in the usual way, with long black dresses, wimples and veils, but because of the weather, they also wore thick overcoats. The black outfits clearly stood out against the white of the snow and there they stood in humility, with their outstretched collection tins. They were all of middle age, although one of them actually looked older than the others, but that was down to her genes and not to her years.

The odd thing was that they collected more money when the weather was bad and on those days, they would usually trudge back to the convent with full tins—it seemed that people felt more generous when the nuns looked as if they were suffering from the cold—they just couldn't bring themselves to walk past without dropping some money in the rattling tins.

"God bless you, my son, for your generosity to the poor! You will reap the benefits of your kindness." It usually worked every time and the givers walked off feeling better. The voluminous outfits were warmer than they looked and the veils and wimples kept their heads well covered from the falling snow. But who could have resisted them—the little, old ladies who chose to help the poor of the town in this way? Mind you, some people could and walked quickly passed with their heads bowed, 'What nuns? Were there nuns there? I didn't see them.' It would have been nice if they'd felt guilty afterwards—but that didn't seem likely.

Sister Mary Theresa liked to stamp her feet on the ground as she stood there, highlighting how cold she was—but still willing to collect for the poor—she continued to smile and nod her gratitude. Sister Bernadette on the other hand—and at the other gate—liked to sniff rather loudly and cough regularly. 'Oh, that poor nun—see, she has a terrible cold and yet is willing to help the poor—I must go back and give her some more money, she deserves it.' Words she'd heard more than once. Now Sister Claudine was a natural collector of money as she made sure her collection tin was never too full and emptied it from time to time in the deep pocket of the dress under her coat—this encouraged some passers-by to feel they must help her fill it up more.

So, each gate was covered at the time when people were going to work or covered when they were coming home again after a nightshift. Those crucial time was too good to miss and the nuns made sure they took up their stances at the right times. Tomorrow they'd stand in a different location—it was better to change their collection spots so that people didn't get used to seeing them there.

On this day, Sister Mary Theresa was busy stamping her feet to fight off the cold, when a young man came up to her and said, "Wotcha Sister—how're you doin' today?" He was a gangly youth and wore a baseball cap back to front, but his clothes were of good quality and at least he wasn't being confrontational—as so many youngsters often were when they saw her there.

"I'm alright, young man, but rather cold. What about you, where are you off to?" She didn't really care but she was being pleasant.

"I'm off to my job, Sister, in the big hotel across the park—I'm a bell-boy there, running messages for everybody and carrying suitcases up and down the stairs. Still, it's a job, I suppose." He reached into his pocket and brought out a packet of cigarettes.

He offered her one and was told, "Really young man, I don't smoke, thank you."

"Don't suppose you drink either," he laughed at her reply.

"I have been known to have a glass of wine, but I have to admit it's usually communion wine when the Priest has blessed it at Mass." She was being truthful with him, but she knew he was really laughing at her.

From his pocket, he brought out a small leather bag which he held out to her, then dropped it into her collection tin. "That's for you, Sister—not for 'the poor people' but for you. I found it at the hotel but don't need it—but you may do." He walked off quickly and almost ran out of the park.

She shouted after him, "You're a good boy—and God sees what you do!" But he was gone. She didn't bother to check what was in the small bag—that could wait till she got home—her fingers were too cold just then. Anyway, it was probably only a few sweets—but she was very fond of those.

She heard the town clock chime the hour of ten and she realised it was time to meet the others in their special coffee shop. Off she went, grateful to be able to move her frozen feet again. She was struggling along because the tin was so heavy with all the coins but she was still the first to arrive, followed closely by Sisters Bernadette and Claudine. All three had lived in the same convent for almost 30 years and had become close friends—they even shared a room and had their narrow beds all in a row for convenience. It was a comfortable room but in no way luxurious—very plain and with few personal possessions. The blankets however, gave the room a cheerful and cosy look—Sister Claudine was very good at crocheting and always found cheap wool at the local charity shop. The blankets were right and colourful. Yes, it was their home and they were grateful for it.

Their convent was shared by 15 other nuns, some much older, but with a few much younger—the young ones were still only novices and not fully fledged nuns. The convent had a good atmosphere, mainly because the Mother Superior was a kindly and caring woman, who loved the thought that all her nuns were happy to be there. The sisterhood was Anglican and linked to the church just next door—the nuns' lives were very methodical and structured with all the gardening, cooking, housework and general maintenance undertaken by the women themselves. The small library was overseen by one of the older nuns, Sister Clementine, who'd had a love of books all her life and, as Sister Claudine was always proving, she had a knack for sewing and knitting—crafts of all sorts.

Sister Bernadette was the convent Bursar and kept the books in order—she'd always been good with figures since her school days. Mother Superior watched over her 'chicks' and listened to their moans and complaints when she had to, but generally they were a pretty happy bunch who still manged to spend an acceptable time in prayer and contemplation. The Bishop was their spiritual leader but didn't live at the convent—he was however, always there if he was needed. He tended to visit the convent once a month to make sure things were running smoothly.

Staring out of the shop window, the three nuns were comparing how well they'd done with their collections and enjoying mugs of steaming coffee and home-made scones. They told themselves they needed the sustenance having been standing in the cold for so long.

Sister Mary Theresa was speaking, "Isn't it odd how generous people always are when the weather is bad—it's as though they feel sorry for us and give more to make us feel better."

"Well, whatever the reason, it's good news for us and for the convent." Claudine liked to look on the positive side of things whenever she could. She reached for a second scone and Bernadette tutted and reminded her that gluttony was a sin. "Look, I've just stood in the freezing cold for the good of the poor people and I think I deserve a little treat." She scoffed the scone before Claudine could say anything else.

Mary Theresa asked, "Now ladies, have we done what we always do and halved the collections into two separate sums—one for the convent and of course, one for us?"

"Of course, we have—it's a good thing our skirts have such big pockets, or it wouldn't be so easy. We mustn't count it here in case someone sees us—we'll do it when we go to our rooms tonight. Isn't it good that you're the bursar, Bernadette, or we'd never manage everything."

"Oh, I think we'd find a way—we've always managed, haven't we? By the way, will we be going out collecting tomorrow as well—I think the snow will stay around 'till then—and it's too good an opportunity to miss."

"'Course we will, Claudine, now get your things together—it's time we were off or we'll be late for prayers at noon and we don't want to upset Mother Superior, do we?"

The nuns left the coffee shop and struggled back to the convent a mile away. They almost fell over a couple of times, it was so slippery. They arrived just in time to get out of their damp coats before the hall bell was rung for prayers. The other nuns looked at them when they came in—they were already kneeling in prayer with their heads bowed. The silence was complete and no one even coughed. They stayed like that for two hours and when the hall bell rang again, there was a lot of 'Oohs and Ahs' and creaking of bones as everyone rose in one movement. A light lunch had already been prepared in the large kitchen and they all sat at the table, grateful for what they were about to receive.

"What's our total now, Bernadette?" The three had retired to their room after evening prayers and changed into nightclothes. They had given her their collection tins earlier and she had deposited half the money into the convent's bank account—later to be transferred into different charity accounts supported by the church—but from their own 'large' pockets, they had kept the money to be added to their 'personal' savings. Claudine was quite excited and asked again, "The total, Bernadette—tell us the total now."

She liked to keep them waiting and enjoyed their impatience, "Well, after five years of collecting, we're fast approaching £40,000. An amazing sum, isn't it?"

Mary Theresa had been praying with each gem of her rosary beads—a little prayer whilst waiting for Bernadette to speak and possibly helping to increase the sum she might say. When she heard the figure, she dropped her beads and said, "Holy Mary, Mother of God, that's amazing. I know it's been a few months since we last counted it, but I never thought it would be as much as that." She made the sign of the cross and fell onto her bed laughing.

"We're rich—we're rich, aren't we, Sisters?" She wrapped herself in her bright blanket and rocked back and forth with pleasure. "Should we treat ourselves—just a little? What do you think?"

Before the others could answer, she jumped off the bed and ran over to the small bureau where she kept small, personal items. "I'd forgotten this—a young man gave it to me today and wished me luck. I didn't look in the bag—it was too cold." She undid the string and tipped the bag upside down on the blanket—and there, sparkling and shining in the light of the candles, were several differently-coloured gems. The others crowded around her bed and tentatively touched the stones. "What do you think they are?" she asked the others.

"Why, I think they're precious stones, that's what I think." Bernadette was a bit more practical than the others and believed she was more worldly wise. "Why else would he have given them to you—it's obviously a donation for the poor—and we're poor, aren't we?"

"Yes, but we're meant to be poor—we've sworn to live by poverty, chastity and obedience—and we're not poor like really poor people. We always have something to eat." Claudine liked to believe she always stuck to the actual truth—although deep down, she knew she didn't.

Between the three of them, Claudine was the prettiest—or at least she had been when she was a girl—and she was popular with her colleagues as well. Even Mother Superior treated her like a pet and forgave her small misdemeanours, like when she forgot to clean out the candlesticks and gather all the stubs to boil together and make new ones—or when she forgot to collect the eggs before the hens stood on them—there weren't many eggs for breakfast when Sister Claudine was on duty. But she was one of those people whom

294

everybody liked and to coin a phrase, 'she could get away with murder if she tried.'

Bernadette was a more serious person—she stood tall with a straight back and always knew the right question to ask when the situation was difficult. She held out her own small ledger for them to see and at the same time, told Claudine not to be so pious as it made her feel sick.

"I know what we should do," Mary Theresa closed her bible, which she was pretending to read, "I think we should give the Reverend Mother some of the stones to go towards the convent funds. We can just tell her exactly what happened, that a young man donated them into the collection tin. Best to be honest, I think."

The others laughed and Bernadette said, "It's a bit late for that, I fear—with our thousands of pounds under the floorboards."

They decided to vote on that suggestion and were unanimous in the decision. "But before we do, I think we should visit the jeweller's shop in town and ask him to appraise them. It would be dreadful if we gave them to Mother Superior as if they were valuable—and it turned out they weren't. In fact, if it turns out they are valuable, we should perhaps sell them and give her a share of the result." A new decision made, the three tired nuns climbed into their beds and were soon asleep—sleeping like the innocents they claimed to be!

Following bowls of milky porridge and early morning prayers, the three of them pulled on their rubber over-shoes, their heavy coats with the veils tucked into the collars. It was still cold and snowy and their cheeks were red as soon as they left the convent, but they did their duty and chose different collection spots. They did well that morning and after their usual hour, they went to the tea room in town. As they always did, they, they shared the money between the tins and their own deep coat pockets. No one ever seemed to see them doing it, but then who watches a group of little nuns enjoying their morning coffee?

The jeweller's shop was just a few doors along and they went there before returning to the convent. "Yes ladies, you have a few lovely stones there—may I ask where you got them?" Then he realised that was perhaps an inappropriate question and coughed to cover his embarrassment.

"Can you give us an idea of how valuable they are—that is, of course, if the convent chose to sell them. Mother Superior will only ask us for the valuation when we go back—so it would be useful to know the answer."

"If you'd like to leave them with me and come back in two days, I'll make sure I have the answer for you." He wanted to show them to someone more expert than himself.

"Will you give us a receipt for them please—it would be awful if they were lost, wouldn't it?" He reassured them however that he would take good care of them and they left his warm shop back into the cold.

"Do come in out of the snow, Sisters!" Sister Celine opened the door as wide as she could without allowing too much snow to blow inside. "We need your help later—we've all been instructed to re-categorise the library—now that'll be a big job." As she walked away, she told them there was extra coffee in the kitchen today because it was so cold.

"Jolly good." Was the response and they quickly removed their outdoor clothes and boots and almost ran into the warm kitchen. There was a huge fireplace there, where a caldron hung over the flames and the smell of simmering soup filled their nostrils. Lunch was being prepared! The bells began to ring to call everyone to mid-day prayers and the hot coffee was drunk rather quickly. As they hurried along the corridor, Claudine managed to whisper to her friends, "Have you managed to separate the money yet?" She was reassured everything was okay.

After Prayers and in the library, all the nuns were working on great piles of books but at least the work was keeping them warm. Mary Theresa was given the task of working on the Dickensian section and removing all his books from the shelves, after which she'd dust them and ensure they were put back in the correct order. She'd just pulled out *The Old Curiosity Shop* when a piece of paper fluttered from between the pages. She opened it and read the words:

I know what you three have been up to and if you don't share your ill-gotten gains—I'll tell the Bishop.

She quickly scrunched up the paper and thrust it into her pocket. She just continued to work on the books, wondering how the person had known who it was who would be working on Dickens' books. The work was taking so long that it was agreed to stop for the day and continue tomorrow. After supper and evening prayers, the three friends changed into their nightdresses and lounged on their beds. Three nuns who should have been classed as innocent as children—but who knew very well, that in their case, this wasn't the case.

"Who could it be? We've never told anyone about our collections, have we? It must have been whoever arranged the book categorisations—someone who gave me the Dickens section and knew I'd find the note." Mary Theresa felt very anxious. "Do you know who handed out the responsibilities, Bernadette? Was it Sister Margaret—I bet it was Sister Margaret. Well, was it?"

Neither of the other two knew who'd arranged the rota. "But we'll find out tomorrow, don't you worry." Bernadette would find out. They all slept badly that night—that was conscience and fear of being caught. Bernadette was first to awake next morning and the other two were just beginning to stir when she came back into the room.

"It was Margaret. You were right, Mary Theresa—it was our dear Sister Margaret—I don't know if she wrote the note but she did arrange the rota of workers." Bernadette was furious and the others had to calm her down, fearing she would have a seizure. They agreed not to panic and to go about their normal tasks—but to watch Sister Margaret closely for any odd behaviour. They went about their collections—they thought it important as the snow was beginning to thaw and the generosity of the people would soon thaw as well.

Immediately after mid-day prayers, the nuns returned to the task in the library. Everything went smoothly and the end was almost in sight when the suggestion of a coffee break was welcomed by all. Sisters Claudine and Bernadette volunteered to prepare the drinks. In the kitchen, they could discuss the situation without eavesdroppers.

"It was her—she was watching my every move—she couldn't have made it more obvious if she tried." Bernadette was boiling the milk in a large saucepan and Claudine was laying out the cups. "Do you think we should take in some biscuits as well?"

"Certainly, Sister—some biscuits will do no harm—unlike this cup of coffee I'm fixing for Sister Margaret," and she poured into the mug the contents of a small phial she'd produced from her sleeve.

"What on earth do you mean, Bernadette? What are you planning?" Bernadette however just collected all the cups on a large tray and grabbed the sugar bowl.

She paused at the door, "Allow me to hand around the cups, won't you—I have a special one for our friend." And they left the kitchen and walked along the corridor with long skirts swishing against the walls. "Here you are, Sister Margaret—enjoy—and do help yourself to a biscuit—specially baked only this morning." Sister Margaret did as she was bid and greedily took two biscuits—just to be sure!

The shelves in the library were filled again with rows of books and the nuns went their separate ways, some for meditation in the Quiet Room, some for their Arts and Crafts work, results intended for the Christmas Bazaar—but one nun in particular went to her room to rest as she suddenly felt unwell. Sister Margaret had developed strange stomach pains and had asked the apothecary nun for some medication to help ease the pain.

"I don't know what's wrong with me, Sister Clementine, and you're so gifted with your herbal cures, I thought you might be able to suggest something." And Clementine sent her off with some specially prepared cordial, which she swore would ease the stomach pains.

Next morning however, Sister Margaret was discovered dead, and by Mother Superior herself, who'd gone to the nun's bedroom to see how she was feeling. She was very surprised as Sister Margaret had not seemed unduly poorly throughout her time at the convent. The Priest was sent for to pray for her soul and even the police were called in—as the death hadn't been expected. After the body had been removed, nothing further was done about the death—it must just have been one of those things. It had happened to a middle-age to elderly nun dying in her sleep—nothing remarkable about that!

"Yes, I did it, ladies—I had to, she was on to us and meant to spill the beans sooner rather than later." The candles had been lit and the friends' eyes shone in 'round-eyed surprise' at Bernadette's admission. "Look, we're all in this together and have to support each other—what I did I did for you both, as well for myself. What would have happened if she'd gone to the Bishop with her tales? In fact, I can't imagine what would happened—but it wouldn't have been good for us."

"Oh Bernadette, we're not blaming you—in fact, we admire you—but we'd never have had the nerve to do it, that's all we're saying." Claudine stared at her friend in awe and looked at Mary Theresa with eyes, begging her to say something positive to Bernadette.

Mary Theresa obliged and patted her friend on the back, "Well done, old chum—you're a brave lady."

And that was that! They decided not to go collecting for the poor as there was no snow around that day—in fact, it was fast disappearing and pickings would be scarce. After mid-day prayers, Claudine and Mary Theresa joined the Art and Crafts team in the sewing room and Bernadette went to her small office where she did her bursary work. It was about 4 o'clock and already quite dark outside when she sat behind her desk—with three candles spaced around the room—just a solitary nun ready to do her work. As she totted up figures, she glanced towards the window, admiring the candle glow reflected on the glass and there, standing straight-backed with a grim expression on her face, was Sister Margaret in all her glory.

Bernadette looked again, removed her glasses and rubbed her tired eyes—but nothing had changed and there she was, as large as life—Sister Margaret whose body had been removed from the convent only that day. What could she do? Did she speak to the apparition—did she ignore it and hope it would go away? She didn't know what to do. So, she did nothing but stared at her former colleague.

The apparition spoke, "You think you've been so clever—killing me—don't you? Actually, you probably are clever—but why did you do it? That's what I don't understand. I swear to God I have never done anything to hurt you. The Angels in Heaven will confirm that." She didn't move but just stood there—she was frightening and threatening and Bernadette was more afraid than she'd ever been in her whole life.

She attempted to speak but choked on her words. Should she answer the question in her normal voice as though she wasn't speaking to a ghost? And what would she say anyway—'I killed you because you were going to tell on us'—it sounded so weak. Or could she say, 'I killed you because I didn't like you.' Neither excuse sounded feasible.

A gentle tap on the door and the ghost disappeared into nothingness. The candles didn't even flicker. Had Sister Margaret really been here or was it the result of a very guilty conscience? She called out in a shaking voice, "Come in!" and Mother Superior came in, carrying a cup of cocoa.

"I was on my way to my room and I thought I'd bring you this." She put the cup in front of Bernadette. "I wanted to tell you—there was a gentleman looking for you today—but all three of you were someplace else and I couldn't find you. He obviously didn't want to tell me anything, but he said he'd come back tomorrow. I just thought I'd mention it to you." She was just about to go out the door when she turned quickly, "Oh, and just to put the thought in your mind—Sister Angelique told me today that she'd like to share the burden of going out to collect for the poor—she knows how long you've been doing it and she thinks you deserve a break. I believe she's only thinking of you! Anyway, we'll talk

299

tomorrow." And she was gone, leaving behind a very worried bursar. *Take over my collecting—I think not Madame Angelique!*

She finished her work and went to her room where the other two were already in bed. "I was wrong—it wasn't Sister Margaret who wrote the note—I think it was actually Sister Angelique. We'll have to find out pretty quickly." And she undressed and got into bed, leaving two shocked nuns with many unanswered questions on their lips.

"Well Sisters, your gems are worth quite a bit of money." The jeweller was holding the small bag in his hands. The four of them were in the convent's waiting room just off the hall and Claudine had fetched coffee for their visitor.

"Can you sell them on our behalf, and for the sum you've just mentioned?" Two voices spoke at the same. He told them he could sell them with ease and went off to do their bidding, but first allowing Mary Theresa to choose two particular ones to be valued separately. Their value must go to the Reverend Mother, who can use them to help support the renovation work needed on all the windows. The wood was rotting and had been like that for a long time. This helped them to feel better about keeping the rest of the money for themselves.

When the jeweller had gone, Bernadette asked, "What are we going to do about Sister Angelique—she obviously knows how lucrative collecting for the poor can be—and wants some of the action." She'd begun to sound like a member of the American Mafia.

Claudine giggled at the question, "Well, we'll just have to deal with her the way we did with Sister Margaret." She obviously found the prospect quite attractive. "You just leave it to me, Ladies—I'll take care of her. I never liked her anyway." Claudine sounded determined to put a stop to the meddling nun.

The day passed as most days did. It was a very structured and organised life in the convent, but the nuns never found it boring. There was the housekeeping, the cooking, the baking, the darning and sewing, the gardening and of course, the prayers and meditation. Each day was as full as could be, but two days later, there was considerable whispering in the convent and much scurrying about the place.

"Have you heard?" was the question on everyone's lips.

"Yes, it is true—she died in her sleep just like Sister Margaret. No one was there and she'd not even complained to anyone. Yes, it's Sister Angelique, I'm afraid—Mother Superior found her this morning."

"Sister Claudine, can you come to the kitchen for a moment?" Mary Theresa called across the room and led the way. Bernadette was already there, peeling potatoes and carrots for dinner.

"What did you do, Claudine? Have you done something you shouldn't have?" Mary Theresa started tidying eggs into the rack.

"I did what needed doing—she was going to take our collection duties from us—and we couldn't let her do that, could we?" Her voice dropped even more to a whisper, "I waited until I knew she'd be asleep and I crept along the corridor, and placed my pillow over her face, holding it down hard. It took longer than I thought it would and she was tougher than I imagined. She soon stopped struggling though, but I didn't let up for a while—to be sure you know—and then she just lay still, not breathing and her arms fell to each side."

"Oh, Holy Mary, Mother of God!" Mary Theresa said and crossed herself. Claudine was proud of what she'd done and laughed at the other's expressions. She seemed to find the whole thing rather amusing. "It's no worse than what Bernadette did!"

The kitchen door opened and Bernadette was told there was a gentleman who wanted to see her. "Here you are, Sister, that's as much as I could get. Not quite what I'd hoped for, but a nice little sum in any case." The jeweller handed over a bulky brown envelope. "It's all in cash, just like you said, and I've separated what you got for the two separate gems. It's all there!" And he was off very quickly up the path, knowing full well he'd cheated them out of quite a few pounds—but that was his commission, wasn't it?

"Reverend Mother, I have something for you." Mary Theresa handed over an envelope to her superior. "The gems were dropped in my collection tin and I don't even know by whom—but they were intended for the poor, I'm sure—or any other worthy cause you consider suitable. The gentleman who came to see us was selling them on our behalf and that's what he gave me today." She bowed her head before leaving the room. The Reverend Mother looked in the envelope and her mouth fell open in surprise! It was a large amount of money.

Next day, the three nuns went collecting as usual and took up their separate stands—far enough apart to meet different people coming and going about the town. The clock in the tower began to strike 10 o'clock and the women hurried along to their favourite tearoom. It was quite a bright day but still cold and they were glad to sit in the warmth. But their usual table was already taken—and amazingly, by two nuns.

"Well, what do you make of that? Are they from our convent? They've no right taking our places like that. I suppose we'll have to sit at another table." Mary Theresa plumped herself down on a chair and stared across at the strangers. "Oh God in His Heaven, it's Sister Margaret and Sister Angelique! But it's not possible—they're both dead!"

Her friends didn't even sit down but left the tearoom quicker than they'd come in. All three rushed back to the convent—not a word left their lips until they were in the safety of the hall. "Let's have our coffee in the kitchen. It's always warm there."

Sister Clementine was already there, making some of her special herbal medicines. "I should be doing this in the laboratory but it's so cold in there—I hope you don't mind me being here." Sister Clementine had helped many nuns with their minor ailments and she was well liked by everyone. She pushed up her spectacles and rested them on her forehead. "I think I'll join you for coffee, if you don't mind."

They made room for her around the table when she suddenly asked, "How much money do you actually have? I know all about your little secret collections and your hiding place under the floorboards. Did you really think that no one knew? There are many ears around this convent—and mine are sharper than most."

Gasps of disbelief! What was she talking about? The three others concentrated on their cups until Bernadette spoke up, "What on earth do you mean, Sister Clementine? What money are you talking about?" She pretended she was insulted by the normally-sweet nun's accusation. She really hadn't suspected Clementine, of all people!

"Come on, Sisters, you know exactly what I'm talking about. The money you've been squirrelling away for years and which should have really gone into the convent's coffers. Oh, don't look so scared, Reverend Mother doesn't know anything about it. I'm the only one who really knows—and your secret's safe with me—that is, if you share your profits with me." She poured herself some coffee and waited patiently for someone else to speak. "Come along now, ladies, it's getting near lunchtime and others will be joining us to prepare the food. What's it to be?"

Sister Bernadette however was made of sterner stuff than the other two and said again, "We don't know what you're going on about—we have no money under any floorboards. How dare you accuse us of such a thing." She was bristling with anger—an odd thing to see a nun do, but she felt genuinely aggrieved—and scared.

"And don't try any of your tricks with me—Sisters Margaret and Angelique suffered at your hands. They were innocent, you know, neither of them knew your little secret. They were both completely innocent!" She was laughing at them now and enjoying the fear that showed in their eyes. "Come along now—you don't want me to tell the Bishop, do you! And don't go thinking I'll be as easy as the other two to get rid of—I'm onto you!" Her voice changed then almost and she sounded pleading "I just want to share your good fortune and have something to look forward to in my old age. I don't want to become old and decrepit here with everyone feeling sorry for me. What is the total figure now, may I ask?" She stood up and cleared away the cups—she could hear voices in the corridor, so said, "We'll continue with this conversation later."

After discussion, and in their bedroom that night, the three agreed they had no option but to allow her to join their syndicate. Sister Mary Theresa was angrier than the others and said, "After all our hard work, we've just to hand it over to her? I can't bear the thought, but what else can we do?"

"Let's sleep on it and we'll decide in the morning. Perhaps something will come to us in our sleep." Claudine soothed her friend.

"Okay, that sounds like a good plan." And three sleepless nuns fell into their beds, wrapped warmly in their bright blankets—but with heavy hearts and a feeling of dread.

"Of course, we can take up where we left off yesterday and decide the way forward." Sister Clementine sounded as if she was talking about the price of bread and not £50,000, at which their total now stood. "I think we'll do very well, working together—the Four Amigos—better than the Four Nuns—it sounds like a pop group. Anyway, I'd like to learn your techniques." She was obviously feeling pretty good about what she was doing. Later, as they were leaving the convent, they bumped into Mother Superior, who looked surprised to see the four of them leaving together.

"Yes, Reverend Mother—Sister Clementine wants to share our task—and we welcome her." Sister Mary Theresa spoke for them all and smiled as sweetly as she could. They walked into the middle of town together and planted themselves far apart. People were going to and fro about their business—it was a bright day, but bitterly cold and everyone was well wrapped up. Luckily though, nothing stopped them getting out their purses and wallets to give to the elderly nuns. The townsfolk had always been generous to the convent nuns, who were very much respected in the town.

'Well, that's the clock bell.' And the sisters gathered outside their tearoom and waited for each other to arrive. Luckily, there were no ghostly nuns at any of the tables this time and they were able to sit in their usual place. The coffee and scones were particularly tasty this morning and the sums collected very pleasing, but Clementine spoiled it all by saying, "Well, ladies, how will we split the money—and I mean all the money, not just what we've collected today."

"Well, it'll just have to be split in four equal portions, won't it? There's £50,000 to share—not to be sneezed at, is it?"

Bernadette had to try hard to keep her cool with the new enemy, but she knew Clementine would be surprised at how much money there was.

"Heavens Above." Was the only response from the newcomer.

"Tell you what. Let's treat ourselves to a second coffee today; after all it's pretty nippy out there—and the treat is on me—I'll fetch it over, save the waitress's legs." Mary Theresa crossed to the counter and returned moments later with four fresh coffees which she dealt out to each nun. "Enjoy, ladies! I asked for their special coffee which has an almond essence. Let me know if you like it."

For 'some reason', Clementine reached over and changed her cup with Mary Theresa's. "Wrong cups, my dear—this one was mine!" and she slowly sipped the drink.

"Oh yes, I do like it—and I can taste the almonds," Bernadette agreed. "We'll have to have the specials again."

The four nuns headed off home, up the street and back to the convent. They had to walk slower than usual as Sister Clementine was much older than them and her steps were faltering. As they neared the convent, she actually stumbled and reached out to Mary Theresa for support. The nun grabbed her arm and said, "Steady on there, Sister—take more water with it next time."

They walked on, even slower, and eventually reached the door of the convent. Two of the other nuns were working in the front garden, just tidying the weeds from the garden path and clipping back an overgrown bush. It wasn't really weather for gardening although it was bright—and the nuns were eager to finish their chore and get back inside. One of them opened the front door and they all went inside together.

Unfortunately, Sister Clementine tripped over the doorstep and fell into the hall. The Reverend Mother was coming out of the quiet room and saw it happen. She rushed over to help and Clementine collapsed into her arms, without saying a word. All the others gathered around the little tableau but could do little to help. The Reverend Mother looked at them and shouted, "Ring for an ambulance— please, do it now. And one of you others, fetch a blanket and a pillow to make her comfortable whilst we wait." Everyone did as they were told. The ambulance arrived in quick time and Sister Clementine was carried off on a stretcher.

"Right, Sisters, would all three of you like to follow me to my study? I have a few questions for you." It was beginning to get dark by this time and they followed her along the corridor, looking very much like naughty school children. "What happened to Sister Clementine—she seemed perfectly okay when she left here—and yet in a state of collapse when she got back? Did anything happen when you were out together?"

All three nuns tried to speak at once but Bernadette was more forceful and responded with, "Nothing happened, Reverend Mother—it wasn't until we got back here that she began to stumble—you saw it for yourself. None of us touched her. We had coffee and scones in a tearoom and she seemed to enjoy that."

Mother Superior looked thoughtful and the deep lines on her forehead made her look suddenly older. "Very well—but I think we must reschedule our duties and you must allow others to collect money outside. Everyone has become too complacent in their duties and now, we've had two deaths and one serious illness in the past few weeks—we have to do something about it. Make tomorrow your final day of collecting—and then I shall appoint your replacements—some of the others need the benefit of good fresh air, as you're been having—is that clear?" She was speaking with great authority but less gentleness than usual.

"Yes, Reverend Mother, it is clear, but it does make us sad as we've always enjoyed that duty." The three of them left the study and went to their bedroom.

"What on earth did happen to Sister Clementine?" They asked each other and Mary Theresa spoke up immediately, "I honestly thought you'd guessed that I did it. I thought I'd tipped you all off by ordering the special almond coffee and insisting I brought it to the table. There was almond essence in the drinks but in Clementine's, it was cyanide which tastes like almonds. I got it from the medical room here in the convent—of course, it had skull and crossbones on the bottle, but that reassured me it would work. Yes, I did it—but it was no more than you two have already done, so don't look at me like that!" Mary Theresa was adamant that she'd done right. She was really no worse than the others.

"I must admit I wasn't too happy about her having a quarter of the money we'd worked so hard to collect over the years." Claudine was being honest at least, and Bernadette nodded her head in agreement.

"Well, we've lost our money-making task—but we've still got our savings intact—and that's something to be proud of, don't you think?" Mary Theresa yawned widely, which caused the others to do the same. Bed that night was very welcome—what a day it had been!

Before leaving next morning, they heard the news that Sister Clementine had died in the night. But as they said to each other, "What did you expect?"

They spent an uneventful day and collected quite a bit of money. Soon the Reverend Mother would remove them from the collecting rota so they'd have to enjoy whatever time they had left—to feather their nest. They didn't order the almond coffee that day, as it seemed a bit disrespectful—but the normal drink was lovely as usual. They ignored the little group of nuns at the table in the corner although they knew exactly who they were. There were three of them now but, 'what could they do'—they were just ghosts with no power at all. They were just appearing to upset their used-to-be colleagues.

On entering the convent, they found the Bishop waiting for them in the hall. By his side, stood Mother Superior and around her feet were three suitcases and three briefcases. He held up his hand and spoke in a stern tone, "You are not to enter these premises ever again. The Reverend Mother has told me of the things you've done recently—she has always suspected, but wanted to give you the benefit of the doubt. Sister Clementine was the last straw and we are no longer willing to put up with you." It was a long speech coming from him and he couldn't have been more stern, if he'd tried.

"Take your belongings and leave here. You may keep whatever money you collected today. It's tarnished money which God has not blessed and we don't want it."

"But we have nowhere to go, Your Grace—and why does the Reverend Mother blame us for the deaths—we are innocent of what she accuses us." The three crossed themselves and stared at the floor.

Bernadette was the first to look up. "We must be allowed into our rooms to make sure that we've left nothing there. Will that be permitted?"

"It will most certainly not be permitted—the rooms have been totally emptied and cleaned—there is nothing left there—you can be sure of that." She said the last words with extra emphasis as though trying to give them a message. She was most insistent that the nuns were not be allowed to come further into the convent.

Sister Bernadette pleaded with the Bishop, "Please Your Grace, it is not a big thing we ask. Surely, after all our time at the convent, you can allow us this last request."

He looked at the Mother Superior questioningly and she nodded her head slightly. "Only one of you may go—who is it to be?" the Bishop asked.

Bernadette was pushed forward by the others and she quickly ran along the corridor before the Bishop changed his mind. The room was clean and tidy. There was absolutely nothing left there but she scrambled onto the floor and eased up the wooden plank, reaching her hand into the void to find the box of money. There was nothing there! She used both hands and felt around the sides of the space—it was completely empty. She sat back on her haunches. Where had it all gone? Who could have taken it? There was no answer.

She walked back towards the group by the front door and shook her head at Mary Theresa and Claudine. "Come Sisters, we must leave with what we have here—there is nothing else." She looked into the Reverend Mother's eyes, and she knew. She knew who had written the note in the library, who had suggested to Sister Angelique that she should take over a collection tin and who had suggested to Sister Clementine that she should join their group. In fact, Reverend Mother had known everything all along. It was written so clearly in her eyes at that moment—she'd been the guilty party all along. She was almost smiling when she nodded her head just a little, but enough to confirm to Bernadette that she was correct in what she was thinking. She'd planned for a long time to get the money for herself and wasn't the kindly woman she'd always seemed. She'd been in it from the start!

"Goodbye, Sisters—let us hope you are successful in the outside world—I somehow think you will be. You are sharp and seem able to make the best of what God gives you." Mother Superior turned away then and with her, the Bishop—a very much richer Bishop and Reverend Mother than before. The door was closed in the nuns' faces and they suddenly found themselves with no lives, no home and no support. They stood there with their suitcases at their feet and just stared at each other. What a way to end up after all the years in God's service!

They'd lived under the church's protection all their adult lives and suddenly, the outside world looked strange and unwelcoming.

They walked slowly into town—they had to walk slowly with many stops to rest, as the suitcases were heavy. All their life's belongings in one suitcase—small results for such a long time. "We'll have to find a cheap boarding house for the night, before we decide what we're going to do." Claudine was being practical but didn't find it easy and there were tears in her eyes.

"Yes, let's do that—but before we do, let's make one more collection. We need the money now, don't we?" And they all walked towards the park—to their best collecting place. But there were several nuns collecting there already—one at the main gate, one at the side gate and a third at the back gate. The nuns were already 'on parade' and the usual spots had been taken!

Their places had already been taken by Sisters Margaret, Angelique and Clementine, on whose faces were ghostly and knowing smiles. As the three disgraced nuns walked past them, the three ghosts actually had the audacity to shake their collecting tins in the others' faces. "Spare a few pennies for the poor—you can afford it." Their killers just grunted and walked on past.

"What cheek!" Bernadette was heard to say.

A Truly Aristocratic Gentleman

He stretched his arms above his head and yawned widely. The sky was blue and the bright sun was high above a couple of clouds. He looked out of the bedroom window and saw two squirrels wrestling with each other on the lawn—they were debating the ownership of an acorn and of course, the bigger of the two won the prize—and ran away across the grass. The loser quickly climbed a nearby tree as if he really hadn't wanted the acorn anyway.

David smiled, reached for his hairbrush and began styling his blond hair—he had begun wearing it rather longer of late, it came all the way down to his collar. He studied his image in the mirror and tweaked his stiff, high collar. He really looked the part—an obvious aristocratic gentleman. As usual, he dressed himself with care and chose his second-best suit in honour of it's being Monday. Monday was a special day as the whole week stretched ahead full of promise. It was also his birthday and he wanted to spend it in a special way. He had no friends and so, would have to decide by himself what to do.

Before going downstairs, he checked his parents' bedroom as he usually did. It was immaculate, with nothing out of place. It looked exactly as it had looked the morning before, and the morning before that. In fact, it looked exactly the same as it had looked on the day a year ago, also on his birthday, when they were taken away by the nice ambulance men. There was a chair on either side of the bed and he had laid out clothes for each of his dead parents. He changed the shoes he'd left for his mother—as he thought his current choice was better. He liked that touch—it made it look as if the room still belonged to them.

He closed the door and stood looking out of the landing window—the squirrel was still on the lawn, looking disappointed as he discovered there was nothing inside the acorn that he liked. David thought, *Life's like that young squirrel—looks good from the outside—but nothing of interest inside.*

He made himself a cooked breakfast and settled down with his toast, marmalade and his morning newspaper. After about an hour, he got up and methodically washed the dirty dishes. Now, where would he go first today? He picked a small, white rosebud from a bush in the garden and pinned it to his suit as a buttonhole. He didn't work, he didn't have to—his parents had left him well-healed, very well-healed indeed. In his fastidious way, he pulled some dead leaves from a bush and tidied them away in the garden bin. He decided to walk across the park, towards the business sector in the town.

It must be said he looked the part—a successful gentleman going about his business—he flicked an imaginary fleck of dust from his sleeve. The carriages were out in force, it being the right time in late morning when the ladies chose to ride around the park, looking for titbits of gossip to discuss with their friends over afternoon tea—and of course, to show themselves off. *Nothing ever changed,* he thought, and knew that someone, somewhere, would be discussing him. Well, he was worth discussing, wasn't he?

He eventually arrived in the diamond quarter and wandered along, looking in the shop windows, gazing at the fabulous jewels placed there to tempt those with money. Maybe today, he could have one of those precious gems to add to those he'd inherited from his dear Mama. He went into a recently built shopping mall where all the shops were under one roof—he walked the entire length of the corridor before turning back and re-tracing his footsteps. He liked the window, specially decorated for the new Queen's coronation. The one with all the Union Jacks around the door. Obviously, a true patriot!

Victoria was to be crowned soon—and still so young—David was a staunch admirer of her Uncle, King William IV, who had just died. He wasn't sure about the idea of having a woman—a very young woman—on the throne of this great nation, but then as that was something over which he had no control, he could only hope for the best. He was still saddened by the death of William IV, whose time as the King of Great Britain, he had followed closely and he admired him—he was a man's man after all. William had been the last in the line of Hanoverian monarchs and he'd done a pretty good job, at least that's what his toadies told him. He had the reputation for having many amorous relationships with women throughout his life and he was regarded by his subjects as a 'jolly rake'. As said earlier, 'A man's man!'

David had actually hero-worshipped him—even when he was the Duke of Clarence. In truth, the poor man had never expected to be King at all, after all he was only the third son of George III and had already chosen his career in the Royal Navy when he was only 13 years old. He had also fought in the American

Revolution and still somehow manage to have ten illegitimate children with an Irish comedienne—Dorothea Jordan. Alas, he had only two legitimate daughters with his wife, Princess Adelaide. Unfortunately for the continuity of the Georgian/Hanoverian line, both girls died in infancy and so the British crown came next to the King's closest relative—Victoria.

David had decided he would go into the centre of the capital on the big day, to see how everything went. He was an ardent Royalist and loved the pageantry and pomp that came with it. At present though, he cleared his head and got on with the job in hand—enough about Royalty, he told himself! Down to business!

The bell rang softly when he opened the shop door. It was an elegant interior with soft leather sofas, ruby red drapes and occasional tables dotted around the showroom. A young man came towards him and asked him if he would like to take a seat, "The manager will be with you shortly, Sir—would you like some coffee whilst you wait?" He had obviously been identified as a true gentleman.

"I would, young man, that is very kind of you," and he settled back against the plump cushions of the sofa.

The manager appeared as if on cue and bowed slightly from the waist. "How very nice to see you, Sir—how may I help you today?" David liked to be treated in this way—he was quality and liked when others saw it at the first meeting.

"I would like to see an array of middle size to large diamonds, one of which I may choose to have set into a ring my mother left in my possession, when she passed." The manager mumbled his condolences and the young man with the coffee arrived and set the tray down by David's chair.

"When you're ready and when you've finished your coffee, please will you join me at the counter where I can show you some of our finest diamonds." The manager almost bowed which wasn't really necessary—but then, David painted such a dignified figure, it wasn't surprising.

He intentionally took his time over coffee, liking to keep the manager waiting. The man's subservience was almost edible and David liked it. At the counter, a piece of black velvet had been spread over the glass and the Manager stood waiting, with a large box he'd placed on the counter. The two men spent at least an hour perusing the stones, the manager pointing out the obvious charms and clarity of the stones and David waving some aside, whilst looking more closely at others. He discussed the importance of clarity and lack of cloudiness in the stones and the manager recognised him as a discerning customer as well as a dignified one. This was exactly David's intention!

"Do you think I could have some more coffee?" He asked and said he'd have to sit back down again to rest and think things over. "I've recently been ill, you see," he explained.

"Of course, Sir—Charles, fetch the gentleman some fresh coffee." The manager—a Mr MacIntosh—was quite good at being obsequious. He could smell he was on the brink of a potential sale. The man could obviously afford the purchase.

David had now been in the shop for almost two hours and even Mr MacIntosh was getting tired of waiting. He suddenly stood up and went back to the counter, with the manager in hot pursuit. He appeared to be perplexed and unable to decide which diamond to choose. It was between two of them actually—now which did he prefer? He mopped his brow with a large, white handkerchief before replacing it in his pocket.

"Mr MacIntosh, I am going to go home now and discuss what I've seen with my sister. The ring will be for her after all. Please keep these safe and I shall return with her and allow her to choose for herself." Mr MacIntosh looked disappointed but knew he mustn't show it.

"Very well, Sir—will we see you tomorrow, perhaps?" And David confirmed he would, before leaving the shop. Once outside, he moved quickly along the corridor, back along the street and across the park from whence he'd come. In his hand, he could feel the sharpness of the two stones he'd helped himself to. People could be so stupid, it seemed—even managers of valuable jewel emporiums. But it would be a learning curve for him and may ensure more caution in the future.

Inside his home, he retrieved the handkerchief from his pocket and laid the diamonds on a small, glass tray. They really were beautiful and looked even larger than they had in the shop. The afternoon sun moved onto them and they glittered in its light. They cast prisms on the window and walls—beautiful colours reflecting colours all around the room. It was like being in an Aladdin's cave. What a haul! He was very pleased with himself and he muttered the words with a smile, "Well Sister, wherever you are, or whoever you are, I hope you like what I've brought you. Don't ever say I don't give you anything!"

Of course, there was no sister—just in his imagination, but he preferred it that way. There had been a sister once, but she'd only been a baby and he hadn't liked her then either, so he did what needed to be done and smothered her with her own pillow. It was rather easy and didn't take much strength at all—in fact, she died after only a few moments. Sad, but then these things happened and his parents still had him to love and spoil. When she was born, the baby had taken all his parents' attention and all she could do was gurgle and burp, unlike he, who could actually read by the time she was born. He was twenty-five now and she would have been twenty—but he didn't miss her one little bit. He remembered her name had been Isobel and she was six months old when she died.

He carefully lifted the diamonds and took them upstairs. In his parents' room he had a special box where he kept all his most precious possessions—and the diamonds fitted in quite nicely. In fact, his collection was growing—he really was good at what he did—and that was to relieve people of things that either didn't belong to them—or that they had no future use for.

Two days later, he was up with the sun and again planning his day ahead. He liked to do at least two or three daring things each week—it kept him feeling alive and anyway he enjoyed the challenge it presented. He used the back door today as he didn't want to be seen, although his neighbours wouldn't have recognised him, even if they'd seen him. Today his hair was brown and brushed back behind his ears in a rather Bohemian-arty style, he wore dark glasses and a moustache and carried a gold-topped walking stick. He looked and felt dapper, quite like Oscar Wilde, he thought.

He walked in a different direction from the other day and ended up in Chelsea—well away from the Diamond Quarter—he strutted today as he felt that was how such an artistic gentleman should walk. The gallery was small but interesting and he soon arrived at the Art Exhibition which he'd read about in the newspaper. It was rather smart with subtly placed wall lights pointed at the paintings—some of which were large and some quite small. But they were all beautiful and very old.

In the room, there were several potential customers and he was soon mingling amongst them. Twirling his false moustache, he moved from painting to painting, peering at each information disk beside the work. He used a pince-nez which he'd retrieved from his inside pocket.

"If you require any help or information, Sir—I am always here to aid you. Whilst browsing, would you care for a glass of champagne—and there are also some tasty hors d'oeuvres in case you're feeling peckish." If anything, he was even more obsequious that Mr MacIntosh had been.

There was one wall at the back of the main room, in a kind of alcove, and its walls were covered in miniature paintings. David walked closer to them and used his pince-nez—they really were quite exquisite and elegant—some were of people from modern times and some from figures from the middle ages. There were even some of much older religious figures from the Renaissance period and those were especially desirable. He actually didn't care which one he stole—as long as he didn't leave the shop without one. He discussed certain of the miniatures, disagreeing with the assistant about when they were actually painted. It was always good to have a different opinion from those who thought they knew everything.

"May I please have some more bubbly?" And he sent the assistant off to do his bidding, while he scrutinised the wall more closely. He'd already made his choice and cautiously looked around the room—no one was looking as he slipped a miniature from the wall—it was a painting of what looked like Chaucer's *The Wife of Bath*. It wasn't his first choice but it was an easy one to slip off its holder and into his deep pocket.

"Why, thank you, young man—most kind." And he slowly sipped the nectar before moving towards the door of the gallery. He really was good at this—but he'd have to tackle something more difficult next time, as this was getting too easy.

With the miniature placed securely in his Collection Box at home, he changed into more relaxing clothes and went downstairs to prepare some dinner. Stealing things was quite demanding and he felt quite hungry. He set the table—for one—but before sitting down, he went out into the back garden and scattered a present on the grass for the friendly squirrels who played there. He threw what looked like food pellets around the bottom of the trees—that would make them sit up and pay attention. He knew that's where they often played. And he'd check in the morning to see if they'd found the poison he'd put down. The man in the Haberdashery told him he could guarantee their effectiveness. After all, why should the squirrels run around his lawn, enjoying themselves—he hoped he'd put a stop to it now. It was his lawn after all, not theirs.

He enjoyed his dinner and finished it off with a good claret and cigar. Yes, he still felt most like a Georgian gentleman. Watching the smoke curl towards the ceiling, he knew he must 'up' his game and do something more daring than simple theft. It was too easy for an intelligent man such as he. He toyed with the idea of visiting patients in hospital and helping put an end to their suffering, subtly of course, and painlessly he hoped, but not necessarily in that order.

Early next day, he was awoken from a deep sleep by the incessant ringing of his doorbell. He jumped out of bed and looked at the clock. It was only 8 o'clock so he hadn't overslept too much. He opened the bedroom window and peered down below. His next-door neighbour stood there, tapping her foot.

"Can I help you, Clara?" He called down.

"David, I just thought you'd like to know there are dead squirrels all over your garden. I only know because my dog brought one into my garden. What on earth can have happened to them? Did you have anything to do with it?" Clara was an elderly woman who'd always had the reputation for being a busybody. David didn't really like her, or her husband, although his mother and father had always got on well with them.

"No Clara—nothing to do with me, I'm afraid. Poor little chaps, what on earth could have happened to kill them like that?" He tried to look sympathetic.

"David, they're in your garden and I need to know if you've put anything down to get rid of them—it's just that my dog might find something and I'm sure it would do him no good." The woman was obviously upset and worried for her dog, but he could do nothing about that.

Again, he reassured her gain that it had nothing to do with him, closed the window and threw himself back onto the bed. He was smiling, happy that the poison had worked so well—the man in the Haberdashery had been so right. *I'll have to use him again sometime!* But in the meantime, he went downstairs and boiled a couple of eggs! A new day full of promise, and his morning newspaper was lying on the mat waiting for him. He tucked into his food and wondered what he could do to annoy miserable old Clara next door—yes, he'd like to do that and she was always asking for it.

He didn't leave home till gone twelve that day and his mode of dress was a bit less flamboyant than usual—a muffler, jacket and flat cap was his choice of apparel to go hospital visiting. He needed to look just like anyone else and fade into the background in the wards. He picked up some cheap flowers from the market and a couple of boxes of chocolates—these were for the patients who were trusting enough to talk to him. He went into a couple of wards until he found a very quiet one where all the patients were wired up to some sort of breathing apparatus—and all wore masks.

315

David thought, *Those would fit into my collection very nicely and add a certain 'Je ne sais quoi' to the other more valuable items.* It wasn't necessarily things of value he wanted—just things that were difficult to obtain. It didn't really matter to him that the patients would probably die without the masks—so what, they were probably going to die anyway? His concern knew no bounds—and caused him to smile at his own lack of sympathy.

He sat first by the bedside of an elderly man and chatted about the weather, "It's a glorious day outside—you should try to get better so you can go out there." The old man nodded but said nothing. David put some flowers in an empty vase on his bedside table, "That's much better, isn't it?" Again, the old man smiled and said nothing. As he collected the rest of his flowers, he bumped against the table and, using small nail scissors he'd brought with him, he snipped the tube attached to both the mask and the machine at the side of the bed. *That was easy*, he thought.

He moved off quickly and stopped three beds further on. He did exactly as he'd done before and left the second sick, old man breathing heavily and looking very distressed. But he had given him flowers, hadn't he, so he should be grateful? *Two masks—what fun*, he thought, and quickly walked out of the hospital, the masks safely in either pocket. Another successful day doing something out of the ordinary and making a difference to the people he met. Ah, that's what life was all about! No one could call him lazy, could they?

Tomorrow was to be the new Queen's coronation and David dressed himself with great care that morning. The year was 1838 and the month of June—it was a Thursday—and London would be so packed, he hoped he wouldn't be hurt in the crush. Mind you, with it being so crowded, he may try his hand at pick pocketing—something he hadn't tried before. You see, every day had its challenges.

He looked incredibly smart when he left the house and followed Clara and William, her husband, down the street—they must be going to see the procession as well. He'd keep well behind them and pretend he hadn't seen them. As he neared Buckingham Palace, the people all along the Mall and around the palace railings, must have been standing twenty deep at least—with so many red, blue and white flags, it was almost blinding. The newly-built railways had brought thousands into London to see their Queen on her way to be crowned and all the London parks were full as well, full with catering and entertainment needed to relieve folk of their hard-earned pennies.

There was line upon line of scaffolding for the people to climb on and see better. In fact, the Government had laid aside £70,000 to meet the costs of the celebrations. On the other hand, for William IV's coronation, they'd only spent £30,000 and it became known as his 'Half-Crown-ation.' An insult if ever there was one and aimed at his hero too!

From Trafalgar Square, the smart Georgian gentleman crossed over Horse Guards' Parade ground and began to walk up the Mall, almost having to push his way through the laughing throngs. One man shouted at him, "Hey, ye're a bit of a toff, ain't cha? A bit overdressed for this shenanigan!" He wasn't being offensive but David thought him rude, so he ignored him. One woman crushed herself against him and snatched the flower from his lapel. He didn't know if he liked this crush and pushed harder to reach the palace gates. Then he saw a carriage going past and sitting there, was Lord Melbourne, the Prime Minister himself—and said to be a good friend of the new Queen—he would be on his way to Westminster Abbey as well.

The policemen lined the streets trying to control the unruly crowds. David, of course, behaved impeccably but couldn't resist pushing a young man out of the way—right into the path of a Guardsman on horse. The horse was big and black and powerful. He turned away quickly as a policeman ran over to help the lad—he knew the incident couldn't have had anything to do with the well-dressed gentleman in the top hat. The boy must have tripped! The wounded chap was hustled away and the well-dressed toff just brushed the sleeve of his jacket.

Hyde Park was the scene of a huge fair with a balloon ascent for those who could afford it. It was supposed to be there for two days only but that soon stretched into four days—it was so popular. David didn't think he'd go there—*it was more for the common people,* he thought. Green Park too had entered into the spirit of things by having a magnificent firework display for everyone to attend. It was a great day—the sun was shining and all seemed right with the world.

Then he saw her in her carriage. She was a pretty young thing—only a girl really—but she held herself well and actually looked like a Queen. Her procession was apparently the greatest procession through the streets since Charles II was crowned in 1661. (He'd read that in his morning paper.) It really was an impressive sight. As he stared around, he spotted Clara and William out of the corner of his eye—absolutely amazing what with all the crowds around—but there they were at the edge of the pavement.

He suddenly realised he could turn the situation to his advantage and do some necessary damage he'd been wanting to do for a long time. Everything was confusion and noise and the crowds' screams were deafening. He stepped close behind his neighbours and produced a sharp knife which he'd concealed in his inside pocket—it slid like butter straight into William's back. Roughly, he pulled it out again, actually doing even more damage in retrieving it—and hid it under his jacket. He moved quicker than he'd ever moved in his life and disappeared into the crowd. He'd actually seen William slump against his wife and then fall to the ground. *A job well done,* he thought.

He'd seen what he'd come for and felt he could continue to be a good Royalist—he'd liked the young girl he'd seen—she would do! And he'd managed to rid himself of one of his horrible neighbours—only one to go now! *Watch out, Clara, I've got my eye on you*, he thought.

Back in the house, he sensed an odd atmosphere. In fact, the strange thing was that he could smell his mother's perfume. She'd always used lily-of-the-valley and the smell was very distinctive. He went into his parents' room and saw the crib that had been there since the death of their baby. They'd never got rid of it, despite his frequent requests. The strange thing was it was moving, as though someone had just rocked it. Of course, that was impossible—he was the only person in the house. Then, he saw her—his mother—just as she'd looked in the days before her death. She was dressed in the self-same clothes that still hung over the chair by the bed. There was, however, no sign of his father.

"And what have you been up to, young man—some of your old tricks, I suppose. You were always a naughty boy who never knew right from wrong." Her voice was exactly the same as he remembered and for a moment, he felt ashamed about what he'd done to her friend William—but the shame didn't last long. He hadn't seen his mother for more than a year now and he didn't know how to speak to her. He hesitated for a moment.

"What do you want, Mother? Where have you come from?" He managed the words at last and spoke in a rather hoarse voice.

"I've been here quite some time, David, and watched the way you're living your life. Why do you go out of your way to hurt people who haven't hurt you? Why did you kill William next door?" It wasn't surprising that her son wasn't too happy to see her as she inevitably scolded him on each and every occasion. And he really resented it!

"Mother, you have no right to question me like this! You don't live here anymore—in fact, you don't live at all." He decided the best way to tackle his mother was to be upfront with her and show no remorse. When she was alive, he'd been scared of her—nothing he'd ever done had been good enough for her—and he was glad when she died. "Why don't you disappear to where you've come from—you're not welcome here. This is my home now—not yours."

"Why did you kill William?" she asked again.

"Because he's always annoyed me—even when I was a child, he'd carry stories to you and Father. I felt he was watching me all the time." David thought his reasoning was logical.

"You'll be caught, Son—stealing things is one thing, but killing people is quite another!" Her voice was slightly softer than it had been. "The Law will catch up with you sooner than you think."

"No one caught up with me when I got rid of you and Father—did they? I'm quite happy with my life now and William next door was of no importance, whereas I am important." He was less afraid of her now—she could do nothing to him—he must learn just to ignore her.

She was fading away now but managed to say, "I'm going to get your father to speak to you!"

"You do that!" he shouted after the disappearing figure—and then he was alone in the room. He could still smell the scent of lily-of-the-valley—but that would soon fade as Mother had done. His doorbell was ringing—someone was very impatient. When he opened the front door, William stood there. He was quite pale, but otherwise looked okay! David wondered why a ghost had to ring the doorbell!

Bill spoke up, "I believe your Mother's just been to see you—she tipped me off, you see—we're both in the same place now and she told me what you did to her and to your father. I wanted to tell you, I'm going to hang around your garden and your house, just to make you miserable. I feel it's the least I can do in the circumstances—don't you? After all, you killed me!"

The damned ghosts were beginning to gang up on him—so he turned around and went indoors. Unfortunately, William was now standing in the hall. "You can't get rid of me, David—you were always a bad boy and someone I never liked." And the man settled down in an armchair by the fireside.

319

"Bloody well get out of my house and don't think I can't make you—I know how to do it. I'll contact an exorcist I know—she'll soon move you!" But William just made himself more comfortable in the chair, looking quite relaxed.

David thought a stiff drink and a cigar would help the situation. He had his mother upstairs and neighbour William, downstairs—it seemed he'd never be alone again. When he eventually climbed his weary way to bed, he thought he could hear voices coming from his parents' room. Cautiously, he opened their door and Mother was sitting on her chair, with Father on the other side. Their conversation sounded serious and he knew they were talking about him. "Why don't you two just disappear—neither of you have a right to be here. What's happened—would Heaven not let you stay there? I bet that's what happened."

"We've been allowed to visit you to try to stop your terrible behaviour here on earth. You were never a nice child but you've become an unbearable monster now." His father used his most stern voice and David knew he was in for a telling-off. It was the same voice he used to use when David brought home a bad report from school. Both ghosts stood up and came towards him—but he backed away. "We're going to stay here until you turn over a new leaf and start behaving better."

The young man turned and swiftly left the room—he'd soon see about that! He didn't sleep well that night and tossed and turned until dawn had broken. He dressed carefully and crept out of the house, so as not to bump into any of the visiting spirits. Mind you, he did pause on the landing to listen—and he heard it quite clearly—a baby crying. He'd only heard that once and thought he was imagining things. Had his baby sister joined his tormentors then?

He did actually know of a spiritualist who lived in Putney and he hailed a carriage for speed—walking would be too slow. As soon as the spiritualist held her séance, the sooner they'd all be gone. Mrs Breckenridge lived in a terraced property and he knew of her because he'd seen her once when she'd come to his house to see his mother. It was just after her baby had died and she'd been a great believer! He rang the doorbell tentatively and waited. A dog began to bark and he hoped it was a small dog, as he didn't really like dogs. The door opened a crack and a pale, haggard face looked out, "Yes?" she asked. *At least he thought it was a she.*

"I'd like a consultation, Mrs Breckenridge, if you can spare the time."

"Time is all I have, young man." She stared at him. "Don't I know you—you look familiar as though we've met before." She pushed back a small spaniel with her foot.

"It couldn't have been me, I'm afraid—the only time I saw you was when you came to see my mother just after my sister died. I could only have been about five then and you didn't see me." He wondered if perhaps she was senile—she was very old—but he hoped she was still compos-mentis enough to help him.

"No, I'm quite sane, young man. I did meet your father then and you're the very spit of him—that's why I thought we'd met before." She stepped back and invited him inside. The hallway was dark and foreboding—maybe she had no electric light—just gas mantles. She showed him into a small sitting room and offered some tea, which he quickly refused.

"I have another appointment I'm afraid and am in rather a hurry," he lied.

"Well then, let's not waste time—how can I help you?" She poured herself some tea and watched him closely. He explained what was happening to him and how he couldn't live like that. He told how his mother and father were now dead and his neighbour who had just died, kept on turning up in his house. "I need you to get rid of them please. Do you think you could do that?"

"I remember now why I came to your house many years ago. Your mother had just lost a little child and was grieving badly. You were just a little boy then—but if I recall correctly, you were a pushy little chap! Is that right?"

"Well, yes I suppose you might have seen me but you're wrong about me being pushy—I don't think I was." He didn't like her and thought she might be a good subject for his 'next project'.

She agreed to come to his house to get 'the feel of it'. Until she'd done that, she could make him no promises. He left her then and decided to walk home— it was a lovely day and there were lots of people in the streets. He was about half way home when he suddenly felt tired—probably all that tossing and turning the night before. He stopped at a hackney carriage queue and joined the back. In front of him, he recognised an elderly man—who used to be his history teacher. He'd been obnoxious then and was probably worse now—he was probably the reason he'd never liked History.

On impulse, he decided to act. One little push when the next hackney was approaching the stop—and it could all be over. It wasn't right that old Mr Smithers had lived this long and he knew he'd be doing him a favour, before ill-health set in. Yes, that's what he would do. The man was frail now, but hadn't been when he'd handed out punishment with his leather strap—David could still remember the smarting pain.

There was a hackney carriage approaching and David stooped down to tie his shoelace. As he got up again, he fell slightly forward into the back of the old man's legs and off he went, rolling into the path of the oncoming vehicle. It actually was a bit of a bloodbath as the horse and carriage wheels went right over him and actually came to a stop on top of him. *How easy this killing business was,* he thought, and quickly moved away from the gathering crowd—because although he'd have been quite willing to help, there was absolutely nothing he could do. He decided not to take a carriage the rest of the way home after all and walked with new energy, as though he'd just had a pick-me-up. As indeed he had!

Two nights later and at the agreed time, Mrs Breckenridge arrived at David's front door.

"Do come in please." And he waved her into his sitting room. She thanked him for his offer of a sherry and drank it greedily. He topped up her glass again. It had to be said she looked the part—dressed all in black and carrying a big black handbag. She wore a hat with a veil that came down to her nose—and black, fingerless gloves. The veritable picture of a witch.

"Let's get right down to business, shall we? Show me where your 'visitors' appear and then we might sit down together and try to chase them away. By the way, have you been involved with someone's death very recently—I seem to sense that you have."

"No Mrs Breckenridge—not that I'm aware of." *That must have been old Mr Smithers*, he thought.

Upstairs, Mrs Breckenridge immediately went into his parents' room. "There has recently been a child in that cradle—or was it the spirit of a child whose bed it once was? Yes, I think that's it! The spirit of a child who has passed on. And I recognise that man and woman sitting on either side of the bed—I met them before, when they needed my help." The figures never moved or spoke—David and the spiritualist went back to the sitting room. There sat William from next door! He'd just realised what David was up to.

"Yes, I see your problem—and that gentleman over there in the armchair—I take it that's the neighbour you spoke of. Well, they're certainly filling up your home." She eyed the sherry decanter and David filled her glass again.

Rising from the sofa, she told him she was going home now but that she'd be back the next night when they would hold a seance to rid the house of the unwelcome spirits. "If we can't do it, you'll have to get a priest to exorcise them—you realise that, don't you?"

"Of course, I do—but I believe you can do it." He played up to her vanity.

Almost as soon as she'd left, his doorbell rang again and he went to answer it. Clara stood on the doorstep—a more subdued Clara than ever before. She'd come to ask him if he would attend her William's funeral, as 'he always liked you, you know.'

"No, I didn't know that, Clara—but I'll most certainly come to pay my last respects to your husband." A husband, who was sitting in his usual armchair, watching them both. David felt most uncomfortable and turned his back on the ghost.

"Why would anyone want to do that to him, do you think? He was a good man, you know—and never hurt anyone," she was crying into her handkerchief.

David didn't respond to this, instead he poured her a glass, all the time thinking, *What about all the times he told tales on me when I was a youngster? He used to watch my every movement, in the hope I'd do something wrong.*

She went on, "Actually, I thought I saw you in the crowd at the Coronation—I did, didn't I? Didn't you spot us? The police have asked me to try and remember if I saw anyone I knew when it happened—I forgot about you. But I can always tell them tomorrow, can't I? Did you see anything, David?"

"Nothing unusual, Clara—I'm truly sorry. Have some more sherry, why don't you? It'll help you sleep." And he whisked her glass away to the sideboard.

He knew he wouldn't have to keep his word to her and attend the funeral, because she herself would pass away that night—quietly and in her sleep—possibly heart failure brought on by sudden stress. He'd use the same poison as he'd used for his own parents—it had no taste and wasn't discernible in the organs after death. But then an autopsy might not even be considered necessary. He dropped a few drops of cyanide into her sherry and she finished it in one gulp—now he'd gotten rid of both his tiresome neighbours. And Mrs Breckenridge was on the case to deal with his other problem. Life was good again!

He washed the glasses, had a bite of supper and climbed the stairs to bed. His parents were quiet that night—probably the visit from the spiritualist had upset them. He laid out his clothes for the next day because, no matter what had happened—he had to appear smart and in control.

Again, next morning he was awakened by the doorbell ringing. It was very early so he peeped from behind the curtain, to see who was there. Two large gentlemen stood there, one carrying a notebook in his hand. They both wore long blue tunics and pointed helmets—both had striped duty bands around their arms, which showed they were there on official business. What could they want with him? He scratched his head in dismay before pulling on his dressing gown and slippers. *They really should allow a chap time to dress before coming knocking on his door*! He felt quite indignant.

"Good morning, Sir. Just a few questions, if we may—we're hoping you may be able to help us." Both men had handlebar moustaches and looked so similar, David almost wanted to laugh. They were like characterised comic bobbies. "Of course, gentlemen, do come inside—would you like some coffee perhaps? I was just going to put the kettle on." He bustled them inside and hoped they wouldn't spot William sitting in the armchair—nor his wife Clara, who now sat on the other chair. *God! It hadn't taken her long to manifest herself as a ghost*, David thought. The room was really getting quite crowded.

The three men drank their coffee and the police explained that David's next door neighbour had been found dead by the milkman when he called to collect his money. Apparently, she hadn't been dead for long. "How awful, gentlemen— and her husband was murdered only last week—in fact, she came around to see me last night to invite me to his funeral. Isn't that just dreadful, Officers! Could his murder have brought it on?"

"Most certainly it is dreadful, Sir—and that's the main reason we've come to see you. The coincidence is amazing—both man and wife dead in a week! We were hoping you had seen something unusual that might help us—and there was an old gentleman who fell in front of a carriage just a few days ago—he died at the scene, and we believe he may have been pushed—were you perhaps there at the time?"

David told them all he could—which was nothing—and offered more coffee, but the policemen declined and left the house. "We may have to talk with you again, Sir—you're not planning to leave town, are you?"

And that was that—David breathed a sigh of relief! *Managed to swerve that ball, didn't I?*

That evening, Mrs Breckenridge came as promised and before starting her séance, she performed a few strange physical exercises, which made her look even more ridiculous than before. She jiggled and danced around the room and then, they both sat at a small, round table and joined finger tips in the expected way. He'd seen it once before, when she'd visited his mother all those years ago but he'd never heard his parents talk about it afterwards—so he didn't know how good she was as a spiritualist.

"This house is rather full of wandering spirits—you know that, don't you?" she whispered in a voice he could hardly hear.

"Not that many surely?" and was told, "Well, there's your mother and father upstairs with your baby sister, a man and his wife on the sofa, two elderly men in their hospital gowns and several people who claim you ran them over, one by one, when you used to drive your own carriage. And there's another old man in a gown and mortar who looks like a teacher. That's all I can sense just now, but there could be more. In fact, there's two new boys just joined—apparently, you were at school with them and on a cross-country run, you made sure that one cracked his head on a low branch of a tree—and the other somehow fell off a rickety bridge—or at least you helped him fall."

David started to defend his actions, "Well, they were both planning to stand against me for the school's Head Boy—and I couldn't let that happen, now could I? Well, could I?" He needed her reassurance, but she ignored him.

He knew she was enjoying this—and began to feel an icy chill up and down his spine. She went on, "You killed them all, didn't you? Killing your sister when you were only five must have been when it all started. How many have you actually murdered in your life? Why you haven't been caught before now, I can't understand." She tutted loudly. "There's no need for a séance as all these people have already volunteered to contact you. They want to see you get your just desserts. I think it's time you went to the police, don't you?"

Now that he didn't expect! How dare she? If she thought she was going to charge him money for this consultation, then she had another think coming. He'd give her nothing, he decided. Well, that wasn't strictly true—maybe he'd give her a couple of sherries—she was very partial to them. And so ended Mrs Breckenridge. As a spiritualist, she might have anticipated her own death, but no—nothing so clever as that.

He waited until the middle of the night and dragged her slight frame down the road, placing her against a stone wall. He did at least have the grace to cover her face before going back home and reading himself to sleep. He'd been meaning to read that book for a long time—it was all about his hero, King William IV. He enjoyed anything to do with Royalty and William was his 'min man' after all.

Just as he was about to switch off his bedside lamp, he noticed a movement by the window—and there she stood, in all her 'black glory'—Mrs Breckenridge. She cackled at him—not a laugh, but a cackle. "Thought you'd got rid of me, did you? Well think again, young man—I'm here to stay, or at least until you're gone from this place. I'm going to join all your other visitors now." He ignored the old crone and switched off the light—soon his soft breathing could be heard in the room—he slept just like a baby with no conscience at all. The sleep of the just!

Next morning, he washed, shaved and combed his golden hair. He chose his very best suit as he felt the day was going to be special and he must dress the part. His cravat was a shade of blue, stiff and shiny—and he leaned out of the bedroom window to pick a sweet-smelling rose from the rambling bush on the wall outside. The rose carefully held in his buttonhole, he collected his best top hat and went downstairs to prepare breakfast. However, there seemed to be something stuck behind the sitting room door. He pushed but it was stuck fast— and so he took a step back and charged at it with a mighty push. He ended up right in the middle of the room and was surrounded by a crowd of people, some he identified easily and some he vaguely recognised. At the forefront, stood old Mrs Breckenridge, her black veil pushed back from her face. *Not a pretty sight*, he thought.

"Good morning, David—are you happy to see us all here? You are looking smart today—is it a special day or something?" Her voice was rather croaky but then he realised she had only recently 'passed over' and may not yet be used to her present condition.

His mother pushed forward through the throng, first thrusting her baby into her father's arms. "You were warned, weren't you? I told you myself to stop your old tricks or they'd find you out." She was angry and plumped herself down on the sofa, between Clara and William, who obligingly moved to either side. There were several young men playfully pushing and shoving each other out of the way—boys from his old school perhaps? God, how many people were here? The two old men whose breathing masks he'd stolen were supporting each other to stand upright and neither had any teeth, so looked even more grotesque.

Everyone was talking at once and he could hear his own name being repeated over and over again.

He held up his hands and told them to be quiet. "I can explain everything if you'd just give me a chance—I had to get rid of all of you because you were annoying and wouldn't let me have my own way." It sounded perfectly acceptable to him.

The two old men mumbled and mouthed the words, "That's not true—you know you picked us at random. We'd never hurt you." At least that's what the rest of the crowd thought they'd said—their lack of teeth impeded the words. The really odd thing was, there were also several squirrels darting about the room between the people—then he remembered he'd killed them too—but he wasn't sure that squirrels could become ghosts; *did they have souls?* he wondered. Now, that was an interesting thought.

One of the boys shouted, "They're coming now and they're wearing their duty arm bands, so they mean business. The Peelers are coming—the Peelers are coming." And the other boys took it up as a chant. The two burly policemen passed the window and rang the doorbell. David invited them inside—although there wasn't much room. It didn't matter though, because they didn't seem to notice the crowd of ghostly figures in the room. David now realised his 'victims' had all come together to see him get his just desserts—how many of them there were—he didn't realise how many he'd killed. Whatever the number, at least the policemen couldn't see them.

"We've not come to question you more, Sir; we've come to escort you down to the station. I'm afraid we're going to arrest you for murder. Mrs Breckenridge, the spiritualist, was found dying in the streets outside—although she died before she reached the hospital, she had time to tell who had tried—and succeeded—to kill her. She named you, Sir—so if you'd like to come along with us, we'd much appreciate your cooperation. There'll be other officers along in a moment to search this house—we've had several reports of theft of valuables involving yourself. Apparently, in the past, you've tried to alter your appearance—but not as successfully as you thought. Everyone always mentions your arrogance, something they all agreed."

The police couldn't hear nor see anyone but David. However, he could hear the 'Hoorays' and 'Bravos' from all the people he'd killed. They were treating it like a football match. *How strange and uncouth! And he such an aristocratic gentleman!*

"Of course, I'll accompany you to the station—let me first get my hat. I must look my best, I'm sure you understand. However, just before we go, I must insist you have a last drink with me—just to see me off properly, after all I am now a Victorian gentleman—and should at least be allowed to celebrate that fact." He reached for the decanter of sherry and filled three glasses to the brim. "You must drink with me—or I won't come quietly." He smiled at his own little joke.

"We wouldn't normally do this, Sir—but as you've been so obliging, we will join you." One of the Peelers said with a smile. The three men drank the sherry and replaced the glasses on the sideboard.

The room had mysteriously emptied as if the show was over—as indeed it was—and David donned his shiny top hat. "I do look like an aristocratic Victorian gentleman, don't I? I wonder what the young Queen would think of me. She'd probably say, 'What a true gentleman—he's the sort who makes this great country even greater.'"

As he spoke, he stumbled against one of the policemen, who himself fell against his colleague. A moment later, all three were lying in a heap on the floor. The sherry had done its work! David knew he'd have to stay in this house forever, with no friends or relatives to keep him company. The ghosts had all disappeared from the house—they could rest now he'd got his just desserts—after all, hadn't he now committed the ultimate crime of taking his own life—the most precious thing given by God to an aristocratic Victorian gentleman? Perhaps he should have stuck to killing other people; after all, Plebs didn't matter, did they? And he flicked a piece of fluff from his immaculate—and ghostly—sleeve!

My Life's Not My Own

I write stories about famous people from history and I've always enjoyed doing it. Believe it or not, but I've recently discovered it can develop into quite a dangerous pastime. When I write about those people, I do a lot of research and really get to know them. I check the accuracy of dates, sometimes more than once, and I like to believe I understand the reasons they did the things that made them memorable. Some are pleasant and some not so pleasant.

Like, for instance, why did Henry the Eighth execute and reject five of his wives? Why was Charles the First so determined to stick to his stubbornness with Parliament when a quite small admission would have allowed him to keep his head? (i.e. That he wasn't God's only chosen and there was room for Parliament) Personally, I'd have voted for keeping my head. And why did Lizzie Borden give her mother and father forty whacks with an axe—then deny it, first getting her evidence upside down and back-to-front at her trial?

When you begin to look closely into their times and into the decisions and actions they took—you really begin to understand how their minds must have worked. This knowledge however tends to stay with you and live on in your mind and sometimes, you find yourself arguing with your imaginary visitor. As an example, only last week, I found John Wilkes Booth resting in an armchair in my sitting room. I recognised him immediately—he was the handsome actor who shot President Abraham Lincoln in the back of the head and then ran away to save his own skin. He was apparently an ardent Confederate sympathiser but never fought for them during the four years of the American Civil War. He was only thirty-two years old when he died at the hands of a Yankee sergeant who'd helped to corner him in a country barn.

"Mr Wilkes Booth," I said, "good manners make me say it's a pleasure to meet you, but I have to say I don't approve of what you did to Abe Lincoln in 1865. May I ask why you've come to see me? I am not one of your Confederate sympathisers."

"It was easy to sense when you wrote about me that you thought I'd done wrong when I went to the theatre and killed the President. I wanted to put my side of the case directly to you—you weren't there when it happened and so you couldn't possibly appreciate what people were feeling at the end of the American Civil War." He spoke rather dramatically with an actor's voice and gripped his coat collar as he spoke in an obviously theatrical way.

I had to concede the point he made—I hadn't been present when it happened—but I knew a lot about the President and about John Wilkes Booth and his famous brother. I also knew a lot about the effects the Civil War had had on the people—both in the North and in the South—how those in the North had idolised Lincoln and resented the action Booth took that fateful night at Ford's Theatre.

And then he appeared in the chair opposite Booth—Abraham Lincoln himself, dressed in his stiff collar and cravat, in fact exactly what he wore that fateful night when he set off with his wife Mary, to Ford's theatre in Washington—and never came back. The two men seemed at ease with each other—almost as though they knew each other. Typically, the first thing Lincoln said was, "How's the leg Mr Booth—I heard you broke it when you jumped from my box onto the stage below—after shooting me that is."

"It is good Sir, thanks to Dr Mudd who set it for me—and was arrested for having done it. Treason or some unjust claim—he was just a doctor living up to his Hippocratic Oath." Booth looked defiant as though proud of what he'd done—in fact, he probably was proud of it.

"Glad to hear it, Mr Booth—and I agree with what you say about Dr Mudd, but I cannot agree with your decision to kill me. I thought I'd been quite a good President." Lincoln spoke with a hint of a smile and even looked at me for confirmation. I nodded my head.

"I'm sure you were a good President, Mr Lincoln—you were on the wrong side however—the Confederates should have won the Civil War." Booth stuck to his guns. "They were not industrialised like the North but rather preferred to live off the land—hence the need for slave labour."

"Ah, that's a different opinion altogether and one with which I cannot agree. The South favoured slavery and were willing to break away from the United States just to maintain it. People were thinking differently and Jefferson just refused to see it."

The discussion was getting heated, so I interfered and asked if I could get them anything. The two ghosts looked at me as though I was quite mad. I did break their train of thought however and they both became quieter. I realised it was my presence that was keeping them there and I left the room, glancing back just in time to see them both disappear.

What a pity those two gentlemen didn't have the opportunity to talk things over before Booth did the dastardly deed. You never know, it might have changed American history as we know it.

That day, I stayed out of the lounge—just to be sure the air was clear of people from the past. And it was—but on going there next day, I was to find quite a different character sitting on the chair by the window. There was no mistaking that figure. It was Adolph Hitler in full uniform and when I entered the room, he stood up and gave the 'Heil Hitler' salute. I couldn't stop myself from saying, "Don't Heil yourself to me Mr Hitler—I don't agree with what that salute implies." I knew I was on dangerous ground, but I couldn't help myself. *Who could ever respect what this man had done? Certainly not me!*

Adolph spoke in his guttural accent, "Who do you think you are, to disrespect me like that? I am the Fuhrer. The people of Germany loved me and I was going to make them great, but those damned men, Churchill and Eisenhower just wouldn't give in. It was all their fault and that of their European allies—so many pointless deaths and all caused by their stubbornness."

I couldn't let that one go, "How dare you speak like that of those heroes who saved the world. They kept the spirits of Europe high—well some more than others—but enough to make you surrender and shoot yourself in a cellar. You obviously knew at that moment what you'd done to the world."

"You're just another one who doesn't understand what was going on in the world at the time. I was the saviour of my people and Germany was becoming great again—they loved me, you know, no matter what you believe. I started off in a very lowly position, you know—a house painter in fact and then a corporal in the army—and I rose to be the most powerful man in Germany and in many other territories as well. I know for a fact, it was that damned, small island Britain with America behind her, who stood in my way! Mind you, at one point, I was pretty close to beating both those nations." He was on his feet and shouting in the same way he'd once made speeches.

"And what about the Jewish people—what about them? Who were you to decide the world would be a better place without them? And the way you did

331

it—it was inhuman and cruel beyond understanding. You were a monster where they were concerned." Even I was getting louder and told myself to be careful. *Remember who you're talking to!*

"You see, that shows you know nothing about what was going on at the time—and about what had to be stopped. I was meant to save Europe from destruction and I was doing a good job until Britain and her allies interfered with my plans—but Britain most of all."

I decided I couldn't take any more of the man. He was intolerable—and conceited, vain and opinionated—just what a dictator needed to be, in fact. I spent the rest of the morning baking in my kitchen with the local radio blaring in the background. I found kneading the dough therapeutic—in fact, I pretended it was Adolph's head and I was pummelling some sense into it. But of course, that ship had long sailed. I made a sponge cake as well and spread one half with strawberry jam and the other with butter cream—two of my favourites. I sat at the kitchen table with a glass of milk and a slice of my brilliant cake and enjoyed the peace. No one else visited me for a couple of days. It happened next when I was changing the sheets on my bed and I felt someone tugging at the cover—but I was the only one in the apartment. I'd thought I was alone, but was I?

I keep a small armchair in the bedroom and sitting there was a lady, dressed in a long pale blue dress and wearing white gloves, reaching all the way up to above her elbows. At first, I wasn't sure who she was but then I knew! It was one of my favourite authors, whose books I had grown up with. She spoke gently, "Good afternoon—how pleasant to be able to visit you. I've been moving house rather a lot lately and it's nice to just sit here and converse with you." Jane Austen had honoured me with a visit and I sat down on the bed opposite her.

"Where are you living just now, Miss Austen?" I started to say, but she interrupted me with "Please call me Jane." And so, I did! "Have you been living in the town of Bath recently—I remember you moved house a lot there." I didn't know what else to say. I had admired this lady since I was a child—her writings were amazing but hadn't given her the financial rewards they should have. I believe it was because of a dodgy publisher who took advantage of her—but I thought it might not be politic to mention it.

"Yes, we have moved several times in the city of Bath—my mother just can't settle and of course my father died there with a chill he caught from the dampness in the foundations," she explained. I nodded my head in sympathy—I did remember that had happened—and held out my hand to comfort her, but of course, she didn't take it. I frantically thought of something to say, "You've had a bit of trouble with your publisher, haven't you—and he somehow swindled you out of your royalties?" I thought to Hell with being careful—I needed something to discuss.

"I'm afraid that did happen although my novel *Pride and Prejudice* has done very well and believe it or not, is a bestseller. My other novels are doing reasonably well just now too." She said it quietly and modestly—a very refined lady indeed.

"Whilst I'm lucky enough to have you here, Jane, may I ask a question please? I was never sure in *Pride and Prejudice*; was it Elizabeth Bennett or Mr Darcey who was proud and the other prejudiced—or was it vice-versa/ I get confused, I'm afraid." I was genuinely interested.

"Oh, my dear, it was both of them—and most of the others in the story. She was prejudiced against his vanity and pride and when they first met, he was prejudiced against her middle-class background and of course, against her very middle-class and rather eccentric family, whom you have to agree could behave shamefully—and they always liked to be the centre of attention. In fact, pride and prejudice was a fault on all sides of the characters in the novel—Bingley broke up his relationship with Jane Bennett because Darnley persuaded him she was beneath him. As for Mrs Bennett—ah, Mrs Bennett—she was prejudiced against anyone who disagreed with her and she was such a snob, wasn't she? Darnley's Dowager Aunt was prejudiced against everyone, looking down her nose at everyone in sight. The theme ran all the way through the book."

I really appreciated her words and, now understood clearly the widespread moral in her most famous story. How wonderful that she'd come to see me. I wanted to talk more with her, but she disappeared as quickly as she'd come. I was really disappointed.

The next couple of days passed quietly and I was able to get on with my writing. After a while, I began to stiffen up and decided to take a walk in the park. The day was lovely and warm and I didn't need a coat. I'd brought bread for the ducks and sat on an empty bench near the water. A figure was approaching and I moved along the bench to make room. In fact, I had to move over quite a bit as he was a very large man. He was dressed in rather strange clothes and wore a hat with a feather blowing in the breeze.

The man spoke, "Well Madam, we meet at last—I've only read your words about me but have never met you. Do you recognise me—you should—you've written enough about me and although you don't know me, you quite clearly have formed an opinion of me. Rather audacious really, don't you think?" He didn't have to say more—I recognised him now as none other than King Henry VIII—and he was right, I had written a lot about him. In fact, like a great many people, I had decided he was a monster, a very cruel monster indeed. And from his tone, it was obvious he didn't like it one little bit.

I turned to face him and was glad that no one else around could see him. At least, I hoped that no one else could see him. "You murdered two of your wives and divorced two others, sending them to live away from the court. One poor Queen died after childbirth because you ordered her to rise from her sickbed when she was obviously very ill. She of course, died soon after—and your sixth and final wife managed to outlive you, much to her credit."

"And there you have it—just what I'm here to complain about—you have no idea what happened during my lifetime, have you? You're like all the others—you make up your mind without even trying to see things from my point of view." "Did you know, my father was the last king to have won the throne of England by being victorious on the battlefield—Henry Tudor dealt magnificently with Richard III—and brought to an end the very long War of the Roses? The clever man even chose his bride to unite the red and white roses of the long war. The man was a great strategist and united the houses of York and Lancaster forever."

"He was the one who actually won the throne of England and then, I inherited it—but the biggest challenge of my life was to keep it. To secure the Tudor line for the next generation, I had to produce a male heir. Until Jane Seymour gave me Edward, none of the others could give me a son.

Oh yes, there were illegitimate boys born but that was of no use to me." As he finished talking, he looked quite crestfallen and I almost felt sorry for him.

"Okay, okay, I see the point you're making." I butted in, "But for all the dubious decisions about the queens and their failures, it was one of your daughters who became the best and most loved Queen of England. Your son, whom you craved so much, only lived for fourteen years. So, wasn't everything you did through the years all for nothing in the end?" I paused, realising I was perhaps being too judgemental. In fairness he couldn't have known this was how things would pan out—he didn't know what the future would bring. "Mind you, I suppose you could also argue that because she never married in her turn, it was she who ended the short-lived Tudor line. She never made it her life's work to have an heir, did she?" Looking at his expression, I realised I was upsetting him even more, but then he'd chosen to visit me and not the other way around, so he had to let me speak.

"I wasn't the bad man you describe in your writing—I was married to my first wife for twenty-six years—but she gave me no heir—what else could I do? The Pope wouldn't agree to our divorce. Anne Boleyn was unfaithful to me with several courtiers—as did her cousin, Catherine Howard, also with close courtiers. Jane Howard gave me a son, but then died—and Ann of Cleves was so repulsive, I couldn't stand her—but after our annulment, we became good friends. Katherine Parr, my last wife was an angel and looked after me when my health failed. Can you perhaps appreciate my problems a little better now?"

I didn't like the direct question and I started to say so, but when I turned towards him, he had already gone—and I was alone on the bench. It was at this point that I finally began to think that perhaps writing about people in history, wasn't such a good idea. It seemed I couldn't get them out of my head once I'd researched them. But I had to finish my current book, I couldn't leave it half finished, could I?

I walked slowly back towards my apartment, thinking about what he'd said to me. Maybe I could see his dilemma a bit better now—how desperate he was to have a male child and how hurt he must have been when two of his wives made a fool of him and carried on behind his back. But did they—who could tell—it was too long ago? As I put the kettle on to boil, I told myself that I'd just been given a sob story—and that Henry could have had better judgement and not marry so often—and with such wickedly short times between ceremonies. It was odd but his moral code which made him marry so often, was actually the reason for his terrible dilemmas—but then, he needed that elusive heir!

"No, Your Majesty, my thoughts will have to remain as they were—you haven't managed to change my mind." I settled down on the sofa with a cup of creamy coffee and some chocolate digestives. The fresh air and the King's lecture had made me tired and I soon fell asleep, thinking about the book I was still writing—about Robin Hood this time. Maybe when I'd finished it, Robin Hood himself would pay me a visit. I'd have to wait and see!

"Wake up, wake up, I believe my father has just visited you." My God but the woman looked magnificent—she had vivid red hair and wore a beautifully embroidered gown of gold threads, which was too full to allow her to sit in one of my chairs. She wore a ruff around her neck and had rings on every finger. There was absolutely no doubt who she was!

I stuttered, "There's no need to tell me who you are Your Majesty, and yes, your father has recently been to see me."

"I suppose he was pleading his case—he really believes he'd done no wrong you know—when he cut off my mother's head. What can I say, the man was a monster—and yet, I have to admit I loved him. I didn't like him, but I loved him. Having spoken with him, what do you think?"

She tapped her foot impatiently, waiting for my reply.

"I thought he was saying what he wanted me to believe, rather than what he knew to be the truth. No, I don't think he should have had your mother executed—she denied over and over again that she was guilty of his accusations and that they were not true. I believe that a Queen's role in that period was to be pleasant and kindly to all the courtiers—it was expected of them—and your mother behaved no differently from other ladies of the court but your father chose to think the worst of her without giving her a chance. That's what I think, Your Majesty."

As I had worked on my research of the period, I had thought Anne Boleyn to be innocent—but not so with her cousin, Catherine Howard, whom I believed did deserve the accusation of adultery. But even so, she shouldn't have died because of that. She was just a child and had had a strange upbringing. If anything, Henry himself should be blamed for choosing such a young girl to be his wife—her short-comings were those of youth and lack of wisdom. She still had to grow up and he never gave her the chance.

"That pleases me." Elizabeth managed to rest on the arm of the sofa, her dress spread before her. "I was never close to my mother but then, I was only two years old when he had her executed. I didn't get a chance to get to know her and I regretted that very much. Turning to me, you've also written about me, so what conclusions did you reach about me?" She looked at me expectantly with a 'Don't you mess with me, young lady' expression on her queenly face.

I thought for a long moment and said, "I thought you were one of the wisest, most competent and loved monarchs ever. You wrote the best speeches and were an excellent orator—that probably sounds over the top—but it's what I think anyway. As to whether you deserved the title of 'The Virgin Queen', well, that's another question. I think you had many suitors and many favourites whom you encouraged in their love of you."

She laughed and almost choked but seemed to enjoy what I'd said. She laughed again. "I can't deny I had a few favourites in my time—but Robert

Dudley was the best. I think I loved him since I was a young girl and I know for a fact, he loved me. At one time, I might have married him but the time was never right, so I remained a virgin."

I couldn't resist saying that marrying him and remaining a virgin were two different things. I think she understood my meaning as she added, "When we were young, we did discuss marriage, but he was a married man already and so we couldn't. Then his wife died suddenly and we thought again about marriage."

"Yes, I remember—that was Amy Robsart, wasn't it? She fell downstairs in her home and broke her neck—and everyone talked about it, hinting that it was no accident. Was that true?" Although I thought I knew the answer, I couldn't resist asking the question.

Elizabeth stood up and crossed the room, "Yes, I know you knew about his first wife and in your writing, you implied that it had been no accident. Did you believe Robert arranged it? Is that what you believe?"

I had to admit that I did think it. She looked angry, so I added, "And what about his stepson, Robert Devereux—did you love him as well?"

"I may have loved Robbie once but I don't know how you can ask that question—you know I had him executed for treason. I had no option—he'd gotten too big for his boots."

Our conversation was getting out of hand and I knew it had to stop, so I jumped in with: "What about your speech at Tilbury Docks when you rode your grey palfrey and addressed the troops? That speech will never be forgotten— people still refer to it today." I knew I had to appease her and it seemed to work. She raised one hand in a gesture of goodbye and smiled—the smile of a true Queen.

"Goodbye, young lady—I am tired of our conversation and must go." And the incredible woman and her incredible dress swept out of my sitting room, back to wherever she'd come from.

I'd really been in the company of royalty over the last few days and I was eager for whosoever would visit next. I went to bed that night and dreamt quite disturbing dreams. My imagination could run wild when I allowed it—and when I was asleep, I couldn't very well control it. Mind you, I didn't only write about historical figures but I also indulged my fancy in pure and utter fiction—making up characters in my stories as I saw fit. And as though echoing my thoughts, next morning I awoke to the figure of a young girl sitting on the end of my bed. I knew her right away as the 'Lass of Lincoln's Inn.' She was dressed in a torn dress and apron, with a plait hanging on each side of her head. She wore a sad expression and had obviously been waiting for me to wake up.

I stuttered, "Hello" and rubbed the sleep from my eyes. "I know you, don't I?"

She nodded and said, "Well, you knew me well enough to write about me and how I started the 'Great Fire of London', something of which you couldn't possibly have known. Yet, there it is in black and white in your book—the blame clearly lying on my shoulders. I believe before you point the finger at anyone, you should first be sure of your facts." She was speaking in an angry voice and even pointing a finger at me.

I was awake by then and I answered, "I'll have you know I did a lot of research about that incident and I only formed my opinion afterwards. Your father trusted you to dampen down the oven fire and then he went to bed, leaving you alone in the bakehouse. You were not as careful as you should have been and so the embers fell onto the straw-covered floor—and so the fire spread from house to house along Pudding Lane—and then much further until many of the London streets were ablaze." Luckily, my memory was quite good and I could clearly remember writing about the incident.

"You wrote that but you didn't base it on proven fact." The girl was not going to let the matter rest. "Why do you think I helped so many of the London homeless by providing food and water—I sought out those who needed help the most. Even King Charles was grateful to me and had a plaque erected for me in the field of Lincoln's Inn. A poor little bakehouse girl couldn't have fooled a King—now could she?"

I pulled on my dressing gown as I felt vulnerable in my pyjamas with a ghost sitting at the bottom of my bed. "I'll tell you something, Rosie Farynor—I've searched every open piece of ground around Lincoln's Inn and I've never managed to find any plaque that immortalises you. High and low I've searched, and it's just not there."

She interrupted me, "Oh yes, it is—I've seen it myself. How dare you make me out to be a liar. The King himself had it erected—and I did help a lot of people by finding and giving food to the worst-off—until London began re-building the city again and the people had homes once more. You can't deny that!"

I agreed with her words but added, "I believe you did try to help but I don't know whether you manged it. Your reputation lived on and superstitious people made you into a heroine, that's all. How you could help the people was questionable—you were a ghost after all and not physically able to do all the things you claimed to have done." I was getting tired of the argument as it looked as if neither of us was going to win.

Looking at the little ghost, I suddenly felt sorry for her—she needed me to say something positive. "Mind you, I must admit that your spirit and reputation cheered the people in their make-shift tents and pulled them together. Lincoln's Inn became a place of hope and that was probably due to you." I hoped that appeased her and for a while, I think it did as she fell silent.

"If you write about the Great Fire of London again, will you make sure you put that into your story—that I helped the people at the worst time in their lives." Now, that was an easy promise to make—as I believed she had.

"I will certainly do that, Rosie—it's the least I can do. If I've tarnished your reputation, then I apologise and will do better next time." We parted friends and I was able to start my breakfast—needless to say, I burnt my toast! And there was no Rosie to cheer me up.

My meeting with Rosie had been a different one from the others—although names and incidents were real enough, both Rosie's acts of kindness to the people who'd lost their homes and her friendship with the King, were however untrue—they were straight from my imagination and nor was there a plaque raised in gratitude for her kindness. I made that up too! As I said above, meeting Rosie was quite different from the others and not many of my completely fictitious characters had visited me before. I must be careful too what I say about them in the future, or they might all decide to come back and haunt me.

The day passed quietly and I accomplished quite a few pages of my book, being extra careful not to say anything untoward about the characters—unless the facts told me otherwise, then I have to be true to the text. I stopped for a break and wondered who would visit me next—from amongst the people I'd written about. Then I heard the argument coming from my spare room—and I thought I recognised one of the men's voices. Yes, I was sure it was Abraham Lincoln came to visit for a second time but who could he be arguing with? Then I heard another voice—a woman's voice this time.

He shouted, "Mary, stop being so difficult; you will accompany me to the theatre tonight. I have promised various people that we will attend. I am not asking you to forget the death of our son, but life has to go on and you along with it. I miss Willie as much as you do, but the play will cheer us up—it's a comedy starring Laura Keene and everyone says it's really funny. Its name is *Our*

American Cousin." He was getting exasperated with his wife Mary, who was becoming more and more difficult of late—in fact, some people thought she might be developing dementia.

"Stop ordering me, Husband—I resent your bossy way. I am my own woman and can think for myself. I have an odd feeling that is telling me I shouldn't leave the White House tonight. Nor should you—my feelings are usually right, you know."

I listened to the argument but decided to keep out of it, as it had really nothing to do with me. I couldn't resist however moving over to the wall and placing a glass against it—I wanted to hear as much as I could.

"We will go together, Mother"—his special name for her—"and afterwards, we'll have a lovely meal for our supper. Move quickly, or we'll be late for the performance." Mary obviously did as she was told, because the scene changed and they were talking about something completely different.

Her voice was soft and she said, "Let me hold your hand, Husband—I feel better that way. Although Miss Harris over there will think it odd of me hanging on to you so urgently." (Miss Harris was the fiancée of an officer and they'd both been in the theatre box with the Lincolns and now, were still with them, standing beside the President's deathbed). The President told Mary the young lady wouldn't mind it at all—and after saying another few words, he died. The great President Lincoln was no more. There was a deathly silence and I could hear the ticking of my clock. I knew I had to go into the room to see if there was anything I could do and the scene that met my eyes was truly moving. Mary was crying and saying, "I told you so, Husband—I told you we shouldn't go to the theatre, but as usual, you wouldn't listen." She bent and kissed his hand. "If only you'd listened, you'd still be with me now."

I went into the room and told Mary Todd how sorry I was. I really didn't know what else to say. She replied, "Thank you, my dear—but you know better than anyone that he wouldn't listen to me. I should have been more insistent, shouldn't I?" She obviously thought his death was her fault and I knew I had to think of something reassuring to say that would make her feel better.

"Ma'am, please don't think that. He knew how much you loved him—but he could be a stubborn man. Maybe that stubbornness was the reason he was such a good President and won the Civil War. You must believe you were his rock and you know how much he loved you." It must have been the right thing to say

340

as she seemed to pull herself together and leave the room on the arm of her eldest son, Robert.

I breathed a sigh of relief and actually began to consider moving house, as I didn't know how much more I could take. But would that have made any difference—those I write about would still be able to find me. The stress was beginning to affect me—and affect my writing as well, as I became afraid of which of my characters would visit next—and complain. It was odd, but although I knew full well none of them were real—only ghosts from the past—their visits still left me feeling exhausted. I'd enjoyed them at first but they were becoming too intrusive now.

It was two weeks later before I had another visit—almost as though they'd decided I needed a break. I had been getting on well with my book and felt I had made good progress, so I knew I was probably due for some of my characters to come and see me. I was having breakfast one morning. I had slept late and felt very relaxed—then I heard it—a hub-bub of different voices, getting louder and louder—like a rising crescendo. I didn't recognise anyone in particular, so I knew I'd have to go into the sitting room to see who was there. You'll never believe this but I swear it's true.

In my sitting room against the window, Grigori Rasputin of Russia was arguing with Nell Gwyn—about what I didn't know. Boudica, the Warrior Queen was nodding her head as though in agreement with Blackbeard the Pirate, who hadn't drawn his cutlass or sword so they seemed to be getting on all right. And on the sofa sat Beau Brummel in all his Georgian finery exchanging views with Jupiter, Head of all Roman Gods—he wore flowing robes and a small, golden coronet. What a roomful of misfits and yet, if asked, I'd have to admit to having written about each and every one of them so they had every right to visit me. Individual conversations seemed to be working well and the characters managed to both ignore and yet comment on all that was being said.

Jupiter's voice was the strongest and loudest, "As the most senior person here, I think you should all listen to me." There was mumbling amongst the others and I could hear the word, 'why' and 'who does he think he is?' following his statement.

"I am Jupiter and I shouldn't have to tell you who I am—you should know however, as I don't mind blowing my own trumpet, I shall tell you. I am the King of the Roman Gods and sometimes referred to as Zeus in Greek Mythology. My father, Saturn tended to eat his children as they were born—he feared they would steal his throne you see, and that would never have done. My mother, Rhea, tricked him and I was allowed to live—she wrapped a stone in a blanket and told Saturn that was his latest child, he ate the stone, thinking it was a child—and so I lived.

"When I grew up, my mother and I played another trick on Saturn and we gave him his favourite honey drink—but we laced it with salt and mustard, which made him sick. He was so sick, he regurgitated all of his children—plus the stone—and we all joined together and attacked him. Thus, I was voted as his replacement—Jupiter, King of the Gods." He looked pleased with himself and looked disdainfully on everyone else in the room.

Beau Nash almost burst his waistcoat in raucous laughter and shouted, "Well, who's going to believe that? He certainly can't take charge of us if he talks such rubbish and expects us to believe it." Blackbeard and Rasputin cheered him on and then tried to take charge of the group themselves.

I thought it was time I interfered and, to calm everyone down, I said, "I am in charge—it is my house after all. Now what are you all here for? There really isn't room for so many people."

They seemed to accept that and Nell Gwyn stepped forward and said, "We're here because some of the things you've written about us are not correct—and we want to know why. In your story about Charlie Boy and myself, you make me out to be a cheap trollop—you can't deny that, can you?" She really was a pretty woman but I didn't know how to answer her because she had been exactly that— a cheap trollop. A likeable trollop, but still a trollop.

"Mistress Gwyn, the reputation you left behind told the world how you'd behaved—so how could I write anything different? Your behaviour was well noted and I certainly wasn't the first to write about you. Is that fair?" King Charles' mistress looked rather crestfallen but nodded her head.

I decided that attack was my best form of defence so I began to address them individually. I told Jupiter he wasn't even real—he lived in people's imagination and was part of mythology; I told Beau Nash he was nothing but a dandy and was more interested in what people wore, than in their characters and morals. Shallow, or what? In his turn, he looked sheepish and began to polish his lorgnette closely. He was far too fashionable to use a monocle—anyway, he had two dodgy eyes so one glass wouldn't have done.

I turned to Boudica, the Warrior Queen and if my memory served me correctly, I had only said positive things about her. I wondered what she was doing here—the others had come to complain about my writings, but I only spoke the truth about her. "Well, Warrior Queen—what have I done to you?"

Boudica rose to her full height—she was a strong woman, not only in body but in mind also.

"I have nothing against you—you recorded the details of my life very well and I am happy with them. I only came along since the others were coming and I felt like a trip out. Life can get boring when you're a character from the past—even a famous one. The only thing I'd say perhaps is that you might have told how cruel the Romans were to me, my family and my people—they locked my people in a building and set it alight—everyone died. They treated both my daughter and myself viciously and cruelly and I would have liked people to know that."

"I'm sorry, Warrior Queen, but I thought I wrote of what they did to you— you certainly didn't deserve that—but you have to admit you were a thorn in their flesh, weren't you? They were monsters to you however and I thought I made sure the readers knew that. Please forgive me if I didn't make it clear. I really meant to." I felt quite put-out at the criticism, but she seemed okay now.

It was time to turf them all out—not an easy task—but I managed it. "All right, you lot, your time is up. Go back to where you've come from and take your complaints with you. I do my best and thought I'd treated you all fairly. But there you go, you can please some people some of the time and most of the people some of the time—but never all of the people all of the time." And that was that—they all grumbled and muttered but at least they left my sitting room. They really had exhausted me and I fell flat out on the sofa, arms folded—and dropped off to sleep right away. *This has to stop* was my last thought before I started to snore.

I'm writing this story so you'll understand the pros and cons of dealing with famous people from the past. You read their story and it gets under your skin and embeds itself in your brain. You wonder exactly what you would have done in the situations in which they found themselves—you might have done the exact opposite—or indeed exactly the same. Who can tell?

In King Charles I's case, would I have been stubborn enough—or committed enough—to insist that I was God's anointed with no need for Parliament—the result being that they took me out to a specially erected scaffold in Whitehall, and cut off my head? I don't really know—but I suspect I might have accepted

Parliament. It came in the end after all, but he didn't know that. Was he too stubborn, or would I have been too weak?

Blackbeard didn't have to let himself be caught by the British Navy and allow himself to be keel-hauled and then executed as a pirate. He could have escaped from that predicament and gone home to Bristol from whence he came. But oh no, he was convinced he would beat the Navy at his last battle—but of course he didn't. Instead, to prove his superiority even after death, his decapitated body swum three times around his ship before finally giving up. Again, I think I would have given in to the Naval authorities, after all there were a great number of Pardons being handed out by the British at the time, and all you had to promise was that you'd finished piracy and given up being one of them.

Also, why was Queen Elizabeth I so stubborn about marriage? She had had several 'favourites' who wanted to marry her and she declared love for more than one of them. She believed that having a husband was a way to lose her absolute control of England—she would have to share her power with him and that she didn't want to do. However, had she married and had a baby, she would have safeguarded the Tudor Line and not had to hand the crown of England to her relative, James VI of Scotland—whom she'd never even met. Her lack of action meant the end of the Tudor line!

These types of questions live on in your mind and you find yourself debating with yourself as to what you would do in similar circumstances. There is no right answer but that doesn't stop you trying to find one.

I was given another two week's respite from my visitors so I got on with my book. I wasn't sleeping well; my mind was full of jumbled thoughts—I was writing well into the night and sleeping late in the morning. I didn't really like this as I was turning my life upside down but I was nearing the end of the book, so I knew I'd get a good rest soon. Until I started my next book that is.

I met one of my friends for coffee and we sat in the sunshine, relaxed and content. We laughed about our school days and the friends we used to share. Luckily, we both had good memories and the conversation was along the lines, 'Do you remember when...' or 'That was the day when you...' or 'He was my boyfriend first...' I started to tell her about 'my visitors' but it all sounded so stupid, I stopped halfway.

"Go on, don't stop there. What's wrong?" and I explained how the characters in my books kept coming to see me—some to complain about things I'd written about them. She asked me if I was sleeping okay and I told her I wasn't. She was thoughtful and had a fixed look on her face. Eventually, she said, "I really think—if you're not mad and I don't think you are—that you should take a break from your writing. Your research is filling your head with so much from the past—and from your own vivid imagination—that you're actually beginning to live their lives."

She took my hand and asked if I was listening. I nodded, but she still repeated it all again. We separated then, promising to meet the next week and in the meantime, I was supposed to let up on my writing. I promised her I would, but I was so close to the end of my story, that I wanted to finish it.

Two days later, I was sitting watching a programme on the television, when I felt someone watching me. And there stood a man, dressed in a strange costume. It was obviously a military uniform but the right side was that of the American Army and the left side was the British uniform loyal to King George of Britain. It was a man split in two and his expression was both sad and confused. I waited for him to introduce himself as I wasn't sure who he was— then the penny dropped—the split uniforms meant that he belonged to both sides in a war. He was both American and British.

"Are you Benedict Arnold, by any chance?" I asked, knowing the answer.

"I am he, Ma'am, and I wanted to see you about how you portrayed me in your story. I wasn't as bad as you made me out to be—I admit I was confused and unsure of where my loyalty lay—so I suppose I hedged my bets. I first fought hard for my American country and attained a senior rank—I was even given command of Westpoint Fort, a prestigious position indeed. George Washington thought highly of me but the British offered me the kind of money I couldn't possibly refuse. I needed the money and as my wife and her family favoured the British—they were very loyal to King George—I saw no problem with helping out the British. Surely you can see my dilemma." He paused to see what I would say.

"Now that's a difficult question—a man has to decide where his loyalty lies and stick to his decision. George Washington recognised your skills and ability and rewarded you with the command of Westpoint—something you actually asked him for, if I remember correctly." This was one man from history whose actions I didn't respect—but how could I tell him that? I couldn't at first—I'd have to work up to it.

"I had to think of my family, don't you understand—they were all British sympathisers and they looked to me to do something to help the cause. I really was trying to be loyal to both countries—for instance, did you realise George Washington and some of his officers came to my home on the day I ran away to sea—my wife entertained them and it was only afterwards that they learned of my negotiations with the British. You see, nothing was as straightforward as you think—I was already deeply involved with the British and had no option in the end." He looked defiant, but it didn't wash with me.

"You were to receive a large payment from America's enemy, weren't you? It sounds as if you'd have done anything for money—is that fair? That's the way the American population saw it, wasn't it? And King George did give you a reward as well and the Queen did the same to your wife? Not really a sign of your loyalty to George Washington, was it?!" I sighed—I was tired of discussing what he'd done. To me, it was black and white. "Why don't you go now, Mr Arnold—we've talked long enough—and you won't change my mind."

He stood tall in that strange uniform—neither British nor American—a man with one foot in one country and the other foot in another. A man with no real country. He left me then, knowing he wasn't going to change my mind. Funnily enough, I enjoyed that discussion more than most—I suppose it was because I believed I was right. I didn't admire the man and that's all there was to it. I'd written what I felt about him.

I finished my current book and was just going through it to do an initial proof-reading when I finally decided I was going to stop writing for a while and take a rest. I was getting too involved with my characters and I had to escape from the stress it was creating. Halfway through the reading, I stopped to get a sandwich and a cup of tea—proof-reading is a tedious thing to do, you have to focus carefully on every detail. I rubbed my tired eyes and carried my snack into the sitting room—and there he sat in all his glory. It had to be him—it couldn't have been anyone else. Will Shakespeare himself had come to call.

"Good-day to you—you will note I have come alone, as I fear my colleagues overpowered you recently, coming all together in a mob, as they did. Such thoughtlessness is all I can say." He spoke with a pleasant accent but there was a lot of London in it. I felt really privileged and wondered if I should offer him a sandwich, but decided against it—he wasn't real after all.

"Mr Shakespeare, I am honoured to meet you. I have read nearly all your works and enjoyed every one of them." I couldn't think what to say to the great man, so I just waited. I hoped he hadn't come to complain about my work—I didn't remember writing anything amiss about his life.

"I haven't come to criticise your work—in fact I enjoyed most of it. Too many people are only waiting to complain about something but never to offer praise. I experienced such things every time I put pen to paper—my scenes were too long, or too short, my characters were wooden or even unreal, my stories unlikely or impossible. I could go on forever. I thought therefore I'd come and see you to tell you you're doing a good job—and to keep on doing it."

I spoke at last, "But I told about your young life and how you went from one job to another, of how you made your sweetheart pregnant, of how you frequented most of the taverns in London and left your wife to cope at home alone—and of how you moved your theatre from one side of the Thames to the other—although the land owner had told you not to do it. And yet you say you enjoyed my work? How can that be?"

"The things you said were true—you didn't lie, so how can I reproach you? What you also said was that my writings were superb—and you didn't lie there either. No, all in all, you did a fair job—and that's all I've come to say. No, that's not true, I came to tell you one other thing. Because of my own experiences, I learned that writing can take it out of you and that you must rest from time to time. You must break off from researching other peoples' lives and concentrate on what's best for you."

I listened to his words—this man admired by so many—and I paid attention. He disappeared out of my life as suddenly as he'd come and I was sorry. I'd liked him—and not just because he was positive, but because he seemed nice. I would finish off my proof-reading and take a short holiday, that's what I would do. I completed my manuscript and sent it off to the publisher. I retrieved my suitcase from the attic and began packing. I'd rented a small seaside cottage in Devon where I'd been before and liked it. I knew it would do me the world of good—and God knows, my mind was in such a turmoil, with all the characters I'd written about that I really needed a complete break. And so successfully managing to book the same cottage I travelled down to Devon that afternoon—and there stood the cottage, as though it had been waiting just for me.

I put my case inside and the basket of food I'd brought with me. Before settling down, I walked along the beach which was literally across the road. I filled my lungs with the good, sea air and felt wonderful. I smiled, knowing none of my visitors would find me here and began to collect the prettiest pebbles I could find. I placed them in a bowl on the kitchen table and took my glass of wine outside the cottage to sit on the stone wall. This was the life, I told myself. I went inside to re-fill my glass and there on the sofa, I saw myself resting against the soft cushions. I know it sounds crazy, but that's what I saw—clear as crystal.

I didn't speak at first, just stared. What was I seeing—was that really me? Yes, it was, the figure was wearing identical clothes to mine. She stood up from the sofa and smiled, "It's my turn now to visit you. Now, you've written about yourself, you've become of one of your own characters and as everyone else has had their turn, now it's mine. I've come to say—I'm going nowhere. From now on, it's you and me together." Then she added the sting in the tale, "You'll need someone to help with your nervous breakdown, won't you?"

I plucked up courage and said, "I think you should leave now, I don't want you here—I came to be alone and get better. I've been poorly, you see, and keep getting visits from people who aren't really there—and I can't take any more of it. You'll have to go now and no matter what you say, I'm not having any nervous breakdown."

"Make me go!" she defied me. "You'll have to make me—and it won't be easy, I assure you. From now on, everywhere you go, I'll be there. When you wake up in the mornings, I'll be up before you. I'll start to anticipate your movements and reach your destination before you do. I'll stick to you like your shadow." She was smirking now—not a nice smile—but a twisted one.

I knew I couldn't bear it and I turned and went out of the cottage. She was already down on the beach where the tide was out and the sands were shining with lovely puddles sparkling in the dying sun. She was standing at the shoreline and she beckoned me to join her. I didn't move at first but then I realised it was inevitable and meant to be, so I walked slowly towards her. She stayed at the water's edge but I went in deeper until the water was up to my waist. I could feel the strength of the current which seemed to pull me further out to sea. I glanced back at her but she hadn't moved. She was waiting there for me. But I fooled her, I walked on and the sea eventually took me as its own and I began to go under. It was lovely and quiet and I felt quite safe with the lapping waves caressing my tired body. I was on my own—just what I wanted. If this was having a nervous breakdown, then bring it on. And fate took me at my word!

Of course, I wasn't safe at all, was I? I drifted out to sea and my lungs filled with sea water—soon my lifeless body sank beneath the waves. It felt both comforting and welcoming. I died that day but welcomed the solitude of death—no more uninvited visitors to bother me and no more proof-reading to do.

The shoreline was empty—no one was there at all—not even me!

Christmas Eve Is Full of Surprises

Two little foreheads were pressed hard against the window and four eyes peered into the darkness. Snow had been falling all afternoon and a thick blanket of white covered the ground—it also covered the walls, roofs and trees and the moon and stars were reflected on the snow, like little, shimmering candles. The scene couldn't have been more beautiful, especially when Simon grabbed his sister's arm and pointed into the darkness.

"Look Sis—over there, under that big tree. It's a fox and it looks black against the white." The fox moved slowly, his paws obviously unsure of the new texture of the ground. It walked tentatively, feeling its way as it went.

"It's beautiful, Simon—it looks like a shadow—except it's not. It's obviously looking for food—but that'll be difficult tonight, won't it with so much snow around?" Mary was very excited and bounced up and down on her bed.

And so, she should have been, after all it was Christmas Eve and the two nine-year olds had already sent their letters to Father Christmas—up the chimney in smoke in the usual way. It had always been a tradition, taught by indulgent grand-parents some time before. Anyway, the twins were smart enough to realise their letters were a good way of letting the parents know what they really wanted for Christmas. Smart yet cunning! They believed Santa would bring them gifts as well, but they also wanted to keep on the right side of the parents. Hedging their bets was the best way to do it.

"Look over at those trees—look at the tallest one. It looks magical with the moon sitting on its top branches. It looks just like a special Christmas tree and the moon its decoration. I know it's usually a star at the top, but the moon looks even better, doesn't it?" The glass was beginning to mist up from their breath.

"Yes, it's lovely, just like our own Christmas tree downstairs, except it's more special. Listen, I can hear Dad moving around, we'd better get back into our beds before he catches us." They both lay down and pulled the covers up to their chins. Dad however didn't come into their room but went back downstairs again.

"Shall we get up again and watch out the window?" Mary whispered. "By the way, what are we watching for—do you think we might see Father Christmas?" She was hopeful.

"We're just looking, Sis—to see what we can see—you never know, we might see him. Yes, come on, let's get up again and have a look." The bright moon was still sitting on top of the tree sending winding beams of light down its branches. Simon peered harder, "Look Mary, what's that? Oh my God, there's two men and they're coming up our drive. Maybe Dad knows they're coming, maybe they're delivering something for our Christmas—or maybe they're thieves!" He liked to scare his gullible sister.

"Are you sure it's not the fox again—perhaps it's caught a rabbit?" she asked. "I'd much prefer if it was the fox."

"No, I don't think it is. It looks like people alright and they're carrying something—something big. Oh my God, they're coming towards the side of the house. Don't be scared, Mary—it's only men after all. Let's wait and listen."

The two children suddenly jumped back from the window. A big, moon-shaped face had appeared at the glass and stared right into the room. He was dressed like an elf—his tunic was red and green and he wore a little cap on his head. He seemed to be fiddling with the window lock and within seconds, he had opened it and dropped onto the carpet. He was wearing those special shoes that elves wore—with curling toes that went around and around in circles.

The children were too scared to move but fell backwards onto their beds. The moon man had come into the house and stood there smiling as though he was doing something quite normal. "Hello Simon—Mary—I hope I didn't scare you." He sat down on the floor and crossed his legs—he looked just like one of Santa's helpers they'd seen at the store in town. "You're probably wondering who I am and who my brother is." He obviously had climbed up a ladder as the window was quite far from the ground. Another face had appeared at the window and was dressed in the same red and green tunic as his brother, with the same feathered cap.

"We're Santa's little helpers and we've been sent to give you a Christmas treat. The Chief's been watching you and knows you've been good children, so he wants you to come with us and meet Mama Christmas—she's waiting at home for you with lots of chocolate and candy canes." He took two canes from his belt and gave one to each child.

"We're not supposed to take sweets from strangers." However, Simon still held out his hand for the candy.

"But we're not strangers now—you know who we are. I'm called Eddie and that's Joe." He pointed to the face at the window who'd still not spoken. "Now, all we want you to do is to wrap up warmly—are there clothes in your wardrobe? Good, choose nice woolly ones and put on your wellies as well—there's a lot of snow around." Eddie was actually a nice elf and the children liked him, so they did as they were told. After all, they were going to meet Mama Clause.

"Won't we have to tell Mum and Dad where we're going?" Mary asked, but Eddie reassured her they already knew and were quite happy for them to go.

"You like the snow, don't you—and look at that bright moon—he's come out in full to show you the way? We're going to Santa's own house—but you won't see him till tomorrow cause, as you know, he's busy tonight, delivering presents to all the good children. Don't worry about yours—they'll be waiting for you when you get back." Eddie helped them on with their coats and boots—and they were ready!

He showed them how to hang on around his neck and he and Joe would take them safely down the ladder. It wasn't difficult and soon they were standing in the soft snow beside the two elves. They all wandered down the drive together, Joe carrying the ladder over his shoulder. On the snowy road there was an orange transit van waiting for them and the elves put the children into the back and tied the ladder to the roof, before climbing in and switching on the engine.

And it was as simple as that to kidnap two young children from right under their parents' noses and drive away with them to God alone knew where. Simon and Mary were excited, but quiet. They were looking forward to seeing Santa's house and meeting Mama Christmas.

"Maybe we should have brought a gift for them—after all, it's Christmas." Mary suggested, but Eddie reassured her it wasn't necessary as Mama Christmas already had everything she needed. It was odd but neither child was concerned that they were driving off into the darkness with two men they didn't really know. But then, they were Santa's elves so they must be good!

"Did you remember to leave the note somewhere obvious?" Joe asked his brother, who nodded, "Left it on top of one of the kids' beds—so they can't miss it." Eddie was concentrating on driving through the thick snow. Luckily, the snow was still falling, so the tyre tracks would soon be obliterated. "It was a good idea of yours to wait until tonight—even the weather is helping—and those two in the back don't realise what's going on."

Their destination was a small farmhouse on the outskirts of a village—it actually looked lovely covered in its white blanket and Simon and Mary thought it looked just like the sort of place where Santa would live. "Look at the little windows, Mary—it's an old house, isn't it? The window panes have that very old glass with dimples in the middle—it must be quite an age." Simon was first to climb out of the transit van and Mary followed. They were told to wait until Eddie had put the van into an old shed and then they were led up to the front door.

Inside, it all looked welcoming and warm—and there was a roaring fire in the grate. The lighting was soft which made the room look even more inviting and the twins stood inside the front door on the mat. At the side of the fireplace, an old lady sat on a rocking chair, rocking back and forward—she was plump and had two rosy cheeks with round spectacles resting on the bridge of her nose. Her hair was snowy white and piled on top of her head and around her shoulders, she wore a lovely, red shawl. She was the picture of Christmas and exactly what Mama Christmas should look like.

"Come on over to the fire, children! You, Joe, get the bairns a drink of milk and a slice of Christmas cake each." She didn't move from the chair but helped the twins take off their coats and boots. "Sit by me on the rug—you'll soon warm up." She was lovely and cuddly and her hands were soft and warm as she settled them on the floor. Simon and Mary felt quite comfortable in the house and gratefully took the drink and food from Joe, who'd already changed out of his elf's suit and wore denim trousers and a white jumper. In fact, he was dressed identical to Eddie, who'd just come back downstairs.

"Charles! Charles! Wake up, it's gone twelve!" Ruth touched her husband's shoulder and shook it gently. He'd fallen asleep in front of the dying fire and woke up with a start. He mumbled, "Have you put all the presents under the tree, dear? The kids will be sound asleep by now." Charles got shakily to his feet and reached for his unfinished drink.

"Not only have I finished the presents, but I've prepared the turkey and veg for tomorrow. The sherry trifle is ready as well—the children are going to love tomorrow." Ruth plumped up the sofa cushions and backed down the already dying embers of the fire, before accompanying her husband upstairs.

"Just peep in quietly—check on them."

Charles did as he was told before calling out, "Come here Ruth—come here—there's something wrong."

Both beds were empty with only crumpled blankets to show that someone had once been there. Both parents ran around the house, calling out, "Where are you, kids? Come on out now—it'll soon be Christmas morning and Father Christmas could be on his way now." They looked everywhere—inside and outside, ending back in the children's bedroom. Charles spotted the note on Simon's bed and read it out loud:

Dear Parents,

I have your children and I intend to keep them until you've done what I ask—which is to arrange for Peter Winship to be released from your prison within 72 hours and to be given £100,000 plus airline tickets and a passport. He should be transported to the airport and allowed to leave the country the same day. You will be contacted by phone after 48 hours for confirmation that these arrangements have been made. When it's seen that Peter Winship has left for Russia—where there is no extradition agreement with the UK—your children will be brought back. If you don't do what you're being instructed— your children will be killed. It would be no great deal for us!

The choice is yours! And, by the way, Peter Winship is and always was innocent.

It seemed whoever had penned the letter, was well educated and could spell.

Ruth burst into tears, "Oh Charles, what are we going to do? Our dear little twins are in danger. Whoever has them might be mad and will kill them anyway—what can we do? Oh, my babies, my babies—where are you?" She ran downstairs and grabbed the phone.

"Yes, I need the police—I need them now." And she fainted clean away onto the floor. When she woke up, she was lying on the sofa and there were two strangers talking with Charles. She listened for a while as she didn't want to join the conversation just yet. One stranger was asking for photos of the children and asking when they'd last been seen. One of them also asked Charles about the prisoner Peter Winship and why he was in prison.

"Your position as Prison Governor, Sir, places you in a difficult position—so, Winship still has 20 years to serve and his crime was using a knife in an assault where the victim died. Is that right?"

Charles nodded and said, "Officer, I just can't release any prisoner I choose but I also must look after my children." He was obviously shaken and scared. "What happens now?" he asked.

Ruth intervened, "I'll tell you what happens now, Charles—you'll just have to arrange for the man to be released and set up whatever else the kidnapper wants—you have no choice. I want my babies back." She looked appealingly at the policeman. "Why aren't you out there searching for them?"

"Madam, you must allow us to gather the facts—and I assure you people are out there looking already." He closed his notebook and stood up. "Meanwhile, Sir, it's Christmas day but you must contact the Home Office and tell them what's happened—and I'll do the same from my end. I'll be in touch later this morning with an update." Both policemen departed, leaving two grief-stricken parents clinging to each other.

Ruth said through tears, "Couldn't we pay them money instead—that would be easier than what they're demanding, wouldn't it? I mean, I know we're not rich but we could scrape together some money, couldn't we? I've got my jewellery, don't forget—I know it's not the crown jewels, but they must be worth something."

"Darling, you must understand money isn't an option here—they want Peter Winship to be released."

She brightened up a little at that. "Well, you can arrange that, can't you? You're the Prison Governor after all—just tell your men to let him go."

"It's not that simple, Ruth—and they want £100,000 and a current passport as well. I need you to calm down and help me with what I have to do—and the first thing is to contact the Home Office and see what they advise." They sat together for a while, arms around each other and picturing their frightened children, maybe in pain and certainly scared.

Ruth crossed to the mantlepiece and lifted down the snow globe that sat there. She shook it and the snow swirled around, eventually settling down to reveal a small farmhouse with a couple of wooden sheds at the side. The windows were lit up and she could see two little heads looking out of the window. It was them, she just knew it—she'd never looked closely at the snow globe before, but she could clearly see it now.

"They're sending us a message, Charles—look at this. I know it's tiny but those figures are Simon and Mary—I feel it—they're trying to tell us where they are. They're in a farm, that's where they are—ring the police and tell them they have to search small farms. I just know that's where they'll find them."

Charles was looking at her as though she was mad. "Come on, darling—you need to take a rest, before you crack up." And he led her upstairs and made her lie down. She was shivering and crying at the same time. The odd thing was that the house in the snowstorm looked just like the one Mama Christmas lived in. That was as far as it went however, the snow globe just looked like the one where the children were being kept.

"What would you like for breakfast, children—are you cereal people or fried egg and sausage people? The boys like their cooked breakfast and it is a special morning after all. They'll be in in a moment looking for food." Mama Christmas was busy in the kitchen, "It's still snowing out there—you can play in the back garden later—I think Santa would like if you'd build a snowman there for when he gets back from delivering the presents."

She plonked down two boiled eggs on their plates, cooked at Mary's request. "And when you've finished breakfast, you must look under the tree—there's a present each for you—I wrapped them myself—Santa was too busy." She liked to talk while she was working and chatted on while the children ate their eggs and eyed the parcels under the small tree. Joe appeared and sat down beside them for his bacon and eggs.

"Joe, why are you not wearing your elf costume anymore? I thought you looked great in it—is it that you're not Santa's helper now Christmas is almost over?" Simon asked between mouthfuls of toast.

"Most of the helpers' work is over for this year and we can have a rest for a little while, before starting again for next year." Mama answered the question before putting a heaped plate in front of Joe. She asked where Eddie was. "He's fetching fresh straw for the animals—they'll soon be coming in from the fields." He watched the twins enjoying their food, "Are you two okay? You're not missing anything, are you?"

"Don't think so," Mary replied, "although I'd quite like to see Mum and Dad again—and all our presents Santa will have brought." Simon nodded in agreement.

"Well, in that case, fetch the parcels from under that tree—and as for seeing your Mum and Dad, you will see them—we'd just like you to spend a few days with us cause we have no young children here—and Christmas is better when there are some around—we're just borrowing you for a few days. Is that all right?" But the twins were already scrabbling under the tree.

Mama Christmas brought a small swivel mirror into the room and stood it on the table. She turned to the children, "When you're missing your mum and dad, just look into this mirror—and you'll see them. You'll see they're quite safe—but obviously wondering where you are." She went back into the kitchen.

Looking into the mirror, the twins could clearly see Mum and Dad sitting on the sofa, reading magazines. "They're fine, Mary—you don't have to worry. We'll go back soon. What a great mirror—do you think it's magic? It must be! Aren't these presents wonderful—I've always wanted a Jack-in-the-Box."

The Prison Governor and a police Chief Inspector were visiting the Home Office to discuss the situation. The Inspector was adamant that they must be given more time to find the missing children but Charles was more concerned about their welfare. The Home Office Minister knew he'd have to be careful what he said—after all this man was not only the Prison Governor but also the father of the kidnapped children.

"How do you think they'll be dealing with their kidnap?" he asked, not really expecting an answer, but Charles did answer, "I think they'll deal with it quite well—of course, it depends how they're being treated. They're very trusting of people and depending on what they're being told, they'll go along with it for a while. I feel they'll eventually get fed up and want to come home—and that's when the kidnappers might get impatient with them—and perhaps hurt them or release them, I really don't know—they're only nine years old, you know." He didn't know whether he was answering as a Dad or as a Governor. "Is the money and passport a problem, Sir—or could we arrange that in such a short time? I know it's a great deal of money but I'll contribute whatever I can."

The Police Inspector broke into the conversation, "Let's not pursue that way of thinking just yet—give us the time to find the children first."

But Charles shouted, "For God's sake, man, we have to make plans in case it becomes necessary to obey their instructions." His head fell forward into his hands and he looked like a broken man. The meeting was over temporarily and the men went their separate ways—the police to continue overseeing their widespread search around the county—and Charles, to comfort his wife as best he could.

"My snowman's better than yours, Eddie—yours is rubbish!" Simon had been busy for at least an hour, whilst Mary had been building a huge pile of snowballs, shaped like an Egyptian pyramid. She took two from the pile and threw them at Eddie, who threw more back at her. For people who'd met so recently, they seemed to be getting on well together.

Joe appeared outside the kitchen door. "I've made the call—and just as we thought, they're stalling. Perhaps it's time for the photograph—what do you think?"

"We'll do it after tea—you get the gun from the barn and hide it in the house." Eddie went on throwing snowballs and Mama Christmas called, "There's mugs of hot chocolate here." And they all went indoors to the warm kitchen. "How are the children?" she asked her son.

"They're okay so far, but it's still early days." Eddie looked grim.

The police had spread a wide net around a radius of land in the county. The snow didn't help their search—as Eddie had said, any tyre marks were obliterated by the next day—all marks hidden under a blanket of innocent white. Because the children had been taken from their home so late at night, questioning neighbours produced no information as no one had been around.

It was a dreadful situation as the police kept hitting a brick wall whichever way they turned. The Home Office had set in motion the procurement of money, airline tickets and a quick passport, the latter being put together using Peter Winship's prison photograph, obviously removing the prison number which sat across his chest. Everyone was doing their bit—well, as much as they could in the circumstances, but Charles and Ruth were frantic with worry.

Ruth had taken all of her jewellery, including her wedding ring, for valuation at a jeweller's in the city, but it came to nothing like the money being demanded. She handed the bulky envelope containing the cash to Charles that evening, just as the telephone rang. The policeman in the house sprang into action and used another phone to request a trace on the caller. The voice was a man's and it sounded muffled, *Look in the telephone box at Maple Tree Corner in Summerton village.* That was all he said before hanging up.

"No good," the policeman on the tracer phone said. "He used a pay-as-you-go mobile—not the sort we can trace." Charles and the other policeman grabbed their coats and rushed out of the house, arriving in Summerton village fifteen minutes later. There was a girl in the telephone box, just finishing a call. When she came out, she was carrying a brown envelope which she willingly gave to the policeman and he took it from her, first putting on rubber gloves.

"Let's return to your house before we open it—then we can do it carefully. Okay?" The girl who'd discovered the envelope looked confused and walked away, tutting, "Well really, some people!"

Back in Santa's farmhouse, Mama Christmas was polishing the gun. She'd worked hard to make it shiny and Mary and Simon were intrigued. They'd never seen a gun before—except on the telly, of course. "Why are you cleaning that gun Mama Christmas?" Simon asked.

She looked up at him and smiled, "Well, after seeing that photo of Mary with the gun to her head, I realised it needed a good cleaning."

"Yes, why did Mary get chosen for the gun photo—and not me?" he asked.

"Well, we're saving that for another day when you can be in the photo—and then you'll have a nice shiny gun." Eddie took the gun from her and tucked it into his waistband. It made him look quite menacing.

After checking for finger prints, the police showed Charles the photo—it would be better if he showed it to his wife, rather than the police. It seemed somehow kinder! And there were no finger prints on it—it had been wiped clean.

The photo showed little Mary's sweet face; she was smiling into the camera, not looking in the least afraid—but just behind her to one side, was a heavily gloved hand holding the gun against the back of her head. Ruth broke down when she saw her little girl looking so innocent and unafraid. Whoever stood behind her must have been a monster—he obviously felt nothing for the child or he could never have done that.

"If that man isn't released, they're going to kill our children, aren't they? If they don't achieve what they want, what have they got to lose? The children are unimportant to them." Ruth was beyond crying and looked haggard and defeated—Charles was just sitting in an armchair, his head in his hands.

One of the policemen came into the room, "We've had a small breakthrough at last—our men have visited Winship's brother, hoping to find the culprits there—but unfortunately, they had no luck. The brother however became very excited and kept shouting that Peter was innocent—and that he'd never carried a knife in his life. What he said was 'If I could arrange his release, I would do it in the blink of an eye and whatever kids get hurt in the process—well, that's just bad luck. The damned legal system in this country is full of holes and I wouldn't help you find those children, even if I could—they mean nothing to me.' He was obviously a very angry man and one the police would be keeping a close eye on, in the hope he'd try to contact whoever had the children. Before leaving his house however, they warned him he could be accused of with-holding evidence—if he knew something that would help with their enquiries—and subsequently be arrested. Unfortunately, that was all they could do at present.

"Another contact is due tomorrow and the Home Office tells me they're ready to move forward and meet the kidnappers' demands—should the police fail to find the children in the meantime. I'm afraid that's what's going to have to happen. What I'm particularly afraid of is they'll kill my twins just to tidy things up." Charles seemed to have made his mind up about the fate of his youngsters.

Mama Christmas told the children to go upstairs and put on their pyjamas and "Then I'll read you the story of *The Night Before Christmas*—and we'll all have a mug of hot chocolate. Does that sound good?" And they skipped off to do as they were told. They both felt quite safe with these kind people.

"I can hear mum's voice, Simon; she's crying cause we're not there. Look Simon, look at the mirror—there she is." And sure enough, Ruth's face looked back at them, telling them to be brave and keep each other safe. Her face was shimmering and rather unclear but there was no mistaking it was her.

"How can Mum's face be there, Mary—we know it's not really possible. Have we conjured her up? Maybe she's not really there at all. It makes me better for having seen her though—let's go down and get our hot chocolate." Simon's mind was more on his stomach than on anything else. And Ruth's face had disappeared from the window.

"I want a photo of Simon this time—in fact, in his pyjamas would be good. A gun at his head should show the authorities that I mean business." His mother looked sad but knew Eddie was right. She knew that Peter Winship would never have hurt anyone—and to stick a knife into a living being was something he could never have done. But all the evidence was against him and his trial was very short—he was convicted after a few hours and still had almost all of the 20-year sentence to serve in prison.

"I know he was your best friend and I know he was innocent of the crime—but the children!" Mama persisted, heating the milk in a saucepan. She'd actually become quite fond of Simon and Mary in the short time she'd known them—but she knew her loyalty had to rest with her sons. They were absolutely sure that

Peter Winship was innocent—and the plan they'd put together to get the children out of their house, was incredibly clever. So, she had to go along with them.

This photo was even better and more threatening than the first one. Simon actually looked scared and had turned his head slightly towards the gun. In the middle of the night Joe took the photo to another phone box in another village and left it there, before ringing the Governor's number and telling which village he should go to. On arriving home again, he was alone in the sitting room with Eddie, when he suddenly asked, "Eddie, why are you so sure that Peter didn't knife that bloke?"

"I just am! Okay, Bro? You know I've always been a friend of his and know him better than anyone else. You weren't there the night it happened—I was and I saw everything." Eddie was very defensive and poured himself a stiff whisky.

Joe refused the whisky and went on, "But if Peter didn't do it and you saw him not doing it, then you must have seen who did do it." Although it sounded non-sensible, Joe was right. He went on, "Was there anyone else there that night—and why didn't you go as a witness at his trial?" He was confused and had been so for several months, since it had all happened. But Eddie was his brother and had always been his friend.

The lads had been out together on a boys' night out and the beer and wine had been flowing freely. They began to argue about football and two of them got into a serious argument. It was a hot and sultry night and the alcohol had fuelled the men's tempers, when suddenly one pulled out a knife and held it against his opponent's chest. Someone at the back, wanting a better view of the scuffle, pushed too hard and knocked the man in front into the two antagonists—unfortunately, the knife, which probably wouldn't even have been used, slipped neatly into the other man's stomach.

"And that was that." Eddie finished the story. "It's not as if I haven't told you before—I have. We all ran away like cowards—all except for Peter who stayed by the bleeding man to see if he could help him. He picked up the knife and the blood sank into his sleeve, so he put himself right into the picture for when the police arrived."

"And whose knife was it—if it wasn't Peter's? I've asked you that before but you've never told me," Joe insisted.

"That's none of your business—I'm no grass, so stop asking." Eddie was angry.

"What's a grass?" a little voice asked from the other side of the Christmas tree—and the brothers realised Simon and Mary had been there all the time.

Without time to think, Joe blurted out, "He didn't say grass—he said mass—he asked me if I was planning to go to Christmas Mass, Cloth Ears! By the way, Eddie, isn't it time to make that phone call—they'll have picked up the envelope by now."

The Home Office contacted Charles and told him everything had been arranged for the prisoner to be released the next day and taken to the local airport. The authorities had given in to the kidnappers—they had no option if the children were to be seen again. It had to be a covert collection of Winship from the prison and the same to get him through Customs etc. The passport was hard to arrange—but there he was—with his prison mug shot on it—luckily with his prison number obscured. The Home Office had been efficient in light of 'the police's incompetence' at finding the kidnapped children and time had completely run out. The TV news followed the whole story, but of course, left out the finer details.

"Let's think positively, Ruth—everyone's on our side—look at the number of good wishes we've had from members of the public. Please God, let the kidnappers keep their word and that they watch the specially televised programme on the continuous loop—to show Peter Winship being put on the aircraft bound for Russia. This will be the proof they're waiting for and they must release our children then—and give them back to us." He tried to sound as positive as he could but Ruth's expression told him she'd already given up—and thought she'd never see the children again. The image of Simon's face with the gun to his head was with her every minute of the day—and she was scared.

"I'm actually very sad, Mama Christmas, that I haven't met Santa himself yet. He can't still be delivering presents, can he?" Simon was just a little more astute than his sister and he wouldn't let the subject of Santa drop easily.

"Well now, young man, Santa doesn't only work one day a year—contrary to what some people believe—he has to look after his animals, renovate the sledge which takes quite a battering every year, deal with the mountains of letters he receives and begin making toys for the next Christmas—so you'll have to forgive him, I'm afraid. Are you okay with that?" She really was a special old woman and in the few days the children had known her, they'd come to love her—just a little.

That evening, Eddie and Joe watched the television with interest. They saw their friend Peter taken to the airport, escorted through customs and actually climbing aboard the plane carrying a holdall. It was done! The TV was delighted to be allowed to show this—they knew viewers would lap it up—and such a thing had never been shown before on television. Eddie and Joe were delighted— they'd managed to save their friend from another 20 years of punishment in prison for something he'd never done in the first place.

"You have to say bye-bye to Mama, children. You're going home to your mum and dad now—as we always promised you would." He made sure they were wrapped up warmly and wearing the wellies they'd arrived in. "Bye-bye, Simon—Mary—I'm going to miss you. It's been lovely having you to stay for a few days and I hope you've enjoyed yourselves." Mama had tears in her eyes. "Go back to your parents who love you—they'll have missed you a lot. Have you got your Jack-in-the Boxes from under the tree—mustn't forget them! And think, you've still got your presents at home where Santa left them. You must take this mirror too—it's a special one—and if ever you miss me, just look into it and call my name and I'll come to see you. But it's our secret mind and you mustn't tell anyone about it."

She kissed them both on the cheek and waved goodbye from the kitchen door. The old transit van was waiting for them and they climbed aboard, waving furiously and with Mary wiping her tears away.

They drove quite a distance towards the coast. Great heaps of snow were piled at the sides of the road and a few times, the van slithered on dangerous ice. They arrived safely at a small harbour where the fishing boats were all tied up— no one would venture out to sea in such conditions, so there was no one around.

"Now kids, this is where you have to be brave and you'll soon see your mum and dad again." Joe was the more sentimental of the two and felt quite sad at leaving the two little ones in such an open, desolate spot—but there was no option—it was the only safe way they could hand back the children.

"As soon as we've started to drive away, we'll ring from the mobile and tell the police where they can find them—it's not traceable I sincerely hope—well it hasn't been so far. To be on the safe side though, I'll chuck it away before we get home. We'll have to drive pretty fast to get out of the area."

They turned to the children again, "See that boat over there—the one dragged onto the beach—well, we're going to open it up for you and you can settle there until your people arrive. Is that quite clear? Now, you mustn't be afraid, nothing's going to happen to you—and by tonight, you'll be in your own little beds. Stay here until I come back." Eddie crossed the beach and broke the lock on the boat—the door swung open and there was a little cabin inside—just big enough for Simon and Mary to be comfortable.

And that's where the police found them just half an hour later—two little children who actually looked as though they were enjoying the experience of being abandoned in a strange boat in a strange part of the country. They were bundled into a police car and covered with shiny, Teflon blankets which they loved and they were taken to their own home, where a police doctor and a nurse were waiting.

"Mum—Dad—great! We've missed you." Simon ran over to hug Ruth. Mary was a little apprehensive—it felt strange to come back after being away for so long. She thought she might be told off.

Ruth reached for her daughter and said, "You can tell us all about your adventure later—I think both of you should have some supper, a bath and then tucked up in your own little beds." And that's what happened until the next morning when Mary continued to be tearful and Simon very quiet. Breakfast was usually a noisy affair, but not today—they seemed to need to settle back into their surroundings. A police lady came to talk to them, first asking who they'd been with.

"We've been with the elves—Santa's elves, that's all—and they were really nice to us—except maybe when they took our photos with the gun—that was a little scary." Simon looked as if he was trying hard to remember.

"And did the elves have names? For instance, what did they call each other?"

The twins looked at each other and Mary shrugged. "They were just called elves—I didn't hear them use any names."

Simon looked at her curiously, but said nothing—he took his lead from her and echoed what she'd said. "It was two men; that's all I remember."

The police woman insisted, "Was there a woman, or was it only men?"

"It was only men—there wasn't any woman—the men fed us and cared for us," Mary continued and Simon again nodded his head in agreement. He wondered what on earth she was doing!

And that was the story they stuck to—they didn't know the men's names and there was no woman around. They said the house was nice and they had a room all to themselves—Simon reached for his Jack-in-the-Box and explained they'd been given one each on Christmas morning.

It was odd the way they both remembered exactly the same things—in effect, nothing—and agreed with each other, as though reading from a script. They even spoke about the snowball fight they'd had with the elves and how their snowman was better than the grown-ups.

Some childlike wisdom told them not to tell about Joe, Eddie and Mama Christmas—they'd been good friends after all and they didn't want the police to hurt them. It was an amazing concept for such young children to have—but it was as it was.

Ruth didn't know whether to be happy or sad that they'd suffered so little whilst she and Charles had been out of their minds with worry for three days. And even now, with their children safe at home, she didn't think they'd ever get over it. Charles took another week off work but knew he'd have to go back soon, there was a lot of paperwork to get through because of Peter Winship's release. The workmen had been in to fit extra locks everywhere to make the house more secure. The talk with the children would have to wait a few days—they would have to stress they must never go away with strangers again and must scream and shout if anyone ever approaches them again.

That night, snuggled beneath the blankets, Simon and Mary whispered together about their experience. "We mustn't ever tell people about Eddie and Joe—and definitely not about Mama Christmas. They were all so kind to us—and I don't think they'd ever have used the gun on us—it was just for effect." Simon was sure about that.

"And now we've got all these lovely presents that Santa left us—I think we've had quite a good Christmas this year, don't you—and I loved Mama Christmas, did you?" They agreed on that as well—funny how you could know someone for such a short time and yet, love them.

Simon smiled, but went on playing with his Jack-in-the-Box, his favourite present that year. "Maybe we'll see Santa next year—as long as we keep wide awake all night. In the meantime, Mary, let's have a look in your special mirror."

Back in 'Santa's House', the three kidnappers were sitting around the fire when Mama Christmas said, "I really miss those children—I even think I loved them in the end. Ah well, how would you like a mug of chocolate?"

Her sons looked at her and nodded their heads. Joe answered, "It's funny, but mugs of hot chocolate aren't so good as when the kids were here."

Mama went into the kitchen and the two brothers sat there looking sad. Eddie said, "Come on, Bro, let's try to cheer up; after all, we've managed to save Peter from 20 unjust years in prison. Let's try to be cheerful for Mama."

"Before we leave the subject completely, Eddie—I've helped you all the way through, but I still have one question. I know you won't want to answer it—but I feel you owe me that much. You say you saw the man being knifed and you know Peter didn't do it—but you wouldn't tell me who did. You've always wanted to help Peter—even from the start –and yet, I can't imagine why you should feel so strongly about it."

Eddie swallowed hard, put another log on the fire, before turning around and looking straight into his brother's eyes. He said quietly, "It was me, Bro, I did it—I knifed the bloke and Peter took the rap for me. He wasn't a grass either—not even in court when he was sentenced for such a long stretch. Now you know why I felt I owed him big time. Big Time!"

Cluedo—Or Whodunnit?

Maggie looked over her glasses with very blue eyes and shouted triumphantly, "Miss Scarlet with the gun in the conservatory." And she looked around the table at the others, waiting for them to scoff 'Rubbish' or 'Try again, old dear'—but the room was silent. None of them knew the correct answer. She reached for the envelope in the middle, which contained the right answers and scattered them across the table.

"Miss Scarlet with the gun in the conservatory," her friend Liz repeated incredulously. "She's right—would you believe it? I haven't got even one yet. You're just a smarty-pants, Maggie." And all six of them relaxed against their chairs in a state of semi-collapse. It took a lot of concentration to play this game. Mind you, the alcohol they'd drunk played its part in relaxing them.

Bill stood up, saying, "I think we all deserve another drink after that," and he crossed to the sideboard where there was a still generous selection of spirits and soft drinks.

"Don't overfill the glasses, Bill—you always do and spill it everywhere." His wife, Jenny admonished him, before he'd even started to pour.

"Yes Dear—No Dear—three bags full, Dear," he mimicked her.

There were six of them and they'd all been friends since their University days. For a few years after that, they'd kind of lost touch and gone their different ways, but now in their late forties, and with their families behind them, they'd formed a group again and met up regularly. Three men and three women, who knew each other very well—and all of whom had a fascination with the game Cluedo and played it regularly at each other's homes.

Tonight, they were at Jenny and Bill's new house which had been recently built on a posh estate. Peter and Maggie had a house at the end of the same estate—a large and rather nice house with every possible mod-con. The new houses were comfortable and spacious and sought after by those with money. All six of them were settled in the dining room around a large circular table. Liz was sitting beside Dominic, her husband—and Peter was beside his own wife, Maggie—who'd just won the game. They normally sat anywhere—they were all so at ease with one another.

"I could have sworn it was going to be in the kitchen, judging from the decisions some of you made—but I was wrong. But then, I'm a man—I can take it," Peter lied badly—he liked to win, but then they all did.

"Whose turn is it to host next weekend?" Dominic asked and was told by his wife that it was their turn.

"Oh goody," Maggie said, "I always like when it's at your house—it's so big and old—I love the atmosphere, just right for playing something like Cluedo. There's a library, a party room and a conservatory—as well as all the more usual rooms." She was getting quite excited at the prospect.

"Yes, Maggie," Liz looked rather bored, "I know what rooms I have! There's no time for another game, is there? It's getting quite late." So, the small group separated and went their separate ways—Bill started to put the game away, as it belonged at his house, when he suddenly bent down and started searching around the floor.

"What are you doing?" Jenny asked impatiently and was told he was looking for a piece of the game that seemed to have disappeared. "Professor Plum has upped and gone, I'm afraid—I can't find him anywhere." He was puzzled but too tired to do anything about it then.

Jenny looked into the kitchen where Pam was still washing up the dinner dishes. "When you've finished those, Pam—there's nothing else to do—just go home." The home-help was a local woman who lived in the town and on the nights of the 'Cluedo' parties, she'd visit whoever was hosting, to serve dinner and clear away afterwards. She never said much, just got on with her duties. When the couple retired for the night, they left Pam to lock up, which was quite usual. In fact, she had a key to all their houses, so trusted was she.

Next morning, everything was pristine and Bristol Fashion—everything in its place, with no trace of the dinner party of the night before. Bill left early for work, as he had a meeting that morning—he was a lawyer and enjoyed the challenges of his work. He was tall and strongly built—had been a rugby player in his younger days, now he'd let himself go to seed, just a bit. It didn't matter though as Jenny had done the same—she'd been a gym teacher, but once the children had started to come along, her figure faded with each birth—and they had two children!

She went shopping next day and actually called into a couple of charity shops in the hope that she'd find a cheap game of Cluedo—so she could replace Professor Plum, he who had mysteriously disappeared, but she had no luck. *One of the others must have taken the figure home—for what purpose, I can't imagine*, she thought as she sipped coffee in her favourite café. Across the street, she spotted Liz coming out of the Chemist's and stood up, calling out to her— but her friend quickly disappeared and shot up the street in the opposite direction. *Well, I never*, she thought, then she saw Liz meet up with their friend, Bill. *Perhaps she had some legal business to discuss with him. She certainly must have heard me call out, as I shouted loud enough.* She felt rather disgruntled, finished her coffee quickly and made her way home. Liz had always been a bit stand-offish—even at University—she'd come from money and that made a difference when they were students.

That night, after dinner, Jenny and Bill were sitting side by side, watching a film on television. "I saw you meet up with Liz this afternoon—what did you need to talk about? Surely, you could have discussed it after the game last night." There was just a hint of suspicion in her voice.

He cleared his throat. "It was about her shop and business—she wanted some advice. It wouldn't have been right to discuss it last night in front of everyone."

"Don't see why not—we're all friends together." But she stopped talking about it when Bill tutted to remind her they were watching a film. "By the way, did you find a Cluedo figure of Professor Plum today?" and looked disappointed when she told him she hadn't. "It's a real mystery—where could it have gone?"

Jenny said, "Perhaps someone took him home, but why would they?" It was her turn to tut so she could watch the film in peace. She spoke to herself then as Bill was in another world, *I must remember the window-cleaner's coming tomorrow—I want the inside windows done as well, so I'll have to leave a key for him in the usual place—it's so good to be able to trust tradesmen.* Bill, who couldn't have been as interested in the film as he claimed was now fast asleep. *I'm not going to tell him the ending—that's what he deserves.*

Winter was really here now and the walk to Dominic and Liz's home on the edge of the village was more difficult than usual—the snow was quite deep and still falling. They persevered however and the big house soon came into view. It was of Georgian design with some later Victorian additions and had many tall windows that seemed to welcome passers-by. Tonight, the windows were brightly lit and a wreathe of green foliage and red berries adorned the big front door, with a shiny red ribbon hanging down from the middle.

"Isn't it a picture—a beautiful picture!" Jenny held her husband's arm and made him stop to admire it.

"Yes, it's incredibly beautiful," he agreed, "I just wonder how Dominic managed to afford it—it must have cost a fortune!"

"His father—it was his father—don't you remember, Bill? The old chap died when Dominic was a teenager and then his mother too, passed away a very few years later. He inherited everything, so he's never been short of a bob or two. When Liz married him, she knew she was onto a good thing—but then, she had some money of her own—and with no children, they never had to meet the expenses we've had. She's always treating herself to something or other."

"That's a pretty mean thing to say, Jen—they're our friends and I thought Liz was your friend in particular." Bill was being rather defensive. Before they reached the door, they heard their names being called out.

It was Maggie and Peter, holding on to each other to stop falling over—the frozen snow was slippery. "Wait for us; we've come to beat you soundly," Peter called out. All four fell into the hall when Dominic opened the door. They took off their snow-covered boots and rushed into the sitting room where a glorious fire burned in the hearth. They playfully knocked each other out of the way to get closest to the flames.

"Now, that's what I call a fire!" Bill won the place at the front of the group—his rugby-playing body came in handy on occasion. He really knew how to push people out of the way.

Liz appeared in the doorway with a silver tray holding six goblets of hot sherry. "Now there's a pretty sight, if ever I saw one." Peter elbowed his way towards the wine, took the tray from the hostess and placed it on the coffee table.

"I've always admired that fireplace, you know—how old do you reckon the house is?" Maggie loved the house and didn't attempt to conceal the fact. They all settled around the flames and enjoyed the drinks.

"It's 250 years old, I've seen the deeds," Liz told them and Dominic got up to put another log on the fire.

"Yeah, my family's only had it for a hundred years—my grandfather bought it, then my father, then me—it's become a tradition now, for us to live here."

"Why, Dominic, you're very smart tonight—I don't think I've ever seen you looking so dapper." They all looked at the host who was wearing a plum-coloured smoking jacket and a white cravat.

"Thank you, Maggie,—you always say the nicest things."

Bill grunted and coughed out, "Bit poncy, if you ask me."

"I've just heard Pam arrive in the kitchen—I'll just pop in and make sure she knows what's for dinner—I've left it all ready for her." She hurried from the room, gulping down her sherry before she went. The others moved an occasional, round table into the middle of the sitting room, so they could play Cluedo beside that wonderful fire.

"We can't play anywhere but near that glorious fire!" Maggie always liked her comforts.

Spread over the table, the Cluedo board showed its beautifully designed rooms—as well as the Secret Passages, where someone could slip secretly from one room to another. Everyone had their favourite character and chose the same every time—but on this night, a small Lego man stood in for Professor Plum. He looked rather silly, but it was only a game after all.

"Time to call for Pam, so we can begin," and Liz called for the home-help to come into the room and choose 'in secret' the murderer, the weapon and the location of the murder, then hide them in the special envelope, which she placed in the middle of the board. No one else was allowed to touch it and Pam said nothing, but returned to the kitchen to finish dinner preparations. As usual, Pam's cooking was exceptional and was quickly gorged by the hungry six. It was followed by one of her spectacular puddings, which always made Bill call her a witch, they were so yummy. And as usual, most of them had seconds.

The six players began the game very seriously—they always played as though their lives depended on winning. Maggie suggested an answer, but was wrong and so she was out of the game. She left the table and languidly stretched herself along one of the two sofas in the room. Another wrong guess from Bill meant he too, was out of the game. "Does anyone mind if we make this a natural break and I nip down to the cellar and fetch a couple more bottles of wine?"

Of course, no one did, so he left the room quickly. As he went, he said to Liz, "That was a great dinner, Liz—please give my compliments to the witch, will you?" Promising to do that, she cleared away the crystal bowls and took them into the kitchen. Jenny asked if she could use the telephone in the study, just to check with the babysitter that the children were okay. She disappeared as well.

Dominic jumped up and said he would fetch some logs from the garage as the fire was burning pretty low. It was great to have a regular delivery of logs from the local farm and the wood always smelt so lovely. He only had to leave the garage open for the farmer and he'd deliver the logs without disturbing anyone—everyone was so friendly and trustworthy. In fact, one of the farm workmen, Jonathan, was Dominic's gardener and he could be trusted as much as his boss (who happened to be his father). The house ran smoothly and that was because of the lovely people from the village.

Peter excused himself to use 'the facilities', and with the drink and the warmth of the fire, Maggie had fallen asleep on the sofa. She was actually snoring, although she'd have been mortified had she known. Luckily, she was all alone in the sitting room, so her secret was safe.

First to return was Liz who smiled to herself at the noise Maggie was making. Peter came back from having used the facilities and Liz asked him, "Does she make that noise in bed, Peter?"

"I'm afraid she does—but always denies it." He sat down at the table and waited for the others.

Bill came into the room then, pulling off a couple of spiderwebs he'd picked up in the cellar and plonked the wine on the sideboard. "My God, I envy Dominic that cellar. Lucky Blighter!"

Jenny came back then, telling everyone the children were okay—but no one was particularly interested. "They're home from boarding school for the holidays," she added but again, no one paid any attention.

"My God, he's taking his time." Bill crouched down in front of the dying fire and rubbed his hands together. "Can we get on with this game—I want to know who did it and with what."

"I'll go and find him," Liz said, "I know his routine—he'll be coming back through the conservatory, dropping bits of wood as he goes." She left the sitting room where her three friends were waiting patiently to begin. (Maggie was still sound asleep).

A minute later, she came back with her handkerchief stuffed into her mouth. "I've found him—he's in the conservatory as I thought—but he seems to be dead. Please come and help me—see for yourselves!" She was clearly very upset and shocked—she obviously didn't know what to do. They all crossed the hall and went into the conservatory.

Dominic was lying on the floor just inside the wide-open door of the conservatory—the basket of logs had spilled onto the floor amongst clumps of snow and grass. Peter, the doctor rushed over to him and felt for a pulse, but there was none. He was lying on his side—sort of crumpled and twisted—then Peter saw the knife protruding from his stomach. He was lying in a pool of blood and his mouth was twisted in an open grimace. Strangely, there was also a look of surprise in his open eyes, as though he couldn't believe what—or who—he'd been looking at last.

Bill rushed into the hall and called for an ambulance—although it was obviously too late, but he didn't know what else to do. When he put the phone down, he just kept repeating, "Who could have done this—he was the most likeable of us all. Who could have done it?"

The ambulance arrived, and then the police. Statements were taken about who was where when it happened. Who knew what? Did anyone see or hear anything unusual? No one was much help as they'd all been someplace different. Maggie ticked them off on her fingers, "Liz had gone into the kitchen to speak with Pam; I had fallen asleep on the sofa and was apparently snoring loudly, which I dispute; Peter had gone to the toilet; Jenny was in the study telephoning her babysitter to check on the kids; Bill was down in the cellar choosing the most expensive wines he could find. No one had even gone looking for Dominic, but then we didn't know he was missing then."

Bill suggested, "I suppose it must have been an intruder—after all, he'd been outside in the garage to get the logs and someone could have been waiting there and followed him into the house."

The Detective nodded and said that was a possibility, then he asked Liz to check around the room to see if anything was missing. "She can't do that just now—she's distraught—in deep shock. Can't that wait until tomorrow?" Peter used his doctor's voice. The Detective agreed that would have to do, but added he'd have to leave a couple of men in the house to look around for clues and also, for Liz's protection.

Jenny said she'd stay overnight, "We can't leave her on her own, can we?" She looked at the others, who were glad she'd volunteered herself. In the circumstances, the others just wanted to go home.

Everyone left the house, Bill saying he'd come back next day to collect the Cluedo game and, of course, to see how Liz was. The police arranged for Dominic's body to be taken away during the night, but not before the forensic team had done their work around the murder scene. What was strange, when they moved his body, they found a little figure of a man underneath him and the stamp on its base, said simply 'Professor Plum'. When they heard, everyone agreed that was strange. In fact, the mystery was solved—that's where the figure had gone! Dominic must have taken it! But that was too ridiculous—why should he?

The mystery deepened however when Bill called at the old house to check on the women and to pick up the Cluedo. Not only was Professor Plum missing—although they knew where he was now—but now Miss Scarlet had completely disappeared, and despite crawling under the table and over the carpet, she couldn't be found. Ah well, with all the strange occurrences of the previous night, it wasn't all that surprising. But why on earth would anyone have taken her as well?

The next couple of days passed as if in a dream. Liz was especially confused—how could it happen? Dominic had no enemies—in fact, everyone liked him. He was one of nature's gentlemen. It wasn't surprising that he went to fetch more logs for the fire—it was certainly low, but the poor chap never managed back again. She felt bitterly cold all the time and realised it was the shock. Jenny tried to comfort her with the inevitable deluge of tea, but also with several glasses of brandy, but nothing seemed to make much difference. She remained in a state of shock for several days, but her friends rallied around her and were always there if she needed them.

Jonathan, the gardener, worked on the hedges and trees but as there was still so much snow around and the ground was hard, he was really just tidying up bits and pieces. Liz made him a couple of coffees which he drank in the kitchen. The silence was awkward; after all, what did you say to a woman whose husband had just been murdered?

"Do you still work on Bill and Peter's garden as well Jonathan?" she asked for something to say and was rewarded by a grunt from Jonathan. He was quite a shy young man, but a good gardener and she knew was lucky to have him. The figure of Miss Scarlet never did turn up and it was put down to 'just one of those things!'

"I think we'll soon have to get a new Cluedo game—or we'll have to call it the 'Lego game' now that two main figures have disappeared. The police want to hang on to Professor Plum until the case is solved." Bill could always see the funny side of things.

"And that could be awkward," Jenny replied. "What are we going to do about the next night we're due to play—it should be at Peter and Maggie's—I think I'll ring her and see what she says—and we'll go from there. Liz is so vulnerable just now, we mustn't do the wrong thing." Bill agreed.

"It seems wrong to play a game when Dominic is lying dead, but it seems the obvious thing to do—to help everyone get a bit of normality—especially Liz. We'll be damned if we do and damned if we don't. I'm off to the office, Jen— I'll see you later."

"I think we should go ahead with it," Maggie seemed convinced. "Peter will fetch Liz and take her home afterwards." She thought for a moment, but it still seemed like a good idea. "Don't forget to bring the game, Jenny—we don't have one." And the decision was made.

Jenny left the window cleaner in charge and went into the village—she had some things to do for Liz and as she left, she shouted, "Don't forget to lock up and hide the key."

Bill had originally drawn up Dominic's will and Liz went to his office to discuss it—so many things to attend to, it was unreal. After having coffee in her usual café, she went to Bill's office. The couple had had no children, so she would be the sole beneficiary, except for various bits and pieces Dominic wanted to give to friends. She tapped gently on Bill's office door and waited for him to call 'Come in'. Once inside, Bill came from behind his desk and swept her into his arms. "Oh my darling, you've been through so much." And he kissed her passionately.

"Bill, Bill—I'm free now, but you're not, so we must play it safe. I wouldn't want to hurt Jenny for the world." Liz sat down and lit a cigarette. "At least, you'll be able to come and visit me now—with no one there to stop us—and you're my lawyer after all."

"Yes, but I didn't expect this to happen—not to poor old Dominic. He was a good chap!" Bill looked rather sheepish and poured them both a sherry.

"I know he was—you know, for a moment I thought it was you who'd killed him, to get him out of the way, but when I saw how shocked you were, I knew it couldn't be so." She inhaled deeply and looked like the 'femme fatale' she was. She'd been having a relationship with Bill for a few months now and no one suspected anything, but now things could change—well, at least as far as she was concerned, they could.

The secretary tapped on the door and opened it cautiously, "Excuse me, Sir—but you have a visitor. Your wife's popped in to see you." The two culprits could do nothing and he told the secretary to show Jenny in. Disbelief and surprise showed on her face as Liz was the last person she expected to see there. She stuttered, "I brought you a chocolate éclair to have with your tea, dear—sorry if I've disturbed you. Hello Liz, you're looking well—better than when I last saw you." She crossed the room and sat on Bill's chair. She found the situation embarrassing but she had more right than Liz to be there.

The femme fatale stood up, saying, "Well Bill, I think we've covered everything. Will you bring me a copy of Dominic's will tomorrow—there's a few things I know he would have wanted me to give people. And I need to discuss my own will unfortunately—as I'm on my own now."

"I didn't realise Bill had drawn up Dominic's will—so that's why you're here. Now I understand." She turned to Bill. "Have you told Liz we're having a game of Cluedo at Maggie and Peter's next weekend? It's to try to lift your spirits." She smiled at her friend.

"That'll be a couple of days after the funeral—I know you'll all come to that. It wouldn't be right if you didn't. But goodbye for now—I have an appointment with the funeral director." And she left the office, leaving an awkward atmosphere in the room, which Bill tried to cover up by offering his wife some tea.

"No dear—you keep your tea. I'm not sure how much I believe of what you and Liz were saying." Jenny stood up to her full height, which wasn't very tall, and left the office.

What a strange afternoon, was all she could think. Next day, Bill asked his secretary to deliver the will to Liz—allegedly he didn't have the time to do it. The truth was, he didn't have the brass neck to do it.

After the funeral service, they all gathered at Dominic's place—at least at Liz's place now—there were only a very few friends and three relatives gathered in the room. Dominic had been an only child and his parents had died when he was still young. There were a couple of teachers from the University where he'd taught and they'd come to pay their last respects. Dominic had been a popular teacher. Looking awkward, Jonathan the gardener and his father had also come to pay their respects. Dominic had been a good person and a good customer and they felt it only right to attend his funeral.

As is usual at such events, everyone stood around, not knowing what to do or say—Liz tried to be a good hostess and made sure everyone had a drink and something to eat. Pam had answered Liz's call to come and help with the buffet food and the clearing away afterwards. She hadn't been invited to attend the funeral—but she had done in any case—it felt right to her.

"By the way, Pam—would you like to look through Dominic's clothes and see if there's anything you, or your family, could make use of. I don't have to show you where everything is cause you already know. I mean it, Pam—take what you want, I have no further use for men's clothes."

Pam agreed to do it but she said she would show her what she was taking—just in case. She did actually think it was all a bit quick—and insensitive to get rid of Dominic's clothes so soon—but then who was she to argue?

The afternoon went quite smoothly and, one by one, people began to drift away, leaving only the closest friends—only five in number now. Bill and Liz kept away from each other as it seemed Jenny was watching them closer than she should have been. It was an odd occasion but then funerals always were—especially when the deceased was so young and his death, so sudden and unexpected.

The following Saturday was to be the Cluedo evening at Peter and Maggie's house, so when they all left after the funeral, they promised to see each other at the weekend—and Peter reminded her he'd pick her up at seven o'clock. But it was not to be. He drove into her drive at quarter to seven and had no answer when he rang the doorbell. He waited a few moments and rang the bell again. *Funny*, he thought, *all the lights are on.* He decided to walk around to the back of the house towards the conservatory, which might be unlocked—although after what happened to Dominic, it should have been. But he didn't get that far—before he reached the door, he almost tripped over something lying on the stone patio.

He recognised her immediately—Liz was lying in a crumpled heap with blood oozing from a horrific head wound. He shouted her name and then again, but she didn't move. He felt for a pulse in her neck, but there was none. Liz was well and truly dead. Automatically, he looked up at the balcony which was outside her bedroom but there was nothing unusual there. For a moment, he froze, not knowing what to do. His brain just wouldn't function properly and he stood up slowly, stumbling a little before his eye caught something shiny at the side of her body.

Picking it up, he saw it was the Cluedo figure of Miss Scarlet—the one that had gone missing after the last game. He knew he shouldn't have touched it—he'd watched enough TV dramas to know—but he couldn't resist it—something told him if he left it there, it would implicate her Cluedo friends, of which he was one of course. He slipped the little figure into his jacket pocket and then immediately forgot all about it.

After the police had arrived and the ambulance had taken away Liz's body, the police wanted to talk with him. There was nothing he could tell them—he'd arrived at the agreed time and after failing to get an answer at the front, he'd walked around to the back and almost fell over Liz's body. He hadn't gained entrance to the house at all, "Just stood there like a moron—I didn't know what to do—it was the last thing I expected to see."

The police made a point of getting the names of anyone who worked around the house—like the gardener, the home help and the window cleaner. Peter could tell them, as he employed the same people.

After his talk with the police, Peter went straight home, where Maggie and the two others were waiting to begin the game. "Where on earth have you been, Peter—we've been waiting ages." Maggie was rather cross, supper would be spoiled and she and Pam had spent a lot of time preparing it.

"You found what?" Bill was the first to speak. "But I saw her just today—she came to my office to discuss making her Will. It was a pretty simple will, so it didn't take long and afterwards, we had a cup of tea. It had to be drawn up by my colleague, Malcolm, as I actually figure in it as one of the beneficiaries—but that wasn't a problem. She signed the document and left—that's the last time I saw her."

Jenny interrupted him to stop him from blabbing on, "Methinks the Lady doth protest too much, Bill," she couldn't help saying. "Nobody's asked you to account for your movements—yet!" So, they'd been together again just today! "What do the police think happened?"

"They won't commit yet until they've had a good look around the house—but their first thought seems to be it was suicide. It certainly looked like that—there was no one else in the house and it seemed as though she'd thrown herself off the balcony. Apparently, it's not unknow for a spouse to commit suicide following their partner's death—especially where it was unexpected. Oh, and by the way, I found this beside her body." And he held out Miss Scarlet in the palm of his hand. There were gasps all around and everyone was speechless.

"By the way, I'd better tell Pam the police have her name as they asked me for it and for the gardener and window cleaner as well. They want to talk to anyone who saw Liz recently." Peter left the room.

Much later, and after a few stiff brandies, they'd talked the subject to death (which Bill remarked was a poor pun in the circumstances). It won him a disapproving look from his wife. Liz was the last person they'd expected to end her own life—she was too full of vitality and energy. "I don't think I can believe it. Not her, she had everything to live for."

Maggie was talking to herself, but Bill answered, "Is that true though? She'd just had her husband murdered and had to bury him, she had no children to lean on—all she had to look forward to was playing Cluedo with us. Not much of a prospect really!"

Jenny turned to her husband, "So, did she complete her will today? Did she actually sign it—and who witnessed it? Did she perhaps make her will because she planned to kill herself? My God, that's too horrible to think of—and then went home to get ready to play Cluedo with us. Her mind must have been in a turmoil." Bill just looked at her in silence.

"I don't think I can ever play that game again—there's fewer of us all the time." Jenny was obviously upset and then she said, "Oh and by the way, we did bring the game with us to play here and we discovered yet another figure is missing. We brought the game anyway, as we could play with just the named cards."

A pointless explanation as no one was really interested, except for… "Which figure has disappeared now?" Bill asked.

"It's another woman—Mrs White this time! She has just disappeared from the box." Jenny looked perplexed. "Isn't it time we told the police about the missing figures—it seems to be happening regularly now and it might imply a death amongst us. Well Maggie, who is Mrs White—you or me?"

"Oh, don't be so sick, Jenny—the figures can't have anything to do with the deaths—you've been reading too many mysteries." But Maggie actually felt a chill run up and down her spine.

Another funeral! Another dead friend! What was happening to their world? The friends had told the police about the figures and they certainly didn't regard it as trivial—in fact, they told them off for withholding information. Bill had hidden Professor Plum from Dominic's murder, Peter had removed Miss Scarlet from beside Liz's body and now they'd concealed Mrs White's disappearance from the box. They knew they deserved the telling-off.

"I'm sorry, Sir, but I must ask you to come along with me—there's a few questions I need to ask." The police Detective had arrived unannounced at Bill's office and was accompanied by a burly Sergeant.

"What on earth do you want me for—and why me?" Bill felt himself begin to sweat. In the end, he had to go with the detective as it didn't seem right to discuss it there—offices have many ears and his secretary had especially big ones—he believed she sometimes kept the intercom open to hear more.

"Why you?" Jenny asked. "Is there a reason I don't know about? I had begun to think of late that you and Liz were as thick as thieves—but I certainly never thought you'd kill her. However, Dominic's death is quite another matter." It was time it was all brought into the open—she knew now there'd been something going on between Liz and her husband.

"It's not what you think—they wanted to speak to me because Liz left everything to me in her last will. I remonstrated with her and said it wasn't a good plan—everyone would find it odd—especially you. I told her it didn't seem right for me to draw up her will with myself as the main beneficiary—but she wouldn't listen—and the only thing she'd agree to, was that I fetched another lawyer from the firm to do it—Malcolm did it in the end. She said if I didn't do it, she'd just go to another firm, so what could I do? What have you got to say now?" He looked shattered and fed up—not at all like a man who'd just been left a fortune. "I like to believe she was thinking of you and the children—you'll all benefit as much as I will," he ended lamely.

The police knew they had nothing on him, although he'd been the last person to see Liz alive. Since she'd left his office, and his secretary confirmed the time as she'd been watching as usual—he'd been with Jenny until they'd both gone to Maggie and Peter's house together. There was no time he could have hurt Liz. However, he'd learned something from the police that shocked him—Liz had drunk a heavy drug in a glass of milk just before she died—a drug that induced a heavy sedative to work on the system. She could have gone onto the balcony and staggered towards the edge—or she could have been pushed over quite easily. She was probably in an unbalanced state.

Now, it looked like murder and not suicide. He was even more relieved that his alibi had stood up and was believed. The police seemed to be interrogating everyone in sight and for a while, held onto Jonathan and his father at the station, only releasing them after six hours. They'd even tracked down the regular window cleaner to check if he'd seen anything. After his interview, he bumped into Jonathan in the village and they talked about what they'd just been through.

"As if any of us would ever hurt that lady! She was always nice and friendly—if a little stuck-up sometimes." The window cleaner was quite angry. "All I do is clean windows. Okay, sometimes I see things I shouldn't—but that's not my fault, is it?" Jonathan agreed with him.

"What on earth are we going to do now—there's so few of us? Should we play again in loving memory of our two friends—or should we never play again? I think we should vote on it." Maggie and Peter had met with Jenny and Bill for an afternoon coffee in the local pub. To break the silence, Maggie said, "I think we should play again in memory of Liz and Dominic—we've now buried both of them and we should do something to celebrate their lives. We'll ask Pam to come in and prepare the food and drink and make a special night of it. All of you come to our house next weekend and we'll really push the boat out." She raised her coffee cup in salute to her lost friends.

And that's what they did—Bill had set up the board game with three little Lego figures to replace Professor Plum, Miss Scarlet and Mrs White—it didn't seem right to replace them with real life-like figures—that would have seemed disrespectful! Neither Maggie nor Peter mentioned Bill's recent good fortune as that too, seemed disrespectful—and anyway, Jenny had told them in confidence. They all sipped their drinks and could smell the delicious aromas coming from the kitchen.

"Sorry to bring this up, Bill—but did Liz leave anything to Pam—she'd been her home help for years? Maggie and I just wondered." Peter looked ill at ease asking the question. They'd heard the police had just finished questioning Pam—little, meek Pam who just did her work and never asked for anything—in fact, who never spoke until she was spoken to. Ridiculous, or what?

"The will is to be read on Tuesday—10 am at the couple's old house—and I think we should all attend. I know you're both astounded at Liz leaving me the house and the rest of her Estate. I don't know what to say except that I honestly tried to change her mind, but she was insistent. She said she had no relatives and only us as friends. That's all I can say at this time—but everything will be revealed on Tuesday." And he made it obvious he was going to say no more on the subject.

They played a good game and, in the end, Jenny chose the right murderer, the right weapon and the right location. "Well done, old fruit." Bill had been stumped himself and was glad his wife had won. Pam had produced a tasty meal and a lovely, calorific pudding which they all loved. "Seconds. Please?" Bill was first to say, but they all eventually joined in. In silence, Pam brought the extra food. She still looked upset about what was going on and being questioned by the police had been no picnic. It had scared her more than ever.

"There you are, chaps—Mrs White, whichever one of us she is—remains well and alive—in the game anyway—only her figure is missing. I think we must be over the curse!" Jenny actually felt relieved.

Next day… "Maggie darling, are you planning to go into town today by any chance? If you are, would you mind depositing this cheque in the bank for me—I have a meeting first thing, so if you could do it, it would be a tremendous help." Peter was obviously in a rush.

"Of course, Peter—no trouble. Give me the cheque. I'm going to town to get some ingredients for the quiches and pies I mean to take along to the will reading—I think someone should make the effort and it would be wrong to depend on Pam to do everything. She won't be there in her usual role, will she? She'll be more like one of us. I wonder what Liz has left for Pam."

"That's kind, Maggie—trust you to think of the 'eats'. There'll be plenty of drink for everyone—Bill already knows his way around the cellar, doesn't he?" He kissed her cheek, handed her the cheque and was gone. Maggie had a quick cup of coffee before she left for the shops. Jonathan was working in the garden and she shouted out 'Good morning—just help yourself to coffee—the kitchen door is open." It was a very cold morning and she wrapped up well, pulling on her favourite woolly hat and thinking how just over a month ago, both Dominic and Liz had been alive and part of the gang. She couldn't help shedding a tear or two when she thought of how much life they should have been looking forward to. What a waste! And if they were both murdered, who could have done it? She wasn't surprised the police had questioned Bill so closely—his position was pretty suspicious—but then, they'd let him go so it obviously wasn't him.

The bank was busy as it was lunchtime before she got there and people were obviously on their dinner breaks. She stood in one of the queues—and of course it was the slowest one—she always picked the slow queue—and moved forward very slowly. Suddenly, the front door of the bank was thrown open and a man ran in pointing a gun at everyone. Another man stood at the door to stop people coming in and going out.

The man with the gun shouted to all the cashiers, "Pass over the money from your drawers and don't take too long about it—you've only got one minute. I know you'll all be pressing your panic buttons now, so when I say one minute, I mean it." He waved the gun in the air and told all the customers to lie on the floor—everyone obeyed, including Maggie. Someone jostled her from behind and made her fall forwards—she hadn't seen who it was—probably just someone as scared as she was.

As soon as the man had some money, he began to back away towards the door, where the other man was still waiting. He seemed to aim the gun at the customers and fired once. Everyone thought he'd fired into the air, but he hadn't—he'd fired at the woman in the woolly hat. Both men ran from the bank and disappeared up the street—the police arrived very quickly and a couple of customers crossed the bank to see if Maggie was all right. But Maggie was dead, her shopping bag spilling onto the floor and blood seeping through her warm coat. A customer who'd been in the queue bent down beside her and spotted a small figure lying on the floor; it was a woman in a white dress and had been part of the spilled contents of her bag. Had the figure always been in the bag, or had the robber thrown it there? No one knew! Everything had happened so quickly and when the police spoke with the other customers, there were several different accounts of what had happened. Even the man who'd found the figure, told a garbled story.

There were no quiches or pies at the will reading. In fact, there was no will reading on the day. Everyone was in a daze—people were dying all around and everyone was scared and confused. Peter was devasted, "She wouldn't have been in the bank at all if I hadn't asked her. My God, that makes it my fault."

Before Maggie had even been buried, Peter went home with a bottle of whisky and a large bottle of sleeping pills. He felt he had nothing more to live for and indirectly, he felt he'd caused her death. His dear Maggie with the lovely blue eyes—eyes he'd never see again. He poured the whisky and took a handful of pills and swallowed them down—then he did exactly the same again. In a strange way, he actually felt relieved as if he'd paid for what he'd done. Conscience can be a cruel thing!

And so, Jenny and Bill had to attend a double funeral—again. "That is one of the saddest things I've ever had to do—and those teenage children looked bereft and so alone. There are grandparents and I suppose they'll all live together now. Oh Bill, there's only me and you left—our lovely circle of friends have gone." They stood by the graveside and saw the wreathe they'd brought, placed on the grass—it was yellow roses, four large ones for each of their friends—and there, leaning against one of the flowers, Bill spotted a small figure of a man.

He picked it up and turned it over and clear as crystal, it read 'Colonel Mustard'. Peter had served in the army for twenty years and, although he'd never reached as lofty a rank as Colonel, he'd enjoyed his time there.

Jenny turned ashen. "Oh Bill, this is uncanny—who's doing this? We must have hardly any Cluedo characters left now and how on earth is someone managing to get into our houses, find the game and remove the figures. Have we any left now?"

"Oh, we still have two—Mr Boddy and Mrs Peacock—but nothing's going to happen to us—we'll take care of each other. And there's still the business of reading Liz's will—that's something I still have to arrange again—people are beginning to ask why it hasn't been done yet. If only they knew what we've been through lately."

The two lonely figures left together and got into their car. They spotted Pam walking away from the grave and asked if she'd like a ride home, but typical of Pam, she smiled and said, "No, the walk will do me good." And that ended another horrific day! Jonathan, the gardener, was walking just behind her—he was thinking how amazing it was that he was losing so many clients.

It was surprising to think almost three months had passed since the night Dominic had been found stabbed. It seemed time also flies when you're not having fun. The police were questioning everyone in sight—the newspapers had got wind of the weird and sudden deaths—murders and suicides—and were writing up the story with great gusto. Bill thought that people were looking at him suspiciously and he tried to keep a low profile. Just wait until they learn Liz had left him her estate—then they'd really have something to talk about.

Life had become very difficult and each evening—when they were sure they were still safe—they'd draw the curtains and have a glass of brandy, watching each other with ill-disguised suspicion. No more talk of playing Cluedo—it seemed that part of their life was over. And good riddance!

The will reading had now been set for two weeks ahead and it was to be at Liz and Dominic's house, the biggest property—the interested parties had been alerted, although there were only very few of them. It would be a day Bill dreaded!

Jenny decided to go to town and, to avoid parking problems, she went by bus. It was only a short journey but it was pleasant to sit back and enjoy the ride. She'd gotten some nice steak for supper as she felt both of them were in need of a treat. There was a queue at the bus stop and she watched out for a Number 37, as that stopped almost at her door. People in Britain always queued well and she was surprised to be jostled from behind—she glanced behind and gave a little old man one of her dirty looks—and then realised it hadn't been him at all.

There was a double-decker bus coming—it might be a Number 37; she couldn't quite see, so she strained forward and peered up the street. Suddenly, she felt something hard poke into the small of her back and it made her lose her balance. She tripped into the gutter and fell right into the path of the bus—which turned out to be a Number 37 after all.

She knew nothing after that as she was unconscious and her prized steak was lying squashed in the gutter. Jenny was quite squashed too and several people tried to come to her aid, but it was useless. Someone rang for an ambulance and she was whisked away by the paramedics to the hospital. Bill was contacted and he came very quickly—she looked dreadful, not like his Jenny at all. All night, he sat by her bedside, but she never again gained consciousness.

In the morning, he went out into the corridor to have a cup of coffee and was surprised to see Pam, the home help, standing there. She looked quite out of place and uncomfortable.

"I've just popped in to see how your wife's doing. I heard about the accident in town and I've been praying that she'll be all right." It was the most Bill had ever heard Pam speak.

"Thank you for that, Pam—I appreciate your concern—but she's not looking good," Bill whispered. "If you'd like to pop in to see her, I'm sure it would be all right—but just for a moment."

She was back in the corridor in two minutes, shook his hand and left the hospital. *That woman is dying*, she told herself. And she was right—by six o'clock next morning, Jenny had passed away. The hospital had done all they could for her, but she'd been too badly injured by the weight of the double-decker bus. The doctor could only make her last few hours as comfortable as possible.

Bill was allowed to stay in the room with his dead wife, to say his goodbyes privately. He sat there, his head in his hands and cried. What was he going to tell the two children—oh, they were old enough to understand but not old enough to accept their mother's death—two little teenage boys, who'd adored Jenny. He'd have to fetch them from their boarding school to attend their mother's funeral. What a reason to have an extra break from school!

He bent down, kissed her cheek and touched her forehead. Then he spotted something very familiar—a small Cluedo figure lying just under her right ear—it was Mrs Peacock. He removed the figure and threw it into the waste-paper basket. *My God, someone is still playing their tricks—I suppose it'll be my turn next*, were his last thoughts as he left the room and went home.

It was a small group of people who stood around Jenny's graveside. They'd come to say goodbye to a popular lady who'd always been liked. The vicar gave a beautiful memorial service at the graveside and described her perfectly. "It was a terrible accident that took her away from us—one of those things in life we can never understand. She was a lovely lady, lovely mother and wife, and a lovely friend to all who knew her. God rest her soul."

And that left Bill, the last of the group of friends who'd played Cluedo. The gang had gone! He'd never felt so alone in his life and a heavy depression descended on him like a fog. He'd have to get this reading of Liz's will out of the way and then he'd have to pull himself together and form a plan for the rest of his life. He'd even considered bringing his boys back from boarding school permanently and have them taught locally, just to have them close and enjoy their company—but he knew he couldn't affect their young lives so drastically when they'd just lost their dear mother. He heard his letterbox clang—something had been pushed through. A folded piece of paper lay on the mat and when he read it, he was deeply touched.

Dear Bill Sir,

I know you'll be feeling very sad and I'd like to help cheer you up. I'll come around on Friday evening and cook you a special meal—it's all I can do, I'm afraid.

Regards Pam

What a kind thought and he loved Pam's cooking—people could be so kind! He smelt the delicious aroma the moment he stepped into the hall that night. Pam had worked her magic and had already left for her own home—a little note on the kitchen table told him what she'd made and where the pudding could be found—also telling him not to clear the table after his meal—she would come in the next day to do that. *Perfection*, he thought!

The meal was huge and beautifully cooked. Rich beef cut into slices with lots of roasted vegetables and a strong mushroom sauce. He found the pudding in the fridge—an artistic creation, if ever there was one! A baked Alaska covered in extra cream and heaped with strawberries—all washed down with a bottle of his favourite wine. He went to bed that night, if not a happy man then certainly a full one. Sleep was close and experiencing a sudden exhaustion, his head sank into the pillow—then his sleepy eyes fell on to his bedside table and standing there, he saw a Cluedo figure. He raised a tired arm and picked it up and could just make out Mr Boddy on its base. He realised this was it, and it was now his turn to be one of the figures—the last one—with all the other characters having appeared at the very end of his friends' lives—and of course, of Jenny's life.

His head sank deeper into the pillow and he fell into a sleep that seemed almost welcome—he could forget about everything now, all the sadness of the past few months. Now he could sleep in peace forever. All six of the Cluedo group had gone now and all in a very short time. His colleague would have to do the will reading now—and at least, everything in the end would go to his children. His glass was half-full in the end.

At five o'clock next morning when it was still dark, Pam used her own key to open the front door. She went upstairs first to check on Bill and found exactly what she'd expected. He was cold now so he must have died quite some time ago. All she had to do was to remove the Cluedo figure of Mr Boddy—but then she decided against it, why make it easier for the police? They were already looking for a serial killer, so why disappoint them? The rest of the room should remain as Bill had left it. She certainly wouldn't be ringing for an ambulance nor notify anyone that the man had passed—after just two days, the cyanide in his system would have cleared and with it, the proof that he'd been poisoned. She wasn't inclined to help the police and even if they eventually found traces of it in his system, who would ever suspect meek little Pamela, everyone's loyal home-help?

In the kitchen, she tidied away every scrap of food and all utensils—and cleared the dining room table as well, washing up everything and putting them away in their proper place. Everything was cleaned and polished to her exacting standards. She used a thick black sack to take away all remnants of food—she would get rid of those at home. Looking around carefully, she saw the rooms were immaculate and just as they should be. She also removed the note she'd left for Bill—now there was absolutely no evidence of her having been there. Everything had worked according to plan.

One of Bill's colleagues—Malcolm—took over the reading of the will. They all assembled in the old house's sitting room and the rather pompous-looking lawyer cleared his throat to make everyone be quiet. It wasn't difficult as there were so few people there, other than himself of course. He mentioned first the smaller bequests for Liz's acquaintances. Of course, they thought they should have had more but then, they hadn't been close to Liz or to Dominic. The most difficult part of the will was rather easy to explain—the whole of the Estate and the big house itself, with all its contents had been left to Bill, who unfortunately couldn't be there that day—" I believe he's come down with some sort of flu and hasn't been at work for a couple of days." Malcolm explained.

And that was the contents of the will. It was short and to the point, with no mention of Pam. Liz had promised her so many things and yet, she hadn't even left her as much as a penny. She sat in silence—sad and angry at the same time. From her bag, she took out the will she'd witnessed for Liz several months ago. Its words were clear and duly signed by Liz and witnessed by herself.

'I leave my house, its contents and my whole Estate to my friends Bill, Jenny, Peter and Maggie to inherit in that order. They have been good friends to both myself and to my late husband, Dominic, and I wish them great happiness. Should, however, these friends die before the reading of this will, my house, its contents and the rest of my Estate, should pass to Pam, my loyal and hardworking home help who has looked after me for many years.

'In this will, I attest my wishes and want my requests to be actioned as I have directed. I am of sound mind and body.'

Her signature was clear as was the date—and Pam's witnessing signature was clear too. The date was several months before the date of the will the lawyer had just read, so making the one in her hands null and void. She couldn't produce it now—Liz had obviously done the dirty on her and didn't tell her it had been changed. Should the authorities see the will she had, suspicion would immediately fall on her regarding the recent deaths—although she'd always been careful in their execution. Why muddy the waters unnecessarily –she'd destroy her version of the will?

She'd caused all those deaths, both directly and indirectly, and all for what? For nothing, she'd just learned. As she packed away her things, she was actually smiling. *You win some, you lose some.* She realised she'd really enjoyed ending the lives of those people she'd worked for throughout the years. She'd worked hard for them, but they'd never once asked her to sit down and join them for a drink, never once invited her to join them in their pathetic games of Cluedo. They'd only ever treated her as a servant, never as a friend, and only ever paid her meagre wages with no little presents or bonuses. *And I've been out of pocket paying those men to rob the bank and shoot Maggie—still it was worth it!*

All these thoughts rushed through her head. She'd done it all for nothing— what a waste of effort, but then she'd been pretty shrewd the way she'd used the figures from the game. It had added mystery to the deaths—and had been quite a challenge. She'd made sure she was never near any of them when they'd actually died—oh yes, she'd been pretty clever. A pity she'd received no reward for her efforts after everything she'd done to deserve them.

She walked slowly down the drive, thinking she'd never be coming here again. "Hello," she said to Jonathan who'd just arrived, spade in hand. "It's bitter this morning, isn't it?" She didn't notice the shiny, black car sitting outside the main gate nor did she hear the conversation the men inside were having.

"Do you think it's too soon to take her in for questioning, Sir? Should we continue monitoring her movements for a while yet? But we're going to have to be careful about the man, Bill—the only one left of the group. His safety is of paramount importance and she might try to harm him as well."

"Oh yes, Sergeant," the police Inspector smiled. "But do remember—Softly, softly, Catchee Monkey! And we've been on to her for a while! Let's pay a visit to the gentleman inside and make sure all is well with him—he's bound to be concerned after losing his wife and friends, and as you say, his safety is of paramount importance!"